LAND WITHOUT ECHOES

Land
Without
Echoes

A NOVEL

JOHN HOPKINS

Z

First published 2019

by Zuleika Books & Publishing

Thomas House, 84 Eccleston Square
London, SW1V 1PX

British Library Cataloguing in Publication Data

A catalogue record for this book is
available from the British Library

ISBN: 978-1-99-931256-5

Designed by Euan Monaghan
Printed in England

Dedicated to the memory
of Tessa Codrington Wheeler

PART I

The Barbary Shore

CHAPTER I

City On The Strait

Mrs. Adams stood on the foredeck of the ship as it approached Tangier. A fierce wind was blowing down the Strait of Gibraltar, making the sea heave and crash. All around were green mountains, the sight of which confused her. Some were in Morocco and some were in Spain. She had thought Africa and Europe would be different, but it was hard to tell which was which. She had been seasick the whole way from Barcelona.

"I hope you're not going to be disappointed, Daisy!" she said, hanging onto her hat to keep it from blowing away in the wind. She herself had been disappointed by the Pillars of Hercules, having expected something more impressive than the two distant hills guarding the entrance to the Strait. "I don't see the desert anywhere!"

Mrs. Adams was a tall, brown-skinned American lady, with a mane of hair dyed jet black and a bosom men stared at. The skin around her eyes was soft and creased. In her eyes was a look of pain; her face, when she wasn't talking, subsided into a residual expression of exhaustion and hurt.

Daisy was leaning on the rail gazing at the Moroccan coast. Tiny white villages clustered around the summit of each green hill.

"Not a camel in sight," Mrs. Adams observed doubtfully. "Surely we've come to the right place?"

Mrs. Adams had travelled all over the world, she spoke several languages fluently, but she was ignorant of geography.

Daisy's hair stuck out from under a fisherman's cap she wore at a jaunty angle. Five foot nine inches tall, she had inherited her mother's Mediterranean complexion and, from a distance, you might have guessed she was a Spanish or an Arab boy. Even close up her sex was difficult to determine. She wore a coarse coverall made of blue cloth. A pink scarf knotted about her neck seemed to add a feminine touch; yet similar dainty bandanas were currently in vogue among the toughest of hombres. Beneath the grizzled jaw of a Barcelona dockhand, a silk hanky looked like a trophy awarded by a high class lady for incredible feats in bed. You could look at one side of her face and be certain her beardless cheek belonged to a country lad; she turned her head and there, like Tiresias, was the smile of a young woman. Her smile was marred by a discoloured tooth in the middle of her mouth. She was what the French call *une jolie-laide*: a rather plain boyish face with a hint of beauty that emanated from her large brown eyes.

Her costume had confused some of the passengers who thought she was a member of the crew. This was not surprising since she'd spent most of the voyage below decks playing cards and drinking gin with the sailors. She had been very, *very* naughty, and Mrs. Adams was glad the trip was nearly over. Ahead lay Tangier with its frightening reputation for debauchery. She preferred not to think of what scrapes her daughter might get into there.

Trailing a wide arc of wake, the ship swung into the Bay of Tangier.

"Look over there, mother." Daisy was pointing to the shore. "There are your ships of the desert."

With languid and undulating step the camels were making their way along the beach toward the city – a glittering blur of white in a field of green. Tangier is built in tiers on the side of a hill that slopes to the sea. White, flat-topped houses and multi-coloured minarets are girdled by old ramparts and crowned by the Casbah, the fortified inner city.

"Actually, it looks quite attractive, doesn't it?" Mrs. Adams remarked hopefully. "At least from a distance."

An order was shouted from the bridge. The anchor dropped into the water, making a huge splash, and the chain chased after it with a loud clanking noise. The ship's engines fell silent. A lady approached.

"Hilda, you're wearing a new outfit to come home in," Mrs. Adams said.

Mrs. McGregor, the wife of a Scottish doctor, had lived for many years in Tangier. A stern, censorious expression masked her face. As soon as her mother started talking to her, Daisy edged away down the rail, as though she were afraid of catching something.

In Mrs. Adams' view, Mrs. McGregor might prove to be a valuable acquaintance in Tangier. She or Daisy might fall ill and require the doctor's services. She decided to seal their friendship then and there, before they went ashore.

"I hope it will be a happy home-coming, Hilda," she offered brightly.

"My home is in Dundee." Mrs. McGregor was looking with disapproval at Daisy's boiler suit.

"Her father insisted she wear working clothes, not only at home, but also in public even when she was a child," Mrs. Adams said quickly, hoping to head off a critical remark that seemed about to spring from Mrs. McGregor's lips.

"Even on Sundays?"

"Our ranch was thirty miles on a bad road to the nearest church."

"And why ... " Mrs. McGregor persisted, "did her father insist on it?"

"It made it easier for her to do the chores, and dispensed with that ridiculous invention, the side saddle."

This explanation seemed to fall on deaf ears. "Are you coming to Tangier on holiday, Mrs. Adams?"

"Lord, no! What with all the troubles Morocco has been having, it's hardly the vacation spot it used to be."

"If you ask me America should stay out of it."

"We're only here to help."

"You'll only make things worse."

"Morocco is one of our oldest friends, Hilda."

"Sooner or later you'll put your foot in it. You always do."

"Well, I think it would be unchristian for a rich country like

America, with our surplus of food, to stand by and do nothing while our friends suffer."

"Moroccans don't want American soldiers in their country."

"Well, one of the sad facts of this day and age is that it seems necessary to send soldiers with the food so it gets distributed to the people who need it most."

"We've come to see my brother," Daisy commented from far away. Her voice was a dry nasal twang as flat as the desert she grew up in.

Mrs. Adams wiped away a tear. "The poor boy was bitten by a snake and had to go into the hospital. We've come to Morocco to make sure he's all right."

"You must go straight to the American Consulate. They'll be able to help you … " Mrs. McGregor paused ominously, "if anybody can."

Mrs. Adams produced a hankie. "I pray to God a thousand times each day he's safe … "

Mrs. McGregor was dressed in a gray pants suit she had had made in Scotland especially for "the landing." Long sleeves ended at the wrist, and the high collar buttoned tightly around the neck.

For the past two days, Mrs. McGregor had talked non-stop about "the landing," and now it was about to take place. The port had been commandeered by the Moroccan army for the unloading of relief-aid arriving from America; the few passenger ships that still bothered to call at Tangier were required to drop anchor in the bay. Disembarking passengers were brought ashore in boats manned by native rowers. Even these were unable to reach the beach because of sand bars and shallow water. The ladies had to be carried ashore if they didn't want to get wet. This task was performed by a team of stevedores who charged out through the surf whenever a boat came into sight.

A flotilla of landing craft was approaching the ship. Above the heaving shoulders of the rowers a shouting match was going on. Insults and threats were already being exchanged in the competition over the passengers. There were almost as many boats as arriving tourists, and these were commanded by merchants who wanted to be the first to sell to unsuspecting visitors the items that Tangier was famous for – camel saddles, curved daggers, and hashish pipes.

"Don't buy any of it!" Mrs. McGregor commanded.

"We're not here on a shopping spree," Mrs. Adams reminded her.

"Now remember," Mrs. McGregor was saying. "As soon as you reach the beach, take a taxi to the Minzah. It's the only hotel for a respectable woman to stay in. Every other place is full of drunken American soldiers."

"From what I hear, all American military personnel are stationed south of the Atlas Mountains," Daisy corrected her firmly. "That's 500 miles away."

"Will you and the doctor join us for cocktails, Hilda?"

"I'm a temperance woman."

"Tea, perhaps … "

"I'll ask the doctor. Now remember, when you get to the hotel, lie down until you feel rested. Everything is different in Morocco. Everything is strong – the smells, the colors, the noises, the languages. You'll go crazy trying to take it all in."

The boats were clustered about the bottom of the ladder. Men in turbans were waving daggers and shouting with a vehemence that startled the passengers.

"They seem so violent!"

"That's their way of bargaining," Mrs. McGregor explained.

Mrs. Adams leaned over the rail and began to haggle with the merchants in Spanish.

"Come down, señora!" shouted one, admiring her voluptuous figure. "Ride in my boat! It's the only one that's safe! The others are full of holes and might sink with you in it!"

"Don't listen to him, señora!" interrupted another. "He went fishing last night, and the bottom of his boat is full of dead and stinking sardines! Ride with me! Look – my boat has just been painted!"

"Look at these rowers, señora! Feel their muscles! The strongest in Tangier! They'll get you to the beach quickly and safely!"

"Ah, yes, but for how much?"

"You name the price, señora! Anything you say!"

While the bargaining was going on, Daisy listened to the babble of background comment from the rowers as they rested on their oars. She had studied Arabic in Spain and was able to understand some of the North African dialect.

One by one the passengers descended the ladder and stepped into the boats. Daisy and her mother took seats in the stern. Mrs. McGregor was helped into the bow. She looked ashen.

"Are you all right, Hilda?"

"I think she's saying a prayer."

Daisy attempted to strike up a conversation with the fellow steering the boat, but he just grinned and pointed at the beach.

"He doesn't understand a word I say."

"Your Arabic sounds wonderful to me."

"I knew it was a mistake when Antonio hired Sulimein. Why didn't he get a Moroccan when Spain is full of them?"

"Egyptians speak the purest Arabic, dear."

"Now I probably speak it with some weird accent nobody here can understand."

Mrs. Adams wiped her eyes. "Just keep it up and you'll be speaking like a native in no time."

"Why are you crying?"

"It seems like only yesterday that Arturo used to stick his little foot up for me to tickle while I changed his diaper."

Daisy put her arm around her mother. "You know perfectly well he knows how to take care of himself in the desert."

"Those terrible pictures in *Paris Match* ... "

"That was Casablanca. The Americans have been sent to the desert to do just what you said – making sure the food gets to the people who need it the most."

"I hope you're right."

After a while the boat was nearing the shore.

"Look, mother. There are your camels."

The camels were couched on the beach being relieved of their burdens of charcoal. A crowd of Muslims had gathered to see the Christians arrive.

"Look, mother."

"Heaven save me!" Mrs. McGregor was gray with fright. "Here they come!"

"Just shut your eyes, Hilda," Mrs Adams called. "Pretend they're knights in shining armour."

Mrs. McGregor let out an hysterical squawk.

"Goodness!" Mrs Adams eyed her with concern.

The sea was growing shallower, the waves were breaking all about, and water was splashing into the boat. The stevedores arrived not a moment too soon. Thigh deep in the water, laughing uproariously, shouting at one another in an incomprehensible tongue, they were wading strenuously among the boats. They wore nothing but flimsy cotton shorts. Their naked torsos gleamed with brine; their shorts were soaked through and clung to their bellies and legs.

"It's quite a sight, isn't it? I mean … "

"What, mother?"

"I mean, I didn't I expect such an unabashed welcome to Africa."

Their heads were shaved. Grotesque ivory grins wreathed savage faces incised with tribal markings. Amidst the babble of tongues and salt spray flying, brawny arms reached down and lifted up the ladies one by one.

Mrs. Adams was amazed by the gentleness with which she had been snatched up and borne above the waves. She could almost shut her eyes and dream she was flying.

"Are you all right, Hilda?"

"I think she's passed out."

Daisy was studying, from the distance of about twelve inches, the architecture and scars on the temples of the African who carried her. The gentle giant averted his eyes from her gaze. He deposited her, safe and sound, on the sand. No fee was charged, no tip was asked; the service was supplied free by the Port Authority of Tangier.

The beach was vast, and Moroccans were swarming all over it. A hot wind was blowing out of a bright blue sky, but nobody was sunbathing or in swimming. Uniformly dressed in long brown robes, the men were walking aimlessly around. Some knelt on the sand. Veiled women, swathed in yards of white, huddled together like so many bundles of laundry. From a crowd a few yards away came the sound of drumming.

"Isn't it wonderful to see people in native dress when the rest of the world is wearing blue jeans," Mrs. Adams commented.

A line of taxis was drawn up beneath the palm trees. There was going to be a delay while the stevedores carried the luggage ashore.

Daisy shook the hand of Dr. McGregor, a distinguished-looking gray-haired gentleman in a straw hat. He had a firm grip on his wife's waist.

"I'm going to help the doctor put Hilda in the car," Mrs. Adams said. "Stay here and wait for our bags. There are eleven in all. Be sure to count them so they won't get lost or stolen."

They went off, and Daisy walked over to the crowd of people where the music was coming from. The Moroccans were packed so tightly together that it was only with difficulty she managed to wedge herself among them.

Four musicians were kneeling on the sand. One was blowing on a flute that let out a spooky, moaning wail. Another wielded a pair of ringing, clacking metal castanets. The drums were going a mile a minute while a coal-black girl, with a perfectly round, moon-like face, danced. A long piece of cloth was wrapped around her waist and held by another woman. This restricted the girl's movements, which was just as well, for she was strong and her dance violent. Flinging her arms out and then crossing them over her chest, she bobbed to the rhythm of the drums. As the tempo increased, she threw back her head. Her face was contorted by pain or ecstasy – Daisy couldn't tell which. Her braids were whipping back and forth across her face. Her eyes were rolling and wild. She seemed to be completely crazy or lost in a trance – maybe both. She tugged like a calf on the end of a rope.

The spectators watched impassively. Their eyes were glazed. The drumming seemed to have put them into a trance, too. Daisy, who had disliked the sound of the alien Moorish music from the minute she heard it on the radio in Spain, began to feel dizzy. She didn't know if it was the music, the heat, or the smell and pressure of so many bodies packed together.

The girl began to slap her shoulders with her fists. To Daisy's horror blood appeared. The girl, she now saw, held two small knives, one in each hand, and she was stabbing herself to the rhythm of the music. Faster and faster she slashed until her clothes were torn and stained red.

The Moroccans looked on in silence, as though they were watching a chess match. One woman raised her baby high to see the blood. By degrees the music slowed, and the girl sank to her knees on the sand. The front of her robe was soaked with blood, but she did not seem to be in pain. Her bewildered, rapturous expression appeared to be the result of having stabbed herself.

The crowd broke up, and Daisy walked back to where the stevedores were piling the suitcases on the sand. The drumming had put her in a kind of daze, too. But she felt mysteriously rejuvenated, as though she had just woken from a catnap. She had just witnessed a native ritual which, without understanding it, she knew to be truly amazing. She made a mental note to find out what it all meant.

"Are you all right, dear?" Mrs. Adams asked. "You look pale."

"All eleven suitcases present and accounted for." Daisy did not want to upset her mother with a story about blood.

A taxi driver loaded the bags into his car.

"It's just like Matisse said ... " Daisy said when they were settled in the back seat. "Morocco puts you back in touch with nature ... with Africa ... with the elements, with real people! The natives! Did you hear those drums?"

"Where to, ladies?" the driver asked in Spanish.

"The Hotel Minzah, please."

"Mother, are you sure we can afford it?"

"Mrs. McGregor said the Minzah is the best hotel."

"She's anti-American. I don't like her."

"No one is more anti-American than your father, dear."

"Will you please stop referring to Antonio as my father."

"He raised you. He gave you his name."

"I didn't have any choice in the matter. And that doesn't make him my father." Daisy had a knack for making her mother feel guilty. "Anyhow, he has his strong moral reasons for being anti-American."

"Moral reasoning is the biggest obstacle to forgiveness."

"He can't forgive America for what it did to the Indians, the blacks, and the Mexicans."

"Forgiveness is everything, dear. It purifies the soul. It purges the mind. You'll learn that sooner or later. Any person who cannot forgive cannot think clearly or be truly happy and at peace."

"Can you imagine Antonio turning the other cheek? Well, I'm proud of you for standing up to Mrs McGregor. She's a bully."

"She said the manager is a Frenchman so the food ought to be good."

"We have no idea how long it's going to take to get in touch with Arturo. What if our money runs out?"

"Let me worry about money. Mrs. McGregor said the position of the hotel gives it a psychological advantage. We might be put off by the maze of the Arab town with its veiled faces and hordes of nagging urchins. At the Minzah we'll have a view of the sea. On a clear day we can see Gibraltar."

"We didn't come to Tangier to watch the boats go by."

"I travelled all over South America with your grandfather. He said that when you enter a strange town, always stay at the best hotel. People will come to the best hotel to tell you what you need to know. The most important locals always meet in the bar of the best hotel. We may have to entertain people, and the best hotel is the place to do it. People will respect us more if we stay at the Minzah."

"You're going to feel awfully guilty if you've spent all your money entertaining freeloaders in the bar of the Minzah."

"Your grandfather said that in a poor country wealth, even the illusion of wealth, is the best guarantee of safety."

"I would have thought that to appear to be absolutely penniless would be the best way to avoid being robbed or conned."

"No one will hurt us if we stay at the Minzah."

"Mother, you said so yourself: if we return from Morocco empty-handed, life won't be worth living."

The taxi was grinding up Cuesta de la Playa, a steep hill leading to the medina, or Arab quarter. It was market day, and the taxi was nosing its way through a human moraine of Moroccans intent on getting their shopping done before the day stoked up. From his blackened cave a charcoal vendor blinked like a mole into the morning light. A weathered fisherman hawked sardines with piercing, guttural cries that seemed to echo the harshness of his life. Fresh-faced country girls in floppy straw hats and red and white striped shawls sat primly before shiny piles of home-grown vegetables. The shouting and the haggling, the flies and the confusion, the sickly-sweet smell of uncollected garbage: the scene was enough to send tourists home in strait-jackets.

A boy darted in front of the taxi and was nearly hit. The driver slammed on his brakes.

"*¡Dimasiado niños!*" he said fiercely. "Every year there are more of them – every day! A man with no job, with children all over his house, what is he going to do?"

"Children are the blessing of God," Mrs Adams said.

"Our schools are like movie houses. The first group goes in at eight and comes out at twelve. The second lot arrive at twelve and leave at four. The third lot after that. And when they grow up, there's nothing for them to do. They have to swim to Spain to find a job. Education is a lie because it prepares our children for a life of work that does not exist. And our women keep pushing them out like sausages!"

At an intersection a policeman put up his arm to stop the traffic. A trickle of tiny schoolgirls in cornflower blue smocks was crossing the street.

"Look at the children, Daisy. Aren't they adorable?"

The driver stuck out his head out the window. "¡*Putas*!" he shouted.

"What?"

"Whores, mother."

"He's gone mad! Imagine calling little girls that!"

"Driver," Daisy said, "do you know of a less expensive hotel? What about an Arab hotel?"

"There's no such thing as an Arab hotel," the driver responded irritably. "The closest thing we have is a *fondak*."

"What's a *fondak*?"

"A caravanserai, where travelling merchants stay."

"A caravanserai. Mother, it sounds perfect. We'll learn more about what's happening in Morocco in a *fondak* in one day than we would in a month at the Minzah."

"Horses, mules, and donkeys are tethered in the courtyard." The driver rattled on like a guide. "Rooms on the ground floor are reserved for the merchants' wares and maybe a servant or two to guard them. The rooms upstairs are for travellers."

"Do you think we'd be comfortable?" Mrs. Adams asked doubtfully. "My bedroom is so important to me."

"No beds, no furniture, no running water. Food has to be brought in from the outside or you cook it yourself, if you have a stove. The Moroccan toilet is the great outdoors."

"Oh dear. That sounds absolutely impossible."

"You can see for yourself." The driver stopped the car. "Here's one right here. *Fondak* Waller."

"Come on, mother. It won't hurt to have a look."

Stepping among piles of steaming dung, they followed the man through a tunnel that opened onto a wide interior courtyard. The animals were milling restlessly in the dust. The building, multi-balconied and several storeys high, echoed with loud, shouted voices. Loaded laundry lines criss-crossed the sky above their heads.

A woman heaved a bucket of slops over a balcony. She shrieked with laughter when they had to jump out of the way.

The donkey stallions, in a sexual frenzy, were chasing the mares and attempting to mount them with much kicking, bucking, and loud braying.

"Heavens!" Mrs. Adams retreated from the cloud of dust. "It's like a mad-house!"

"El Minzah, please," Daisy told the driver. "Hurry!"

CHAPTER 2

Tangier Tales

The next morning at dawn Daisy rose from her bed and stepped onto the balcony. The air above the hotel garden was cool and fresh, yet already heavy with the great heat to come. A smudge of low cloud lay like a curtain across the Strait of Gibraltar. Against a sky that was almost colorless, swallows swooped and dove for invisible bugs. The massed hulls of the fishing fleet were reflected on the glassy water of the harbor. A lone boat was making its way out to sea, towing behind it the great spreading V of its wake.

It was a grave, utterly silent hour, as though time had stopped for the Creator to take a breather before starting another day. As if in recognition of this, a man carrying a rolled-up prayer mat and blue plastic bucket emerged from a door to one of the flat white rooftops below the hotel. He squatted down and splashed water over his face. His teeth he scrubbed with a finger. He rinsed his feet, pouring the water between each toe. He then bowed toward the East, and began the morning prayer.

Brushing the air with silent wings, a brown owl threaded the palm trees of the hotel garden. A mother cat, followed by two emaciated kittens, stepped from the shadows. She lay down in the sunshine, rolled on her side, and let her babies feed.

The sun, which had been pushing upwards, filling the sky with gold, suddenly jumped from the curtain of cloud. The light threw the coastline of Spain into relief, illuminating hillsides speckled with white houses.

The grace of the owl's flight, the stealth of the cat's step, the deep shadows in the hotel garden where pockets of night still lingered, and, above all, the astonishing quantity of light that was pouring across the watery horizon between the Pillars of Hercules: it all seemed so wild, so silent and mysterious that Daisy didn't dare move. She could have watched it forever because she loved being part of it.

Mrs. Adams had passed a restless night. The mournful hooting of the owl she took to be a bad omen, and the screeching of alley cats had disturbed her sleep. Despite having been up half the night comforting her, Daisy felt so exhilarated on this, her first morning in Africa, she couldn't go back to bed. She dressed quickly, let herself out of the hotel and walked downhill into the medina.

The narrow alleys made her wary. She walked slowly, looking back at turnings and memorizing street signs. The only others moving about at this early hour were the garbage men, removing trash from where the cats had been feeding all night. Dressed in thread-bare tweed jackets, baggy pants, rubber boots and wide-brimmed pal-metto hats, these bearded paupers saluted her heartily as she went past.

Rounding a corner, she nearly stumbled over an elderly man lying on the pavement. He was nobly dressed in a white cotton djellaba ribbed with silvery stripes. A creamy woolen burnoose was draped over his shoulders, Roman-style. His flat brown feet were sheathed in pointed yellow slippers. Clutching a painted lemonwood cane, he was struggling to get up. A tasselled fez lay on the street.

Daisy picked up the fez. "Can I help you, sir?"

"Yes, please … " The man grimaced.

She lifted him to his feet. He took the fez and placed it on his head. "That way," he said, a little breathlessly, pointing with the cane.

She led him, at a shuffling pace, to a doorway at the bottom of an alley. A sign read CHANCE BAR.

What with the yellow paint peeling off the walls and reek of cat urine, the place seemed seedy enough from the outside, but, once through the door, Daisy was pleasantly surprised to find herself in a sunlit, cobbled garden.

A waiter shouted, "*Madame, viens vite!*" and helped Daisy settle him into a chair. A woman in black, followed by a tiny black dog, darted from a cottage. She ran over to the old man and made a fuss over him.

"Are you all right, sidi?" She spoke French in a raspy voice. "Do you want me to call the doctor?"

"No, no, Babette. I lost my footing, that's all. Thanks to this young ... lad ... lady ... I'm all right."

Daisy had taken a seat at the next table and was admiring the hibiscus shrubs that flowered in whitewashed tubs. Blood red geraniums flowered in pots hung on the walls. A jasmine vine piled on the cottage roof showered blossoms onto the cobbles. An old Moor in faded bloomers was sweeping them up with a twig broom. The garden was overspread by the fronds of a colossal palm, itself swathed in the powerful grip of a night-blooming cereus.

The woman came over to Daisy and asked what she wanted for breakfast. Her face was a mass of wrinkles, which she still took the trouble to rouge. A yellow cigarette dangled from a flaccid lip. The toy poodle danced at her heels.

Daisy didn't speak a word of French.

"He wants to buy you breakfast," she croaked in English.

"Who is he?"

"That's old Jâafar Tazi. He used to be the Moroccan ambassador in London. Now he's the Mendoub – the Sultan's Representative in Tangier."

"He has the most beautiful clothes."

"Yeah, I guess he does. Every morning he sneaks out of his ramshackle palace while his wives and children are still asleep and comes here for breakfast."

"How many wives does he have?"

"No one knows how many. Some say four, some say forty. Now, what'll it be?"

"Coffee, please."

"Look, it's on his tab. He doesn't care how much you spend."

"I'm not much of a breakfast person ... "

"Suit yourself."

"All right. I'll have a brandy."

"Courvoisier?"

"I like the Spanish kind."

She went back into the cottage. Daisy took out her tobacco and began rolling a cigarette. The waiter and the fellow leaning on his broom were furtively scrutinizing her and conversing in whispers.

"This is the quiet hour for us café-dwellers," she heard Jâafar say in English.

"This is my favorite hour, too. Before the world wakes up and the noise begins."

He beckoned her over to his table. "Are you enjoying your holiday?" he asked. "In Tangier, east meets west. Have you come here by yourself?"

She sat down beside him. "I'm here with my mother."

"Did you and your mother buy *round trip tickets*?"

"I think so." Daisy was startled by the hollow intonation of his words. "Why?"

"Because many people come on holiday to Tangier for the weekend or even one day," he said, "and they like it so much they don't go home. They stay for the rest of their lives."

"We've only been here one night. Already I've seen a girl slash herself with knives. My father never stops telling me – 'Go back to the basics, the primitive and the elemental.' When I saw her smiling while the blood flowed ... I felt I'd arrived."

"You're not English?"

"American."

Daisy asked the waiter for a fresh pack of tobacco. He bowed, murmured a reply, and went away.

"He understood!"

Jâafar smiled. "You speak Arabic."

"A little. Not very well. My father insisted I study it before coming here."

"I commend you."

"Mine's pretty basic. I think I've got the wrong accent."

"Very few American, English or French people bother to learn our language."

"My father said that Arabic was once the language of Spain."

"That is true."

"And one day it will be so again."

Jâafar smiled. "Morocco and Spain are brothers in history."

Daisy ran her tongue along the cigarette paper. "We've come to Morocco to see my brother. We got a postcard from a place called Tafilalet. Where is that?"

"The Tafilalet is an oasis near the border with Algeria."

"Is it safe for a woman to travel down there?"

Jâafar smiled. "In the Sahara ... a great chief ... if God has not chosen to give him sons ... might ask a favorite daughter to disguise herself as a boy so she can accompany him on his travels."

"In other words, your advice is no."

"I would say ... a woman on her own in the Sahara must be very wise."

"I was raised in the desert. We live in Spain now, but home for me will always be the Guadalquivir Ranch near Douglas, Arizona. Guadalquivir – that means Big River in Arabic, doesn't it? Like the one in Sevilla."

Jâafar thought for a moment. "*Wad al Kebir*. Big River. Yes."

He watched her light the cigarette with her *mechero*.

"You're very good at making those ... "

"Heck, I can do it at a full gallop." She exhaled some smoke. "Well, that's not quite true."

The color of Jâafar's skin might be described as purple, not as dark as the eggplant. This, combined with thick pinkish lips and dark hooded eyes, gave him a rather morose, even cruel appearance. But, when he smiled, his features lifted into a comical, almost clown-like mask. He had a good sense of humor and loved nothing better than a good gossip in English, a language he prided himself on speaking.

Breakfast arrived. Daisy poured half the brandy into her coffee and drank off the rest.

She glanced at her watch. "I better get back to the hotel. My mother will be worried if she wakes up and I'm not there. She has an aneurysm."

Jâafar frowned at the word.

"That's when a blood vessel inside your head balloons out. She's supposed to lie down three hours a day, but she never does. She didn't sleep much last night. The only thing that soothed her was the call from the mosque. It was like a lullaby – it put her right to sleep."

Jâafar's fingers plucked her sleeve. "I would like to invite you and your mother to my home."

"Well, thank you very much."

"Some friends are coming this evening ... "

"Tonight? I don't think so. She's supposed to take it easy, especially the first day here. I'll have to ask."

"My guest of honor will be a gentleman of grand standing in the desert. He can tell you what you need to know about the situation in the Tafilalet."

"My mother would be very grateful for that!"

"Which hotel are you staying in?"

"The Minzah."

"Your name?"

"Daisy Adams. But that's not the name we're registered under. We're registered under my mother's – Toledano."

"Toledano?"

"Yes. It's a Spanish name."

Jâafar smiled. "It is a very grand name."

"You know it?"

"It is a Spanish name, yes. It is also a Moroccan name, a Tangier name and a Jewish name."

"Jewish?"

"The Toledanos came to Tangier from Spain many years ago ... 1492."

"The year Columbus went to America."

"Also. Also the year of the fall of Granada, our last Muslim capital in Spain. In the years following, the Spanish Muslims – called Moriscos – and the Jews – Sephardim – left Spain to seek more tolerant lands. Tangier was where the Toledanos settled, guarding the keys to their homes in Spain and speaking Ladino."

"What language is that?"

"An antique form of Spanish."

"These Toledanos. Are they still in Tangier?"

"Not as many as before."

"So my mother may have relations here?"

"It is possible, yes."

"It's like she's come home!"

Jâafar nodded. "To a very old and historic family. They distinguished themselves before the battle of Trafalgar."

"My father told me. Admiral Nelson."

"Correct."

"He said the word admiral derives from the Arabic."

"*Amir al* ... yes. Your father must be a very learned man."

"Mister know-it-all." Daisy snorted some smoke through her nose. "He thinks he knows everything."

Jâafar smiled. "Before the battle the English fleet provisioned in Tangier. The Toledanos and other great Jewish families supplied Nelson's ships with water and food, mainly beef. As a result they were granted English citizenship in perpetuity."

"Like the descendants of General Lafayette are entitled to American passports."

"That is so. Legend has it that herds of cattle were gathered and driven to Tangier. Fresh beef was supplied to Nelson's ships. History tells us that the English sailors were more disciplined than the French and the Spanish. They were also better fed – with beef just before the battle – which made them stronger and braver, and so contributed to Nelson's victory."

"That is truly amazing."

"Tangier is full of history."

"It explains why my mother has an English passport!"

Jâafar smiled.

"Do you think she could be connected to all this history?"

"It is possible."

"She hasn't told me any of this."

"No?"

"I'm going to have to have a talk with her as soon as I get back to the hotel."

Jâafar placed two fingers on her sleeve. "You mustn't."

"Mustn't I?"

"No, you mustn't. You must not disturb her."

Daisy had the uncanny feeling that this elderly gentleman, whom she had just picked up off the street, seemed to know things about her mother that she did not.

"All right, I'll let her sleep." She finished her coffee and stood up. "But I better get going."

"I will send my car at nine o'clock, Miss … Adams."

Daisy bent over, put her arm around him, catching the back of his neck in the crook of her elbow, and planted a kiss on his cheek.

"Nine o'clock. I'll tell her! Goodbye!"

Jâafar sat back in his chair. The carefree impetuosity of her kiss, the odor of her perfume, and especially the pliant strength of her embrace sent a tremor of delight through the old man.

"Allah be praised!" he sighed.

CHAPTER 3

Hammada

The thump of a chopper making a long low curl over the desert snapped Arturo awake. A sun that was nordic in paleness had risen from the plain. Somewhere a bird was singing – a solitary bird – a bird he could not see. The song was magical and seductive. It seemed to be beckoning him into the void.

Waiting for the chopper to disappear, he crawled from the fist-like clump of boulders where he had spent the night, and set off again. The mineral silence of the Sahara was broken only by the crunching of his boots. He put on his dark glasses as the day stoked up. The air seemed to ignite like a blast from a furnace. The silence murmured in his ears like the echo within a seashell. He swore he could hear the lowing of cattle.

Mirages crowded in, cutting off the horizon. The quicksilver puddles crept to within a few yards from every direction but windward, where a sneaky little breeze opened the door a crack. Palm trees floating on mirror-water islands were swallowed by the reflection of the double sky. He crossed a wadi plugged with stones rolled from the Atlas over millions of years – spherical stones the size of marbles, golf balls, billiard balls, baseballs, softballs, bowling balls, soccer balls, basketballs, medicine balls! Ankle-breaking stuff and a chore to walk over. When kicked aside they clicked together like steel. The plain was alive with dust-devils. Like mysterious marionettes they swooped, bounced and danced along, emitting a plaintive hissing song as they sent sand and dust spiralling into the air.

On his map this stony plain, the *Hammada du Guir*, looked about a hundred miles wide, to Kenadsa, maybe one fifty to Colomb-Béchar, which was once in Morocco, but now in Algeria. When the French ruled the desert, a general could shift a border with the stroke of a pen. The frontier was a vaguely defined line. Otherwise it was no-man's land, laced with mine-fields left from the Algero-Moroccan war. Vultures would tell him where the mines were.

At the end of the gruelling day, with a molten sun sizzling on the horizon, his shadow stretching a hundred feet, something flashed up ahead. He threw himself down and dug out the binoculars. What he saw was not shiny but a white-washed dome that glowed like a pearl against the swarthy background of the desert.

He made for it.

The dome was the roof of a *koubba* or saint's tomb, which dot the landscape all over Morocco. He ducked inside and fell exhausted onto a dune that had drifted through the door. Lying on his back, he sliced off a lump of cheese and sipped water from the bottle. Through a gaping crack in the dome he watched the curved shadow of the earth, like a gigantic eraser, sweep across the sky, removing the last light from the day. In its wake, a few stars clicked on.

Thrusting his hand into the dune, he felt the cool sand beneath the layer of warm. Signs indicated that the tomb had once been inhabited. A number of broken pots lay scattered on the sand. The ground outside was littered with them. Three blackened cookstones huddled in a corner. The wall above was smudged by smoke. A fire had burned there, maybe the day before, or a year. In the frozen landscape of the *hammada*, where nothing ever seems to change, it's not easy to determine how old the marks of human habitation might be. In the Sahara yesterday is the same as BC.

He could hear nothing, absolutely nothing, save for the beating of his heart. There was no soughing of wind in the grass, no motor murmur, animal squeak or human voice. Stars like flares spilled across the heavens in an avalanche so bright and dense and he felt he could reach up and stir them with his finger. If there is a God, He is but One, and He is silent.

CHAPTER 4

Jâafar's Roof

The heavy door thumped behind them, shutting out the curious children gathered in the street. The young woman who slid the bolt across wore a billowing yellow caftan tucked at the waist by a green embroidered belt. A braided halter across her shoulders held back voluminous sleeves. Her hair was covered by a red silk handkerchief. Heavy silver bracelets encircled her wrists and ankles; henna tattoos speckled her hands and feet. From this finery her face shone like a ripe blue grape. Leading the way, she padded along barefoot with a seductive clank of jewelry.

A row of slender columns, reminiscent of the Alhambra in Granada, supported an arcade that encircled the courtyard of Jâafar's palace. The ceiling was adorned by stalactite vaulting, the walls ornamented with geometric designs.

A stately palm dipped its head over the dripping fountain. Hibiscus blossoms floated on the pool. Black women in sumptuous costumes glided here and there.

"Do Moroccans dress like this all the time?" Mrs. Adams wondered out loud.

"They're slaves."

"In this day and age?"

"Mr. Daoudi, the concierge, said that when Jâafar was named ambassador to England, he moved his entire household from Marrakesh to Tangier, including the servants, some of whom had been with his family all their lives. They come and go as they please, but they are happy to stay under Jâafar's roof. He feeds them, he buys their clothes, he calls the doctor when anyone is sick, he sends their children to school. Under his roof they feel safe."

A group of brown men, in spotless white shirts and woolen robes of military uniformity, their heads swathed in tightly-packed orange turbans, sat in a semi-circle on a carpet. Their pointed yellow slippers were lined up like a row of boats on the marble floor. Clouds of scented smoke billowed from pots of charcoal where they warmed the skins of their drums.

The great hall, decorated head-high with mosaic tiles, led the eye upward to Suras from the Koran chased by hand into the plaster frieze, and on to the fabulously painted wooden ceiling.

One corner of the ceiling had fallen in. The carved frieze was stained by water. The hole had been crudely patched with a sheet of blue plastic. Stiff with the unbled pond of last winter's rain, it stared into the room like a great unblinking eye.

Jâafar, in a white robe, greeted them ceremoniously. "I have a special guest tonight."

They followed him across the huge Wilton rug, past a dozen or so mute grandfather clocks, onto a terrace overlooking the Strait.

The area had been arranged like an upholstered nest. The tiles were layered with carpets, the low walls banked with pillows. Ornate candle lanterns supplied a dim light. Charcoal blazed in pots, sending up pillars of heat. Shadowy robed figures sat looking in different directions while a boy made noises on a flute.

Beneath a starry sky, the Strait was sprinkled with lights. Close to shore, fishing boats shined beams into the depths to attract the catch. The fleets of every nation constantly funnel through this busy bottleneck between the Atlantic and the Med. The lighthouses of Tarifa and Gibraltar flash reassuring signals to be answered from the Malabata light, on a point of land across the Bay of Tangier. The sea captains are thus able to triangulate their positions on this narrow waterway.

Jâafar led them across the terrace to a man who stood alone, looking out to sea. He was not a tall man. His turquoise robe was slit down both sides to reveal a darker garment beneath. His turban was black, his yellow slippers shiny and new. This solitary figure bore an aloof and grave formality among the other chatting guests.

"The Marabout Si Mohamed," Jâafar introduced him as. "The Grand Master of the Jilaliya."

He did not smile. Neither did he seem unfriendly. His soft grey beard was accentuated by the bluish shading of his weathered skin. He could have been fifty or seventy. He moved with a limp.

Mrs. Adams put out her hand. He did not take it, but inclined his head and murmured a greeting. He then said something which Jâafar translated.

"He says it is so seldom that he sees the sea."

"That's the one they call 'The Rogue,'" Daisy whispered to her mother when they were alone. "The holy man who's been stirring up trouble in the desert."

"How do you know these things?"

"Mr Daoudi dixit."

"I swear I've seen his face somewhere before."

"The Sultan has put a price on his head for putting up a fight against the Americans. What's he doing here? I wonder."

"He doesn't look very fierce to me. Look how sad his face is."

"Stay away from him, mother! Don't talk to him."

"But isn't he the one we've come to see?" Mrs. Adams crossed the carpet, performed a kind of curtsey before the Marabout and settled herself on a cushion beside him. They soon discovered they spoke a common language – Spanish.

"My daughter made me stay in the hotel before coming here, so I've been resting in my room all day. Our bathroom has a wonderful view of the city. I stood on the edge of the tub watching the women doing their laundry, washing rugs, and feeding the sheep. In Tangier the sheep live on the rooftops."

"Ah yes." The Marabout smiled. "Because the feast is near."

"Is that similar to the feast of Abraham when the sheep are slaughtered?"

"That is correct, Señora."

"I haven't seen your country yet, but I'm told it is one of the most beautiful in the world."

The Marabout inclined his head. "That is also true, Señora. A beautiful country, blessed by God, which we love very much."

"I wish my husband were here. The desert appeals to him very strongly. All the great prophets – Moses, Christ and Mohammed – they all heard God's message in the desert. Isn't that so?"

The Marabout nodded. "That is correct, Señora." The round face, the sad eyes, the soft gray beard – she had an urge to stroke it – had an irresistible effect on Mrs. Adams.

"I think you would like my husband, sir, because he dislikes authority. He is a rebel like you."

She accepted a glass of orange juice from the tray being passed by an ebony-skinned child in a silver robe. "The clothes you people wear make me realize that I am in a very old and cultured society that has not given up its traditions."

The Marabout nodded.

"My husband used to belong to the Mexican Socialist Party, but now he has given up politics. He pins his hopes for a happier life on the education of the young. Sir, have you heard of the anarchist philosopher Peter Kropotkin?"

The Marabout shook his head.

"He's Russian. Like Kropotkin, my husband envisions a society in which men and women do both manual and mental work. Instead of being taught from books alone, he believes children would be better off if they received an active outdoor education, and learned by doing and observing first hand."

She noticed the Marabout looking at Daisy.

"She may look fluffy in that toreador jacket and pantaloons, but physically she is very strong. When she was fourteen my husband sent her into the desert with the .22 and a blanket and told her not to come back for two days. He taught her to ride and shoot. I know you Arabs can ride like the wind, but I'd put money on my daughter in a riding contest any day. She won her first rodeo ribbon when she was ten."

"Mother, dinner is ready." Daisy had been eavesdropping. "Jâafar wants us to sit down."

"My son is in the desert." Mrs. Adams got to her point. "He's already been hurt once. Can't you and the Americans make it up?"

"We are not in America, Señora," the Marabout's eyes flashed. "I do not make war on America. We are in Morocco, and the Americans have come here."

"But the Sultan asked for our help."

"It would have been wise to consult his people before extending such a rash invitation."

"Maybe there wasn't enough time."

"We Moroccans have been solving our problems, in our way, for thousands of years."

"Oh dear, I do understand." Mrs. Adams was wringing her hands. "If my husband were here, he'd agree with you. He'd probably be on your side."

"It is not my wish to fight your country, Señora, but it is my duty to defend my people from American soldiers who occupy our land."

"Do you mean you want to make peace?"

"I would make peace with America, yes, but does America wish to make peace with us? American soldiers march across our land; we do not invade theirs. We Saharans consider that we have the right to enjoy the possession of our territory in preference to any other people," the Marabout said heatedly. "I am sure your son is a civilized man. Can he imagine what it is like to be the party being invaded? The history of America tells us that every man and woman fights until the enemy is defeated, as they did when they won their independence, as they did in two great wars. Now American soldiers occupy our oases while we, the rightful owners of these places, are forced to wander the waterless plains. Is this civilized behaviour? No, it is the worst kind of barbarism when a rich and powerful nation preys on a poor and helpless one in the name of civilization."

"Come on, Mother. Jâafar wants us to sit down."

The guests took their places around a low round table. A copper basin and pitcher containing warm water was passed to wash their hands. The first course was a massive pink *pageot* that lay whole upon the platter. As a traditional host, Sidi Jâafar did not sit with his guests but circled the table, directing the servants. Mrs. Adams and Daisy were the only women present. He showed them how to eat Moroccan-style, with their fingers.

Next came chicken with pistachios, accompanied by a cool radish salad. The couscous was a more complicated matter. The Moroccan guests pinched off gobs of semolina with their fingers, deftly rolled them into little balls, and popped them into their mouths without a grain being wasted. After observing a few unsuccessful attempts, Sidi Jâafar handed the ladies spoons.

Despite its abundance, the food was light and digestible. Dessert was sliced oranges sprinkled with sugar and cinnamon. The basin and pitcher were passed again.

The musicians filed onto the terrace, their drums humming like the engine room aboard ship. Daisy recognized the rhythms she had heard on the beach. One of the musicians and the woman in yellow, the one who had let them in, danced side by side. She was hopping from one foot to the other as though the floor was on fire. The man came over and beckoned Daisy to her feet. She tried to imitate the bouncing movements. The servants of the household poured through the doorway to watch. The surrounding rooftops were crowded with Jâafar's neighbors.

By degrees the music slowed, and Daisy sank to a cushion next to the Marabout.

He invited her to a game of parcheesi. A board was brought.

"When you think about it," Mrs. Adams commented in the car on the way back to the hotel, "eating with your fingers that have just been washed is more sanitary than with knives and forks that have been used by countless others we have never seen."

"I was full after the fish."

"He speaks beautiful Castillian, not the mongrel Andaluz you hear on the street."

"He studied at the University of Salamanca."

"Now I remember where I've seen his face before. He's the spitting image of Robert E. Lee – the photograph taken at Appomattox, when he handed his sword to Grant. He was sad and worn out from fighting to preserve the way of life he loved. Jâafar said we must address him as *Sidna*."

"What does that mean?"

"It means 'Our Lord.'"

"Mother, for goodness' sake."

"Like Lee he is a rebel leader fighting to keep the Yankees out of his country."

"The reason he's sad is because he lost his children."

Mrs. Adams remained silent.

"A little boy and a little girl. They were twins."

"No!"

"They both died of meningitis when they were six. One after the other. The little boy died first. The next day the little girl. This all happened in the desert where there was no hospital and no doctor. His wife was so grief stricken she committed suicide."

Mrs. Adams was silent for a few minutes. Then she began to whimper.

Mrs. Adams made that sound in her sleep when she was having a nightmare. Her defenceless soul was crying out, but shed no tears. A puppy might make a noise like that when he's been locked out of the house at night, with no warm body to cuddle against. Mrs. Adams struggled to be happy, but she had been made to suffer terribly, and she did not have a happy life. It was in her defensive nature to think in advance of all the awful things that could happen to her children. By invoking a worst case scenario she forged a breastplate for herself. Her imagination armed her with a shield and a spear to beat fate to the punch. But when the shield shattered, as sometimes happens in a dream, and the black coyote moved in and breathed on her face, she whimpered pathetically like that scared little puppy alone in the dark. Daisy used to creep into their bedroom, give her shoulder a push and say, "Mother, you're having a nightmare!"

True to form, Antonio Adams lay sound asleep beside her, snoring like a bear in a hollow log.

CHAPTER 5

Koubba

In the wintry light that precedes the dawn, Arturo was woken by the sound of tapping. During the night he had drawn his knees up and thrust his hands between them. Beneath him the sand was cold.

He smelled smoke.

Peeling back the burnoose, he raised his head above the crest of the dune. Hunched in the far corner of the tomb, his back turned, a man was crouched over a fire.

Heart pounding, Arturo fell back. He lay still, listening and looking up. The crack in the dome gaped crookedly at the sky in which a solitary star still shone.

Again the tapping came. Once more Arturo lifted his head above the dune. The fire had subsided. With a stick the man was scraping some embers into a shallow basin scooped from the sand. He filled a tiny blue teapot with water from a skin and nestled it among the embers. Reaching for a small metal hammer, he tapped it against a white, cone-shaped object wrapped in blue paper. White flakes fell onto a piece of paper that was also blue.

The teapot began to shake. The man withdrew it from the embers. Dipping his fingers into a tin box, he let fall a handful of tea into the teapot, and replaced it on the embers. Two miniature glasses he filled with sand. The inside of each glass he scoured with his finger, poured out the sand, blew the dust off the glasses, wiped them with the end of his turban and set them side by side, on the blue paper, next to the white flakes. The flakes were dropped into the teapot, one by one, and the teapot was allowed to stand once more. Finally the tea was poured into the glasses, then repoured into the pot. He refilled one glass and tasted the brew. Another flake was added, and the pot was left to stand.

34

The meeting of eyes came as a shock. Arturo had been so absorbed by the ritual preparation of tea he had not realized that the man had turned his head. He pointed at the pair of glasses and grinned – a grotesque, gap-toothed, malevolent yet friendly grimace. An upward movement of the chin beckoned Arturo forward.

Crawling to the fire, he warmed his hands over the glowing coals while the man poured out the tea in long, smoking strokes.

"*Assalam alaikoum,*" he said, offering a glass.

"*Was alaikoum assalam.*"

CHAPTER 6

Zero, Place De La Casbah

In the shabby warm heart of Tangier's bustling medina stands the American Legation, our country's oldest diplomatic property and its only historical monument located abroad. In 1821 the original building was given to James Monroe, the fifth American president, by the Sultan Moulay Suleimein as a symbol of friendship between Morocco and the young American republic.

Surrounded by rooftops where women hang out laundry and men slaughter sheep, whitewashed walls and clean architectural lines define this prim New England oasis. Reception rooms display a treasure of paintings of this North African kingdom which has inspired so many artists. A library of rare books on Barbary, staircases hung with ancient engravings, maps, and portraits of American diplomats date from the time when the Legation was the only American outpost on the dark continent. Venetian mirrors and chandeliers ornament Moorish rooms with the elegant furnishings of a shared past touchingly preserved.

During this dimly remembered time of crisis between two friends, which our story spans, when America and its nearest Muslim neighbor worked together and at the same time edged to the brink of war, the Legation, which embodies the spirit of that enduring friendship, housed the offices of a small army of government officials arriving from America, including the military attaché.

"Mrs. Adams, your son joined the United States Army, not a kindergarten where mothers can come running with band-aids and kisses every time a soldier scratches his finger. I suggest you go back to America, ma'am, and wait for him to come home."

"We must find a place to live," Mrs. Adams announced firmly on the way back to the hotel. "I'm not going to leave here until Arturo leaves too, safe and sound."

A few days later they drove to the Casbah. She wanted to look at a house up there Jâafar had told her about.

Horn tooting, the taxi nudged its way through the crowded market square, ground up a steep cement street grooved for grip in a herringbone pattern, passed through a scarred keyhole archway into the fortified inner city of Tangier, where it was chased by children down a dark tunnel before emerging onto a broad sunlit cobbled area known as La Place de la Casbah, and pulled up before a high white wall with pink geraniums spilling down.

Mrs. Adams tapped a brass knocker against a green door. A diminutive Moroccan woman opened.

"You must be Mina."

"*Si, Señora.*"

They entered a courtyard paved with green and red octagonal tiles. White Moorish arches ran along one side. A gnarled old fig tree, whose branches were so heavy they had to be supported by chains – the chains themselves had long ago become imbedded in the wood – shaded the area with its broad leafy expanse. Green figs, each as big as a man's fist, hung precariously above their heads. A heady datura plant looked ready to collapse under the weight of its bell-shaped blossoms.

A bust of Seneca, Nero's tutor, scowled from the top of a Roman column. Water spilled in a quivering glassy sheet from a fountain into a shell-shaped basin. Hanging upside down in its cage, a yellow-crested cockatoo shrieked "*¡Patatas fritas! ¡Patatas fritas!*" Somewhere someone was moaning an old Andalusian lament. The scene was Mediterranean and timeless. They could have been in Rome or ancient Greece, Leptus Magna or Alexandria.

Mrs. Adams peered at the bird.

"Poor thing! It's blind in one eye and has a crooked foot. We'll take it."

"Mother, are you buying the bird?"

"No, the house."

"Please, can we see the place first!"

"You can tell in the first minute whether you're going to love a house."

Another woman peeked from a doorway across the courtyard.

"That's Sobrina, my niece," Mina explained. "She's shy."

"This tree ... " Daisy was gazing up into the colossal fig. "Jâafar said Samuel Pepys wrote his diary under these branches."

"Good. Now you can write your book under the same tree."

Opening doors with keys attached to a cord around her waist, Mina showed them around.

"This house belongs to a Mr. Williams, an elderly English painter, a friend of Sidi Jâafar," Mrs. Adams said. "The poor man is ill in London, and won't be returning to Tangier. His family wants to sell or rent the house and everything in it, to pay his medical expenses."

They were standing in the living room with its painted moorish ceiling.

"Jâafar said Mr. Williams bought a house in Fez, just for this ceiling. He stripped it out and had it brought here, along with these tiles. Look at that beautiful madonna in the moorish niche. That's where I'll pray."

They inspected the bedrooms, the baths, a small kitchen, and panelled dining room.

"This panelling is walnut. Mr. Williams brought it over from Spain. Jâafar said the house is completely furnished, right down to the cups and saucers. We won't need to buy a thing."

An outdoor stairway led to a terrace overlooking the sea. A carpet was spread on the tiles. They sat among embroidered cushions around a low table. Mina brought tea.

Poised between the Atlantic and the Mediterranean on the extreme north-western tip of Africa, Tangier is buffeted by the *Levante*, a heavy humid gale from the east. But on this day the wind had shifted to the southwest, pulling in dry air which the Moroccans call *El Rharbia,* the Spanish *El Poniente,* the English a zephyr, to blow the veil of humidity off the city, thinning the clouds and opening up spectacular views. When this happens the barometer shoots up, and Tangerines breathe easier and more deeply. They experience a sense of optimism and well-being, almost a whole new lease on life, whatever their troubles. The Pillars of Hercules edge closer and at sunset stand out with startling precision. The low, lean warships patrolling the Spanish current look like toy boats floating in a bathtub.

"Jâafar said that ever since the troubles began, the bottom has dropped out of the property market. The owner will lower the price if the house can be sold quickly."

"Mother, we already own a house in Spain!"

"Rather than waste our money on an expensive hotel room with orange juice at five dollars a glass, it will be more economical in the long run to have a place of our own. We can enjoy home cooking for a change. Jâafar says Mina is an excellent cook."

"How much is all this going to cost?"

"I'll buy the house in your name. If anything happens to me, you can sell it and have the money." They watched as Mina poured the tea. "I'm going to do everything on this carpet. I'll pray on it. I'll read on it. I'll write letters to Arturo. I may even die on it."

"Take it back."

"All right, I take it back, but I don't consider it bad luck to talk about death. For someone my age it's as natural as making out a shopping list. I told Antonio to spread bread crumbs on my grave, so the little birds will fly down. I will hear them and not feel alone."

"I wish you wouldn't talk like that. It brings bad luck."

"There is no such thing as luck in life. It's like the Muslims say — there's only *mektoub* — the fate that God has written down for each of us. *Gracias,* Mina. I love religion. I love to see people pray. Otherwise we'd all go down the drain like so many tadpoles. Even though I am a Roman Catholic, I may convert to the Muslim religion because both believe in the same god."

"You talk like you're never going back to America."

"Why should I when my children are here? I'm going to stay put in Morocco until Arturo is safe. I feel perfectly at home and ready to accept fate. With an aneurysm it can happen any second. Pop and the lights go out."Mrs. Adams looked at the horizon for a few minutes before leaning over and patting her daughter on the knee. "Don't worry, dear. I'll be around for a while yet."

"Is that all you can do – gaze toward Mecca and dream of eternity? Or are you dreaming of the good old days before you created this mess?"

"Raising a family is not making a mess. And I was not dreaming of eternity. I was saying a prayer for you and Arturo."

"There are happy families and there are unhappy families. What did Tolstoy say?"

"Please, darling, don't make me feel more guilty than I already do."

"Our family mess would have defied even Tolstoy's wisdom to untangle."

"Let's not go into it again."

"The ranch is gone. We have no place in America to go back to. We've only been here a few days, and already you're talking about staying forever."

"My home is here in my heart." Mrs. Adams pressed her chest with both hands. "I carry it wherever fate takes me."

"You made gypsies of us, which means we'll never be happy."

"Take it back."

"We may be more interesting than other people, mother, but you've condemned us to lives of rootlessness and dissatisfaction."

"You can't see into the future."

"You deprived us of our father's family in New York and the relatives we never knew, and left us with a nostalgia for a past we've only heard whispers about, like the ashes of a fire you can warm your fingers over but can never be rekindled, a past that rightfully belonged to us but which you extinguished forever. This nostalgia is like a slow, lingering death – like one of those Amazon rivers of yours that seems to flow along forever but ends in a swamp, a morass of quicksand and weed, with no way out. If we'd stayed in New York, Arturo could have gone to Yale like our father did, instead of winding up as a soldier in Morocco. I should be in college, too, not here in Africa wondering what's going to happen to us."

Mrs. Adams wiped away some tears. "Arizona was paradise ... " she said in a little voice. "Our little ranch in that big desert."

"Paradise it was not. No rich grannies, no aunts, no cousins, no uncles or generous godparents, no family reunions in a big house on the Hudson River, zero Christmas and zero Christmas presents."

"Money isn't everything, dear."

"Well, it's *something*! Fifteen years in Douglas, and we hardly knew a soul. No wonder the Greeks thought exile was the worst punishment – worse than death."

"Antonio adopted you. He's been a father to you."

"He's old enough to be my grandfather." Daisy was rolling a cigarette.

"Believe me, he's been a better father than your own father ever was. He devoted himself to your education."

"Do you call being employed as agricultural slaves and subjected to the atheistic jargon of my mother's Mexican lover an education? Oh, sure, your toenails were painted bright pink. They still are. You floated around the house in caftans while Arturo and I sweated in the garden. He never sent us to school, did he? We never had any friends."

"The nearest school was thirty miles away."

"So we had to learn the three R's in the bunkhouse. Whenever we got bored he sent us out to chop wood. He made us take cold showers, sleep all winter on the porch, and taught us how to light a fire in the rain."

"He taught you first aid and astronomy, and how to survive in the desert."

"He bullied us to be individuals or nothing."

"He wanted you and Arturo to be physically strong."

"Physically strong with the equivalent of an eighth grade education."

"You read *Don Quixote*."

"Only because of Rocinante and Rucio. When I have children I'm not going to experiment. They won't be human guinea pigs to test my theories on. I'm going to send them to school so they can grow up with other children, see how other people live, and lead a normal life. If they want to do something crazy after that, that's their business. Now we're condemned to exile because the central question has never been answered – where are we going to fit in?"

Mrs. Adams winced. "All my life my only concern has been for my children."

"Did you think of us when you uprooted us from our real father's home in New York and dragged us out west?"

"You're a great believer in original sin, aren't you? My life in New York was unbearable ... yes, I did think of you then ... I took you with me."

"And condemned us to this rootless life."

"Antonio taught you must be free."

"He barked at us to unshackle ourselves from rules that govern normal society, throw off our oppressors and so forth; but did it ever occur to you who we thought the tyrant was? We thought it was *him*."

"He wanted you to have the courage and confidence to say 'no' to the conventional world."

"And go out and liberate ourselves through wild deeds." Daisy finished rolling her cigarette.

"I wish you wouldn't smoke ... "

With her thumb Daisy flicked the little wheel of the *mechero*, which sent a spark into the soft rope wick. She blew on the wick until the spark glowed, touched the cigarette to the wick, took a couple of drags until the cigarette was fully lit, then snuffed out the wick by pulling it back into its tube.

"I keep telling you to stop smoking and stop drinking, to stop putting those poisons in ... "

Daisy blew out a cloud of smoke.

"You'll ruin your beautiful complexion, your hair and your health."

"It's my body."

"You used to be so conscious of your body."

Daisy ran a hand over her hair. The white scalp showed where her fingers ploughed furrows through the curls. "When I was sixteen."

"You used to run up with hugs and kisses when our friends came to the house."

"That was before I had my baby."

"They were all so impressed by your affectionate nature."

"That was the dazed expression of an absent personality."

"I forgive you. I forgive Arturo. I forgive you both a million times."

Daisy had been hit over the head at an early age by the facts of life. Her face could assume an almost madonna-like reverie when she reflected on a vanished chastity.

"Tell me the truth, mother. Our baby – was that the real reason we left Douglas?"

"The ranch was a dead duck. It didn't make financial sense to keep it going any longer."

"Not the shame of my having a baby?"

"No, dearie – the money."

"Shame must have had something to do with it. *La vergüenca* in that hick-town. That old school marm Miss Maplethorpe had her spies everywhere. Sooner or later she would have got wind of it. That's why we left in a hurry."

Mrs. Adams was saying a prayer.

"Well, Arturo might find the army a relief after being forced to haul in the wood, hoe the corn, and listen to Antonio's dreary lectures on nihilist philosophy."

"We're going to stay here until he's out of danger," Mrs. Adams said. "Even though we can't see him, it's a deep consolation for me to be here in Morocco. We breathe the same air he does. We see the sun rise and set at the same time. He sleeps when we sleep. He hears the call to prayer, and so do we. We have Jâafar to bring news. To be in another country, especially the next country when his life might be in danger would be absolutely unbearable."

"Did you tickle my feet, too?"

"I love you both the same. They can't keep him down there for ever. When peace comes, I want to be here. Sooner or later he'll be posted to a quieter spot. Then we'll all be together again. I'm going to call Antonio and tell him to come, now that we have a house to live in."

Mina reappeared with a plate of Moroccan pastries.

"Mina, we would like you to go on working here. You and your niece. Will you stay here with us?"

"*Sí, Señora*," Mina brightened. "*Con mucho gusto.*"

"Servants are always afraid when the house changes hands," Mrs. Adams said when Mina had gone away. "There, that's settled. I'll tell Jâafar we'll take it. He knows a lawyer who will handle the paperwork."

"Wouldn't it be more sensible to rent with an option to buy? That way you won't have to sell stock and part with any capital."

"Real estate is the best investment, dear."

"Money and history – those are two subjects you don't like talking about. You keep your past a mystery, but dole out the cash like there's no tomorrow. You never say how much there is or how long it will last."

"There's enough to keep us going until we're all together again."

Mina returned with Sobrina, an overweight girl with a bad complexion. All that was lost behind dimples and a shy smile. She went down on her knees before Mrs. Adams and pressed kisses onto her sleeves and shoulders.

"She made the cakes," Mina said.

"Aren't they delicious, Daisy?"

"That they are."

Sobrina crawled to Daisy and gave her the same blessing.

"Was that her we heard singing?"

Sobrina blushed.

"She's happy now," Mina said, "because someone else will eat the cakes besides herself."

The four women laughed together.

They all kissed at the door.

Mrs. Adams settled herself in the back of the taxi. "Isn't it exciting? A house, all to ourselves."

"Mother, will you please consider renting before you jump in at the deep end?"

"All right, dear. We'll rent."

CHAPTER 7

Mejdoubi

He was an old man, fifty or a hundred, with stubbled face criss-crossed by deep creases. From a nest of wrinkled skin a pair of pale, yellowish-brown eyes glowed like precious stones embedded in weathered rock. His lips were thin and black, his nose aquiline, his teeth few, but white and very sharp. A turban lay in loose folds about the crown of his head. Between the layers tufts of hair protruded. A number of scars shone through. The entire top of his head seemed to be a mass of livid scars. Around his neck, little leather packages sewn with cowrie shells hung on leather twine. A ragged robe enveloped him like a tent.

Arturo sipped the brew. In silence they downed the requisite three glasses. The sugar lift was electric. The man produced a loaf of bread. Arturo contributed a lump of cheddar, a luxury unheard of in the desert. The man's eyes glowed.

His name was Mejdoubi.

Breakfast finished, they walked into the dawn. Once more came the sound of bird-song. Mejdoubi listened; he cupped his ear; he frowned and he smiled. Through a series of interrogative shrugs he indicated that he had not heard the bird before. The bird must have come with Arturo, a good sign. He nodded. He approved.

Mejdoubi communicated that he was a descendant of the holy man buried within the *koubba*. They bore the same name and he, Mejdoubi, was the guardian of his ancestor's tomb. He pointed forlornly at the crack in the dome, the flaking paint peeling off. Pulling at his tattered robe, he indicated that he had not the necessary means to implement the important responsibility of maintaining his illustrious forbear's tomb.

Leading Arturo into the desert, he sank to his knees. With his hands he scuffed away a shallow layer of sand to reveal a leather disk, about two yards across, stretched over a wooden frame. It had been concealed beneath the sand. Together they lifted the leather, taut as parchment, to reveal a hole.

A well!

Mejdoubi nodded. He picked up a stone and dropped it in.

Yes!

Mejdoubi made all the signs that it was good water, clean water, pure water, fit to drink water. He groped in the sand and drew out a length of rope, frayed at one end. He spread his hands and pointed: the bucket and the rest of the rope were at the bottom of the well. He shrugged, rolled his eyes and pointed at the sky: no rope + no bucket = no water. It was Allah's will.

Arturo went to his pack and came back with money.

Mejdoubi backed away. He couldn't bear the sight. His eyes were shining at so much cash, but no – a man of his lineage could not accept. Holy ancestor would roll in his tomb!

Arturo pointed to the gap in the dome, he pointed at the broken wall; he picked up the frayed end of rope and waved it. He pointed down the well. He picked up a pebble and dropped it in.

The splash persuaded Mejdoubi. Kissing Arturo's sleeves he murmured a blessing. He pointed at the sun, made a clock-like movement with his arm, raised three fingers, and without another word strode off across the desert.

Still weary from yesterday's slog, Arturo went back to the *koubba* and spread the burnoose. Morning naps are the best.

Right on time Mejdoubi returned with blue rope and a galvanized bucket. In the bucket was a loaf of bread, a box of tea, a blue-wrapped sugar loaf, a haunch of raw meat, blue desert onions, carrots, potatoes, four eggs, a bunch of mint and another of coriander, and a folded paper containing *sudaniya* (hot pepper powder).

Down went the slinky new rope with the shiny bucket; up came the H_2O. Neither ice cold nor crystal clear, tepid and a bit murky, but water it was. Mejdoubi drank deeply, smacked his lips and declared it safe and good. Arturo sipped a little to quench his thirst.

Shadows lengthened. Mejdoubi dug again into the dune. This time he uncovered a blackened pot. Abruptly, he stopped. His eyes brightened, he lifted his finger and placed it against his temple. He listened. Arturo heard it, too. The bird, the invisible bird and its singular song. Mejdoubi's finger was pointing past his temple toward the sky. He nodded and smiled at Allah's acknowledgement. All was well.

Not a tree in sight, but Mejdoubi produced twigs for a fire. A jolly fire, throwing shadows against the mud wall of the *koubba*. They dipped bits of bread into the stew, which was followed by the strong sweet tea, now mint flavored.

Mejdoubi shared his pipe (*sebsi*), a reed-thin tube ending with a tiny clay bowl (*shkaf*) which he filled from his pouch (*metoui*) with the weed (*kif*).

CHAPTER 8

East Wind

Normally the East Wind, or Levante, which the Moroccans call the *sherqi*, lasts for three, six or nineteen days, but this summer, it seemed, it would never stop blowing. The air was filled with sand and flying dust. Windows banged and broke. Shutters were closed, confining people to stuffy semi-darkness.

Dr. McGregor came and went. Mrs. Adams was suffering from neck pains, which he attributed to a pinched nerve brought on by stress. The rims of her eyes were red from crying. She stopped going out and saw no one but Daisy and the women of the house. On her bedside table lay an English translation of the Koran, a gift from Jâafar.

One night she was woken by what she thought was the sound of tapping on the door. In the hubbub rising from the street, she was certain she heard Arturo's voice. Daisy went to investigate, and found that the noise was caused by a branch of the fig tree bumping against a shutter in the wind.

Mrs. Adams dreamed powerfully of her son. She saw him resting in an oasis. Beneath the palm trees women were singing as they hoed the plants. Arturo's feet were bathed in a basin of water, and the women were bringing him dates.

Each day she telephoned her husband in Spain, but there had been no further communication since that postcard from the Tafilalet.

"We are praying to the wrong God," she said. "We must bow to the One who rules over the place where Arturo is."

In a simple ceremony arranged by Jâafar, Mrs. Adams and Daisy declared before an Imam their sincere wish to become Muslims. The Imam (he who directs prayers) questioned them briefly on religious matters and heard each recite the *Shahada*, or profession of faith. "I affirm that there is no god but Allah, and that Mohammed is his prophet." Thus satisfied, he wrote on the inside cover of Mrs. Adams' Koran that they had both been converted to the religion of Islam. He added the date and signed his name. That was that: they were Muslims.

CHAPTER 9

Ladrillos

Next morning, fast friends now, they toured the premises. Again, the bird. Where was it? Mejdoubi smiled. No matter: the bird was here and the bird was there. A little song. Some music to fill the void. The great mysterious nothingness contained a voice. It was a part of the mystery; it was the mystery.

They inspected the broken-down wall surrounding the *koubba*. With his hands Mejdoubi demonstrated how to make bricks. He pointed at the hole in the dome. He could repair that, too, but ... again he pulled at his tattered robe. Arturo went to his pack for the cash.

Mejdoubi pointed at the sky. In three hours' time the sun would be in that place. Once more he strode off into the open desert, flat as a tennis court.

With time to kill, Arturo did some exploring. Much fresher, and a diversion from human considerations, were the tiny tracks among the dunes. A night's theater had left its traces on the sand.

A mouse highway connected two clumps of bushes atop separate dunes. A vulture or eagle had landed and stalked from one mouse castle to another, seeking the weak or the unwary. The scorpions had gone on parade. A serpent had glided from one bush to the next, leaving a sinister track of a stealthy mission. The beetles had held a dance or a war, and lizards raced by.

He followed the dramas where the eagle had stamped on a mouse, where the snake throttled a lizard, and where a gerbil crunched its favorite insect. A scuffle among bugs had temporarily rumpled a palimpsest of sand. Soon the wind would erase those marks, leaving the stage clear for another evening's entertainment.

The beetle's trail was haphazard. Arturo watched it toil uphill, like Sisyphus, fighting a miniscule cascade of sand created by its own weary efforts.

The day before he had spotted gazelles; now here were tracks where a swift shy one had wandered from one bush to another. The prints of a stalking jackal followed. His trail was straightforward and purposeful as he followed the scent. He was catching up.

Almost true to his word, Mejdoubi was back in four hours, this time riding a donkey! Behind trailed a bouquet of palm fronds. The donkey was burdened with a collapsible ladder, a rope net bulging with straw, a pair of wooden boxes, a bag of quick-lime, a plastic bucket, a shovel, a basket of vegetables and, trailing behind the donkey, attached by a string, a goat, a young goat, beige and white, fresh-looking, friendly and clean. Heck, it was just a kid.

Arturo thought: a pet? There was nothing for him to eat here. The penny dropped. They were going to eat *him*!

A few yards from the *koubba* was carved an ancient wadi, a gully where water once flowed, maybe a year ago, or a decade, or a century. In this wadi was deposited alluvial clay. Onto this powdery clay Mejdoubi poured water, bucket after bucket, until the powder became mud. He discarded his sandals and started to walk around barefoot in the mud.

Arturo pointed. New sandals!

Was it possible for that wizened, grizzled, wrinkled, stubbled old face to blush? Mejdoubi hung his head and looked at his feet. Yes, he mumbled, he had bought new shoes. It was shameful (*shouma*!), he had done it without asking. But look at the old ones ...

Arturo agreed: those old army-issue sandals with rubber-tire soles, Morocco's answer to huaraches, had given up the ghost.

Back to business. It so happened that Arturo was entirely familiar with the making of mud bricks. Their ranch house in Douglas was made of adobe brick. When the children were approaching that age when they should no longer be sharing the same bed, Mrs. Adams declared she needed an extra room for her daughter's privacy.

Too late, mother!

Antonio Adams was not one to walk away from a physical challenge. He tugged the garden hose to the eucalyptus grove, turned on the H_2O and let it run all night. The next morning the area was flooded. He forked up the saturated soil, took off his boots and started walking in the "playa" clay, as he called it. Arturo and Daisy joined the fun. So lovely to go barefoot in the soft warm mud! Antonio pulled apart a bale of straw and sprinkled it on the mud. More walking around in mud and straw while listening to another of Antonio's dreary lectures. Adobe brick-making was introduced into the Americas by recently Christianized Muslims from the Estremadura region of Spain, whose ancestors had developed the technique in Africa.

So, while enduring their step-father's socio-political diatribe, the children learned to make adobe bricks (*ladrillos*).

Adams had held up a piece of straw for his children to see. You can crush it in your hand, but try pulling it apart. You can't do it: straw has great tensile strength. Reinforced concrete was developed on the same principle as adobe brick.

Adams had proudly presented to his wife the bill for adding on a new wing:

Playa clay	$0
H_2O	0
Straw	1
Labor	0
Eucalyptus beams	0
Quicklime for sealing roof	1

Mrs. Adams got her new bedroom for $2.

But let us leave the polemicist and his crack-pot theories and get back to the actual job-in-hand.

Mejdoubi emptied the straw into the wadi; Arturo took off his boots and helped him walk it into the mud. Mejdoubi produced a pair of open-ended, shoebox-sized wooden frames. They shovelled the mud and straw mixture into each. By the end of the day, both working together, they had produced about 140 bricks, lying in rows, side by side, rapidly drying in the desert heat.

Cost: 0.

Somewhere, behind a dune, the kid was mysteriously dispatched. That first night they ate the intestines and internal organs.

It took two days for the bricks to dry and harden in the kiln of the desert sun.

The second night they dined on baby goat's head and shins.

Using the extra adobe mud as mortar, Mejdoubi, with Arturo's help, began laying the bricks.

The third night: back and forelegs.

The repair of the dome required a more complex procedure. Using a wooden mallet, M tapped together the rungs of the portable wooden ladder. The tough palm fronds he ingeniously wove into a tight ribbed mat, which he attached to the underside of the dome with sharpened stakes driven into the existing bricks. A rigid convex frame was created from the fronds to support the weight of the new bricks which Mejdoubi inserted keystone-style from above and sealed with mortar.

The final day they splashed whitewash over the edifice. The *koubba* shone like a pearl in the desert. Mejdoubi, too, glowed with pride and satisfaction. But the bird was no more. Time to move on.

The donkey, the ladder, the shovel, the brick-frames and the mallet were returned to wherever they came from. Nearby village or nomad encampment? Arturo never learned where. The well was recapped and covered with sand. The rope, the bucket, and the cookpot were put back inside the dune. Nothing was left behind except those three blackened stones where fires had been burning forever.

The last night they feasted on the kid's hind legs.

CHAPTER 10

T'beeb

One night in September the first rain of autumn fell. It wasn't much, just a few drops, but enough to settle the dust that had been blowing around Tangier all summer.

In the morning a flock of brown sparrows alighted on the sill of Mrs. Adams' bedroom window. The Moroccans call them *t'beeb*, in imitation of the noise they make. This also happens to be their colloquial word for doctor. Hopping forward, they flew boldly to the floor of the room to peck the bits of sunflower seed ejected by Patatas Fritas from his cage.

Mrs. Adams had grown extremely fond of this disadvantaged bird. During her South American days she had owned many parrots, but not in Arizona. Antonio hated birds, he was afraid of them; but in Tangier she was out from under his thumb. She shared her breakfast with Patatas Fritas, feeding him bits of cheese and fruit. She trimmed the flight feathers of one wing and let him hop around the patio. He shinnied up the luncheon table and plowed among the dishes, nibbling here and there. At dusk he hoisted himself up the Coppa de Oro vine to her window and sedately climbed into the cage for the night.

It was nine AM. The east wind whistled, the old glass rattled, with the cocks crowing all around. From the street came the sound of chanting. Each morning at dawn the stick-women filed silently by the house on their way to the country. Now they returned, carrying on their backs bundles of wood they had collected for the bread ovens. Chanting away their pain, they moved with a jerky, stiff-legged trot beneath burdens few men could lift. The bent-over older women used canes to support their bodies under the weight;

their strong grown daughters panted beneath mountainous stacks of packed sticks; the children struggled with smaller loads.

A clank of bells announced the goats. With a rain-like patter of hooves on cobbles they crossed the Casbah square on their way to the hills for a day of grazing. An excited whinny and brief gallop meant they had sniffed out the figs. The nanny goats stood on their hind legs and strained for the fruit that dangled tantalizingly from branches overhanging the wall. Unable to reach the figs, they nibbled spitefully on the spilling geraniums. The goatherd loaded his sling and … snap! … down jumped a goat from a place where it shouldn't be.

He had rigged crude leather aprons to hang from the shaggy bellies of the billies to discourage incessant copulation. Their red, dripping penises were extended, their testicles colossal; and the nanny goats' vaginas and teats were grotesquely swollen. The sexual organs of goats, it seems, are oversized, just as the noises of copulation are fiendishly excessive. No wonder the ancients portrayed the devil incarnate as a goat-like figure with cloven hooves.

Our goatherd was a curly-headed fellow. Like Pan, he was dressed in skins which gave off a powerful odor. Mina opened the door and exchanged an American cigarette for a jug of fresh milk. It was the only item she ever filched from the house.

Mrs. Adams was usually awake by this hour. A movement from her bed was enough to scatter the timid scavengers. Downstairs in the kitchen Mina could be heard conversing softly with her niece. She was under orders to keep the household quiet until the señora rang for breakfast: coffee from Brazil, milk from the goat and figs from the tree.

The ripe fruit produced by the ancient tree that grew in the *riad* of o, Place de la Casbah, enjoyed a certain sexual fame among the young married women of Tangier. During the paired fig seasons – June, when the figs are encased in a green pulpy shell – and September, when the leaner, sweeter second crop comes wrapped in carbon paper-thin, blue-black skin – they arrived with long cane poles to bat down the fruit in the belief that a taste of the moist, red-centered figs – timeless symbol of female sexual parts – would make sweetness between them and their husbands.

Daisy had risen early to go to the port. Even now the Spanish ferry could be seen from the rooftops as it approached Tangier.

From the courtyard came the sound of clicking. Sobrina was pounding coffee beans with mortar and pestle. With the kettle coming to the boil, Mina arranged Mrs. Adams' breakfast tray. Like many unschooled Moroccans, she was neat and efficient. Everything she put her hand to had a naturally light, artistic touch. The covering cloth and napkin had been embroidered in the Convent of the Adoratrices and peddled door to door by the nuns. With the Antichrist absent, Mrs. Adams had invited them in for tea and bought the lot. A blue and white Fez vase held pink geraniums snipped from the wall. Mina peeled and quartered the ripe fruit and lay the sections in four spokes on a bright green fig leaf, itself the classical male *cache-sexe*.

The finely-pestled coffee powder she mixed with hot water in a saucepan and placed on the fire. At this point the brew had the consistency of chocolate sauce. When it began to bubble she poured the mixture through a cloth filter ("the sock") and added a little boiling water. The cup and saucer rested in hot water and had to be lifted out with tongs. The sugar went in first, followed by the coffee.

Mrs. Adams never went anywhere without her Brazilian "sock." It was the only way she allowed her coffee to be made. The caffeine lift was electric.

Mina could not read, write her name, or tell the time of day, but she knew it was late. She carried the tray upstairs.

When the door opened, the flock of sparrows rose up with a rush of wings. Mina let out a little gasp of fright.

"Señora," she whispered. "Señora … " She pushed back the shutters. "Time to wake up."

An intrepid sparrow was still perched in Mrs. Adams' hair. Perhaps its feet were entangled there. Finally, almost reluctantly, it flitted through the open window.

Mina was certain it was Mrs. Adams' soul she saw fly away.

CHAPTER II

Antonio Adams

The blast from the ship's siren could not drown out the wails of lamentation that rose from the little house in the Casbah.

"This was her favorite place, daddy. Her *sitio*."

"Jesus Christ is a son of a bitch!"

Daisy's nose was running, tears were spurting from her eyes as she lugged a chair up from the patio to the terrace. Her stepfather's legs were too long, his knees too stiff to sit on the carpet.

"This was the place she loved to be, where she could look down the Strait at the Pillars of Hercules and pray."

Antonio Adams had arrived too late to see his wife alive again. With huge brown fists wrapped around the pommel of his stick, the old philosopher stared gloomily out to sea. Daisy sat among the cushions at his feet.

"I don't want to live without her!" she sobbed.

"I don't want to hear about that now."

He was a tall, leathery man with the rugged appearance of one who had spent most of his life outdoors. Deliberately cultivating the dirty, uncivilized look, he rarely washed his hair and let his beard grow down his chest. He wore battered boots and a Stetson. A thick leather belt – the heavy silver buckle adorned with a turquoise vulture – held up his trousers, along with a pair of logger's suspenders.

"I want to see her!" he rumbled.

"You can't." Daisy sniffed back her tears. "Mina and Sobrina are washing her body according to the Muslim rite. Christians are not allowed to watch. You'll have to wait."

"Emptiness and humbug." the old man growled.

"What?"

"Next to death, everything is emptiness and humbug."

The heat of the long African day was abating. Darkness comes on quickly in Tangier, and lights were already twinkling from hilltop villages across the bay. Swallows wheeled through the colorless sky. Smoke from rooftop cook fires drifted through the air.

"Why her?" Daisy asked angrily. "Look at Consuelo Billings. She has a terrible relationship with her mother. But Consuelo's mother's still alive and my mother isn't! Why her? Why me? Why us?"

"What was that thing in the cage?"

"Patatas Fritas, her parrot."

From the Casbah mosque came the muezzin's song.

"What's that noise?"

"The call to prayer."

"Death is all around us here."

"I can't bear the thought of her away from the light, under the hot dusty soil of North Africa." She leaned against her stepfather's leg. "I want my dust to mingle with hers!"

Adams opened his coat. From an inside pocket he pulled a small gray pistol with a short, square barrel. He handed it to her.

"Go ahead if that's the way you feel. Get it over with!"

Daisy held the pistol in both hands. She was surprised how warm it was. She had a sense that some kind of power had been transferred to her, because he had taught her how to use it.

She handed the pistol back. Adams put it in his pocket, buttoned his coat, and re-addressed his silent stare at the sea.

"This is what happens, isn't it?" Daisy said. "The world goes on. People are preparing soup, oblivious of the pain all around them. Mother loved this hour, when the swallows fly. That's the sadness. The senses are dead – no more to enjoy the sweetness of the world."

"She's part of the sweetness now," Adams muttered.

Daisy walked to the edge of the terrace that overlooked the sprawling medina. It was a long drop to the street below. "It would be so easy," she said. "Just the two of us, lying side by side in the hot shade of Islam. No noise and no needs – for time and eternity."

"Jesus Christ is a son of a bitch!" Adams was pounding his stick on the tiles.

"Tell me about her, daddy ... " She returned to where her stepfather was sitting.

"Eh?"

"What was she like when you met her?"

"Get me a drink."

Daisy disappeared downstairs and came back with a bottle.

"What is it?" Adams scowled. "Arab moonshine?"

"Scotch whiskey."

They both drank.

"She was vivacious and talented," he said at last. "She played the guitar. She knew dozens of South American folk songs. She used to travel with her father down there."

"Where?"

"Bolivia. He had a trading post on the Chaparé River. A place called Todos Santos. He loaded a balsa raft with beer, rum and machetes. He and your mother floated down the river trading those items for gold dust panned by the Indians in jungle rivers."

"Did you know him?"

"Toledano? No. He died down there. Dropped dead in the Andes. Your mother loaded his body across the horse. He froze solid in the mountains. She would have been about your age." Adams drank again. "There she was, up in the snow and ice, wondering how she was going to get him into a coffin with him bent in two like a wishbone." He chuckled. "The body thawed. She straightened him out and buried him in the Jewish cemetery in Cochabamba."

"Are we Jewish, daddy?"

"You are."

They listened to a lullaby drifting up from the courtyard.

"What's that noise?"

"It's Mina's song – the song of the corpse washer."

Adams moaned. "I'm not waiting any longer!" He got to his feet. "I'm going down!"

He lost his nerve and had to be led into the room where Mrs. Adams' body lay. Their work down, Mina and Sobrina sat by the bed. A candle was burning in the corner. Adams saw the shape of his wife's body beneath the sheet but came no closer. It shielded a reality too potent even for the old revolutionary. After a long wait he lifted a corner of the sheet. There were the toes with the bright pink polish. It was enough. He dropped the sheet and went out.

Daisy stayed by the bedside for a few minutes. When she came out, her stepfather was nowhere around. The urchins in the street informed her he had left the house. An hour later she found him wandering in the medina.

"Daddy, what are you doing?"

"Ice," he moaned. "She must have ice."

She led him home. She never did discover whether, in his delirium, he intended to bring his wife a cooling drink, or whether he wished to preserve her body from the stifling North African heat.

CHAPTER 12

There is No God But God and Mohammed is His Prophet

The chant was repeated over and over, back and forth, as the little procession filed through the narrow streets of the Casbah. Four men carried the wooden litter on their shoulders. On it lay the body, strangely reduced, wrapped in white and fastened with string.

Daisy, Mina and Sobrina were dressed in the snow white robes of mourning. Daisy had a firm grip on the arm of her stepfather, who walked unsteadily and seemed to stagger with each step. Jâafar.

Adams picked up a stone and threw it at a flock of sparrows.

"Daddy, what are you doing?"

"I want them to fly. I want them to come with us."

The group passed through the Casbah Gate and threaded its way along a cane-lined lane, passing tiny farms amidst groves of eucalyptus. The wind picked up and blew sand in their faces. The green tops of the live cane fence were thrashing in the wind. The sun was coming up, but the air felt cold. Out there toward Spain something strange was happening: the gale had flattened the sea. The Strait looked as though it was covered with pale blue ice. Death was out there flying. You could walk out there with Death.

The cemetery was located on a hill in cactus country. There was neither wall nor gate. Unmarked tombs marched to the horizon. Few bore names or dates. It was the Muslim way of saying the dead need not be named because the faithful are in heaven.

A shallow trench had been scraped from the sand. The litter was set on the ground. The imam spoke a few words. Daisy and her stepfather stood at a respectful distance. As a non-Muslim, Adams was not expected to participate.

The body was lifted from the litter and lowered into the trench, her head toward the east. Sand was showered upon it. The Muslims stood in a circle, chanting the prayer of farewell.

The solemnity of the occasion was broken by a loud groan. Antonio Adams' legs could support him no longer. He sank to his knees.

"*Conejita*, don't leave me!"

Daisy tried to restrain him. Her dusty cheeks were streaked with tears. She managed to hold him at the edge of the mound that the wind was already beginning to smooth. He dug his hands into the sand groping for the body of his wife. One by one the mourners drifted away. Adams pulled from his pocket a chunk of bread, crumbled it with his fingers, and spread the bits on the sand. The sun rose resplendent over the Strait of Gibraltar.

A few hundred yards away, unseen by the mourners, a black Plymouth station wagon with diplomatic plates was parked in the shadows of a grove of eucalyptus. Two men in business suits were standing beside it. One was watching the proceedings through binoculars and providing a narrative. The other was taking notes.

Daisy helped her stepfather up from the dirt. Their roles were reversed; she was the strong one now. She led him home, as one would lead a child.

CHAPTER 13

Bab Al Bhar

Wrapped in a burnoose, Daisy stood on the clifftop outside one of the Casbah gates, known as Bab al Bhar, or Sea Gate, watching her stepfather's ship disappear down the Strait of Gibraltar. A sea mist, wind-whipped from the scudding waves, suddenly enveloped the ship, leaving its wake trailing into nothingness. Mewing gulls wheeled about her. A lone fishing boat, returning from the tuna nets off Cape Spartel, rocked through the choppy sea. Pulling the burnoose about her shoulders, she waded through a happy throng of school children playing and running. The elements of man and nature conspired to echo her loss. The call from the mosque reminded her of the lonely mission that beckoned her from the withered edges of this alien land.

Beneath the folds of the burnoose, she felt the hard outline of Antonio Adams' parting gift: the Ruger.

"Where you're going, babes, you may need it."

In the kitchen Mina was singing to herself and occasionally letting out little cries of despair. When she heard the door shut, she rushed into Daisy's arms. They sat down together on the garden bench to cry on each other's shoulders. Mohammed the gardener came forward. Trying to be manly, he placed his hand on Daisy's shoulder.

"She was a good woman," he said. "She loved Morocco. Allah will reward her. He will place her in a comfortable corner in women's heaven."

While all this was going on, like winds blowing away veils, the reality of her mother's death swept over Daisy. Her stepfather's masculine presence in the house had inhibited the servants from giving full vent to their feelings. She realized that she, too, had bottled up her grief. It took the sound of hoarse and muffled cries to convince her that her mother was gone forever. It was the end of an era, and the Moroccans had understood it more quickly than she had. She went upstairs and lay down on her mother's bed.

That night asthma gripped her. She sat on the edge of the bed, wheezing and coughing out her lungs. The next morning her ribs were sore.

Mina brought coffee. The caffeine lift made breathing easier. She lay back, rested the coffee cup and saucer on her stomach, and let her eyes wander about the room. Her mother's things were all there, but her mother was not. And never would be again. Like the *t'beeb*, she had flown away, never to return.

Her abdominal muscles heaved as the tears came. She lifted the cup and saucer to keep the coffee from spilling. Gradually the convulsions subsided. She placed the cup back on her stomach. Through the blur of tears a glittering object caught her eye – the tiny Andean bell her mother used to ring for breakfast. The silver handle was fashioned in the shape of a Bolivian llama.

The wardrobe door hung open, revealing a layered sandwich of colorful caftans, with brown and white striped hatboxes piled on top. The dressing table forested with bottles. The plastic glow-in-the-dark virgin from Mexico she never went anywhere without. The silver-framed picture of Arturo on the bedside table. The Potosi rosary, also in silver, entwined with wooden Muslim prayer beads – a present from Jâafar – symbolized the mingling of faiths. The crazy collection of shoes, from Spanish riding boots to Moroccan slippers. Hats perched everywhere, some with feathers sticking out, like so many stranded birds.

Her mother's room, like her life, was a colorful hodgepodge. Her existence had been dictated solely by emotion: next to love everything else – order, reason, routine – took second place.

CHAPTER 14

The Legionnaire Clock

There is something heavy about the air in Tangier. People say air-planes slow down as much as forty miles per hour when they pass overhead. Apparently the air is thicker and acts as a brake. Daisy didn't know whether to believe that or not, but what she did know was that once the rains began, the house never dried out. Patches of mould began to appear on the walls. Jâafar had mentioned that it was a summer house; now she knew what he was talking about.

People say the dampness in the walls has to do with the sand the Moroccans made the cement with when the house was built. Apparently they take it straight from the beach, full of salt, which of course absorbs and retains moisture. The sheets never dried out. The mildew was pretty bad, too; Daisy had to wipe it off her boots at least once a week.

As central heating is unheard of in Tangier, no room in the house was warm enough for her. She went down to the local woodyard, bargained with the woodchoppers over a ton of olive wood, and had it delivered by truck to the front door. She and Moe lugged in the logs and stacked them against the wall in the courtyard. They had to act quickly before the scavenging urchins whisked them away. It was the kind of hard physical work she was used to and almost missed. It felt good to lift the logs – the first solid exercise she'd had in months.

Daisy had grown up quickly in Arizona. Handling horses had made her tough. Until she was twelve she could whip any boy her age in a fair fight. That came to an end when cowboy Slim put his hand down her pants while they were wrestling in the hayloft. In retaliation, she bit his ear. He let out a yelp and smacked her in the face. The blow split her lip and loosened her front teeth, deadening one, which accounted for the roan tooth in the middle of her mouth.

To light a fire gave her peace. When she held a match to the crumpled paper and watched the flames travel upwards and touch the kindling, saw the twigs ignite and crackle, she felt her spirit soften and body relax. The fresh flames were hot on her face as she followed their progress through the wood. With warmth radiating into the room she rose from her knees, stiff from kneeling on the hearth, and returned to her studies.

She moved Mr. Williams' walnut desk in front of the fire and made learning Arabic her chief activity. Jåafar sent Fatoma, an albino negress from the Drâa Valley, for Arabic conversation and to teach her how to pray. Her other aim was to write a page a day in her diary.

A minute before each hour she sat back to await the chiming of Mr. Williams' legionnaire clock. The portrait of a Zouave was painted on the clock face. The Zouaves, she learned, were an infantry unit composed mainly of Algerians, created by the French during colonial days for service in North Africa. Seated cross-legged in front of his tent, he wore the colorful uniform of his native regiment – baggy red trousers and waist-length blue jacket embroidered with yellow thread. On his head a red fez was wrapped with a white turban. The fez's red tassel hung over the soft white cloth. In his fingers he held loosely, upside down, a white clay pipe which he seemed to be on the point of filling, that is if, from sheer Moorish *insouciance,* he didn't drop it first.

The Zouave's cruel, morose expression was accentuated by his black beard and thick red lips. His eyes were a disconcerting shade of greenish blue – disconcerting because they seemed to belong to another than the swarthy mulatto face – evidence, perhaps, of the Vandal who had slipped into his Berber bloodstream somewhere along the line and was peering out, fearful, the European trapped inside the African, all confidence lost. As the pendulum swung and the clock ticked, a mechanism caused the Zouave's pale eyes to flick nervously back and forth, giving the gorilla-like features the shifty, insecure look of a slave.

Each hour the clock chimed – it was more like a clank than a chime – a little door opened and an old legionnaire, palsied by the vibrating mechanism, tottered out to croak what sounded like *tout va bien*. The words were nearly drowned out by the creaking, unoiled wheels of the clock.

Twin weights in the shape of pinecones were suspended by chains. A third chain Daisy pulled once each day to hoist the weights. Somehow the clock came to represent her brother in the desert: Arturo too might be sitting in front of a tent; probably he would be smoking weed. She wanted to keep the pendulum swinging.

As she crouched by the fire, encouraging it with the bellows (*rhabbouz*), with the cracked chime of the legionnaire clock marking the hours, memories both sweet and painful rose like smoke from the smouldering logs.

One chill December evening, with the family gathered around the hearth at Guadalquivir Ranch, Arturo held up his hand.

"Listen!"

Conversation stopped while the faint peal of a distant bell carried through the still desert night.

Two miles to the north east stood San Mateo, a tiny mission church. No one had ever visited as Antonio's atheistic thunderings eliminated any kind of church-going. The bell was audible only when the wind blew from that quarter, which it did rarely. The next day Arturo rode over to investigate. He reported that he had spoken to an Indian, who lived in the rusting hulk of a pickup behind the church, whose job it was to ring the bell. Mass, he told Arturo, was celebrated twice a year, on Christmas Eve and Easter Sunday, by a Franciscan priest who travelled from church to church on a donkey.

That Christmas, their last in Arizona, the family went to mass. Even Antonio – lured by Arturo's description of a commemorative plaque dating the church from 1541, founded by Francisco de Coronado during his expedition from Mexico to the American southwest in search of El Dorado – grudgingly agreed to come along.

They rode over at midnight. Antonio insisted wife ride side-saddle – it was one of his monstrosities. Like luminous spokes, delicate torch-lit processions were trailing across the desert, focussed on blazing little San Mateo. A generator had been set up and strings of multicolored lights outlined the double belfry. Incense wafting through the open door could be detected a mile downwind. Dozens of trembling candles guttered within, among modest offerings of flowers, vegetables, fruit. Even Antonio came forward while mass was being celebrated. The family was astonished to see the embattled old atheist go down on his knees among the Indian multitude on the cold stone floor of the church.

Riding home that night, they had never felt closer. Mrs. Adams was singing a love song in Quechua:

"Quisiera ser picaflor
*y que tu fueras clavel ... "**

Antonio got out the bottle, and they all had a swig. The simple and striking demonstration of faith united them in the realization that, no matter what Antonio or anyone else had to say on the subject, God existed, if in no other place in the universe, within the heart of the family.

The cracked bell chimed. Daisy felt her soul torn between hope and loneliness. Her mother was gone, the whereabouts of Arturo unknown. Antonio alone in Spain. How she longed for her lungs to

---

* "I wish I were a humming bird, And you were my flower... "

be filled with dry desert air, and to hear again the clear notes of the mission bell in the perfect silence of the Arizona night.

The old legionnaire staggered out to croak his weary message. *Tout va bien.*

CHAPTER 15

Close Encounters

At least Daisy had Mina for company. It was comforting to know there was another person in the house, someone to talk to, even if it was only about the weather. She offered to lend Patatas Fritas to entertain her elderly mother who had had a stroke. Mina's house was immaculately clean, with barely a stick of furniture. Nothing but a photo of the Sultan over the door. It was decorated mainly by a group of gaily dressed women who sat on the floor making cakes, banging away on drums and singing.

Each time Patatas Fritas squawked, a goofy, toothless smile spread across the old lady's face.

"Everyone has sorrows," Daisy said, "but in your house, Mina, I saw that each one does her best to cheer the others up. I would have never guessed that your household has troubles, when I know there are many."

"We poor Moroccans understand that during hard times people must stick together, make cakes and sing," Mina replied. "That way the pain is shared. You eat something nice and no one is left out."

Daisy became a regular visitor to Mina's home. Chatting with the women, she learned about Moroccan life, and her ability to communicate in Arabic accelerated.

As winter approached, her asthma grew steadily worse. She quit smoking and stayed at home, gradually growing immune to the increasingly strong doses of cortisone that Dr. McGregor prescribed.

From Mr. Williams' bookshelf she pulled a volume entitled *Camels into the Void*, about a French adventurer called the Duke de Bremont. It was an account of the trip he made from southern Morocco to Taodeni, the salt capital of the Sahara, from which he never returned. He was assumed to have perished by everyone but his wife, who wrote the book.

Once more it was Jâafar who proved to be an indispensable friend. When she was down with asthma and stuck in the house, he sent his ancient Chrysler to bring her to his palace, where they dined in comfort while the rain poured through the roof.

Jâafar was a *shereef* – he belonged to the Muslim blood nobility claiming descent from the Prophet Mohammed. He also traced his lineage to Moulay Idriss, who founded the city of Fez and converted Morocco to Islam. In America he would be the equivalent of someone directly descended from Jesus Christ *and* George Washington.

Jâafar may have been getting on in years, he spoke in just above a whisper, yet he exuded an effortless authority. A nod of his head, and barefoot servants scurried to remove platters or empty buckets that were constantly filling with water. Around him Daisy felt safe, and she could talk freely about her brother.

She and Arturo had the same birthday, five years apart, nine months to the day after their mother's birthday. Mrs. Adams used to say, "That's the day they should have locked me in a nunnery!" The place where they grew up was isolated, with no neighbors or friends. There was just the two of them. They did everything together – too many things.

Arturo was a talented artist. He could draw like an angel – but he had problems – mental problems. He was pursued by what Mrs. Adams called 'the Black Coyote' of depression. Twice in Arizona he tried to commit suicide. The first time he threw himself down a well but got hauled out. Another time he got treed by a mob of peccaries – wild pigs whose tusks can slash like knives. He jumped down into them but survived.

When the ranch failed Mrs. Adams moved her family to Spain and bought the house in Balaguer, in the mountains behind Barcelona.

In Barcelona Arturo enrolled in art school. He was just a blue-eyed cowboy, first time in a big city. All those girls, standing around on street corners, kind of overwhelmed him. Then something happened – he started wandering. He went out the door and walked all the way to Santiago de Compostela.

Walking became a kind of therapy for Arturo. For a while he had a job on a ranch near Jerez. He worked for a circus in Sevilla. In Cadiz he worked alongside Moroccan stevedores unloading ships. By this time he had grown enormously strong and had the hardened appearance of a habitual tramp. From his companions he learned about the locust invasion south of the Atlas Mountains and the suffering it had caused.

A phone call came from Cadiz. A ship in the harbor – destination Buenos Aires – was taking on crew. His plan was to go to Argentina and find work on a ranch in the Pampas. Mrs. Adams was almost relieved. She believed that Latin American cultures are more tolerant of people with emotional problems.

The evening before he was supposed to sail, in a bar, Arturo was offered drinks by a *caudillo* who seemed to have unlimited funds. He was recruiting volunteers for the Spanish Foreign Legion, to serve in Rio de Oro. He was impressed by Arturo's desert skills and that he was used to handling guns.

Arturo signed up. As soon as he received his bonus of $500, he bolted for Madrid. Another long silence followed. The family assumed he was at sea when a call came from Phoenix, AZ. He hadn't sailed to Argentina at all, but had flown back to America and enlisted in the army. Morocco was where he felt he was needed, Morocco was where he wanted to go, and that was where they sent him – Morocco!

CHAPTER 16

Moon Over Morocco

What a night! The ice-white moon silvered the palms along the edge of the oasis. On the hill the white dome of a *koubba* glowed in the dark like an alabaster thumb. A row of tents cast tongues of purple from the circle of beards where flames shot up. Here and there the nomads had spread their mats and were engaged in their singular act of devotion.

Arturo felt he had come a thousand miles from everything he had ever known, was isolated to a degree he had never before experienced, and had embarked on a journey, backwards, it seemed, through space and time. He had prayed for peace, his soul felt scoured – like Mejdoubi's tea glasses – but expiation was denied him because he knew precisely the extent of his guilt. Guilt clung to him so closely his skin had taken on the color of sand.

For three days they had walked, before joining the caravan. They rose at three AM and walked for seven or eight hours, covering, he figured, roughly twenty-five miles –the distance between wells – before lying down and roasting in the tent. Like a ship which always sticks to the same course, ignoring what lies on either side, Mejdoubi led his ship of the desert from well to waterhole, never looking right or left. To the east, the direction he scrupulously avoided, lay destruction and death.

The limits of the minefield were clearly defined by the corpses of camels. Every few miles they passed by the decomposing wreckage of some unsuspecting beast – picked apart by vultures, dragged by jackals, or simply shattered by the bomb.

Mejdoubi pointed and shouted, "*Minas! Minas*! Ha! Ha! Ha!"

During these troubled times the young men carried guns. Guns were plentiful in the desert. Arturo saw them in every market, where they were bartered and haggled over. The price of a Kalashnikov had dropped from two to five for one bull camel. The nomads wore their weapons proudly and ominously, like jewelry, or trophies, or scalps.

"They listen to their fathers no more," Mejdoubi commented. "They believe that a man who has no gun, his grave is open." Somehow Mejdoubi had latched onto a bottle of whiskey. How he paid for it – perhaps he had bartered one of his wives for it – he seemed to have one in every tent – Arturo had no idea. The drink seemed to have dissolved his bones. He lay there in the tent, a shapeless heap; there was no moving him.

Wandering nomads require from their oases what sailors feverishly seek in their ports of call: fresh water, fresh food and, after long abstinence, women. The desert was asleep, but Arturo heard, or thought he could hear, in the hidden gardens of the oasis, the sobs and sweet trills of love.

The dull thump that snapped him awake told Arturo all he needed to know. As did the empty impression of Mejdoubi's body beside him, and the fresh detritus of vomit on the sand. He made no move as the alarm was raised. As lanterns and flashlights sped by, he deliberately laced his boots, picked up the *guerba*, and slowly made his way against traffic into the night.

Mejdoubi, his amiable protector, stumbling off in the dark to relieve himself, had "mined" himself.

All night Arturo walked. His cover gone, he knew he would be followed. They would have no more trouble tracking him than a buffalo through a corn field. But a miracle occurred. One of those evil little sandstorms blew up out of nowhere and erased his immediate past. Now he would need another. The *guerba* held five liters of water. He had made it last two days. His time was up.

In the mineral purity of Saharan air, every scent is a signal. The jackal picks up a whiff of a gazelle a mile downwind. Arturo smelled smoke and like an animal turned instinctively toward it. By the time he sighted the glimmer of a lantern up ahead, it was dusk. He dared not approach in the dark.

CHAPTER 17

Crossing Over

One thing about Tangier bothered Daisy, and it bothered her a lot. Whenever she went out she was pestered by Moroccan young men. Even a quick walk down the hill to the local *bakal* for cigarettes and a bottle of wine became, instead of an outing to another world and a chance for a bit of fresh air, a kind of dreaded adventure.

Like the ubiquitous cats that patrolled the alleys of the Casbah, one or more of them would materialize from nowhere, sidle up beside her, and attempt to strike up a conversation.

"You like Tangier? I show you market. You want to buy carpet? I know cheap place. No? What you want?"

She didn't want anything; she wanted to be left alone.

When she stopped at the café below Bab el Assa for a glass of mint tea and to listen to the Andalucian musicians who sometimes played there, one of these tomcats might slip into a vacant chair at the next table. Sometimes they sat on both sides, making her feel trapped. They offered to guide her around the city, show her the shops, sell her hashish – any idea that came into their heads to get some money off her. Nothing she could say in English, Spanish, or Arabic would make them go away. She tried to ignore them, but the silent treatment only seemed to egg them on. Mostly polite but maddeningly persistent, they frustrated her ability as a private person to soak up the sights and sounds of this strange new world, and left her feeling angry, humiliated and fed up with Moroccan male culture.

Word seemed to have got out that a single young woman was living alone at o, Place de la Casbah. One or more of them got into the habit of hanging around the front door of the house, waiting for her to come out. So she had to order a taxi to go to market, when she could have walked. In Tangier the taxi service is not always reliable. Upon leaving the taxi rank in the Zoco Grande, the driver turned on the meter which, by the time he toiled up the hill and threaded the street through the tunnel to La Place de la Casbah, registered such a hefty sum that Daisy wondered if he hadn't dropped off other fares along the way.

Even Mina admitted she avoided going out alone. Any woman on her own, it seemed, was fair game for the unemployed, female-deprived young men of Tangier.

One morning, while going through her mother's things, Daisy came across her brother's "holy clothes" which Mrs. Adams had brought over from Spain. Daisy and Arturo were about the same size. She put on the faded jeans, beat-up leather jacket and the *boina basca* he had worn on the pilgrimage to Santiago de Compostela.

Mina let out a little yelp when she paraded into the kitchen. She clapped her hands together – she had an inspiration.

It was fall, and walnuts were in. Sobrina was sent to market. They peeled off the green husks, boiled them up and added pomegranate and some yellow flowers, crushed in a mortar and pestle.

In Daisy's opinion her skin was already dark enough.

"In Morocco," Mina said, "darker is poorer."

To look rich was the last thing Daisy wanted – that would attract them like flies. She let the women paint her hands and face with the brown soup.

Mina trimmed her hair so it would be concealed beneath the beret.

Standing in front of the mirror with the women fussing about her, Daisy was satisfied that she looked like a typical down-at-heel backpacker, rather scruffy, that you see every day in Tangier. Dressing up, she realized, was not just fun; it was exciting because of the risk of being found out. What sort of risk she was not quite sure.

It had been raining all day. Low clouds raced overhead. When summer goes, darkness comes on quickly in Tangier. Sobrina kept a lookout from an upstairs window. It was supper-time, and the rain had chased everyone off the streets.

When it was properly dark, Daisy stepped outside. The fresh air hit her face. The door shut behind her. Her heart was pounding. Suddenly she felt free as never before in her life.

Pausing briefly at the Assa Gate, she set off downhill into the medina, confident in her disguise. Stopping at a *tabac* – not the one she usually frequented – she bought a pack of cigarettes. The boy addressed her as *señor*. Her height was a definite advantage. She worried about her voice, and hoped she was able to lower it enough. Avoiding the brightly-lit tourist shops on Calle Christianos, she hurried along alleys so narrow she could brush her fingers along the walls on both sides. The glare of the street lights along Boulevard Pasteur made her hurry. She didn't dare sit in one of the cafés. Lighting a cigarette, she strode the length of the avenue and back again. A drenched shoeshine boy pointed forlornly at her boots; otherwise nobody looked twice.

Back at the house, she fell into Mina's arms, giddily triumphant. The amazing thing was that it felt completely natural. The sense of power conferred upon her by the disguise was exhilarating. Like Charles Atlas, she had made herself into a new man. No bully would kick sand in her face again.

One Saturday night she was making her way down Rue de la Liberté, a crowded shopping street and the main pedestrian artery between the Arab and European quarters. A woman screamed. Across the street the door to El Minzah Hotel was flung open. Out streaked a large brown rat pursued by two bell hops in purple bloomers. One wielded a broom, the other carried a bucket. The terrified rodent darted across the street and ran right in front of Daisy, who instinctively kicked out at it. The toe of her boot caught it square in the middle, sending it flying in a high tumbling arc back across the street, where it landed on the sidewalk in front of the hotel, back broken, stone dead.

Through the open door Daisy caught a glimpse of a woman in a fur coat, standing on a chair.

"*Gooooaal*!" shouted one of the bellhops. He picked up the corpse by the tail and dropped it into the bucket. "Well done, señor!" he called.

Sundays she dreaded because it was Mina's day off. Normally she spent it alone, marooned in the house.

The morning started cloudy and cold. She worked on her diary, gave that up and paced around the house, brimming with unused energy. With her mother gone, she had nothing. At 11 o'clock she went back to bed. At noon she awoke, nervous and cold. She listened to the news on the BBC. By one, nearly out of her mind with frustration, she decided to take the risk.

Taking the steps two at a time, she raced to an upstairs window to check that the coast was clear. Putting on her jacket and pulling the *boina* over her ears, she let herself out of house and walked quickly through the Arab quarter. Emerging on the Avenida de España, she meandered beneath the double row of palms (presented to the city by King Alfonso XIII of Spain) and crossed the railroad tracks to the beach.

Daisy had the stride of a country girl. She always felt she had to walk fast to keep up. The rain-soaked beach was hard and firm. She took off her boots and walked barefoot for a mile until she came to a place where fishing boats were drawn up on the sand. At the back of the beach stood a whitewashed shack partially concealed by cane wind-breaks, now ragged and broken by autumn gales. Encircled by inward-leaning bamboo stakes, a wood fire burned inside an old sand-filled rowboat. One stake held a large pink fish impaled through the mouth.

Abdoo's Chiringuito is not listed in any travel guide. Most tourists and Tangier's well-heeled foreign residents frequent the French-style restaurants along the boulevard, where meals are served on smooth white table cloths, not rough table tops hammered from driftwood. But many seafood-loving Tangerines, those whose fortunes like those of their beloved city have been in long decline, can no longer afford pricy dishes like turbot and lobster drowned in butter or a creamy sauce. They've learned to love what poor Moroccans catch and cook for themselves – sardines, anchovies, squid and the mussels that fishermen rip from low-tide rocks and sell to Abdoo for next to nothing.

Daisy slipped on her boots and entered the restaurant.

Abdoo did a thriving business in summer, but autumn winds sweeping the beach made the sea too cold for swimming. The only other customers were two women sitting at a table in the corner. The younger one let out a yelp from being pinched by her friend as Daisy walked through the door.

She ordered a beer at the bar, and was carrying the bottle to a table when a voice called out.

"*¡Guapa! ¡Chica!* Come over here!"

The women were waving.

"Sit with us!"

"Sunday lunch you don't want to eat by yourself!"

Daisy approached their table.

"Those boots!"

"Are you a cowboy?"

"Cowgirl."

Hoots of laughter.

"Those boots make you stand so tall."

The older woman elbowed the other. "She's a big girl. I bet she can kick ass with them boots."

"Yessir!"

The waiter brought a chair.

The older woman was tall and dark-skinned. A black cape draped around her shoulders lent an air of patrician formality. Her companion was short, pink and bouncy. Dressed like a schoolgirl, she had a round face and smooth, muscular arms. Black eyes, magnified by heavy horn-rimmed glasses, gave her an owlish look. Dark red lipstick enlarged her mouth.

The older woman said something in French.

The small edition explained: "Amalia said that if she owned a pair of boots like yours, she could kill the *cucarachas* in our apartment. The little oil-stealers run to the corners when you chase them."

"C'est degoutant."

"With pointy-toed boots like those she could kick them to death in the corner."

She let out a merciless shriek, a kind of war-whoop, and drummed her feet beneath the table. Dust puffed from between Abdoo's rustic floorboards.

They introduced themselves: Amalia, in black, aloof and elegant, with sparkling black eyes. Her enormous breasts seemed to have a separate life of their own. Each time she moved, they moved with her, and kept on moving. They rolled back and forth across her chest beneath the cape as though propelled by some mysterious tide.

Carmen was the worker. She taught flamenco and tap dancing at the Spanish library.

"You're American!"

"Amalia's mother loves Americans."

"Americans are so handy. They can do anything."

"Her mother eloped with an American sea captain. Her maid locked her in a trunk and had it delivered to the port. They sailed away and had adventures."

"How romantic. Did they get married?"

"She discovered she loved the sea captain's wife more than the sea captain!"

Squealing with laughter, Carmen stamped so hard Hamdoo's floorboards smoked.

Lunch began to arrive.

Daisy, raised in a land-locked state, had never encountered such a bizarre array of seafood.

Carmen described each dish: *almendritas* (baby squid, deep fried); *almejas* (small clams in their shells); *boquerones en vinaigre* (anchovies in vinegar); *boquerones fritas* (deep fried); *navajas* (long narrow clams the form of straight razors whose limp, tubular inhabitants, having been boiled alive in their homes, reposed penis-like in their coffin-shaped shells); *calamares* (squid); and green tomato salad with onion.

"Amalia used to be a sole meunière girl," Carmen said. "I taught her octopus and sardines."

Daisy thought the squid was fried onion rings. The women showed her how to eat with her fingers, and to mop up the sauce with bits of bread. They washed it all down with icy wine from a unlabelled bottle which once contained cooking oil. Daisy concentrated on the bread and salad while the women tucked in, moaning and slurping and uttering pained cries of delight.

The multiple plates were cleared away. Daisy thought the meal was finished when Abdoo himself emerged from the kitchen bearing an enormous platter.

Daisy recoiled from the repulsive-looking concoction. She had tasted prairie oysters in Arizona and tripe (*callos*) in Spain, but this dish, whatever it was, looked utterly alien.

"*¡Percebes!*"

"Goose barnacles."

"What?"

"*¡Patas de cabre!*"

"Goats feet?"

Something that looked like clusters of grayish black octopi with hooks or claws on their tentacles. On closer inspection the scaly hooks did actually resemble *patas de cabre*, or miniature sharp-toed goats' hooves on the ends of rubbery stalks that were still rooted to rocks at the bottom of the platter.

Carmen showed Daisy. "You can dig out the tip as well, but it's a lot of work. This horny bit on the end is actually the creature's mouth."

Daisy tried one. The texture was chewy, not as rubbery as squid. Not so moist. Sort of like nibbling the eraser on the end of a pencil. She was glad she had filled up on salad and bread.

Sliding back the wrinkled foreskin, Carmen held up the stalk of pink flesh.

"Look – a baby dildil!" she said, biting it off and chewing vigorously.

"Dildo, dear," Amalia corrected.

In her diary Daisy wrote that after lunch she drove with her new friends in their Pontiac station wagon to their apartment on Boulevard de Paris. She described the bedroom: Amalia slept in a throne-like four-poster piled high with feather pillows and stuffed animals. Snug up against it was Carmen's army cot with its tight sheet, brown blanket and one thin pillow.

She did not record what transpired there.

CHAPTER 18

The Haima

Like a dead man he lay in the sand. The tent was a typical nomad affair, woven of goat hair and staked out on the hard desert "street" among the dunes. Poles propped open a downwind flap facing him, but in the blinding morning light he could make out nothing within.

A naked blue-black child, head shaved save for a topknot, toddled out of the tent, a nut in one hand and stone in the other. Squatting down on his haunches, he laid the nut on a rock and smacked it with the stone.

A curtain of time had lifted to reveal a glimpse of ancient Africa. The primitive tent, lost among the creeping dunes that had been shaped by the wind into perfect crescents – the great groaning silence of the Sahara, broken only by a strange clicking sound from within the tent, and the naked child with his first tool – it was a peep into pre-history where nothing had changed for thousands of years.

After several smacks the nut cracked, and the child let out a little grunt of satisfaction. Laying down the stone, he popped the kernel into his mouth.

Arturo whistled. The child froze. His jaw stopped moving and his eyes rolled. Two naked arms, thrust from the tent's opaque interior, yanked him inside. There was a frightened jabbering, the sound of something breaking, and smothered screams.

No point in hiding any longer. Picking up his pack, Arturo got up from the sand, crossed the clearing, and ducked through the low entrance.

The tent was partitioned by a hanging cloth. One side for women, the other for men. As his eyes grew accustomed to the gloom, Arturo saw that the tent was empty save for an old woman with bright orange hair, who sat watching him from a number of blackened pots by the center pole. An open flap at the back of the tent provided an explanation: he had arrived when the men were away, probably herding camels. Another women and the child, (and perhaps others), who but a moment ago were in the tent, were now running to raise the alarm, leaving behind the crone, too feeble to escape.

Arturo greeted her in his Arabic, but she only muttered to herself and bent to continue the work she had been doing before the excitement began – pounding coffee beans with a mortar and pestle. Arturo had never in his life smelled anything so seductive as those crushed beans. Cupping his hands, he pointed to a *guerba* hanging from the pole. The old woman, still muttering, picked up a gourd and filled it from the skin.

While he was having his drink, a woman came back, slipping in through a tent flap, with the child. They stood behind the crone and eyed their uninvited guest.

Arturo realized that he was being examined by three generations of the same family: the grandmother with the circus hair, and the woman with her child, the boy.

Arturo gestured that he needed food. The women gave no indication of understanding what he was trying to tell them. He opened his pack, took out three red penknives, and handed one to the crone, two to the woman with the child. The child's eyes shone, but his mother accepted the gifts with sullen indifference. Finally, she dipped down and stepped forward, holding a gourd full of unshelled almonds. Parting the curtain, she pointed forcefully to a low stool on the men's side. The child came over, sat at Arturo's feet, and cracked the nuts for him to eat.

Even in his weakened state, Arturo could not help noticing that the child's mother was a miraculously stunning, plum-blue beauty.

CHAPTER 19

The Italian Hospital

An acute attack of asthma, especially when it occurs at night, can be a terrifying experience for both patient and witness. The patient breathes with great difficulty. The tremendous effort required to suck in a trickle of oxygen through constricted bronchial tubes quickly exhausts her. She feels like a swimmer trapped underwater, frantically struggling to regain the surface.

The witness looks on helplessly, not knowing how to bring relief. She fusses about uselessly. The fear is contagious, which only makes things worse.

One evening Jâafar knocked on the door of the Casbah house. He paid regular visits before going on to one of his innumerable social engagements.

Mina opened in a panic. "Thank God you've come, sidi!"

"What's happened?"

"She can't breathe!"

"Did you call Doctor MacGregor?"

"The telephone is broken! Mohamed ran to the *zoco* for a taxi! That was half an hour ago. Just when you need one there are no taxis!"

Jâafar was very much afraid seeing Daisy in such a state – gasping for breath, clutching the side of the bed, sweat pouring off her in big drops.

A syringe lay on the table. She pointed to it with a shaking hand. "Give me a shot," she wheezed. "Quick!"

Jâafar had never given an injection before. Like everyone else, he was afraid of needles. Daisy had told him what a powerful drug adrenaline was, and he was fearful of giving her an overdose, lest she have heart failure and die.

Daisy was watching his every move and despairing over his clumsiness.

"Please hurry!" she begged.

His hands were shaking, and he cut his finger on the glass ampoule the adrenaline comes in. There was blood all over everything. In the end, he administered only half the necessary dose without telling her he had spilled the rest.

When it became apparent the drug was to have no effect, Daisy thought she was finished.

"No air!" she gasped. "I'm suffocating!"

"She's turning blue!" Mina cried.

They bundled her into Jâafar's car and drove to the Italian Hospital, where the nuns gave her a proper injection and housed her in an oxygen tent. Gradually the crisis passed. She began to breathe easier. But she was exhausted. She soon fell asleep.

The next morning Mina and Sobrina arrived with *shabakia* – home-made honey cakes. The huge hospital building, spotlessly clean, where each patient had his own room, was all wonderment. They knew from experience that if you faced the misfortune of having to go into a Moroccan hospital, you would be well-advised to take with you your own sheets and pillowcases, your blankets, pyjamas, wash cloth, towels and soap, pillows and mattress cover, and to stock up in advance on food and drink, medicine, bandages and syringes: that is, if you didn't want to come out sicker than when you went in.

During the hour of the siesta Jâafar, a vision in a silvery djellaba and soft red fez, crept in. He was holding a thermos of mint tea, prepared by the women of his household.

Out of respect for his friendship with Mrs. Adams, he felt responsible for Daisy's well-being in Tangier. His informers kept watch over the little house in the Casbah. Upon learning that she went out dressed as a man, he smiled, believing that he had implanted the idea in her head in the first place.

Gazing at Daisy, her pondered over the ways in which the sleeping girl might prove to be a useful emissary between himself and his ally in the desert.

Amalia and Carmen arrived at the cocktail hour. Daisy could hear them joshing with the nuns in the hall.

"How did you know I was here?"

"We saw Jâafar at the British Consulate."

Amalia had smuggled in a bottle of Old Cornstalk sipping whisky beneath her cape.

"Is this what cowgirls drink?"

"A cowgirl will drink anything."

They wanted to see the tattoo. Daisy pushed down the sheet, pulled up her hospital gown, rolled on her side.

"Darling, so original!"

"Did it hurt?"

Doctor MacGregor had a reassuring bedside manner, but confessed that any treatment for asthma was hopeless in a place like Tangier.

"This climate is too damp for anyone with a chronic respiratory complaint," he explained. "Especially when it is aggravated by emotional strain. My advice to you is to leave Tangier for some place where the climate is warmer and drier, and leave your melancholy associations behind."

CHAPTER 20

Tent Love

When the wind rose in the middle of the night, and the clanking began, she parted the curtain, slipped from the women's quarter and knelt over Arturo's body. The gourds hanging from the pole bumped lazily against each other in the breeze sifting through the tent. The cluster of aluminum measuring spoons clicked in the moving air. Corn shucks rustled and dangling cook pots rattled softly in the little desert gale that sprang up like clockwork at two o'clock each morning. Muffled by this tremulous cacophony, her love-making was stealthy – no groan or giggle, no sigh of love or smacking kisses as they writhed together in serious silence. With the old lady sawing wood, a few feet away, their buttoned-up passion became reptilian in its speechless embrace. A seething hiss in his ear stifled the slightest whimper of pleasure. She had to be on top in order to be able to leap away at the faintest dreaming murmur from the women's side of the tent. She pulled apart her blouse to receive his sucking kisses on her breasts, which he loved like a blind man. She was strong, this girl, she had known nothing but hard physical labor all her life. Her knees clamped his hips in a jockey's vice, calloused elbows dug into his shoulders, and hands as hard as wood kneaded his hair while her pelvis rummaged mercilessly for love. Her husband was absent – departed, divorced, deserted – or dead. No stranger to sex, she deftly directed their death-defying tryst. When her child on the other side of the curtain moaned in his sleep, she reached out a soothing hand while covering Arturo's lips with her own. Her tongue wanted his tongue out of his mouth.

CHAPTER 21

Uncle Bernon, Rucio and Elvis

When she left the hospital Daisy telephoned Antonio in Spain.

"I'm going to the desert, daddy. Asthma is killing me in this place."

"You won't be welcome down there, babes. According to *The Herald Tribune* the Americans are sending over more troops, all because one soldier got killed. These new numbers are beginning to make people nervous. It's mission creep all over again – like in Vietnam. It's not just famine relief going on down there but a full-blown military operation. The longer the Americans stay, the more problems there will be. It may be OK for someone like you to be in Tangier, but with more soldiers arriving – the Moroccans don't like that. The religious Muslims don't like that. They worry about the number of Americans in their country. More are coming, and ordinary Moroccans have no idea what's going on. The Moroccan opposition leader came on Spanish TV to say these new numbers were 'humiliating.' That's a bad sign."

She promised to be home by Christmas.

Mina and Sobrina helped pack her mother's things. A Spanish shipping agent came from the port, boxed them up, and took them away in his truck.

She drew down her mother's bank account, converting the dirhams back into dollars on the black market. She took a beating on the exchange, but she wanted the dollars. In the desert dollars would have more clout, or so she thought.

On the way to the station she stopped at the cemetery of Bou Arakia. While the taxi waited she scattered bread crumbs on the grave and with her lips wet the headstone she had had engraved and placed there. With tears in her eyes but already feeling lighter and breathing a bit easier, she caught the night train for Marrakesh.

The feeling of melancholy induced by riding on a train at night revived childhood memories of lying in a hospital ward, also at night. She was alone among strangers, confined to a space she could not leave. Her fate was in the hands of others. There was a helplessness or passivity in both situations.

It was cold. During the night the compartment filled with soldiers. One of them spread his cape over her. After that she slept better.

In Marrakesh she checked into the CTM hotel next to the bus station. Nervous about venturing into a strange city in her new disguise, she stayed by the window and watched the buses arrive from the country. The unloading of sheep and goats, and chickens tied by their legs in bunches – along with bundles and boxes brought down from the roofs of the dusty vehicles – created scenes of incredible mayhem. Compared to their city brethren, most of whom went around in shabby second-hand, western-style clothes, the country Moroccans looked like nobility from another planet. Shaved heads were magnificently turbanned. Hand-woven robes billowed regally. The gaily-dressed women went unveiled. They gesticulated. They shouted. They haggled over everything. Some arguments verged on violence, but not one degenerated into a physical fight. This was an improvement over Arizona, Daisy concluded, where boys her age prided themselves on the scabs on their knuckles. One of the reasons was that Moroccans, especially traditional country Moroccans, do not use alcohol.

She had expected to see Americans in Marrakesh – soldiers on leave spending their money. Abdelouahaid, the proprietor of the hotel, said they were confined to their base at Ben Guerir, north of the city, a situation he regarded with contempt.

"Big strong American soldiers afraid to go out? Afraid some little Moroccan will bite them on their heels? *Shooma!*" (Shame!)

The crisis in the desert having chased away most of the tourist trade, the merchants were angry that Marrakesh had been placed off limits.

When Daisy wished to continue her journey southwards, Abdelouahaid told her that tourists were forbidden to cross the Atlas Mountains without permission from the Wali, the Assistant Governor of Marrakesh. She checked this information out at the Tourist Office and found it to be correct.

After making inquiries Daisy made her way by bus to Ait Ourir, a village on the Marrakesh plain at the foot of the Atlas range, where there was a Tuesday horse market. For the equivalent of about one hundred and twenty-five dollars she bought a sturdy, fifteen hand, orangey-yellow gelding with one black sock, which she reckoned could carry her over the mountains. She named him Uncle Bernon. For another fifty a second-hand Moroccan saddle, plus a bridle from Algeria in the style once used by Franco-Algerian cavalry. This the Moroccans found stronger than their own. Finally, she paid thirty for a pair of fine leather-trimmed, hand-woven palmetto saddle baskets.

She figured she had been gotten the better of on all three deals, but the saddle baskets were of good quality. Uncle Bernon didn't have much spark or character to speak of, he had been worked long and hard, but Daisy reckoned he was still strong. She went to the *haddad* (the local blacksmith) to have his forefeet shod. He shuffled along, slow and steady, rather like his namesake.

The original Uncle Bernon was also a bit of a gelding. He used to turn up at Guadalquivir ranch unannounced in his pick-up. A virginal bachelor in his sixties, he was born and raised in Tennessee, but his skin, after years in Arizona, had taken on the color of hot dog mustard. He was a man who, from his youth upwards, had been filled with the profound conviction that the softest way of life was the best. Thus, his philosophy in life which he summed up in three words: "Take it easy." He puttered in the garden and didn't pay much attention to the few head of cattle that wandered about his place. The macho Adams ignored him, but Mrs. Adams appreciated his courtly southern ways. She poured him a tall glass of her clove-flavored iced tea, which he spiked with a shot of Virginia Gentleman from his silver hip flask (dented from being sat on during Vanderbilt University football games), and listened to him philosophize about the Civil War. The whole family was addicted to his bread-and-butter pickles, red pepper jelly and pecan pies which he brought over each Thanksgiving.

Uncle Bernon belonged to the "what-if" school of history. His theory stemmed from *what*, from a southerner's point of view, might and should have happened after the battle of Chicamauga (Cherokee for "River of Death"), fought in the wilderness of North Georgia in September, 1863.

If General Braxton Bragg had followed up the famous Confederate victory and chased the shattered Union army out of Chattanooga, it was unlikely that General William Tecumseh Sherman could have launched his celebrated march through Georgia the following spring. Atlanta, the strategic southern railhead, fell to the Federals in the summer of 1864, giving the Union war effort a huge boost. *If* Atlanta hadn't fallen, President Lincoln may well have lost the election of 1864 to the Peace Party headed by General McClellan. The war-weary north might have come to terms with the Confederacy, the unconditional surrender at Appomattox would have been avoided, and the southern way of life, or at least most of it, would have been preserved. Minus the slavery.

Antonio Adams branded Uncle Bernon's theories "hogwash." His view of the Civil War was colored by the fact that many of the most prominent generals on both sides of the conflict, from Robert E. Lee on down, had won their spurs as young officers inflicting a humiliating defeat on Mexico during the war of 1846-48.

Daisy drew up a list of provisions to get her over the mountains.

Nosebag for U.B., iron stake with blue rope to tether, barley (no oats available) – 25 kilo sack, screwdriver (to dig stones from hoof), a pair of heavy duty pliers (to prise up a faulty, loose, or twisted shoe), ground sheet, a ball of string for tying things on. Also a rope halter for tying up U.B. at night.

Also: coffee pot and cups, cookpot with tight-fitting lid, kettle, teapot with glasses, soap with towel, 2 plates, 2 spoons, 1 knife.

Plus: coffee, tea, sugar loaf, salt, *sudaniya* (hot chilli powder), rice, oil, bread, beans, two 6-packs of Coke, 24 Mars bars, and two cartons of Marlboros to ease her way over the Atlas.

After assembling her shopping she realized that in addition to herself Uncle Bernon could not possibly carry it all. Therefore she went back to the horse market, where for $25 she bought a fuzzy grey donkey with spots along his back. She dubbed him "Rucio" or "Dapple." For this new member of her team she added to the pile a second nosebag, plus stake and tether and lead. That she was unable to find a tent worried her. She expected to see big snow up in them thar hills.

The whiff of money drew a crowd of bumpkins. A boy came forward leading a dog on the end of a rope. A big black male dog, tall as a Labrador, but without a Lab's chunky build. He had the physique of a racing animal. His coat was dull and dusty, his belly rubbed raw from scratching, and his ears, what hadn't been torn off in fights, were armored with engorged ticks. Unlike most xenophobic Moroccan dogs he was subdued and friendly, shyly swinging his tail as he regarded her with soulful brown eyes that seemed to say, "Buy me. Feed me. Deliver me from this miserable existence and I shall serve you for ever."

His name was El Malik ("The King"), and the price was a dollar.

She handed over the money and led her pet to a hardware store where she had spotted a plastic tick collar. She bought several of those. Following her instructions the man punched Arabic letters into a brass disk. She cut an old leather belt in two, awled a hole through the piece with the buckle, attached the disk and hung it around the dog's neck next to the tick collar.

AL BEECE (ELVIS)

At a butcher's shop she purchased a meaty bone. With loud crunching noises Elvis crushed and swallowed it. After that he never left her side.

Riding along at a leisurely pace, with Rucio trailing and Elvis trotting beside, she made her way eastward. It was rolling, hilly, shadeless country, alternately lashed by autumn rains and baked by the African sun.

Dressed in a patched burnoose and turban bought second-hand at Souk el Khemis in Marrakesh, she was travelling under an assumed name – Moha ben Abdu – "poorest of the poor" – Egyptian student (*taleb*), wandering from *zawiya* (monastery) to *zawiya* to be instructed. She'd had her battered boots resoled. Her saddle and bridle were ancient. One of her saddle baskets was stuffed with provisions; the other contained the cash, the Ruger and the bottle of Old Cornstalk. Rucio carried the barley, the pots and pans, but she had no tent. She never went out of a walk so he could keep up.

With few provisions she was dependent on the hospitality of those she met along the trail. She camped with shepherds in a field. An amiable farmer walked beside her for a few miles before pointing the way. Yet each encounter contained a potential threat. As the Sultan's grip on the countryside loosened, banditry had become common. She was careful to make no show of wealth. A student's dress was expected to be modest. So far language hadn't been a problem; they accepted her accent as foreign. She was glad she met no women along the way: surely a woman would see through her disguise. For two or three miles each day, to stretch her legs and to take some weight off Uncle Bernon, she walked.

Another thing to her advantage: Moroccan men pee squatting (bearing out Montaigne), backs to the wind, private parts tactfully concealed by the comfortable billowing robes all wear.

Spring comes twice a year to Morocco: in March, when the warming sun fills the bursting fields of grain with the red shine of poppies; and in November, when after seven dry months the rains return to reclothe the parched landscape in green. Beneath an enamelled blue sky, the hills were decked out in loud patches of color. In the valleys below, laced with running streams, autumn ploughing had begun. Mixed teams of donkeys and camels drew behind them strings of white egrets to pluck worms from the freshly turned soil. She never let an opportunity go by to water her animals at one of the gushing, tumbling, sparkling mountain torrents.

The Atlas Mountains began to concern her. She had on-again off-again glimpses of snowy peaks beyond the palms. The view was inspiring, but she began to wonder how she was going to get over them.

In the village of Demnate it was *Souk el had* – Sunday market. For herself she bought provisions, another sack of barley, plus a kilo of carrots for transport, a cooked cow's hoof for Elvis and two heavy woollen blankets. Then she rode on for a few more miles before stopping for lunch in a grove of cork oaks. A natural bridge (Imi-n-Ifri), hollowed out by the river, was hung with gray fang-like stalactites. Beneath the bridge, she read in the guide, was a grotto where Muslims and the mountain Jews of Demnate once sacrificed animals to appease a fearsome *jenoun* (genie) who dwelled down there.

With Uncle Bernon and Rucio cropping grass and munching acorns, Elvis made grinding noises on the hoof. The transformation that had come over her pet was truly amazing. The ticks had dropped off his ears. On a diet of bones and bread, he was beginning to fill out. His black coat gleamed in the sunshine.

She spread a blanket on the grass, loaded the Ruger, and picnicked in the sun. Behind and below her was a view of Demnate, with its old walls and olive groves. According to the map, the town was three thousand feet above sea level. The sun warmed her back, sheep-bells provided the music, but the afternoon air was beginning to have an edge.

For Uncle Bernon and Rucio the fresh grass was like chocolate. She let them eat as much as they liked. With snow ahead, this might be the last square meal for a while.

Tapping a hard-boiled egg on the butt of the Ruger, on the map (Michelin no.171, *Maroc Sud*), she picked out the Forest Lodge of Oazzennt about eighteen miles from Demnate. Beyond that was a Mountain Lodge at Ait Tamelil, and a pass over the mountains. There were many passes: Tizi-n-Tirlist and Tizi-n-Ait-Imi (9,600 feet!). A dotted line looked like a track. Although it was already late in the afternoon, she resolved to make the Forest Lodge at Oazzennt her final destination for the day.

Balancing the empty Coke can on a rock she walked away, Ruger in hand, turned and fired.

The can disappeared. So did Elvis.

CHAPTER 22

Snow

Reverberating in the grotto, the gunshot caused a cloud of black birds to rise up in a spiral. Like a sinister umbrella unfurling, they fanned out above Daisy. She quickly mounted up and rode away.

As she rode along, the sun began to go down, and the snowy flanks of the Atlas Mountains turned pink, then orange, then purple. The track paralleled a roaring river. The minute the sun set, the temperature dropped several degrees. She pulled on her gloves and tightened the turban. (The turban is the warmest of headwear.) The moon made an appearance. After a time she began to pass patches of snow glowing like milk in the moonlight. It was spooky but exciting. Ahead loomed the formidable outline of the High Atlas, still a long way off. The lights of Demnate twinkled in the valley below. They looked warm and inviting. She hoped she was doing the right thing.

After about two hours she spied a light up ahead. A few minutes later she rode into a village consisting, so far as she could make out in the dark, of two rows of stone huts along a street that lay deep in snow.

She dismounted. A village dog ran out to challenge Elvis. There was a brief, savage encounter. The smaller dog ran off, squealing.

Some goats trailed by with bells clanking, followed by a man in a djellaba. He shined a light on Uncle Bernon. Other men came out of the houses.

It was difficult to see their faces, which the hoods of their djella-bas cast in shadow. In the silence that followed, dogs could be heard barking all over the mountain, as they spread the news of the arrival of strangers in their midst. Elvis whimpered and stayed close by Daisy's leg.

"*Salaam alikoum.*"

They murmured as one. "*Was alikoum salaam.*"

She produced a pack of Marlboros and distributed them around. As the cigarettes were lit, she peered at their faces one by one.

Berbers, she thought – like our American Indians, with ruddy skin, high cheekbones and oriental eyes. The Berbers were the original inhabitants of North Africa, long before the Arab invasion. They kept to the mountains and spoke their own language – *tashilhite* or *shleuh* – and remained true to their traditions and their intense dislike of the lowland Arabs. All had their eyes on Uncle Bernon.

Goddamned rustlers, she thought.

"*Cigarette americaine,*" said one. "*Toi aussi – americain?*"

Daisy pretended not to understand. What with so much anti-American sentiment being whipped up in the country, Jâafar had advised her not to reveal her nationality.

"Any place to sleep here?" she asked.

No answer to that.

"How far to the forest lodge at Ouazzennt?"

One of them pointed up the track. "*Cinq kilometres.*"

"Well then, goodnight."

It was pitch black in the woods. She shined her light to keep from getting knocked out of the saddle by a branch. Gradually the trail broadened. The moon cast a dull glow on a tin roof. She tried the door, but the place was locked up tight. Flashing the light through the windows, she walked around the cabin. It looked cozy in there, with wood stacked against a stone fireplace. She could have smashed a window but, after that less than friendly reception in the village, thought it not wise to trespass. Behind the cabin stood a low shed. She shined the light inside. Some hay bales were piled up. A rat scurried away.

Uncle Bernon was going to be her central heating for the night. Leaving the saddle on for warmth she loosened the girth and spread one of the blankets over him. Gathering the corners, she bound them with string and tied them together so the blanket wouldn't slip off during the night. Rucio had his own fur coat. Pulling apart a bale, she let the animals feed and made a nest with the rest. Elvis lay down and started licking. It had been a long day. Everyone was bushed. She took off her boots, stretched out in the hay, pulled the burnoose over her, jammed her feet into the hood and spread the second blanket. She ate some bread and cheese, washed it down with a slug of Old Cornstalk, and for a few minutes felt quite snug.

She was thankful for her companions – Uncle Bernon's and Rucio's body heat to keep the frost from the shed and Elvis to guard. With the Ruger by her crotch, flashlight under her chin, and saddle-bag for pillow, she lay in the hay and looked through the open door at the stars. It was completely still and icy cold. Elvis had curled into a ball. In a ghostly universe that rang with silence, somewhere far away a dog began to bark. It was a short, persistent yap that never seemed to let up. Elvis lifted his head, moaned, and went back to sleep.

As she lay there, her thoughts returned to the Guadalquivir Ranch in Arizona. On clear nights she and Arturo used to spread cushions on the roof and gaze at the stars while Antonio told stories.

In the market place, an old Yaqui squaw was selling olives for $300 a pound. The olives were as old and black and wrinkled as herself. They did not haggle over this unheard-of price because, as the olives were doled out, she told secrets of immortality. She had a map of the stars which revealed the center of the universe. Soon they were flying through the night on their Flexible Flyers. The way across space was black and frightening, but they could steer like they were gliding on snow. Ahead floated a glowing coal, which they knew to be the mind of the Creator. It gave out warmth and light, and they made for it.

"Children! Antonio! Supper is ready!"

Mrs. Adams welcomed the young astronomers back into the warm bosom of her house. It took a few minutes for them to recover their senses and get their appetites back.

The memory made Daisy's nose run and her eyes fill with tears. They came out hot and froze on her cheeks. She drifted off to sleep.

Something dropped on her legs. It was walking on her! She switched on the flashlight as a rat jumped away. Elvis snapped at it and bit off its head. She heard him crunching up the rest.

She was woken by a roar. Silhouetted in the moonlight, an animal was standing rigidly in the doorway of the shed. She groped for the Ruger before realizing it was Elvis. His silhouette against the luminous snow made him look twice as big. She had never heard him bark before. He had a powerful voice – barks strung together into a baritone howl. Breath steaming, she played the light around the shed. Roof beams bearded with cobwebs. She checked Uncle Bernon's blanket and gave him and Rucio each a hug. Heart still pounding, she crawled back under the covers. Elvis, hackles up, lay down again and groaned reassuringly.

Although she dozed from time to time, she spent most of the night shivering and fearful her asthma would return.

Just as well I can't sleep, she said to herself. Sleepiness is the first sign you're freezing to death.

At first light she rolled out of the hay. Her blanket was frozen stiff. She lifted it up in one big piece like a crab shell and stood it in the sun to thaw. The air was bitterly cold, and she jumped up and down to warm up. The effort nearly made her faint. With the sun coming up she noted on the map that the forest lodge was nearly five thousand feet above sea level.

While Elvis gnawed on a loaf of bread, she filled Uncle Bernon's and Rucio's nosebags. She ate two boiled eggs and some macaroons. It had snowed during the night; there were footprints.

So! They had followed and spied while she slept! She patted Elvis. The best thing was to get going. She saddled up. The little team set out on a path where the snow had been trodden down.

The climbing became steep. The snow surface looked deceptively smooth, but underneath the ground was uneven and slippery. Uncle Bernon stumbled and snorted. She dismounted and led on foot. Her feet were cold, but the snow was dry and crunchy, the sun warm on her back. The sky was cobalt blue, almost black, and the white mountains glistened. She felt like an ant on a bedsheet.

She sucked down the pure mountain air and felt a surge of well-being. If she'd stayed in Tangier she'd probably be back in the Italian Hospital!

By degrees the terrain levelled into a long, upward-sloping valley, split by a river that sluiced down the middle. She was able to remount. Whistling *Onward Christian Soldiers* she rode uphill through powder snow. The snow bowl concentrated a light that was almost blinding. Not a breath of air stirred. She was glad for her Ray Bans. The air was cold but the sun incredibly hot. Coming to a place where the river dived over a precipice, she decided this was a good place to stop, to picnic, and to wash.

Bathing was a problem for Daisy. Dressed as a man, she had been turned away from the *hammam*, or public bath, in Marrakesh, during the women's hour, and of course she could not go when the men were there.

She spread a blanket on the snow. Elvis instantly lay down on it.

The water pouring over the rocks had thrown up fantastic ice configurations. Rippled pillars of ice clung to the rock. Icicles as thick as her waist hung down where water trickled in the sun. It was a winter wonderland.

Before undressing she scanned the snow fields all around. Just when you think you're alone in the Moroccan wilderness, a shepherd boy may be spying from behind a rock, ready to dart out and steal.

Naked, she walked across the ice with her towel and bar of Palmolive. She let the water pour over her and jumped back. In Arizona Antonio insisted on outdoor showers, but this was like liquid ice! She soaped herself and jumped back in to rinse. Seconds later, her body burning, she was standing on the blanket, giving herself a vigorous *friction* with the towel. After the frigid shower the mountain air felt like Mexico.

Elvis growled. She looked up. Men! My God, men were coming!

There she was, buck naked, and four men had materialized from nowhere and were walking straight at her!

Still wet, she dressed and jumped on Uncle Bernon. Digging in the iron points of her Moorish stirrups, she set off at a quick pace.

They had been, maybe, two hundred yards away. Uncle Bernon soon stretched that distance to half a mile. They were forging on, single file, following the track Uncle Bernon and Rucio had ploughed through the snow. The icy stillness added to her sense of isolation. Snow plumes trailing from the peaks indicated that strong winds were blowing at higher altitudes. She was glad she wasn't up there. When long blue shadows began to flow down from the ridges, she kept an anxious eye out for the mountain lodge at Ait Tamelil. It would be no joke to spend another night outside at seven thousand feet.

A ray of sun glinted off a tin roof up ahead. The Berber who came out to greet her was wearing knickerbockers and mountain boots, a quilted parka, wool cap and goggles – all in a used condition. He helped her stable Uncle Bernon and Rucio and led her and Elvis inside. His name was Hammu and he was an official mountain guide. He spoke a little English. He made her sit before a pot-bellied stove and placed a steaming glass of tea in her hands.

"How far to the pass over the mountain?"

He pointed out the window at a sheer wall of blue ice rising to a gap between two cliffs. It seemed inconceivable she could scale such a slope, let alone lead Uncle Bernon up there.

Hammu waved away her concerns. "We'll have a go in the morning," he said confidently. "Tomorrow, *Insh'Allah!*"

Before dark the men showed up. Daisy recognized them from the village.

By the light of an oil lamp Hammu prepared a spicy stew which they ate with their fingers, soaking up the sauce with the bread the others had brought. They drank smoky-tasting tea. Despite her misgivings about the new arrivals, Daisy relaxed, a little.

"I met them last night," Daisy said to Hammu. "Why did they follow me?"

He put the question to the Berbers. It prompted a long-winded answer which Daisy, without understanding a word of it, could tell was a fabrication.

"They were worried about you," was Hammu's translation. "They followed in case you got lost in the mountains."

"If they were so worried, why did they let me sleep outside?"

"They saw you under the hay," was the Berbers translated explanation. "They knew you were safe."

While they were speaking, Daisy realized it was improper to question the Berbers' hospitality. She let the matter drop.

Using tin plates as drums, the Berbers improvised a song. While she listened, Daisy detected a change of mood. The song, whatever it was, was the cause of much hilarity, poking in the ribs, and a few lascivious glances in her direction. Hammu looked ill at ease.

The penny dropped. They'd seen her in the raw: that was what the song was about. Judging from Hammu's discomfort, Daisy deduced it was not a nice song. Within the context of the Berbers' strict tradition of hospitality, it was tantamount to an insult, maybe a threat. A chill of fear instantly drove away any sense of comfort.

She jumped to her feet. "I'm going to look after my horse!" she announced, and went outside.

As soon as the door shut behind her an argument erupted. It was Hammu's voice against the others. She heard the word *roumia* repeated again and again. The argument was about her; Hammu was the only one taking her side.

She sucked down the icy air, surveyed the milky slopes in the moonlight, and pondered her options. Should she saddle Uncle Bernon and ride back down the mountain? Night vision in snow is tricky at best, and she doubted her ability to find the way. She also doubted her chances of surviving a night outside at this altitude. Worse, she might ride Uncle Bernon over a cliff and get him or herself hurt or worse. Wherever she went, the Berbers were bound to follow. Here at least she had shelter, and an ally in Hammu. But what chance had they against four men with knives and maybe guns concealed beneath their robes?

She visited Uncle Bernon and Rucio in the hut and fed them carrots. With her heart beating fast, she took a snort from the bottle and came to a decision.

"They're not going to take you away." She pulled the Ruger from the saddlebag and pocketed a handful of shells. "Over my dead body."

The Berbers fell back when she led Uncle Bernon into the cabin.

"Do you like my horse?"

Hammu looked shocked, but he quickly translated.

Daisy had prepared a little speech: "In America … a long time ago … there was a woman called Conchita Billings."

Hammu translated.

"She was an old woman but strong. She lived alone, in a cabin like this … "

Hammu translated. Uncle Bernon snorted.

"She owned a horse like mine. She was dependent on her horse for ploughing and getting to market. This was in America."

Hammu translated.

"Mexican soldiers were combing the countryside, taking people's horses."

Hammu translated.

"This happened a long time ago – a hundred and fifty years ago … "

Hammu translated.

"When the Mexicans came to Conchita Billings' farm, she hid her horse in the house."

Hammu translated.

"The soldiers searched the barn, but they didn't look in the house. So Conchita Billings kept her horse."

The Berbers' eyes shifted when she produced the Ruger.

"This belonged to my father," she said. "He used it to kill many men."

Hammu quickly translated.

"Rustlers used to cross from Mexico to steal our cattle. My father waited by the well."

Hammu translated.

"One time a Mexican took one of our horses. My father chased him. He shot the man *with this gun!* We got our horse back!"

She sat down and laid the Ruger on the table. The Berbers were staring. She took four slugs from her pocket and stood them in a row.

"Four men," she said. "Four bullets." With the tip of her finger she touched the tip of each slug and pointed at the Berbers in turn. "One for you and you and you!"

The Berbers looked grim. Uncle Bernon stamped.

"Here!" She started handing them out.

Each accepted a bullet.

"American!" she said, patting the Ruger. "I'm American and this gun is American!" She produced the Marlboros and distributed them around.

"American!"

The Berbers nodded. Smiles flickered as the cigarettes were lit. The ice had broken.

Uncle Bernon farted. That mouldy straw. At least he didn't crap on Hammu's floor.

Hammu dragged a mattress from the loft and carried it to the shed. With the Ruger next to her cheek, Daisy spent another night outdoors with her transport.

When she awoke the sun was shining. Hammu was brewing a pot of tea. The Berbers had departed. He greeted her in his usual hearty manner and asked if she were ready to tackle the mountain.

Following his instructions, she stuffed the cuffs of her trousers into her boots. He showed her to wrap strips of cloth around her legs from boot to knee, in the form of puttees.

After a jolly breakfast of bread and butter and several glasses of tea, Hammu handed her earmuffs and a pair of ski gloves.

In an hour they had passed from beneath the cliffs into a wide white basin, where they had a view of the surrounding peaks with their trailing plumes of snow. When Hammu began to whoop and holler, Daisy feared his booming peals would loosen the drifts above them. On the contrary, the voice of one small man seemed to dominate the solemn peaks all around. It was inspiring to hear him bellow like that, so she yelled along with him. Together they startled a crowd of croaking ravens, and the impassive mountains returned their voices. It was as though they were the only human beings on earth, and the world was just beginning, or had recently come to an end.

They mounted the basin wall to the pass at Tizi-n-Tirlist, where Hammu presented her with an incomparable view from the edge of the mountain. The precipice fell away a thousand feet or more. Giant eagles swirled below. To her relief, there was no snow on the south side of the mountain. South from the chain of the Atlas, which resembled great scoops of vanilla ice-cream, Hammu pointed out the Sarhro Mountains beyond Ouarzazate and the valley carved by the river Drâa.

Daisy had heard that the Atlas Mountains had no foothills to speak of, and she could believe it. Standing knee-deep in snow and buffeted by a swirling gale, she gazed at the vast shimmering expanse of the Sahara. It looked like another planet. It looked absolutely amazing. Arturo was out there somewhere.

But where?

CHAPTER 23

Trans Atlantic

Somewhere between Colomb-Béchar and Tindouf, on the multi-spoked *Piste de Mauritanie*, Arturo flagged down a Land Rover packed with jerry cans and sand ladders, barrelling across the desert, whip antenna slashing the air. Three cheerful Brits welcomed him aboard. One of their number had come down with malaria and had to be left behind. Arturo could ride as far as Timbukoo, if he could pay his way.

He still had a couple of grand stashed in his pack, along with his Mexican passport.

From Timbuktoo he progressed by *pinasse* (native ferry) westwards along the Niger and Senegal rivers to St.-Louis on the Atlantic.

In Dakar he boarded an Alitalia flight across the narrow neck of the Atlantic to Brasilia, where he hopped on another plane to Panama, and he had to wait three days for the TICA (Transportes Interncionales Centro-Americano) bus to Tapachula, Chiapas.

CHAPTER 24

Schistocerca Gregaria

In the desert, every life form faces a struggle to survive. The rains don't come often, but sometimes fall with frightening intensity. The Sahara has an average rainfall of only a few inches a year, but it can be concentrated into one savage hour. When that happens, flash floods are the result.

The water surges down from the hills and funnels into a wadi, or dry river bed, arriving without warning to smash down the mud dams of the oasis farmer, choking and destroying his irrigation canals. Adobe houses disintegrate in minutes or are crushed by boulders a yard wide that are rolled along like pebbles. Many a slow-moving caravan has been overtaken by a wall of water moving at race-horse speed and swallowed beneath a cloudless sky. In the Sahara more people drown than die of thirst.

The flood soon dries to nothingness as the water is absorbed by the desert. The sun shines down while a miracle quietly unfolds. From where there was only sand and gravel before, a flush of green appears. Within days a mass of vegetation bursts forth – bushes whose stalks had been eaten to the ground, plants whose seeds had lain dormant for years, and many kinds of grasses. Delicate flowers blossom atop thorny trees and shrubs. As long as this vegetation lasts, the wadi becomes a magnet for life. Gazelles come to an alert, uneasy halt on the stony plain of the *hammada*, sniff the air and begin to trot in the direction of the wadi. Flocks of birds materialize from an empty sky. Observing the hawks that hang overhead, scanning for snakes and lizards, nomads hurry their camels across the desert to pasture.

And from the sand beneath this bright green mosaic the *schistocerca gregaria*, or Desert Locust, is born.

Since the beginning of time the Desert Locust has terrorized man
on a scale not known in the case of any other pest. No other insect
in the world travels so far over such inhospitable country, and none
is so swiftly able to expand its numbers when conditions develop in
its favor. The insect emerges from nowhere and multiplies so enormously that the soil where it has bred erupts with hopping nymphs
as far as the eye can see. The hoppers join together in vast marching
bands indestructible by any other creature. All these aspects of its
life cycle combined, even before the flying swarms appear, produce
awe and superstitious terror in its victims.

In biblical times plagues of locusts were reckoned to be the worst
fate that could befall man. Passages in the Old Testament tell of the
sky being darkened by the cloud of approaching insects. Marching
armies of locusts, each the length of a couple of thumbs, advance
across the sand with a fire-like crackle. They invade villages, run up
the walls, climb onto houses and pour through the windows.

The 160 km. long Souss Valley was intensely planted with orange
groves whose fruit was vital to Morocco's export market. The pullu-
lating, leaping and scurrying insects devoured these orchards. They
gnawed the fields down to the roots, ate laundry hung out to dry,
and each other. Having finished off the grass, they fell on the wheat
and barley about to be harvested. Grape vines and date palms were
stripped, and fig trees splintered beneath the weight of the seething
mass.

The catastrophe assumed a sense of doom far greater than any
provoked by human invasion. Muslim priests prayed for divine
intervention to stop the destruction that brought people to anguish
and trembling "like nothing in all their lives."

Farmers fired shotguns into the swarm and lit fires. They dug
trenches and drove the creatures into them to burn and bury. The
women threw blankets over their gardens, but the locusts devoured
the blankets and then the vegetables.

There were incredible scenes among those who had never experienced an invasion. In Taradaunt a group of tourists panicked. A

woman described the horrible feeling of huge insects under her clothes. They writhed and squished beneath her feet to the sound of "millions of jaws biting and chewing." Some of the visitors locked themselves into hotel rooms while others tried to escape. But the insects carpeted the roads up to a foot deep, making driving all but impossible. Cars and buses veered crazily on the slime of crushed insects. Drivers were blinded as windshield wipers snapped beneath a blizzard of bugs.

After the locusts passed, hardly enough grain was left for the mice to scavenge. These mice, too, multiplied as never before, invading villages and eating the inhabitants out of house and home. In the end nothing was left. Tides of rotting insects floated down the Rivers Souss and Drâa to spread disease in their wake. Mountain streams and oasis wells were contaminated. An epidemic broke out among animals drinking from them.

The plague resulted in a 75% loss of the region's crops.

Like medieval prophets, zealots of Morocco's radical underground saw a divine message in the cataclysm. They urged their followers to acts of violence against a government which, in their view, had strayed from the path of God. The army was sent to quell a disturbance in Casablanca. Several demonstrators were crushed by tanks.

Within days, food shipments began to arrive from abroad, but distribution inside Morocco was slow and haphazard. It was rumored that government agents sold the food to recoup the revenue lost by the tourist industry. When the first food convoys left for the plague-ravaged regions of the south, Berber tribes of the High Atlas, whose loyalty to the Alaouite throne in Rabat had been in question since the era of the warlord Thami El Glaoui, mined the roads over the mountains, blasted the stalled trucks with anti-tank guns, and looted the cargo.

The action virtually sealed off the Saharan regions from the rest of the country. Once more the world witnessed television images of African children waiting for food shipments to arrive. Much of

Morocco south of the Atlas reverted to *bled-es-siba* ("wild country") dominated by the warlords of competing tribes, with government garrisons holding out in isolated towns.

The Moroccan situation was debated at the United Nations, and the Security Council reluctantly voted to send a multinational force to Africa. "Operation Groundswell," as it was called, was not expected to last more than six months.

The American Administration was underwhelmed by events in Morocco. Eerie windblown dunes, nomadic blue men blending with the dust, militarized camels, surreal "dune buggy" raids – who needed this desert Vietnam? The U.S. Army should be saved for fighting wars in which America had a clear strategic interest, not frittered away in semi-political tasks like peace-keeping and nation-building.

There was a simple, one-word description of strategic interest: oil. Morocco had none. *Rien. Nada. Walloo.* Maybe a couple of drops.

"But we have to pay attention to the stability of a country which lies only ten miles from Spain across the Strait of Gibraltar," argued the American ambassador. "Morocco sits on the fault line between Islam and Christian Europe."

To the consternation of the UN, Morocco refused to accept a force composed of colonial troops. The Sultan appealed directly to Washington, extending a sovereign invitation to America to come to the aid of its "oldest friend and nearest Muslim neighbor."

Speaking fluent English in an emotional but astute interview that was broadcast on American television, he outlined an area of U.S. history that few Americans knew about. Friendship between the U.S. and Morocco was as old as the Union itself. Morocco had been one of the first countries to recognise American Independence in 1776. The treaty of 1786 between the two countries was the work of Thomas Jefferson, Benjamin Franklin, and John Adams.

The New York Times printed a letter from George Washington dated December 1, 1789 to His Majesty Sidi Mohammed ben Abdellah, expressing his desire to promote friendship and harmony between the two nations.

After the death of the Sultan in 1791, the treaty had to be renewed, and the new Moroccan sovereign said, "The Americans, I find, are the Christian nation my father most esteemed."

During subsequent years many *rapprochements* confirmed the cordiality between the U.S. and successive sultans. In 1871 the Sultan Moulay Hassan, worried about French and Spanish expansionist designs, made clear his willingness to place his country under a U.S. protectorate – evidence of the confidence he would get an "American fair deal."

In 1942, in the first step that led eventually to the defeat of Nazi Germany, America landed its forces in Morocco. President Franklin Roosevelt sent the Sultan Mohammed V a message stating, "I have been highly pleased to learn of the admirable spirit of cooperation that is animating you and your people in their relationships with the forces of my country." In reply, the Sultan noted that American troops "did not come as conquerors but as liberators. We declared to Major General George Patton that as long as our prestige, soul, religion and traditions were respected, they could rest assured that they would find only friends in Morocco."

Calling his father's wartime handshake with President Franklin Roosevelt at the Casablanca Conference, "one of the great moments in the life of our country," and an historic cornerstone in the strong bilateral bond between the two countries, the Sultan reminded Americans that, from the 1950's, Strategic Air Command bases in Morocco formed the front line of American defense against the Soviet atomic threat. There was a navy communications center in Kenitra, and Voice of America transmitters outside Tangier. As a moderate Arab state, Morocco had on numerous occasions supported U.S. attempts to resolve the Arab-Israeli crisis.

Who would have thought that an insect could have caused consternation in the White House, a heated debate in Congress, and an army to be sent across the ocean!

Accompanied by token contingents from France and Spain, American soldiers waded across the same beaches where General Eisenhower had staged the North African landings. Along with the world's press, the Moroccans welcomed them like so many tourists. Children gawked as the world's most expensive hardware rolled ashore.

At first "Operation Groundswell" went according to plan. Helicopter gunships quickly silenced the Berber mountain guns, and the Tizi-n-Test and Tizi-n-Tishka passes were reopened. With American flags flying convoys of trucks crossed the High Atlas and fanned out into the desert. In Ourarzazate, where only a week before the streets had been full of gunfire and fear, people were dancing on the rooftops as the Americans arrived. For the first time, the Red Cross was able to go into the surrounding areas, assess the full extent of the famine, and get food to the oases that had been cut off by banditry and fighting among tribes.

While food shipments were being safely distributed in the desert, a wave of riots swept through Fez, Meknes and Oujda. Calling for open rebellion against the government that had brought "infidel crusaders" to Morocco, fundamentalist mullahs brandishing Kalashnikovs briefly occupied the port of Agadir to keep American military supplies from being landed. A bus-load of German tourists ran over a mine near the Roman ruins at Volubulis. Three were killed. The ailing Moroccan tourist industry, which had received a boost with the arrival of American troops, went into steep decline.

"Let's face it," said one travel agent, "when people go on holiday, they don't want to get shot at."

The American Consulate in Casablanca was holed by rocket fire. When a bomb exploded outside the gate of the Royal Palace in Rabat, wiping out a family waiting to petition the Sultan, he declared a state of emergency. Without consulting Washington, he abruptly withdrew the bulk of his army from south of the Atlas and redeployed his soldiers near the population centers in the north, where they would be available to stamp out further rioting. The Americans were left to deal with the situation in the desert.

CHAPTER 25

Café Zizou

Riding into the pre-Saharan administrative center of Boulmalne-du-Dadès, Daisy halted to adjust her turban, wrapping the end across her face to conceal all but her eyes.

Head down and nodding, a weary Uncle Bernon ambled beneath the red rampart of the old Foreign Legion fort. Where the French tricolor once flew, the Stars and Stripes snapped in the wind. Daisy had crossed the Atlas Mountains and was back in America!

Behind coils of razor wire army trucks were being loaded with sacks of flour. Stencilled on each sack, beneath a pair of hands shaking, were the words in Arabic, Spanish, French and English:

FROM THE PEOPLE OF THE UNITED STATES

TO THE PEOPLE OF MOROCCO

The soldiers, some with their shirts off, lounged around as though they were at the beach. A group of Moroccan school children gaped at the huge vehicles. Country and western music blared from a loudspeaker.

Daisy stopped to have a look. Here were Americans her own age she would like to talk to, but she dared not reveal her identity.

One soldier, noticing the robed and turbanned figure sitting on a horse, strolled to the fence.

For a minute he and Daisy sized each other up through the wire.

"What can I do for you?" He spoke with the raw south accent of an Oklahoma farm boy.

Those were the first words of English Daisy had heard in two weeks. She was more than just lonely; she was desperately homesick.

She made the classic gesture of smoking a cigarette.

He dipped into his shirt pocket, fished up a pack, lipped one out for himself, and tossed the pack over the wire.

It landed in the dust near Uncle Bernon's feet. Elvis sniffed at it.

Stiff from having ridden all night, Daisy eased down from the saddle, picked up the pack and remounted.

To light up she had to pull the turban off her face.

"What's that you got?"

Daisy held up the *mechero*.

"Yeah, that."

"*Mechero*."

The soldier fixed his eyes solidly on Daisy. They were small and close together. Daisy thought them shrewd. He had a narrow, hard-featured face.

"That hoss of yourn looks plumb wore out."

She patted Uncle Bernon. They were both completely bushed. Only Rucio, with burden considerably lightened, was full of perk.

"I left my hoss and dawg back home. You're lucky. You got yourn."

She nodded. She couldn't help herself.

"Too bad we cain't talk. We'd have a high ole time talking about your hoss and mine. Your dawg and Mike. Mike's my dawg."

Daisy desperately wanted to talk about Mike. The boy's down home accent nearly brought tears to her eyes. She hadn't reckoned on having to keep mum among her own kind.

"What's the name of your dawg?"

Her deepest baritone. "Elvis."

"Elvis? Well, I'll be darned. Hello there, Elvis."

Elvis's tail beat the dust.

"Hey, guys!" he shouted. "I got a dawg here named Elvis."

Some fellow soldiers started moving toward the wire.

"This here's Elvis."

"Hello, Elvis."

"Howdy, Elvis."

"How you doin', Elvis."

Elvis's tail was thumping madly.

"You understand what I'm sayin', don't you." The Okie had had a full view of Daisy's face.

Time to move on. Waving the pack of cigarettes as a gesture of farewell, she rode off.

"So long, Elvis!"

"*Hasta la vista*, Elvis!"

"Good to meet you, Elvis!"

"Hey, girl! What's your name?" sang out the Oklahoma twang.

The trek over the mountains had just about finished her off. She had the trots and a case of the chiggers. Plus a sore throat and aching molar. She hoped her asthma wasn't coming back.

With Uncle Bernon going short she found a stone lodged in his fore hoof which she removed with the screwdriver. After stabling him in the *fondak*, she was able to buy an antibiotic, anti-bug and aspirin at the local pharmacy. Café Zizou had zero hot water and no lock on the door. The toilet was a concrete basin with two footprints, but she was able to stretch out on clean sheets. She doped herself up and got her first decent sleep in many days.

It was dark when she woke up, hot and hungry. She dissolved two more aspirin in water, gargled them down, and went to the outdoor café. Beneath stars that twinkled and seemed to beckon toward some distant salvation, the garish light of Café Zizou attracted a swarm of insects, one hollow-bellied pariah (it slunk off into the night when Elvis appeared), and a pair of homesick soldiers.

The desert dogs were talking, and the wind was blowing. Moaning around the corners of the café, it seemed to bear a comfortless message intended for herself. Was there anything to learn from this loneliness? This was something she would like to be sure of at this moment, because all she knew was grim solitude in this one-horse town, and the charge that despair gives as she sat over a beer in that seedy bar.

The aspirins kicked in, putting her into a sweat. Unwrapping the turban from her head, she shook her hair free and gave her scalp a vigorous scratch. The soldiers stared open-mouthed at the transformation going on at the next table. The Moroccan had freed himself from the cocoon of turban and burnoose and emerged as a young woman speaking English.

The effect of the aspirins gave a kind of high. She couldn't hold back. They studied Arturo's photo, but it didn't register.

From somewhere inside the café came a loud bang. A woman started screaming. A hollow bellowing like a bull. The cry of the deranged. A door handle twisted. It rattled but didn't open. There was a hammering noise.

"Vous êtes tous salauds!"

A bottle came flying over the wall. It hopped once off the floor, did a flip, landed on its side and smashed. The waiter grabbed a broom and started sweeping up the pieces.

"A l'enfer avec tout le monde!"

"What's going on?" Daisy asked the waiter.

"That's Zizou's wife."

"What's the matter with her?"

"She's French. She drinks. He keeps her locked up."

"Why?"

The Moroccan shrugged. "When she drinks she breaks things."

On this there was general agreement.

"Watch out!"

A radio sailed through the air. It hit the tiles and cracked open, spilling its guts across the floor.

Now came the sounds of a fight. Physical. A violent struggle. A male voice and a female voice, one Arabic the other French, yelling and not listening. Thuds and screams. A door slammed, muffling the voices.

The next morning breathing was easier, but Daisy was still having to run to the toilet. Leading Elvis, she entered the restaurant side of the establishment, a low, shed-like structure smelling of stale beer and cigarettes.

A red-haired woman, round cheeks and freckles, dressed in a non-descript djellaba with a kerchief knotted under her chin, was wiping the top of the bar with a rag. When she caught sight of Elvis she shouted:

"*Pas des chiens ici!*"

"He's with me."

"Huh? So you must be the 'woman-man' everyone's talking about. Or 'man-woman.' Which one is it?"

"And you must be the thrower of radios."

"Sorry about that. Hope you didn't get hurt." She lifted a dripping bottle from behind the bar and thumped it on the counter. "How about joining me for a little hair of the dog?"

She poured out two glasses. They drank.

"*Mon Dieu* that tastes good!" She refilled their glasses. "Nothing like the first drink of the day."

"Why do you throw radios?"

"The only way to stay sane in this lousy country is permanently plastered. You'd be throwing your house out the window if you were married to a Moroccan. They're handsome, they have lovely brown skin, but they make lousy lovers. Take my word for it. They fuck, they come, they sleep. *Metro, bulot, dodo*. It's not their fault, poor boys. It all has to do with their lousy men-only religion. The sexes are segregated, so the boys grow up in a boys-only society, horny as hell, jacking off and buggering each other. The big boys bugger the little boys. The little boys grow up and get their turn. Then they get married. They go straight from buggery to the marriage bed.

"The only woman they've ever loved is their mother. They fuck for sons and dream of mom – that's what it's all about." She refilled their glasses. "Come on, sister, let's drop this cheesy subject and top up! Now what brings you to Fly Trap? "

"I'm trying to get to the Tafilalet."

"You better see Keller. That's Captain Keller, the American in charge here. Word has it he's travelling down there by convoy tomorrow."

"I'm not sure I should risk it. I don't want to be sent back."

"You don't have to worry. He may act tough, poor lonely bastard, listening to his music. but in my book he's a mama's boy, like they all are. Here's one more for the road. I like your dog. What's his name?"

"Elvis."

"Hello, Elvis."

Elvis's tail banged the floor.

"*Santé*. Are you comfortable in your room?"

"I could use more toilet paper."

CHAPTER 26

Keller

Captain Keller was woken by his orderly who informed him that "a lady" wished to see him. Still grumpy from his interrupted nap, he found in his office what he took to be an impudent Arab youth, sitting in his chair, smoking a cigarette.

"What the hell do you think you're doing?"

Grabbing Daisy by the voluminous sleeve of her djellaba, he yanked it right off her arm. There was a brief scuffle. She stiff-armed him away, sending him staggering backwards.

Elvis growled. The orderly came in.

"How did this hippy get in here? You know the rules! No one comes in here without permission or an appointment!"

"But, sir, the lady … " the orderly stammered in broken English. He had lovely brown skin, a round face and a shy smile. Daisy had already had a little chat with him.

The captain was adamant. "Tell the lady in question to present herself, if she wants business with me, and get this person and that dog out of here!"

"Excuse me, captain … " Daisy slipped her arm back into her sleeve and straightened the djellaba. " … but I am the lady in question."

"What?" Keller looked at her in consternation. "You?"

"Don't look so worried, captain. It's just that I didn't expect this kind of rough treatment from an American officer."

Keller was peering at Daisy as though she were a pane of dusty glass he couldn't quite see through. "Is this some kind of joke?"

She unwrapped the turban from her head and shook her hair free. "I apologize for sitting in your chair. I was out of breath from climbing all those steps. You see, I've been thirteen days on the trail … "

Elvis lay down.

"That's Elvis."

"Elvis, huh? And who are you – Bob Hope?"

"Daisy Adams. Here, if you don't believe me." She handed over her passport.

He grabbed the passport and scrutinized it, but he wasn't taking it in. Daisy took the opportunity to smile at the Moroccan, who lowered his eyes. He had long eyelashes.

Captain Keller's whitish blond hair lay flat on his scalp. His sunburned face was creased with lines. His ears made Daisy think of dried apricots.

"What are you doing here, Daisy Adams?" He spoke in a loud, commanding voice. "Where've you come from?"

"Marrakesh."

He looked her up and down. "You're too young to be a missionary."

"I'm a Muslim."

"Muslim?" This piece of information stopped him in his tracks. "Oh, sure. You're a Muslim, and I'm a Hottentot."

"I have a copy of the Koran inscribed by the Pasha of Tangier, stating that I have been converted to the Islamic faith."

Keller evidently dismissed this as a piece of fabricated nonsense. "I don't believe a person can change religions like a suit of clothes! Travel in the desert is prohibited. I'm placing you under arrest, Daisy Adams, and you're going to leave this place with the first convoy going back to Marrakesh." He started walking back and forth. "I know how you got here," he added. "In the back of Zizou's truck. That drunken wife of his is always inviting evangelicals in here. They think this is the Spanish Conquest or something and start preaching to the natives as soon as they've had a bowl of soup. This is the last straw. I'm going to shut his café, and every guard between here and Marrakesh is going to get a week in jail. You better have some money on you, Daisy Adams … because I know you paid to get here, and you're going to pay through the nose to get out!"

"Zizou had nothing to do with it. I came cross-country on my horse."

"What?" Keller stopped pacing. "Over the Atlas?"

"I rode my horse from Marrakesh."

"What are you – some sort of cow-girl?"

"You might say that."

"The passes are choked with snow this time of the year."

Daisy went to a map that covered most of one wall. "I came this way," she said, pointing. "Via Demnate, and the Tizi-n-Tirlist, Tizi-n'Ait-Imi and Tizi-n'Air-Hamed passes. There was no snow south of the Atlas. The Berbers showed me the way."

"Well, I'll tell you one thing, Daisy Adams." Keller used a more respectful tone. "You're lucky you didn't get your throat cut on that little jaunt of yours. It's the wild west out there. *Bled-es-siba* they call it. We escort the food shipments to where they're needed, and half an hour later some kid is shooting at us from behind the sack of flour we just gave him. That's the kind of thanks we get! I had a soldier wounded last week. I don't have the manpower to protect tourists wandering around. Especially female tourists!"

"I won't be any trouble, captain. I've come to the desert to find my brother."

"Look – the hippies, the back packers, the mountain bikers, the druggies, the movie people – they cleared out like rabbits the minute the first shot was fired. The locusts hit the headlines, but what hit people even worse was when the tourist industry collapsed."

"My brother's a serviceman. I have a picture. Here."

"What, this kid in a cowboy hat? Look, there are maybe a thousand soldiers in Morocco. More now. He could be anywhere. You won't learn that from me. You need to go back to America and wait for him to come home."

"He's here all right. He sent a postcard."

The satchel was on the desk. Daisy opened it. The Ruger sat on top.

"What's this?" Keller picked it up. "It's loaded! Slim, you let her walk right in here with a loaded pistol! What's all this?"

"In case I have to pay a ransom."

Keller stared at the money. "You're crazy to carry so much cash around with you, Daisy Adams. Bandits bother us all the time here. It's a miracle you got this far without being robbed. Maybe a lot worse."

"My mother died in Tangier. Before she died she made me promise to find him."

"I'm sorry about that, but you can't stay here."

Keller was eyeing the cash. He seemed to be trying to make a rough calculation of how much there was.

She pulled *Camels into the Void* from a shelf. "I see you have my favorite book."

Once more the captain failed to reply. Daisy was conscious that she had cast a kind of spell over her would-be jailer. Or the money had.

"What's this on the chairs?"

"Gazelle skin."

The beasts' delicate heads were mounted on wooden shields attached to the walls.

"Do you think the Duke de Bremont is still alive?"

Keller frowned. "Nobody thinks that."

"His wife does."

She stopped by a window where powerful-looking binoculars were mounted on a tripod.

The oasis below the village was spread out in an orderly checkerboard of a well-tended country estate. The saw-tooth summits of Sarhro Mountains were turning pink in the afternoon sun. Light was emptying from the room.

Keller was standing close behind her. She could smell the cologne.

Daisy stepped quickly away. "Maybe the Duke has become a wandering nomad."

Keller's face was red. "Your romantic ideas have nothing to do with reality, Daisy Adams. Why do you wear those clothes?"

"It's a bore to be a woman in Morocco. Do you mind if I smoke?"

"Smoke all you want," the captain growled.

Daisy took out her tobacco. "Do you like the desert?"

"Give me the seashore any day."

"In that case you should have joined the Coast Guard. I'm sorry, captain … I'm not feeling very well … I think I must be dehydrated. Do you have anything to drink?"

"Coca Cola."

"Any whiskey?"

"You'll have to go to Madame Zizou for that." Keller scowled as Daisy sprinkled a paper with tobacco.

"May I use your bathroom?"

"There is no flush toilet in this building."

"Whatever."

"Slimane!" the captain bellowed.

The orderly reappeared. Daisy felt strangely moved by the Moroccan's boyishly handsome face and long eyelashes. She was staring at him. She couldn't help it. Her heart felt full.

"Make some tea, will you. The lady is thirsty. Show her the lavatory."

The toilet was as primitive as the one at Zizou's.

When Daisy came back she picked up her cigarette again, but it fell apart. "I may not be up to this." She felt the tears come. She let them.

"Maybe you ought to sit down."

"Please don't send me back!" she sobbed.

"Slimane!"

Once more the orderly stuck his head into the room.

Cherchez la bouteille sous mon lit!

"Why do you shout?"

When Slimane returned with the whiskey he found Daisy in a better frame of mind. The captain had invited her to join his convoy to Rfud.

"What do you take with it?"

"Coca Cola."

"Best way to ruin a decent drink."

"Will he be coming, too?"

"Slimane? He goes everywhere with me. You're welcome to use my bathtub, Miss Adams."

"That sounds more like what I would have expected an American officer to say. I mean, we've progressed from the guardhouse to the bathhouse. I accept."

"Slimane, light a fire under the water tank! *Allez! Vite!*" Keller poured out the drinks. "Will you stay for supper, Miss Adams? He's a good cook."

"Is there anything he doesn't do for you? What is he – your slave?"

"It's his job," Keller responded blandly, "and he's good at it – when he's not flirting with the market girls instead of keeping an eye on the door. Zizou brought me a case of wine, and I have a can of foie-gras I've been keeping for a special occasion. Do you like foie gras, Miss Adams?"

"Oh, yes, I love it!"

"Goose liver. Have you ever tasted it?"

"I love it."

"My mother is French." The captain raised his glass. "She comes from France."

They drank. Daisy was beginning to worry about the captain's proprietary attitude. She wondered if she were doing the right thing by accepting his invitation. At least Slimane would be there. She wished their roles could be reversed. She would like to fall asleep in Slimane's arms, with the captain to bring them breakfast in bed. Instead, she had this amorous chaperone to deal with.

The bath was an indescribable luxury. She swallowed more aspirin and wandered outside to take in the sunset. It was a balmy night. Slimane was setting a table on the terrace.

"May I help?"

"If you wish," he replied, lowering his eyelashes.

"Is this the way he likes it?" she asked. "With the spoon beside the knife? Or this way, with the spoon in front of the plate."

Slimane showed her. He moved about the table with a nimble, athletic step. He had narrow shoulders, like cowboy Slim's. His eyes were bigger and darker than Slim's, and she loved his eyelashes. They opened and closed like a doll's weighted eyelashes.

"Do you like being a soldier?"

He was taking bread from a basket, and a bottle of wine. "The army takes care of you when you're far from home."

Taps sounded as Old Glory was lowered for the night.

While Daisy rolled a cigarette, the incoming rippleless tide of night slid across the desert. Darkness flooded the oasis and filled the valleys. It washed the rose off cliff faces and saturated an infinity of decked plains, finally drowning the amethyst hill tops. The Sarhro mountain peaks, bleakly silhouetted against the western sky, were still awash with orange light.

Somebody, somewhere out there in the dark, was singing – a reedy male voice punctuated by twanging drum thuds. Eternity flowed about them as Daisy pulled on her cigarette.

"Gang way!" Keller tottered from the *ksar* carrying a candelabra.

"I found this at the bottom of the well! It must have belonged to the French officer who lived here twenty years ago. Slimane cleaned it up, and look – it's in perfect condition!"

"I'll light the candles." Daisy took the box of matches from Slimane. Their fingers touched.

While Daisy lit the candles, Keller set up a record player in the window. With music blaring, they began the feast. Slimane served everything but the peas, which he brought to the table in the same little pot they'd been heated in.

"Do you like this music, Miss Adams?"

"What is it – Dave Brubeck?"

"Casedesus – a French composer." He filled her glass. "Try some of this Sauterne."

"Do you have to play it so loud?"

While Keller went to turn down the music, jackals could be heard barking in the hills behind the village.

Slimane smiled at Daisy. "Are you frightened?"

"Not with you here."

Keller sat down again. "How'd you learn Arabic?"

"Been eavesdropping, captain?"

Keller reddened. "You seem to be completely at home in Morocco."

Keller was tucking into the foie gras with a relish that made Daisy feel nauseous. The temperature had dropped several degrees. A chill ran through her. It may have been a mistake to come outside after that hot bath. She was worried her fever might come back.

"After the bugle blows, the desert seems to close in, doesn't it?"

"You're not eating!" Keller refilled her glass. "Don't you like foie gras?"

"Too rich for me, I'm afraid." The sweet wine, combined with the antibiotics and the whiskey she had drunk before dinner, was making her dizzy. "Not a square meal in two weeks and now foie gras. These baby peas are delicious."

"But you must eat this foie gras! It'll go to waste!"

Passion was getting the better of her. Impatience, too. She wished she had the strength to pick up the candelabra, bang Keller over the head with it, and run off with Slimane.

"Is it true … " She held up a forkful of the soft pinkish flesh. "They nail the feet of the poor bird to a board … " she was slurring her words, "… shove a funnel down its throat, and force feed it until its liver becomes engorged, enlarged, inflamed and diseased?"

"What's that you're smoking, Miss Adams?"

"Golden Virginia – English rolling tobacco. Want some?"

Keller looked disgusted.

Now a little wind arrived to make the candle flames shiver. Hot wax cascaded onto the table cloth.

Daisy felt irresistibly attracted to Slimane. Deliberately dropping her napkin, she reached down and made a grab for his leg as he removed the plates and nearly fell out of her chair in the process.

The next course arrived in a clay pot.

"What is it?" she asked. "Not stewed gazelle, I hope."

"*Cassoulet.*" Keller's expression was stony. "My mother's recipe. I have a bottle of Burgundy wine here."

Daisy put her fork down.

"Don't you want any?"

She smiled drunkenly. "That foie gras was so filling."

"You didn't eat a single bite!"

"I think I'll go now." She reached for Slimane's hand. "He can take me."

"You're dismissed!" Keller bellowed at Slimane.

"Don't blame him!" Daisy protested. "What's he done?"

"You've been making eyes at him all evening!"

"Well, if I have, it's your fault! You've given me too much to drink, and all this rich food. But it's been a lovely evening. Thank you."

"Look at all this food!"

"I'm sorry, but I can't eat any more."

She got up from the table, picked up the satchel and stumbled off into the night.

Keller watched her walk away with a kind of melancholy lust.

CHAPTER 27

War Zone

The next morning she lay in bed with an aching head. Madame Zizou poured another "hair of the dog" and sent her to the back gate of the fort where a black market operated. There she was able to obtain the American medicines she was used to – Tylenol, Listerine, and Immodium. For an hour she sat beside a man operating a pedal-powered sewing machine while he made a robe of glistening indigo. And she couldn't resist a beautiful voluminous but lightweight burnoose woven in Figuig from camel wool. As soon as she put these new clothes on she felt lighter and cleaner, but had to suppress any sign of exuberance. Captain Keller had gone off without her, leaving behind an order forbidding her to travel further south.

After making her purchases, she impulsively reached a decision she had been putting off since the start of the trip.

Against the wall of the Foreign Legion fort stood a row of native barber shops, each identically equipped with a decrepit deck chair, a charcoal brazier (fanned by an infant helper), and once colorful beach umbrella to shield the client from the sun. Offering their services to the Moroccan army, the barbers trimmed the soldiers' beards and mustaches. Saharan men, Daisy had observed, traditionally shave their heads. This wards off ringworm and keeps the scalp clean and comfortable. She had already learned that her hair became itchy from long airless periods beneath the turban.

Taking a seat in one of the creaking chairs, she unwrapped the cloth from her head. Her hair, squeaky clean from her bath chez Keller, tumbled out. The barber let out a grunt of surprise. Stropping his blade on a leather strap, he sized up his customer as a group of women gathered to watch. The razor scraped against her scalp.

Her locks fell to earth. A woman snatched them up. The barber, with a mischievous grin, held up a cracked mirror for her to see. One side of her head was an ugly gray egg while on the other the dark curly hair still grew.

A tear slid down Daisy's cheek. Wiping it away, she told him to finish the job and afterwards listened to a lecture on how to massage the scalp with warm olive oil so the hair would grow back thick and strong.

According to her map, it looked like another two or three day ride to the Tafilalet, depending on conditions.

As Uncle Bernon's shoes had worn smooth in the mountains, she found a *haddad* to put a new set on. She stocked up on provisions – dry bread and cow bones for Elvis and a sack of barley for transport. She had her own cooking utensils but no tent, an omission which had nearly cost her life in the Atlas.

The little team set off along a powdery road that seemed to go on forever. Every now and then a car passed– a dusty Mercedes or French station wagon – desert taxis. They waved, she waved and they went on. She could follow the progress of each vehicle across the desert by its dusty rooster tail. Another period of dreary solitude set in. There was no sign of life, nothing but shadeless silence and the sifting wind. The road ahead looped over the folds of the land-scape like a slack fire hose. At each rise a mysterious little pyramid of stones had been piled up.

To the south slumbered the hills of the Jebel Ougnat, where Keller hunted gazelle. They looked like a long, bony hound asleep with its head resting on big paws. At the base of one paw an oasis was stitched in green.

The road petered out into whimsical vagaries of Saharan tracks. She stopped for lunch beside another pile of stones. Who can be piling them up and why are they doing it? She sliced open half a baguette, squirted mayonnaise from a tube, and filled it with blue desert onions, peeled and split. Beside an irrigation canal was a bank of delicious grass where Uncle Bernon and Rucio stuffed themselves full. She hugged her transport. Where would she be without her companions?

Late afternoon found her atop of one of the paws, gazing down into a wide beige basin. Out in the middle were what looked like two shiny metal scarabs – oil tankers. A third truck piled with oil drums was parked behind. Men were walking around. A tent was going up. They were making camp.

Dusk. With Elvis at her side, she sat on a rug in the tent sipping from a shot glass of smoky green tea, and writing by the light of a candle stuck in the sand. Outside, a few feet away, a fire blazed, men talked, and a pot bubbled.

Si Omar, not the oldest of the truckers but their leader, whom they called *shereef*, had welcomed her in. He had teeth problems for which he chewed tobacco mixed with ashes from the fire. Daisy tried the remedy for her aching molar. (In the Atlas she had bitten down on a pebble imbedded in a piece of coarse barley bread.) It helped a little.

The candle guttered, the campfire crumbled, and the truckers bedded down for the night. The triumphant stars, flooding the heavens, ennobled the perfect stillness of Saharan Africa.

In the hour before dawn a gun shot snapped her awake. Something was poking her hard in the neck.

"Bandits," she thought with a flash of panic as a knee between her shoulders flattened her to the ground.

She tried to struggle, but her powerful aggressor locked her hands behind her back.

He yanked her to her feet and pushed her onto the sand dune. There, by the light of the jaded old moon, she had her first look at the attackers. Six soldiers, kneeling on the sand, each holding a terrified driver. Omar was vainly resisting as a soldier in body armor and goggles tied him up.

Their goggles were glittering. One of them was talking on the radio in a voice that sounded strangely familiar.

The soldier began questioning Omar in bad Arabic.

"We are drivers, and these are my father's trucks," Omar replied. "We are taking fuel to Tinerhir."

"No," the soldier said. "These trucks come from Algeria and you are carrying fuel to the terrorists in the Sarhro. You are providing help to terrorists."

The soldiers marched them over the dunes away from the trucks and made them kneel. They began talking on their radio again.

"Don't try to run," the one behind Daisy said. "Stay down."

"Where's Elvis?"

"What?"

"Where's my dog?"

"You speak English."

"I'm American!"

"Hey, Wayne, this one speaks English!"

"What have you done with my dog?"

Another soldier came forward. He wore a helmet, goggles and gloves. No part of him looked human. "Tell your friends not to move," he said. "If they stay put they'll be safe. We're going to take out your trucks."

"Where's my dog?"

"I saw a dog. I saw him running. I think that dog of yours is a little gun-shy."

She heard the sound of engines coming in. All the earth began to move. It was the rhythmic beat of a helicopter rotor.

"Now get down and stay down!"

There was a surge that sucked the air from her lungs. A rocket slammed into one of the tankers which erupted in a huge fireball. Heat swept over Daisy like a wave. She was lying face down on the sand which seemed incredibly cool when another searing whoosh like the air being torn in two incinerated the second tanker, sending a fist of fire shooting into the air. It mushroomed out and lit the desert, making the night brighter than the brightest day.

The truck carrying gasoline drums didn't explode. One of the soldiers ran forward and started shooting. As the red finger of fire explored every corner of the truck the barrels started leaking flames and blowing up. Unexploded barrels were being hurled into the sky where they burst in fountains of pure fire. The heat was so intense they had to move back, except for the soldier with his gun. He was doing an Indian war dance, shooting and jumping, his leaping form silhouetted against the inferno.

Daisy was aware that a soldier kneeling behind her had cut her hands free.

"Arturo, is that you?"

"Miss, I don't know who you are or what you are." He formed his words in the same slow, deliberate drawl of the original Uncle Bernon. "But if you're American, you better get on home."

A few minutes later she heard the roar of their vehicle as it drove into the night.

Dawn. The acrid smell of burning hung over the twisted skeletons of the tankers. Blackened barrels lay scattered around the charred truck. Bullet holes perforated the side of one of the tankers.

They found the plastic restraints the soldiers had cut from their wrists. Omar pointed out the tracks made by their vehicle, and the footprints left by their boots. His father was the owner of the trucks.

"This is cruel." He shook his head as he surveyed the wreckage. "Farmers buy our oil, not terrorists. In the name of terrorists the Americans are penalizing the common people."

Daisy's satchel was missing. A single hundred dollar bill shivered on the sand. All her money was gone.

Two days later she struggled into the Tafilalet oasis, camped among the dunes and slept. When she felt strong enough to go on, she entered a little white shop where yoghurt was sold. It was cool and clean inside. On the wall behind the counter was a picture of the factory in Casablanca where the yoghurt was pasteurized. The owner, an elderly man in a skullcap, was proud of the factory. He admired Uncle Bernon, saying he had a horse of his own.

Keller made her wait two hours, with a painful strep throat, in a crowd of Moroccans. They were pressed into a narrow corridor with no chairs and no window. Everyone sat on the floor. It was stifling.

Just as she thought she would faint, Slimane appeared. He brought mint tea and aspirin. Holding his hand and feeling strangely light-headed, she told him what happened.

"Will you visit me in the oasis?"

"When?"

"Tonight."

"I'm on duty."

"Daisy Adams!" a voice called.

"You can't be on duty all night!"

She found Keller with his feet propped on the desk.

"I thought I told you," he began in a loud voice, before she had shut the door, "this is a war zone, not a playground. An exception was made in your case because you have a brother in the services and because of your, ah, competence."

"I've been robbed."

"I told you not to carry so much money around with you. These people will steal anything that isn't nailed down."

"I was robbed by American soldiers. Now Omar and his drivers don't have a living and the farmers they were delivering oil to can't run their tractors to save themselves from the famine you're supposed to be saving them from."

"Who is this Omar? Do you fall in love with every Moroccan you meet?"

"Why do you talk like this when I'm trying to tell you something serious?"

"Which one is it then? Slimane or this Omar?"

Daisy felt tears welling in her eyes. "It's unfair for you to talk this way when I'm sick and broke and still reeling from a terrifying act of violence and destruction."

"I give you foie gras, and you fall in love with my orderly."

Daisy waved the hundred dollar bill in his face. "This is all I've got! Since your soldiers are responsible for this hit and run, I need a loan and to see a doctor."

"I don't lend money. The nearest American doctor is in Marrakesh."

"This is uncivilized, captain. You make a show of being civilized with your French food and wine. You could lend me money if you wanted to."

"I could invite you to dinner again, too," Keller answered petulantly. "If I wanted to."

"I don't understand why you insist on keeping this conversation on a frivolous level when you see me sick and in need. What have I done to deserve this kind of condescending treatment? You're adding insult to injury – that's what you're doing. All I require is some elemental assistance which any civilized officer would offer without being asked, so I can leave this place and be out of your hair."

In the end Keller relented. He arranged for her to have the medicine she needed. She bought a bottle of *mahia*, fig brandy, in the yoghurt shop and, gathering firewood along the way, rode back through the palms.

After she had eaten a little supper, she walked away from the fire. She took off her clothes and washed herself with water from the goatskin. She doused herself with Mrakshi perfume and took a slug from the bottle. Feeling luxuriantly naked within the woolen cocoon of her burnoose, she sat down to wait.

While she waited, she took in the stars. They buzzed and whined and sang to her, as though they were alive. They were giving off minute remote vibrations which, in the vast silence of the desert, she was almost certain she could hear.

All of a sudden, Slimane was beside her. They embraced, and he discovered she was naked beneath the burnoose. Overcome by a terrible urgency, he led her walking, then running hand in hand to a little basin between the dunes. She opened her burnoose, and they lay down together.

She yielded to Slimane and to the velvety embrace of the Saharan night. Her lover was moaning, and the stars were singing. Was she hearing the nostalgic melody of love and longing between man and God? It was too much to contemplate. She just shut her eyes and squeezed.

Old Moïses Cohen, proprietor of the yoghurt shop, agreed to lend Daisy two hundred dollars. As collateral he would keep Uncle Bernon and Rucio, feed and exercise them while she was away.

In case of drought, she instructed, they must have three feeds a day: the first at 8 AM, the second in the evening, any time between 5 and 7 PM and the third at 11 or 12 at night. Two kilos of barley per beast per day.

"How can I be sure you'll come back?"

"There are two men here that I love."

The old man leaned closer. "Two?"

"One is my brother."

She agreed to pay fifteen percent interest per month plus expenses. He would keep a detailed list of receipts. If she failed to return to the Tafilalet within six months, she would forfeit the loan. Uncle Bernon and Rucio would become Mr. Cohen's property. She signed the IOU "Toledano." He studied the signature, smiled, and handed over the cash.

The Ruger she also left for safe-keeping.

"I lost my dog in the desert. He's a smart dog and may be trying to find me. If you see a big black dog, call out 'Elvis!' He'll come. He's big, he has a loud bark, but under the rough exterior he's tame. He likes bones and bread."

CHAPTER 28

Potatoes and Meat

Arturo was making his way down Balboa Street in Panama City, looking for a fish restaurant, when he was accosted by a girl with frizzy brown hair.

"Buy me something, Papi."

They walked side by side.

"You can pick it out yourself, Papi. Buy me a feather, I don't care. Only with your heart, Papi. Your heart."

Arturo thought he must be dreaming.

"What do you mean, a feather?"

The girl squirmed with delight. "Oh, Papi, you're so funny! Any feather, a chicken feather."

"How about a peacock feather?"

"What is a peacock, Papi?"

"A bird with big feathers."

"I don't want big feathers. You want to see my room?"

"Sure"

"Right here, Papi."

They entered the Hotel Washington which Arturo was surprised to see was nicer than his own. The wooden walls were painted various shades of green. Cages hanging from the ceiling contained a lively collection of birds from the tropical forest. Green Amazonian parrots and parakeets, love-birds and toucans with their banana beaks, all presided over by a magnificent blue and red macaw, pacing on a metal perch. The girl's room was on the second floor and had brightly painted walls like the corridor.

"Those birds, they sing all day long," said the girl, motioning for Arturo to sit beside her on the bed. "Sometimes I say to myself,

'Little fools, what are you singing about in your cages?' And then I think: 'Paloma, you have the name of a bird, and you are just as much a fool as those birds. You are also in a cage because you don't have any money.'"

Showing little tufts of hair under her arms, she pulled her dress over her head and stood in a pink underslip before Arturo. She was really quite pretty.

"Tell me," she said. "What do you think of those silk kimonos the Hindu men sell in their shops? If I had a rich husband he would buy me a kimono. He would rather buy me pretty things than watch me cry like a baby. A man doesn't like to see a woman cry. You think they like to see women cry, Papi?"

"A man doesn't like to see a woman cry."

"You're right, Papi. A man likes to see a woman laugh. Especially his woman. A woman has got to laugh all night. Watch a pretty girl, Papi. When she laughs she is ten years older. It's because she has to do it all the time. A woman is ten years older when she laughs."

"True."

There was an illuminated aquarium with colorful fish in it, and a Hollywood mirror stuck with postcards from seaports all over the world.

Paloma presented him with a shopping list. A simple lay cost $5. $10 without a condom. To take her bra off an extra $5. Completely naked $5 more. To kiss, a further $10.

Arturo went for the whole package at $30.

While they were dressing Paloma announced she was hungry.

"I'm going for lobster."

"Not lobster, Papi. Meat and potatoes. Potatoes first."

"Potatoes and meat it will be."

"You're so gay, Papi." She rested her head against his shoulder and placed her hand against the small of his back. "When will you be coming back to Panama City?"

CHAPTER 29

Home and Away

Tall, brown, adolescent-thin – stained felt hat with a book of matches stuck in the band, faded flannel shirt, cigarette pack showing through the broken chest pocket, blue jeans with pockets bulging, torn pockets stitched with safety pins – Daisy, burnoose slung over shoulder, walked in her boots from Barcelona to Balaguer, sleeping in haylofts of isolated farms along the way, begging and even stealing.

Stealing is my new vice. A cigarette, a cup of coffee, a glass of beer tastes better when paid for with coins filched from the till of a harassed shopkeeper summoned to the back room by the shrieks of his termagant wife.

Villa Arida Zona bore all the signs of a property that has fallen into disuse. The heavy iron gate opened with a creak, and the drive was carpeted with snow. The greenhouses were cold and dead from neglect. The roof of one had been shattered by a branch blown down from a tree, and snow drifted in where cacti once bloomed.

Snow was falling as she approached the front door of the house. The flakes floating downwards were shaken by the gusting wind before touching the earth. On a cold December evening, full of the peace of falling snow, Daisy returned home.

Wrapped and hooded in a burnoose of brown camel wool, her skin burnt by the African sun, she looked like a monk out of the Middle Ages. Miss Bushy, whose sight was failing, attempted to shut the door on her.

"Please don't, darling! It's me!"

There was a long embrace as snowflakes swirled through the light. Daisy's hood fell back.

"Child, what happened to your hair?"

"It'll grow back."

"What news of Arturo?"

"Nothing, but I haven't given up hope."

"Your father has another postcard."

"Well, that's something!"

"When I see you I see him." Miss Bushy wiped her eyes. "You are so close and so alike. I know because I raised you. New York, Douglas, now Spain ... your dear mother ... how I miss her!"

With a gushing release of tears Daisy sat on the bottom step of the staircase, drew Miss Bushy beside her and buried her head against her shoulder. Dear Miss Bushy, a bag-lady whom Mrs. Adams had taken pity on and picked up one snowy winter night, a night like this night, in the theater district of New York, during the garbage strike, taken her home and installed her as nurse-maid to the children; half-mad but street-wise Miss Bushy, a two dollar bettor crazy for the ponies, but whom Mrs. Adams instinctively trusted, even with her history of Bellevue, where they took everything from her so she wouldn't cut her wrists, including her glasses, and let her walk around naked as a savage; wily Miss Bushy, with half her adult life behind bars, who had stage-managed the escape from the van Renseelaer house in Manhattan to Arizona, relegating Antonio Adams to the role of baggage carrier, and had been with the family ever since.

"It's so quiet ... " Daisy looked about.

"I don't like this Morocco. Arturo goes but nobody knows where. Your poor mother follows and dies down there. And here you are with your hair shaved off and looking like something the cat dragged in."

"Dorothy ... where are the dogs?"

"Gone ... dead."

"What are you saying?"

"They've been put down."

"What? How awful! Who did it?"

"Miss Maplethorpe ordered it."

"Miss Maplethorpe? That old school marm from Douglas? What does she have to do with it?"

"She said she couldn't sleep with so many dogs in the house."

"Miss Maplethorpe is here?"

"Yes."

"Here in this house?"

"She turned up after your father came back from Morocco."

"Douglas is seven thousand miles away! She must have heard mother died and swooped over here like a vulture. Back home daddy never allowed her on the property. Why doesn't he throw her out?"

"Your father is sick, child. Miss Maplethorpe has been looking after him."

"You and I can take care of him. How barbaric of her to put down my dogs! I'm going to push her out first thing in the morning."

"You'll never get her out."

"Why?"

"They were married last week."

"Daddy and Miss Maplethorpe are married?"

"A magistrate came and performed a bedside ceremony."

"Has he gone crazy?"

"The doctor says it's cancer."

"I can't believe this." Daisy shut her eyes and leaned against the door. "Get your coat, Dorothy. I want to make peace with my dogs before I go upstairs. Where are they buried?"

With Miss Bushy carrying a flashlight, they followed a snowy path through the woods.

"Daddy and Miss Maplethorpe ... he couldn't stand her! Don't you remember she called him a tyrant, and went around telling everyone in Douglas how he trampled on mother – the poor woman who sacrificed everything for him – and wouldn't send his children to school? Then there was the time she finally obtained a court order, and we all turned up at the school house one morning, and daddy was stark naked! Miss Maplethorpe took one look and nearly fainted! She regained her senses but was never the same again. She had fallen in love. Her condemnations grew more hysterical until he became public enemy number one." Daisy laughed. "That state of affairs suited daddy fine: at least he could live on honest terms with his neighbors."

"She's still got the fury in her from all those years he spurned her."

"I'll never forget how he insulted her at Consuelo Billings' wedding. We came in, and there was Miss Maplethorpe, his old enemy, sitting by herself in the back of the tent, getting quietly plastered. She must have seen her chance and started to scheme how to get him onto the dance floor. The heady sexual atmosphere of the wedding revived hope even in that old school marm. I suppose she'd never stopped thinking about him standing naked by the school house door. That was how she wanted to see him again. After several glasses of champagne, passion got the better of her. She walked unsteadily to our table and asked him point blank to dance, right in front of mother. I remember exactly what he said: 'You'll get your first dance with me, you old hag, when I'm in my grave!' Those were his words. 'You can dig me up, and we'll do the witches' waltz together, or you can take me for a ride on your broom!' The old girl went white in the face. Her legs buckled. She had to be caught and stopped from falling. She was led away squawking. It was rude, but that was the way he felt about her."

"He's at her mercy now. She takes care of him, but she treats him like dirt."

"Mother hardly dead and he marries that old school marm at the drop of a hat. Disgusting!"

Daisy went down on her knees beside the little mounds of snow.

"Jeudi, Mack, Freckles, Quickie ... My poor family is dead, dying, scattered ... Will there ever be another home for us, except in lonely unmarked graves?"

Miss Bushy pulled her out of the snow, and they walked back to the house. "You were a child of nature. When you ran off, I always knew where to find you – in the dog basket."

"Well, of course. I loved them, and they loved me. Life was so simple then. We were a family. We all lived under one roof, the place where wandering stops and the heart comes to rest, not this going off and dying in different parts of the world."

Adams, pale as the sheets, reached out a long stringy arm. "Well, what did you find out?" Like Samson his beard had been shaved off. Miss Maplethorpe was taming the wildness out of him.

Daisy knelt by the bedside. "He must still be in Africa but I don't know where."

His fingers caressed the outlines of her face. "Sorry about the dogs."

"We'll get to that later." She pulled up a chair. "What does the doctor say?"

"Spic doctor. What does he know?"

"Miss Bushy said cancer of the liver. Are you in pain?"

"My feet are swollen."

"I don't want to be an orphan."

Adams let out a sigh.

"Listen, we can lick this thing, but you must take a positive attitude!" She hugged him. "Barcelona is a big medical center. We'll get a second opinion."

"I'm not the only one who's sick, babes. There's sickness in the world. It's in the air, it's coming out of the ground – it's the despair bred by American greed and ignorance. The U.S. is only two hundred years old, and already we are a decadent society. We're obese. We're addicted to guns, alcohol, drugs, big cars and big oil, no matter what the toll on the environment.

"These new communists – how well I understand them! These fundamentalist movements sprouting everywhere – Hindu, Christian, Muslim. They are violent, intolerant, anti-democratic. They can no longer countenance where America is pushing the world. As Freud said, 'the whole idea of that country is a tragic mistake.'"

Adams sipped from a glass.

"Do they play golf in Morocco, babes?"

"What?"

"Golf!"

"I think the Sultan is building golf courses for the tourists."

"He should be deposed. Show me a country that plays golf, and I will show you a decadent leadership culture of rich white men. Instead of gardening, whittling, teaching their kids how to fish, they play golf. They do it for themselves, by themselves, it profits nobody but themselves, and they do it all day long. Golf is the only sport where the worse you play the more hits you get. In baseball it's three strikes and you're *out!*

"Andalucia is suffering a terrible drought. Every night I see it on TV. With the rest of the country turning brown, the golf courses at Soto Grande are emerald green! Village wells pumped down to the knuckles to water the playing fields of the rich. Those golf courses should be ploughed up and seeded with useful crops, not rolled over in golf carts with rich white men sipping cocktails."

Like all urban Mexicans, Adams loved *beisbol.*

"Baseball is not the American national sport any more. Nor is any team sport, not soccer, football, or basketball. It's *golf.* And they call it sport. When do you see a short-stop holding a cocktail shaker?"

"That's enough golf, daddy. I want to hear more about mother."

Adams eyed his empty glass.

"Wait." Daisy went downstairs for the bottle. They drank for a few minutes.

"Go on. Daddy. I want to hear the rest of the story after Bolivia."

"After Toledano died, she came back to New York and married your father. They lived in a big house on Grammercy Park. While other ladies served up tea and gossip, your mother strummed the guitar and sang Latino songs never heard before in the U.S."

"How did you meet?"

"Like other wolves in sheep's clothing I gravitated to your mother's salon. Neruda was there, Casals, Borges … Your mother was talented, witty, gracious. Your father wandered around in his business suit, serving drinks. A stranger in his own house. No one paid any attention to him. The guests thought he was the butler.

"The fact that your mother got on in the wilderness as well as a man coincided with my belief in female emancipation. Passing myself as a poet who gave private lessons to make ends meet, I got hired on as a Spanish teacher to you and Arturo."

"Did she leave my father because she fell in love with you?"

"She left because the inevitable happened."

"What?"

"He found out she was a Jew!"

"Is that so terrible?"

"Van Renseelaer was a Jew-baiting wasp."

"I don't like to hear that about my father, daddy."

"Forever complaining about 'Jew-boys' – smart young lawyers who challenged the legality of his big-time business deals."

"Don't tell me any more."

"He locked your mother out of the house. Called her dirty, infected. Accused her of scabies, clap, crabs. Made her take a bath before she touched you kids."

"I don't want to hate him for the rest of my life!"

"You asked," Adams thundered. "Now you're going to hear!"

Daisy sipped her drink. "Was that when you took her out west?"

"Your mother wanted to get away from New York as far as possible. Bolivia. Anywhere you could breathe. You were in and out of the hospital the whole time. Seventeen times in one year. You were old enough to know that something terrible was going on in that house. The stress made your asthma worse. Arizona, with its dry desert climate seemed the best place."

"I don't want to hear any more."

Adams sipped his drink. "What was that gadget in your mother's bathroom in Tangier?"

"What gadget?"

"The one that shot water into the air."

"A bidet."

"What was it – a drinking fountain for little children?"

"It's for washing your butt, you nincompoop!"

Daisy refilled her stepfather's glass.

"I kept a diary like you told me to, daddy. I think I'm going to be a writer. I can't live without writing. It's a compelling interior condition, like being pregnant, I suppose."

"Don't tell me you're pregnant again!"

"There's not another baby inside me – not yet – but there are words pushing to come out. When I can't write, or a day goes by when I haven't written something, I get nervous. I can't control my nerves without the balm of writing. I'm like an addict in reverse. He has to put his drug in. For me to have a high, words have to come out. Words on paper. But the pleasure doesn't last long. Like an addict, I have to keep feeding my addiction day after day. In Tangier I started a novel … "

"I told you not to make anything up! At your age a shopping list is more informative than fiction. I told you to wait."

"It fizzled out."

"Write about tramps, losers – loners who seek a personal destiny. People who have not been contaminated by this crap American culture that's polluting the planet."

"What about love?"

"Love will come … it always comes."

"It's amazing you should say that, daddy. It did come."

But the hour was late, and Adams was tired. "Stay close to nature – what's left of it, and away from America – as far as you can!" he mumbled before drifting off. "Maybe you can bring back from the Sahara a message for mankind – that the growth of a man's soul – not his ego – is the only valid reason for his continued existence."

Miss Bushy handed her the postcard, postmarked Tindouf, Algeria.

I bathe in this great soft sea of solitude.
For those this barren shore,

Once sighted and surveyed,
Must sigh forever more.

"What does it mean?"

"It means he has found peace in the desert."

"Bless him."

"He's a genius."

"Bless you both."

Daisy drove her stepfather to see a specialist in Barcelona. His opinion was even more depressing than that of the first. The disease had spread through the lymph glands to the spine and the lungs. It was inoperable and incurable. He prescribed morphine for the pain that was to come.

Following this diagnosis, the fight went out of Adams. His feet swelled. Daisy found a pair of Moroccan slippers for him to slip into.

"Take me to Morocco," he whispered, "where I'll be close to my girls."

"Aren't you forgetting something, daddy? You're married."

Miss Maplethorpe, a leathery brown woman with a mass of snow white hair, hovered in the background.

"You could sew a handbag from her skin," Daisy commented to Miss Bushy. "She waltzes around here in mother's clothes like she thinks she's a flamenco dancer."

She treated Miss Maplethorpe like a servant. She knew it was wrong, but she couldn't forgive her for having the dogs put down. She spoke to her only to give orders.

"I'm Mrs. Adams now," the old woman protested.

"You'll always be Miss Maplethorpe to me. Please bring my father some tea. If I see you wearing my mother's clothes again, I'll rip them off you myself!"

Daisy took charge of the household and devoted herself to making her stepfather's last days comfortable. She did the shopping, cooked the dishes he liked, and took them to him on a tray. In the afternoons, she bundled him into the car and took him for rides through the Spanish countryside. They even got in a couple of games of ping-pong. In the evening she sat by his bed and read from her diary.

"Who is this Amalia and Carmen?"

"My girlfriends."

"I didn't know you went in for that sort of thing."

"I don't."

"And who is this Slimane?"

"The boy I love. He's a Berber – a kind of ideal among men."

"Don't talk to me about ideals or ideal people. We're no better than those locusts that ate up Morocco."

"You'd like him, daddy."

"Those Moroccans looked like a bunch of loafers to me. Sitting all day in their cafés, smoking dope, letting their women do the work. Why would I like him?"

"Because he's polite and hospitable. These qualities are natural. Nothing is assumed, except that I will be the same. You'd like him because he's got something great and durable from his life outdoors. His view of the world is as green as the valley he grew up in."

"Then don't ruin him."

"He's uncomplicated and healthy. He'd never touched alcohol or a woman in his life … " Daisy laughed. "Until he met me!"

"It won't work. You're too different. You can't live his life, and he can't live yours. You'll never make each other happy."

"It won't work if one of us has to lead the other's life. If he took me back to his village in the Riff Mountains I'd never fit in. He wants to go to America, but he'd be a fish out of water. The only way is to live on neutral territory."

"And where is that going to be?"

"He has a plot of land in the oasis where he grows vegetables. He needs financial help. I've got to get a job."

"That sounds more sensible."

"This spring the Americans are going to mount a major campaign to clean the rebels out of the Sarhro mountains. I want to follow, taking notes and recording every detail. I'm going to go to Paris and use my Moroccan experiences to try to get a job as a reporter for *The Herald Tribune*."

On Christmas Eve Daisy sat by her stepfather's bed, keeping watch by the dying fire as the gale, moaning outside the window, spread its cold breath across the room. Adams made a noise and signalled with his fingers. For an instant their eyes met. He squeezed her hand. An hour later he was gone.

A human corpse, recently deceased, shrinks rapidly on itself, as though the flesh contracts upon the space vacated by the departed soul. The body seems smaller with the life gone out of it, and totally, utterly, dead.

Daisy knotted a handkerchief around his head to keep his jaw from dropping open.

The day before, Adams's face was puffy from medications; now his sunken cheeks pressed inwards against the jaw and teeth. When they moved his body, Daisy was surprised how light he was.

A long moaning cry drifted up from somewhere inside the house.

"Dorothy, that bitch howls like a coyote!"

"Well, she loved him, too."

"Everybody who knew daddy loved him."

"Your father never said one thing and did another. He was true to his word."

Adams's will was simple: he left Villa Arida Zona and all his property to Arturo and Daisy. She promptly put the house on the market and instructed Maitre Jacobi, who had drawn up the will, to deal with Miss Maplethorpe.

"Until she's gone, I can't sell this place," she told him. "Our neighbor, Lord Denby, has made an offer, but he can't move in until we get rid of her. Arturo and I need the money. You're a lawyer. You get her out."

She packed a few possessions for Paris.

"I've got to get a job," she told Miss Bushy. "One that will supply a steady income and make me write. I'm too disorganized on my own. I need a deadline. Daddy liked my Moroccan notebooks. He said I should type them up. That's what I'm going to do in Paris. And I'll show them to *The Herald Tribune*. Jacobi paid for my ticket and promised to send money as soon as Lord Denby makes a down payment. He said the proceeds from the sale of the house should provide Arturo and me with steady incomes which we'll share with you. We'll all be comfortable. I need this nest egg because the man I hope to marry doesn't have much money. After Paris I'm going back to Morocco, dear, to help him build a house and stay there until Arturo turns up. The living is cheap and my needs are small. There'll always be room for you."

But Miss Bushy wanted to go back to America. Daisy went to Jacobi and bought her a ticket. She drove her old nurse to Barcelona and put her on the plane to New York.

She had only been in Paris a week when Jacobi wrote that Miss Maplethorpe had produced a codicil to Adams's will which, she claimed, was dictated and signed by him a few days before his death. It permitted her to live in Villa Arida Zona for the rest of her life. Jacobi confidently predicted that the codicil would be quashed as Adams was probably not in his right mind and his signature was barely legible. He regretted that no more money would be forth-coming until the case was settled.

The letter threw Daisy into a tailspin. Just the day before, she had been living comfortably in a little room at the Hotel Lisbonne on rue de Vaugirard, working on her notebooks and warmed, in the freezing French winter, by the prospect that she would be back in Morocco by April at the latest.

Now they were throwing her out!

She didn't know what to do or where to go. The house was tied up in litigation which might drag on for months. The idea of going back to Balaguer to share Villa Arida Zona with Miss Maplethorpe was repellent. The people she loved were gone, the dogs dead.

How she longed for a sea of yellow sand!

Her cherished literary project had to go by the boards. She was down to her last few francs. The hotel manager was pestering her to pay up. One afternoon while he was having his nap, she lowered her suitcase out the window to a friendly Moroccan waiter from the neighborhood café. She tiptoed down the stairs, picked up the bag and disappeared into the streets of Paris.

CHAPTER 30

La Tormenta

At Tapachula Arturo boarded the wetback express for Veracruz, where it stopped for New Year's Eve. His soul may have been scoured by Saharan sand, but south of the border his spirits mellowed. What a relief to converse freely in Spanish after struggling with the Arabic!

He checked into the Hotel Miramar overlooking the Plaza with a view of the harbor. Parting flimsy curtains, he pulled open the French doors and stepped onto the balcony. A vulture lifted from its perch on the railing and floated away. The gleaming freighters of every nation crowded the harbor. Veined with silent lightning, the alabaster walls of an approaching tropical storm piled up on the horizon.

The *paseo* was in full swing. The young men and women walked round and round the Plaza in the hot electric evening, the men one way the girls the other, looking at each other but not speaking. Whole embroideries of lightning now laced the onrushing clouds. It was going to be a monster; already he inhaled the enormous breath of imminent rain.

Mosquitoes droned about his head. It was no good swatting; they owned the air like an alien element.

In the middle of the Plaza, a delegation of vultures, now joined by the one which had vacated Arturo's balcony, gathered about a dying dog. Professorial, conspiratorial, their wings folded like tattered umbrellas, they circled and stooped to inspect their dinner-to-be. Amidst the raucous wind-blown music from the loud-speakers, a primitive ferris wheel was being cranked by a giant of a man in a black sombrero. One by one, the lanterns were blinking out, save for a single light glowing from the last cantina – the fatal red light that never goes out. The meek notes of a marimba drifted upwards. A firecracker exploded.

The rain was now coming on like a froth of thick white smoke; one by one the great ships in the harbor were being enveloped by the seething curtain.

Closing the French doors against the bugs and impending storm, Arturo called room service, ordered a margarita and asked the operator to put a call through to Spain.

Mysteriously, the phone on the other end of the line went on ringing. Arturo checked his watch. What with the time difference it would have been near midnight in Spain. It was unlikely that Antonio and his mother would have gone out to celebrate. Daisy would have stayed home to cook supper. The telephone was located on the night table next to his mother's bed. Unless it was disconnected or broken, there was no way they could not have heard it.

A bolt of lightning blanked the window in white; thunder crashed with an ear-splitting crack, plunging the room into darkness. The power of the sudden gale burst open the French doors.

Hailstones the size of peanuts rifled into the room with a sound like machine-gun fire, levelling the curtains and knocking his margarita to the floor. Just before the line went dead he heard a creaky little voice asking "Is that you, Arturo?"

According to the operator that last bolt of lightning had knocked out the hotel telephones. It would not be possible to make an outside call until the next morning. The lights flickered and came back on. Puzzled, Arturo ordered another drink. Whose voice was that? he wondered.

Three margaritas later the penny dropped. Miss Maplethorpe – that was Miss Maplethorpe's creaky old voice! What in the world was Miss Maplethorpe doing in his mother's house? Or had he mistakenly given the operator his old number in Douglas? His mind reeled just thinking about it.

The next day he was informed that telephonic communication between Mexico and the Iberian peninsula had been restored.

He tried again.

"The Adams residence," that voice answered.

"Who is this speaking?"

"Veronica Adams."

"Miss Maplethorpe, I'm not sure where you are or even who you are, but may I please speak to my mother?"

There was a long silence.

"Miss Maplethorpe?"

"Arturo, I am very sorry to say that your mother passed away."

"What? "Arturo felt like he had been punched in the stomach. "When did this happen?"

"In September, September 5th, in Tangier."

"Tangier? What was she doing in Tangier?"

"You sent a note that you had been bitten by a snake, She went with Daisy to Tangier to see if you were all right."

"I was never in Tangier, or anywhere near Tangier."

"They didn't know that. They didn't know where you were. Daisy said your mother died peacefully in her sleep in Tangier. She spent six months in Morocco trying to find you.

"Please give me Daisy."

"Daisy has gone to Paris looking for a job."

"What kind of job?"

"She wrote up an account of her experience in Morocco and was going to show it to *The Herald Tribune* in hope they will send her back to report on the situation down there."

"Do you have a phone number for her in Paris?"

"I do not."

"Address?"

"No."

"Miss Maplethorpe, if you don't mind me asking – what are you doing in my mother's house?"

"Antonio sent for me to come from Douglas to take care of him."

"Put Antonio on."

"I'm very sorry to say that Antonio passed away on Christmas Eve."

The second blow nearly knocked Arturo off his feet. He had to sit down.

"Arturo?"

"Miss Maplethorpe, why are you calling yourself by his name?"

"We were married a few days before he died."

"Is Miss Bushy there? Please let me speak to Miss Bushy."

"Daisy put her on a plane back to New York. I am sorry to have to be the one to tell you all this, Arturo, but you went off to Africa and nobody knew how to find you. We learned you deserted from the army, but nothing after that. You cut yourself off from your family and left no clue how to reach you. You cruelly turned your back on those who loved you when they needed you the most. I think that is unforgivable. You should be ashamed."

These words felt like a slap across the face.

With time to kill between trains at the Buenavista station in Mexico, D.F., he listlessly wandered the streets of the capital until he found himself standing before the magnificent Cathedral of Santa Maria. In Barcelona he had gazed in awe at La Sagrada Familia and, in Sevilla, at La Giralda, but had darkened the door of neither. He had walked to Santiago de Compostela but cut his pilgrimage a few yards short of the cathedral in a bar across the street. Only the little mission church of San Mateo in AZ had he seen the inside of. Unlike Antonio, he bore no hatred for God. Now the sheer scale of architectural gravitas compelled him forward. How can you hate someone you don't even know ...

Surrounded by hunched figures with their backs to him, he felt like an intruder, a gatecrasher, the uninvited guest who knew no one, who was introduced to no one. The plaster virgin and her child, the Stations of the Cross – it seemed to Arturo that after his travels all that was left for his explorations was the territory of despair. The Lord's Prayer lay mute on his tongue. A service was going on. The priest was moaning, and everyone was repeating: *"Santa Maria, Madre de Dios, ruega por nosotros pecadores, ahora y en la hora de nuestra muerte. Amen."* Pray for us sinners, now and at the hour of our death.

Candles were being lit, one from another, many candles. Arturo pressed a coin into the slot, lit a candle, and sank to his knees.

"Santa Maria, Madre de Dios, ruega por nosotros pecadores ... "

From between his fingers he looked up at the figure on the cross. Watching the priest pour the water and the wine, he thought that any kind of love must deserve a bit of mercy. Incest, too, was a kind of love, not the best kind, but love all the same.

Now there was nobody but Daisy to whom he could speak the truth. But it was not to his sister that he directed his prayers, but to their child, somewhere out in the golden glowing mist of this polluted metropolis, who would never call him father.

From Mexicali, Mexico he crossed the border to Calexico, U.S.A. with a busload of inebriated, hilarious, sunburnt tourists. The exhausted guard waved them through.

From LA he flew to NYC where it was snowing hard, with the Hudson caked with ice. He checked into the Chelsea Hotel at West 23rd St. and 7th Ave., joined the McBurney YMCA across the street, and signed up for an art course at the New School.

In the Manhattan phone book he found the name, address, and telephone number of Duncan van Renseelaer, his real father. Pulling on his boots, he headed uptown.

CHAPTER 31

Elmyr

It's hard to imagine what would have become of Daisy at this point in our story if Elmyr Boutin had not decided to walk home from the Hotel Crillon. Having been wined and dined by some rich Texans, he declined the taxi offered by the doorman and chose instead to brave the freezing January night and make his way back to his left bank apartment on foot. His aim was to pick up one of the impoverished Arab boys who sleep beneath the bridges of Paris and take him home for the night.

Walking along the Seine, he passed by the Pont de la Concorde, where a group of *clochards* had sought shelter under the bridge. Huddled together like so many shivering puppies, shaken by rumbles from above, breathing steam into the frigid air, these exhausted vagabonds were sound asleep. Wide awake among them a creature in a mink coat, head wrapped in a turban, was seated beside a candle, flipping the pages of an Arabic-language newspaper with dirty, tobacco-stained fingers.

Instantly Elmyr thought of a painting by Georges de la Tour.

"Do you read Arabic?" he asked.

"I don't speak French."

Elmyr, a tall pale man, studied her with a blue hypnotic gaze. He repeated the question in English.

"I do, yes. A little. I like your hat."

Elmyr was wearing a green alpine cap with a badger brush. It was one of his fantasies.

"Does that make you Swiss?" she asked.

"Hungarian. And you're ... American."

"How'd you guess?"

"Where'd you learn Arabic?"

"I learned to read and write it in Spain and to speak it in Morocco. You've got an American accent."

"Sure. I lived there. I've lived everywhere." He noticed the prayer beads entwined among her fingers. "Are you a Muslim?"

"Yes, I am. Sort of."

"I was admiring your coat."

"It belonged to my mother."

"I usually spend my winters in Morocco."

"If you spend your winters in Morocco, why aren't you there now?"

"I've had to stay in Paris on business. Plus there's fighting going on."

"Tell me about it."

"There's only one person who can sort that mess out," Elmyr said.

"Who's that?"

"Colonel David Ben Jalloud, an old friend of mine – an American officer who happens to be an Arab."

"That would make him unique."

"His family emigrated from the Lebanon to America. He's been all over the Arab world on secret assignments. Sooner or later they'll send him to Morocco. That's where we met – swimming at Sun Beach in Tangier."

"Nobody's swimming there now."

"That's the fundamentalist influence. They've ordered the entire country to put the djellabas back on. What's your name?"

"Call me Moha. Are you a soldier?"

Elmyr smiled. "An artist."

"I'm an artist too – a writer. Hold on a minute. Are you trying to hornswoggle me? You said you were staying in Paris on business."

"Artists can have business."

"Can they?"

"Paintings must be sold."

"Never thought of that. So far I haven't sold a book. I haven't even written one."

"Moha, can I buy you a drink?"

"That's an interesting idea."

"You're a Muslim. Maybe you don't drink."

"I do drink, but I won't accept an invitation to drink."

"What can I do to change your mind?"

"By inviting me to a square meal."

"You're on."

Born Elmer Button in Idabel, Oklahoma, Elmyr showed rare talent at an early age. After art school at the University of Iowa he came to France on a Fulbright Scholarship and never looked back.

Paris became his home, but he missed the sunshine of Oklahoma. To avoid the cold French climate he started wintering in Morocco. He spent several seasons in a stone hut near the Tafilalet studying the "sun, sum, and substance" of the Sahara. The result of this experience were his miniature, painstakingly executed desert paintings – "interiors," as he called them – tiny men beneath the colossal sky, sandstorms, microscopic views of wind eroded rocks, even grains of sand. One appreciative reviewer called them "the desert seen from the inside out." They were so realistic as to be surrealistic and virtually incomprehensible to anyone unfamiliar with the desert. His work received some rave reviews but did not sell. Eventually he got fed up with being broke. Virtuoso that he was, he changed his name, moved to a new address, taught himself the techniques of *craquelure*, wormholes and yellowed varnish, added a bit of dirt to the linseed oil, and, for good measure, a poorly repaired rip, and started turning out forgeries of Gaugin, Matisse and Modigliani, which he sold to gullible American millionaires. The always sticky matter of provenance was glossed over with tales of impecunious Russians sneaking out from behind the Iron Curtain.

The next morning, in his studio on rue de Grenelle, he started work on Daisy's portrait. Standing before his easel, he made a preliminary sketch of her head and shoulders. There followed a long silence in which he did nothing.

Daisy jumped up to stir a pot she had on the stove. "Is something wrong?" she asked.

"Moha ... " He put down his pencil. "That shaved head ... when you took your turban off in the restaurant last night ... you looked devastatingly criminal and obscene."

"Oh?" She sounded a little disappointed.

"Now I believe it gives you a vulnerable, sensuous look ... if anything, more feminine. Or sultry tomboy ... like the young Rimbaud."

"Well, I ought to," Daisy replied nonchalantly. "He's one of my ancestors."

Elmyr laughed. "You grew up in some awful place like Tombstone, your stepfather was a disciple of Trotsky, and your grandfather was the nephew of J. P. Morgan. How much more of this hogwash do you expect me to swallow?"

"What about you, Elmyr? You've French-fried your name, you tell me you're Hungarian when you're nothing but a low-down cowpoke from Idabel, Oklahoma. The difference between you and me, *Elmer*, is that everything I tell you is the *truth*, as far as I know it, while you hide behind a veil of discombobulating lies ... My mother was like you. She tended to blur her past behind a smokescreen of stories to cover up the fact she was Jewish. One story I got out of her was that her great grandmother had a love affair here in France. While visiting friends near Nancy she got pushed into a haystack by a tramp who called himself Arthur Rimbaud."

"When was that?"

"Well, I know for a fact her baby was born February 17th, 1877 ... that's about 100 years ago, almost to the day."

"Wait a minute. Rimbaud is one of my heroes ... In 1876 he was on one of his tramps across Europe. In May ... he got kicked out of Alsace by the German police and walked back to Charleville on his way to Amsterdam, where he joined the Dutch army and sailed to Java ... He could have passed through Nancy. Christ, I suppose it is possible!"

"He cast a spell over her reciting poems."

"Well, you do look like him." Elmyr took a step closer. "It's amazing ... "

"Better not come too close. Remember all that garlic I ate."

Elmyr returned to his easel. "Last night during dinner while you were telling me these stories, I was looking at your hands, and I was thinking, 'How can those fingers belong to a girl? They're so dirty!' You were eating those garlicky snails. I said to myself, 'This can't be a girl's hand. It's as hard as wood. It has to be a boy's, a boy who's been living rough. Look how hungry he is. Look how he's tucking into that garlic bread.' And you were eating those big chunks of provençal garlic you fished out of the soup, and I thought, 'No girl would do that. No girl would think garlic was sexy.' Then came the bean dish, with more garlic. Tell me, Moha, why do you eat so much garlic?"

"My stepfather said it was good for worms."

"Do you have worms?"

"Well .. I might have."

"It was the garlic that fooled me, more than those shiny, dirty yellow fingers."

"I was so hungry I put off telling you from one bite to the next for fear I might not get another."

"Do I look like someone who would snatch food from a starving writer?"

"I wasn't thinking straight. Besides, you never know how a person is going to react when he discovers that the boy he's picked up turns out to be a grown woman."

"You know, Moha, I've lived in France a long time and ought to be used to it, but you really stink of garlic."

"You don't have to rub it in."

"And you're *still* eating garlic."

It was true. It was the rainy season, and *anguilles* (baby eels) were in. The night before, on their ramble around Paris, Daisy had bought a sackful at a street market. Now she took them off the stove where they had been bubbling in a miniature clay casserole with olive oil, chunks of garlic, and hot red pepper. She had found a tiny wooden fork (the slippery little devils will slip off a metal one) and was waiting for them to cool.

"My girlfriends in Tangier got me to like them. They call 'em *angulas* down there. They're born in the rivers or Spain and Morocco and swim all the way to the Sargasso Sea to breed."

"Their assholes occlude along the way."

"Didn't know that."

Elmyr looked with disgust at the slimy mass of gray eels.

"My stepfather used to swear by garlic." She tucked into the eels with exaggerated relish. "Swore it was a vermifuge."

"What?"

"Worm expeller."

Elmyr finally got down to work on *Girl with the Shaved Head*, in the style of Modigliani. In the picture Daisy wears a djellaba. In her left hand she holds a hashish pipe. A gap between the folds of her dusty black turban, loosely tied, shows a gleam of shaved head. The long neck and dark dreaming eyes convey the sense of sadness and loss. An empty road beckons from behind. The spiritual purpose of the impending trip is represented by the Muslim prayer beads loosely entwined among the fingers of her right hand.

If the face is Modigliani, the background is pure Elmyr. The road winds away and loses itself in the desert. The dunes are puddled with mirages, a vision of water that is not. The road ends in a void of glittering blue beneath a white hot sky. It is a comfortless, mystical landscape. The expression on Daisy's face is submissive, her eyelids heavy. The narcotic smoke and trance of travel have taken possession of her soul.

Elmyr invited her to move into his apartment until she found a place of her own. His studio, on the top floor of a building on rue de Grenelle, consisted of one large room that had been partitioned into areas for eating, sleeping and working. A north-facing window overlooked the slate rooftops of Paris.

He kept the studio tidy. The top of the kitchen table, bleached and striated from repeating scrubbings, looked like it had been made from driftwood.

"Who cleans this place?" she asked.

"I do, and you're going to help me."

"I'm not much good at housekeeping … Ah ha ha!"

"What's so funny?"

"Take a gander at this." She had spotted a pair of cowboy boots in the closet. "These kill-a-bug-in-the-corner boots must date from the days of Elmer Button, cowpoke."

Daisy was fascinated by a series of three unsold "sun" paintings that decorated the walls.

In the first the brown desert, flat as a tennis court, was overhung by a sky of polished lemon yellow. A halo of sinister black specks clusters around the sun that seems to be the eye of an impending storm. In the second the earth has erupted and joined with the air. The sun (or something) gleams through the atmosphere choked with dust. In the third the sun has fallen to earth. Both sky and the desolate gray plain swirl with sand. It was hard to tell which was which. From the bottom corner a forlorn figure in a white robe signals enigmatically. Endless horizontal distances ebb to infinity.

"Are these for sale?"

"Everything is for sale."

"Were they painted near the Tafilalet?"

"There are a dozen kinds of desert around the Tafilalet – rock, sand, mountain – *hammada* – you name it."

"I've never seen desert like this."

"You will when a sandstorm hits."

"How long did it take you to paint these?"

"All my life."

"How do you do it? This is eternity you've created, but how do you stop all these particles that are flying around?"

"With a hair dryer."

"You paint eternity with a hair dryer." Arms crossed, Daisy stood before the paintings. "If I were rich, I'd buy them all."

"If you bought them all we'd both be rich."

"This is the way the desert will always be."

"Loveless. There is no such thing as love in the desert."

"No love?"

"Only alliances and conspiracies. Tribe against tribe. Arab against Berber. The Americans against the Moroccans."

"I found love in the desert," Daisy said, "a little oasis of love."

"That makes you unique. We're here to learn. To love is to learn; those who don't, don't."

Elmyr's pale blue eyes glittered beneath a thatch of gray hair. On his wrist he wore a silver bracelet from Mauritania. A blue star was tattooed on the back of his left shoulder. He was used to an orderly bachelor's life, but for Daisy there was no day or night. She didn't divide up the hours like normal people do. She stayed up until three in the morning smoking, drinking and writing, and spent half the day on Elmyr's sofa. This disturbed his sleep and kept him from working. He was fifty, and she was twenty.

Daisy left her clothes on the floor and littered the place with beer bottles and cigarette butts. As he made his living in secret, his studio was strictly off-limits to anyone but close friends. When she brought home her "bridge buddies," there were loud scenes when he kicked them out.

To raise some cash, she sold the mink coat at a street market for $100.

In the evenings they were joined by Salah, a tall black Moroccan. Dressed in a dove gray jellaba, he had a toothy grin but seldom spoke. The backs of his hands were tattooed with blue dots. He made a living trading in *shira* (hashish).

Elmyr was many-sided, like a prism. One side was his imagination and talent, which could produce rainbows of conversation and color. Another was his paranoia: the illegal nature of his work, the cold weather, and the huge amount of hashish he smoked tended to bring out the pessimism in him.

He slept naked, he walked around the studio naked. Sometimes he painted naked.

"I don't look forward to anything, man. Nothing! I can't remember anymore how human I am, or even if I am human. The simplest problems confound me. I have difficulty in making straightforward decisions. I become more and more mystified by human nature, namely my own. The older I get the less I seem to know. About anything! I've never known what to do. What to do at all. All my life I have been waiting. What am I waiting for?

"You have no idea what it is to die," he told her. "You're too young. That's why people like you make cannon fodder. Death – you don't really believe such a thing exists. Me, I'm beginning to see the end. I'm heading toward it. It's not far away now – the end of this whole pointless existence."

"But you're a genius, Elmyr. Who else can paint a sandstorm approaching? All the land begins to move, in particles. It's as though you are looking into the Brownian movement. The whole earth is rushing, shaking, vibrating … "

"It's not a gradual process at all. You can go for months, *years* without noticing any change. Then, inexplicably, in the period of a month, a week, a single *day*, everything slips. You look in the mirror, and you are older, *much* older than when you went to bed. You can't believe what's happened, but it has! It all begins at twenty-eight or twenty-nine, when the first wrinkles appear next to your ears. It means your face is falling."

While pouring himself a drink he spotted Salah kissing Daisy behind the kitchen door.

He slapped her hard. "You steal my friends!"

"I'm not!" she sobbed.

He made a grab for her ears. She batted him arms away. A heavy push on her chest sent her crashing against the door. He came forward again. Swinging from the hip, she clocked him on the eye with a roundhouse punch. He wrestled her to the floor and dropped to his knees on her arms. Sweeping a kitchen knife off the table he lay the blade against her throat.

"You're corrupting me! Like Rimbaud corrupted Verlaine!"

Salah stood there frozen, his eyes big.

"Salah! Get him off me!"

The minute Salah touched him, Elmyr crumbled. He was sub-dued and sobbing, his eyes wild. Out came a tumble of words, oaths, and accusations.

"Drugs have altered his character," Salah said after they had put him to bed. "He has experimented too much. He smokes too much *shira*."

"Then why do you bring it to him?"

CHAPTER 32

Cajan

The next morning there was a loud knock.

Elmyr went to the door. "Who is it?" He had a splitting headache.

"Me!" came the reply, meaning the Duchess de Bremont, a good friend and patron of his work.

He opened and a lady walked in.

"Wow! Where'd you get that shiner?"

Cajan de Bremont grew up on Plumnelly Plantation near Monroe, Louisiana, where her father was a wealthy cotton and soy bean planter. At an early age she tired of the Delta farm boys and came to London to live it up, spend money, and marry an English lord; but her hard-drinking, loud-talking style and bold sexual manner frightened them away. She decamped to Paris, where rumors of her fabulous fortune brought the impoverished aristos out in droves. She finally married Robert de Bremont, whose family owned a chain of newspapers in francophone Africa. Gluglu, as his drinking buddies called him, was thoroughly anglicized. When Hitler invaded, he was sent with his *nounou* to America and spent the war years in a mansion on Long Island. A big man, he became the first Frenchman to captain the Eton College rugby team before going on to Yale, where he played football. After Yale he never did another stroke of work. Burly and overweight, with bushy eyebrows that met in the middle, he looked more like a truckdriver than the first Duke of France.

They went to Morocco on their honeymoon. Gluglu fell in love with the place and refused to come home. A keen sportsman, he stalked moufflon in the Atlas, hunted wild boar in the Riff, and reportedly shot the last lynx in Morocco.

After gallivanting around the mountains, Gluglu decided to

explore the desert. Disguising himself as a Jewess under the assumption that Saharan tribesmen would consider her so impure they would not approach, he set off to Taodeni, the salt capital of the Sahara. He was never seen again.

Cajan did everything in her power to trace her missing husband. The area where he disappeared was controlled by the warlike Tuareg, but the Moroccan and Algerian embassies were either unable or unwilling to help. She made several trips to Morocco, but was frustrated by the authorities' refusal to let her follow her husband's footsteps into the desert.

The duke's disappearance had made front page headlines, but gradually the thing died down and people lost interest. An air of mystery shrouded the whole affair.

Then one day an old Bedouin turned up at the Hotel Mamounia in Marrakesh with a sackful of notebooks. It was the duke's diary.

He had made it to Taodeni, but his guides let him stay only two hours because of the danger. By this time, according to his own account, he was so ill with dysentery he made the return journey in a sack flung over a camel's back. Weak and helpless, he described how he'd nearly been murdered. On the last page he wrote that he and his remaining guide had missed a well in a sand storm. There the diary ended, and so, apparently, did his life.

Cajan published the diary under the title *Camels into the Void*. The book rekindled the controversy, but in due course it died down again and nothing new was learned.

"Where is she?" she demanded.

"Who?" Elmyr's head was killing him. The boisterous Duchess de Bremont was the last person he wanted to see at ten o'clock in the morning.

"Daisy Adams! Moha ben Abdu! I want to talk to her."

"What about?"

"Business."

"What kind of business?"

"You'll hear in a minute. I've just come back from Marrakesh. The whole town is buzzing about her escapades. She left a trail of broken hearts across the Sahara … "

Hearing her name mentioned, Daisy sidled into the room and dropped into a chair. Brown and skinny beneath her blue Saharan shift, she looked like an underfed waif. The skull cap perched on her shaven head accentuated her gaunt, monkish appearance.

"Glory!" The Duchess studied her for a minute. "She's just a child!"

Daisy's nicotine-stained fingers trembled as she shook a few bits of tobacco onto a cigarette paper.

"Daisy," Elmyr said, "this is the Duchess of Bremont."

Daisy came to life. "Your husband's journal is my bible," she blurted out. "I open it to any page for inspiration. I've read it I don't know how many times. It continues to fill my days and makes me dream mad desert dreams at night. His journey constitutes a myth, like *Moby Dick*, and shows that physical endurance, when pushed to the limit, becomes in itself an act of mysticism. The intensity of his vision, the absurdity of his disguise, his disregard for danger, even the ridiculous introduction … Excuse me, Duchess, but I'm sure those visions were not brought on by fever or lack of water … I can so well imagine his joy, after such hardship, upon reaching his goal. I can see the salt towers of Taodeni, hear the chanting of the slaves, and smell the huge slabs of salt being hoisted from the mines. The camels bellow as the caravan sets off, the slabs like great wallets, sixty pounds each, two to each beast, destined for Timbuktoo. God, it's my dream to take a trip like that! A trip like that, you know … it can never end …it goes on forever."

The Duchess was sitting on the edge of her chair. "What do you mean?"

"Well, of course … " Daisy ran the tip of her tongue along the cigarette paper. "He's still out there … "

Astonished by this outburst, the Duchess leaned forward. "What makes you say that?"

"He couldn't possibly come home after a trip like that. No no.

He made the trip, after all, on a whim, simply to go where few had been before – jumping up from a café table in Marrakesh with a wild blue stare – as you wrote in the introduction. His preparations were scant, he gave little thought to the danger involved ... " She produced the *mechero* and lit the cigarette. "It was a rich man's jaunt that turned out to be a battle for survival. He realized the frivolity of his former life and knew he could never go back to it. How could he take up his old ways again when he makes it clear in his diary that his life had changed forever? No offence intended, Duchess, but I'm convinced he's still alive ... somewhere. Not the same man you knew, but the same man, too, searching ... "

"Searching for what?" the Duchess asked impatiently.

"All the big realities that men have tried to fathom since the beginning of time." Daisy nonchalantly waved her cigarette in the air. "They're all out there."

"All of what? What are you talking about?"

"Oh, God, Yahweh, Allah, the Truth, the Alpha and the Omega, the Ultimate, the Origin of the Universe and the Meaning of Life. The trouble with philosophers ... " she blew out a smoke ring, "they sit in comfortable, over-heated houses trying to figure these things out when they should be out in the cold, under the stars. That's the way you get to know about the universe which, after all, is part of nature – *our* nature – and not just an abstraction to be solved by mathematics. When you lie down, you look up, not through a telescope but with your back on the hard cold ground. And if you look long enough, the answers begin to come. Intuitive answers. That's why the Duke's never going to come home – not after he's come face to face with these realities." She sat back, crossed her legs, and blew out another smoke ring. "Naturally. Why should he?"

The Duchess seemed impressed by the force of Daisy's convictions but found her flippant tone hard to take in.

"How do you know these things?" she argued crossly.

"I was in the Tafilalet before Christmas. If I hadn't gotten sick, I'd be there still. Excuse me, will you sign my book?"

Daisy darted from the room. The Duchess looked at Elmyr.

"She's Rimbaud's great great granddaughter or something," he commented sardonically.

"Is she crazy or what?"

"A little crazy, maybe, but very single-minded."

"That voice! It sounds like a rusty crank! But she's the first person who thinks Robert is alive!"

Daisy came back with the book. "I found this in Tangier."

Her copy was falling to bits and held together by tape. The pages were dog-eared and crammed with scraps of paper on which she had scribbled notes and quotations.

The Duchess signed. "That article about you in *The Herald Tribune* – is it true?"

"What article? I talked to a reporter at the Chance Bar in Tangier after I came out of the desert, but I haven't seen any article."

"It came out around Christmas. Do you really think the Americans could be pushed back to the walls of Marrakesh?"

"Did I say that? Uh, I shouldn't be interviewed while I'm drinking."

"The article said you're a Muslim. Is it true?"

"That's the way to Mecca." Elmyr pointed out the window. "She prays five times a day on this carpet."

"While he parades around here buck naked. I've seen his pecker so many times I could draw a picture of it."

"I hear you're a heavy drinker. I thought Muslims weren't supposed to drink."

Daisy blew another smoke ring. "I'm a Muslim drunk," she said wearily.

"You speak Arabic."

"Moroccan Arabic. *Darija.* Not very well. Duchess, it's an honor to meet you, but would you mind telling me the purpose for this interrogation?"

"I'll get to that in a minute. Call me Cajan. Is it true you travelled incognito through the Moroccan desert?"

"The desert is a big place. I rode across part of it."

"Do Moroccans see through your disguise?"

"I think their reaction is, well, if she wants to dress like that, that's her business."

"Would you go back again?"

"That's all she thinks about," Elmyr put in.

Daisy lowered her eyes. "To go back to the desert is my only purpose," she mumbled. "I'd be there now if I had the cash. The trouble is, as Elmyr knows too well, my money was stolen. I'm broke."

"And if you had the money to go back what would you do when you got there?"

"Go straight to the Tafilalet and track down my brother. He's all I have. That's why I can't rest until I find him."

"How would you live? How would you support yourself?"

"I was hoping to get a job reporting on the Moroccan situation, but *The Herald Tribune* wasn't interested."

"I may be able to help you with that. I can see you're serious. Now I'll tell you the reason for these questions. I disagree with you – I don't think my husband is alive. I think he was murdered, and the Americans know about it and are covering it up."

"Why are they doing it?"

"Because the crime, if it did occur, happened in an area which they've told the world is safe and under their control. If the murder were revealed, it would be proof that they only control a few oases, like you said in the article, and most of the desert is still *bled-es-siba*."

"It's possible. Anything is possible."

"Like you, I want to know the truth. Maybe you can help me. Maybe you're the person who can discover what happened to him."

"Ever since I read your book I've been dying to find out for myself."

"I'm going to make you an offer. I propose to pay your way back to Morocco. In addition, I'll arrange to send you regular monthly sums if you make every effort to find out what happened to my husband. I don't care how long it takes. I don't care how much it costs. I don't want any stones left unturned. Think it over for twenty-four hours and let me know what you decide."

"I don't know … " Daisy inhaled deeply. "Looking for two people at the same time … " she said doubtfully. "I can't promise anything."

"You don't have to promise anything as long as you swear you'll do everything in your power to uncover the truth!"

Daisy ground out her cigarette. "The Americans won't want any questions asked, I can promise you that."

"I don't want to involve the Americans! They'll only get in your way. You speak Arabic and know how to disguise yourself. I would expect you to make your inquiries among the natives. Aside from this romantic notion of yours, do you have any serious evidence for believing he might be alive?"

"Well, an old Jewish gentleman in the Tafilalet told me that he'd heard a rumor about a white hermit wandering in the desert … "

"Heavens!" the Duchess exclaimed. "Could it be him, Elmyr?"

Elmyr shrugged. "As she says, anything is possible."

"Well, if it is him, Daisy, if you find my husband, dear, if you find him alive, I can promise you won't have any more money problems."

"Cajan always keeps her word when it comes to money," Elmyr put in. "Will you send me a camel udder box to put my cufflinks in, Daisy? Why do you look so glum? This is what you've been praying for, isn't it? A ticket back to Morocco?"

"I am excited … " Daisy's lips trembled as she held the book in both hands. "You see … ever since I read your book, I've had this recurring dream … that I would be the one to find the Duke."

"Is that right?" The Duchess looked startled.

"He was poor, he was dressed in rags, he needed nothing and nobody. He was striding along one of those white roads that go on forever – the sacred path to eternity."

The Duchess frowned. "Let's talk dollars and cents," she said. "How much will you need?"

"Well, Miss Cowgirl," Elmyr said after the Duchess left, "Looks like you and I are partners."

"God is great. What'll I call him?"

"Who?"

"The Duke! If he's still out there, what'll I call him if I find him?"

"Your Grace."

"What is he – some sort of god?"

"Some kind of god with the track record of a devil. I'm going to write Ben Jalloud and tell him to look you up if they send him back to Morocco."

"Well, tell your friend he owes me forty-nine hundred bucks."

PART II

Sahara – Leonem Arida Nutrix*

---

* Sahara – Arid Nurse of Lions (Horace)

CHAPTER 33

Fondak Berigou

The streets of Marrakesh were nearly deserted. The earth had given up all resistance to the heat, as the *sherqi*, blowing in from the desert, sucked up whatever moisture remained in the soil. The heat remained constant, day and night. Walls of airborne sand obscured the sun but did not diminish its power. Swirls of dust coasted through the Djmaa El Fna carrying a newspaper gone berserk in the wind. Heat invested the city like an occupying army as the Moroccans sought shelter behind the thick mud walls of their houses.

The lone American soldier, sipping a Coca-Cola on the terrace of the Café Glacier, understood the futility of attempting to bring peace to the Sahara. Even if it were successful, the effort would amount to no more than a temporary disturbance to the vast spiritual peace that is the Sahara; and that man's eternal struggle with the forces of nature is an ingredient of that peace. The unrelenting assault by the sun was more likely to defeat an American army than any Mohammedan horde.

When the sun begins to go down, the citizens of Marrakesh come out of their houses. Dressed in filmy costumes, they glide along, speaking in whispers. This is the hour of the evening prayer. During summer, the cafés of Marrakesh move from street level to roof tops to take advantage of breezes. Rugs are spread on terraces, and customers doff shoes and gather beneath the stars, to smoke the weed and talk, all the while gazing over the cubist rooftops of their desert city. The minarets point toward eternity. If this architectural message goes unheeded, the muezzin's echoing calls inject into the time-absolving conversations of the café dwellers harmonic reminders of their duty before God.

Mr Berigou's *fondak* is such a place. The courtyard is reserved for camels and donkeys, the rooms along the first and second balconies for those who have ridden in from desert or mountain to sell their goods and to indulge, for a few days, in the assorted pleasures of this "Saigon of the Sahara," as the Americans called Marrakesh.

Daisy had arrived by bus from Tangier. Mr Berigou, a tall brown figure in a saffron robe, bowed at the door. His *fondak* was a favorite gathering place for the Jilaliya.

"I have a letter for Sidi Mohamed," she said.

Murmuring salaams, Mr Berigou led her up a narrow staircase – crowded with scowling tribesmen – to the roof where the Marabout was praying.

"He is going to Madrid for talks. This is his last night in Morocco. That is why he is sad. You may go to him now."

Daisy shed her slippers, stepped onto the carpet and sat cross-legged at a respectful distance while the Marabout finished his prayers.

A huge black man came and stood beside her. He wore a dove gray cape which he removed to reveal a lavish red and black undergarment. The fiery colors accentuated his thick neck and bulging muscles, suggesting a volcano about to erupt.

But his voice, speaking perfect American English, was soft. "Sidna prefers to conduct this conversation in his own language. Although I understand you have some knowledge of Arabic, I shall translate."

He handed the Marabout a sheet of paper on which the questions had been written. The margins were covered with notations in Arabic script.

"These questions have already been examined by Sidna, and his answers may be taken as definitive," the translator said.

Without looking at it the Marabout placed the paper in his lap and fixed on Daisy a warm gaze that banished the nervousness she had felt upon entering his presence.

"I would like to express my condolences for the death of your mother," he said in Spanish.

"Thank you."

"Your mother was the first American to express sympathy and understanding of our position."

The first of the questions from *The Herald Tribune*, which Daisy had delivered the day before, was a request for a statement from the Marabout on his attitude toward the Polisario,* and his relations with the Polisario, if such relations existed.

"We have no relations with the Polisario." The Marabout spoke in a firm low voice. "All this talk on television and what is being written in the newspapers has the sole result of frightening the Americans into sending more soldiers to Morocco and therefore earning the condemnation of not only the Muslim world, but of the whole world. Nor do we intend to establish such relations. Our struggle is exclusively a national one and our enemy is not America but the American army in Morocco."

Second question: Are Polisario operatives fighting in Morocco?

"It is true that many volunteers from across the Arab world, and from the whole world, are coming to Morocco. We have turned them away. Our fighters are exclusively Moroccan."

Third question: his terms for peace.

"As for peace, it can come whenever the United States is willing. We desire above all things to live in peace and the liberty to work and to conduct our lives as we have always done. And, before all other nations, we wish for the United States to be at peace with us and to act again as our friend and ally as it has for two centuries.

"But in the terms of peace we have certain irreducible demands. First and foremost, every American soldier in Morocco, from Tangier to El Aâiún, must be withdrawn. Their base at Ben Guerir must be closed, and the bases they have created elsewhere."

The Marabout made these statements slowly, stopping after each sentence so it could be translated. This was a lengthy process. As

---

* Frente Popular de Liberación de Saguia el Hamra y Río de Oro

the Marabout spoke, Daisy had time to study his face. This was not the fanatical, prophet-like figure portrayed in the newspapers, but a cautious leader dealing with a complex national problem.

Question four: his attitude toward the U.S.

"Our attitude toward America is friendly in the extreme, even when their soldiers are attacking us. We have never desired other than peaceful relations, which the Sultan outlined in his speech. However, a grave error was made by inviting American soldiers to Morocco.

"But, if the American army wishes to stay, we are ready to resist for an indefinite term. Our people are hardy and determined to fight. We did not ask for this fight but shall continue to fight until peace can come on our terms.

"I am constantly surprised by what I read in the newspapers and by what is reported on American television. Their media appear to have no idea of geography, or of anything else of importance connected with this conflict."

At no time during the interview did the Marabout display any rancor toward the United States. He briefly reviewed the field of American officers and scorned them principally for failing to have any understanding of the culture or history of Morocco. However, he expressed some respect for Colonel Ben Jalloud, Elmyr's friend, who, in his opinion, was the single American officer with the background, culture and experience to befriend and manage Muslim populations.

"The future of Morocco is unlimited. We were a nation before America gained its independence. We have the confidence to distinguish ourselves in peace as well as war. If America will not give us peace now, when we are ready for it, we shall fight until we have gained it by our swords and the will of Allah."

That statement ended the interview. With a nod of his head he dismissed the translator.

Daisy handed him a letter. "From Jâafar."

The Marabout slipped it into his pocket and spoke again in Spanish. "Would you like a game of parcheesi?" He signalled for a board to be brought. "Parcheesi helps pass the time."

"Will you be away long?" she asked.

He made a gesture of resignation. "For as long as we can go on talking and talking is better than fighting, no?"

"And the cease-fire will hold while the talks last – is that what has been agreed?"

"That is what the government of your country has promised."

"Sidna, have you been able to learn anything about my brother?"

The Marabout shook his head. "My men have been ordered to inform me of any American prisoner. I am afraid I have nothing to report."

She leaned closer. "I have been asked to trace the missing Duke de Bremont. Does that name mean anything to you, Sidna?"

Mr Berigou reappeared, carrying a tray laden with a silvery teapot, colored glasses, and a plate of cookies.

Bending low, he offered the cookies. "My mother made these."

"Mr Berigou's mother is a noble woman." The Marabout smiled. "She has traveled twice to Mecca."

Daisy took a bite. "Delicious!"

Mr Berigou backed away, leaving them alone.

"This man you speak of," the Marabout said. "I have heard of him. Why are Christians attracted so strongly to our desert, Moha?"

"They come to the desert to experience physical pain in the belief it will abolish mental anguish."

"And why do they wish to endure that which most people seek to avoid?"

"Because in America, Sidna, also in Europe, life has become too rich. The pain is still there, and the fear of dying, but for many the anguish is a moral one because comforts have extinguished the need of God. The anxiety of eking out a daily existence has been eradicated. The Duke came to the desert to live beneath the stars, to know physical hardship, and to experience the life his ancestors lived. He wanted his body to suffer so his soul could begin to live."

The Marabout poured the tea. "What has become of this man I cannot say. He may have been abducted by one of the wandering tribes that pass along the Hammada. Those tribes are known to take and exchange hostages among themselves."

"Is it possible he may still be alive?"

"We have infrequent contact with these nomads. In the course of their wanderings they sometimes act as escorts to caravans, a duty which some combine with a bent for raiding, their favorite occupation at all times. I would fear for this man's safety if he fell into the hands of one of these tribes, as the arrival of the Americans has stirred them to a hatred of foreigners, but I have not heard of any Christian traveler being killed."

Cradling a melon in both hands, Mr Berigou returned. Kneeling, he placed it respectfully on the carpet near the Marabout's foot.

"Have you ever, in all your life," he exclaimed, "laid your eyes on such a magnificent specimen? Look at it now. You might never see another like it. Not only did I rise early this morning and go to the oasis to lift it from its patch so the hands of no city dweller might touch it, I kept is guarded this whole hot day in the bottom of my well."

The Marabout smiled at Daisy.

"This melon is ice cold." From his robe Mr Berigou drew a dagger, eliciting an alarmed rustle and clatter of weapons from the bodyguards who had moved from the staircase to the wall. The Marabout calmed them with a wave of his hand.

"Now, what shall it be?" Mr Berigou said, sliding the dagger from its sheath. "Shall we push our thumbs and faces into fat chunks like the ravenous oasis boys do, or shall we cut it into fourths, eighths, sixteenths or thirty-seconds.?" He waved the curved blade at the new moon floating in a pink glow above the Koutoubia tower. "And nibble fastidiously on slivers as delicate as that?"

The Marabout leaned toward Daisy. "Keep the head warm at night. Beware the *lefâa*. Go to the *zawiya* at Hnabu. The brotherhood will assist your enquiries."

CHAPTER 34

The Rogue

The Americans had moved into the desert in force and established what they termed a "safety net" over southern Morocco while food was distributed. Net it was, full of holes. The foreign press reported young fighters arriving from all over the Muslim world eager to repel the unwanted invaders. Among them were the sharp-shooting "she wolves" from Chechnya, blond hair leaking from beneath their turbans. Some of these Soviet-trained biathlon athletes had won medals in the Olympic Games.

While Moroccan troops kept the cities in the north under marshal law, Muslim propaganda that the desert regions were to be forcibly converted to Christianity roused the Saharan populations to a ferment of xenophobia. However, a few skirmishes convinced the resistants that dune buggies were no match for the helicopter. The rebellion seemed to collapse overnight as the fighters melted away into the desert, buried their arms and waited. The tribesmen turned their attention to the next agricultural season, and for the next few months an uneasy stalemate prevailed. Conflict was clearly not going to achieve American aims, and many palms were greased to secure compliance. Huge sums were handed out by the various US-sponsored relief organizations.

In times of emergency the rival shaikhs ultimately deferred to the judgment of the Marabouts, or grand masters of the Sufi brotherhoods, who wielded both religious and secular power across Morocco. In the desert these groups embraced up to three-quarters of the population, and few Saharans did not have some relationship with them.

The most influential of these Marabouts was Sidi Mohamed ould Brahim, grand master of the Jilaliya. His *Zawiya* at Khettamia, deep in the Sahara, was a center for the propagation of Sufi doctrine. For his followers he was the embodiment of a holiness that exudes *baraka*.

Baraka is a potent word in Morocco, with multiple meanings, including grace, charisma and good luck. In the case of a Marabout it implies an invincible spirituality gained through a reputation for strict morality, intelligence, physical prowess, even personal charm. The concentration in a single individual of the multiple definitions of one word is considered an expression of something verging on the superhuman, both holy and godly. The blind obedience accorded to this warrior monk provided him with an army of fanatical followers. His *baraka* gave him such prestige among the brotherhoods that the Americans could not hope to achieve their aims without his approval, or removal.

The Americans therefore congratulated themselves when they persuaded the Marabout to go to Madrid for talks. The letter which Daisy delivered from Jàafar Tazi confirmed an agreement with the U.S. military command to call off the summer campaign against Attaland. This was the Marabout's fundamental condition for leaving his mountain retreat. A cease-fire was declared in his absence. The fighting, except for a few outbursts, died down. Under a pretext of normalcy, the Sahara was re-opened for travel. Daisy, flush with the cash advance from the Duchess, flew over the Atlas in a chartered Cessna.

CHAPTER 35

Tafilalet

The Tafilalet – that green street of palms which leads from the foot-hills of the Atlas to the furnace of the Sahara – holds an important emotional appeal to Moroccans, for it is the cradle of the Alawids, the Sultan's tribe. Rfud, the principal town, numbers a few thousand souls, plus nomadic traders who come and go. Their tents form a semi-permanent camp on the edge of desert. The major importance of Rfud is that it sits astride an ancient caravan route between Fez and Timbuktu. Formerly known as Sijilmassa, it has been on the maps since the Middle Ages. According to Leo the African, a Muslim historian from Andalucia, it was founded by a Roman general who called it *Sigillum Massae*.

From Timbuktu came camel trains laden with gold-dust, ivory, ostrich feathers and, above all, slaves. Slaves and gold, gold and slaves were the life-blood of trade between Morocco and the Sudan. The gold was mined or panned chiefly in Ghana (the Gold Coast), the slaves brought direct from the Sudan. The girls from the Hausa country fetched the best prices, being considered cleaner and more cheerful than those from the west. The prices averaged from thirty to forty Spanish dollars for a boy but up to one hundred and twenty dollars for strong young girls.

Daisy arrived *hors de saison*, when the heat enervates and often crushes. She checked into the Hotel Zizi, a tiny establishment boasting three bedrooms and running water. The next morning she was informed that Captain Keller was waiting in the bar.

In retaliation for their last meeting, she made him wait half an hour while she dolled herself up. Turbanned and reeking of Mrakshi scent, eyes shaded with kohl, she came downstairs in a blue Saharan robe magically picked out with golden thread.

"Good morning, captain." She extended her hand. "This is quite a surprise … or is it?" she added in a mocking tone. "I suppose your spies told you I was here."

Keller was about to shake the proffered hand. Every square inch of it, he noticed, was intricately patterned with red dye. He brought his fingers to within a few inches before changing his mind.

"Afraid of catching something, captain? Don't look so worried – it's only henna."

He squared his shoulders. "Rfud's a small place. There's very little that I don't hear about – like throwing money out the window of the Hotel Mamounia in Marrakesh."

"You must have ears like that fennec over there."

He signalled the waiter. "Would you like a beer, Miss Adams?"

"Do you think I take beer for breakfast? *Un cafe con leche*, Paco, *con pan tostado. Por favor.*"

"You speak Spanish too, do you?"

They went to a table and sat down.

"I hear you've been in Paris." Keller produced a pack of cigarettes.

Daisy took from her satchel a hideous wrinkled pouch that had once been the belly of the spiny-tailed lizard. She sprinkled a mixture of kif and black tobacco onto a cigarette paper. "In Paris I only dreamed of the Sahara. Now I'm back."

"You're smoking that stuff now, are you?"

"Hemp, as they say in Tangier, is good for asthma."

"I wouldn't touch it with a ten foot pole."

"It relaxes the muscles around the bronchial tubes."

"You've come the wrong time of the year."

"Have I?" Daisy pretended to be absorbed in rolling her cigarette. "Is tracing a loved one a seasonal occupation?"

"The heat is infernal."

"There are few flies, I've noticed. Those that are move slowly. They can be swatted easily."

Keller glanced at the big thermometer above the bar, where it presided over a collection of stuffed snakes and sand lizards. Beside a trumpet-eared fennec with glass eyes a dusty, moth-eaten jackal lifted his head in a silent, everlasting howl. The thermometer registered 40°C (103° F).

He took out a handkerchief and mopped his brow. "This heat is … "

"Delicious. It dries out my lungs. I breathe better here. It strips me of desire but for the essential – the right clothes, the right food, the right life … I killed a tarantula this morning."

The captain looked startled. "A real one?"

"What'd you think it was – a fake rubber one? Tarantulas like wood. It was on the window sill." She slashed the air with the edge of her hand. "I whacked it with my sandal." She produced the *mechero* and fired up.

Daisy's face was slightly flushed, which led Keller to think she had been drinking in her room. (OK – she'd had a nip of the Old Cornstalk before heading downstairs.) Her ambiguous appearance fascinated him. One of her palms was tattooed with a fish, the other with an eye that seemed to wink at him when she closed and opened her hand. At the same time he was irritated by the arrogance of her opinions.

"Forgive me, captain. I'm in one of my moods. It's because I'm happy to be here, even though my mission may be a sad one."

Keller was prepared to give her the benefit of the doubt. This haughty, potent young woman confused him. He disliked the way she dressed, but her gamine look excited him enormously.

"I want to help you," he heard himself saying. "I want to be your friend."

"That sounds charitable." Daisy placed both elbows on the table and blew a smoke ring. "Where do we start?"

Paco brought the coffee.

Daisy, chin in hand, dropped in a lump of sugar, stirred and waited.

"I'm throwing a Fourth of July party."

"I love fireworks."

"We don't want to give the wrong impression – that we're breaking the cease-fire."

"Will Slimane be there?"

Keller's face stiffened.

Daisy frowned. "He's still your orderly, isn't he?"

"Not any more … "

"What happened to him?"

"I let him go."

"You said he was the best orderly you ever had!"

"He was."

"What happened?"

"After you left … "

"I know what you're going to say. It's my fault, isn't it?"

"I didn't say that."

"Isn't it! He ironed your shirts! He mixed your drinks! He ran your bath – and mine! He set your table! He cut your hair! He boiled your eggs … did he shave you? Did he trim your toenails and darn your socks?" Daisy's face was now bright red. "Did he get my letters?"

Keller was silent.

"Don't tell me they didn't arrive!"

"How would I know?" he answered blandly.

"You must know because I didn't know where to send them so I sent them in care of *you*!"

Keller struggled to keep his composure.

"All winter in freezing cold Paris writing letters to Slimane. It was my only consolation. The fact that he might not have gotten them – and you did – it's too much!" She walloped the table top with the flat of her hand, making the coffee cups jump. "Did you intercept them? Did you read them? Did you burn them? Don't you see how unjust this is?" Kohl-blackened tears were rolling down her cheeks. "Oh my God! I'm sorry! I want to be friends, too. Just tell me where he is. I don't give a fuck about the goddamned letters. Where is he?"

She wiped her eyes with the back of her hand, smearing the kohl. "I heard he was sent to Marrakesh."

"Marrakesh! I was just there!" Daisy snatched up the *mtui* and got to her feet. "We drove past the Moroccan barracks on the way to the airport. I thought, maybe he's here. Should I go in and ask? Yesterday he was a few yards away. Now it's five hundred miles!"

She circled the table and stood, hands on hips, looking down. "I wish you hadn't got mad at him. It was a good job, no matter how degrading. I'm sure it's all my fault."

She walked away.

"Will you be coming July the Fourth?" he called.

"That all seems beside the point now," she answered without looking back. "I'll think about it."

CHAPTER 36

House-Hunting

Determined to find a place where Keller couldn't get at her, Daisy called on Moïses Cohen in his yogurt shop. He gripped her hands in both of his and looked into her eyes. The unexpected warmth of the old man's greeting brought home the reality that it had been a long time since she had had someone to hold.

"I have a surprise."

She had thought she heard a baby whimpering in the back of the shop. Mr. Cohen opened a door. A huge beast leapt out. His paws were on Daisy's shoulders, his tongue all over her face.

She hugged with all her might. "Where did you find him?"

"He found me. I was standing in front of the shop. My neighbor ran by carrying a gun. 'Where are you going?' I asked. 'What are you doing with that gun?'

"'A big black dog has run in from the desert and is scaring the children. He might have rabies. I'm going to shoot him before someone gets bitten!' We saw the dog. Before my neighbor could take aim I called out, 'Elvis!' He came running. Your dog is not wild, my child, nor is he completely tame."

Daisy held Mr. Cohen in a long embrace. Elvis wanted to join in.

"Thanks to you, my little family is complete."

She paid him the two hundred dollars plus interest. His syce would bring Uncle Bernon and Rucio in the morning.

Leaving the shop in the care of an infant helper, Mr. Cohen took her to a Moroccan with a mass of keys attached to his belt. This "man of many dwellings," led them along a path through the oasis. Daisy was bewildered by the maze of tracks. Where a wall had collapsed she caught a glimpse of a shiny canal. She liked the way huge sunflowers leaned over the wall and turned their sunny faces to her, like friendly neighbors.

At the edge of the trees, where the ever-expanding native quarter spilled into the wadi, they approached a heavy gate, armored with nipple-shaped studs and reinforced with timber. There was a rattle getting it open. Daisy wondered if she were renting a castle.

Ten feet tall and six feet wide, the gate swung on creaking hinges into a dusty courtyard. A looping grapevine crept along a framework of eucalyptus beams, supported by a row of palm trunk pillars, into the heady embrace of a pink-blossomed Liane de Floride.

The gate dwarfed the house. It had just two rooms – one for sleeping, one for living, with the cooking done outside. The place was dusty but clean. No electricity, no running water, not one stick of furniture. The floor of the front room was tiled but the other of earth. The ceiling, fashioned from eucalyptus strips arranged in a pleasing herringbone pattern, was supported by sagging palm beams. An alcove concealed the toilet – the usual crude footprints in a basin.

While Muslim and Jew haggled over the rent, the Christian/Jewess/Muslim, secretly thrilled, paced and inspected. Her mother was right: you make up your mind the first minute! She must have this desert nest – at any price! The shed in the corner of the *riad* would do for Uncle Bernon and Rucio. More than anything it was the *riad* that cast a spell. A well, shaded by a palm, was surrounded by a circular drinking trough. She picked up a pebble and dropped it in.

Yes!

A palm log with steps hacked into it led to the roof. She bounded up and beheld the desert.

"Mister Keys" refused to budge on price but agreed to have the well cleaned. As Moïses Cohen pointed out, a man (or woman) can survive without electricity or the telephone. He or she can get along *sans voiture*, TV, but life without fresh water is not only impossible *mais inimaginable*! On this point there was general agreement. The water was good, the Muslim pledged – clean, fresh and cool. Better to have it tested, the Jew cautioned, in case sewage leaked in from exterior channels.

He handed Daisy the key – about eight inches long, hand-made, crudely wrought but smooth from ancient use and weighing half a pound – and advised her to wear it on a rope around her waist.

CHAPTER 37

Shopping

With Elvis at her side, Daisy made her way to the main square of the town. It was market day, with the nomads and oasis dwellers arriving by camel and donkey, in the dust and the heat, to display and sell their wares. The women, bare-foot and burdened, trailed behind.

The first thing was a collar and leash. Moroccans do not generally keep dogs as pets; they train them to be watchdogs, fierce and noisy. Due to rabies fear, stray dogs are often shot on sight.

The American effort had alleviated some of the worst effects of the famine, but still to be seen were appalling examples of human suffering. By the market gate a line of blind beggars swayed and chanted like a chorus of the dead. Skeletal hands rattled stones in tin cups. Enfeebled children were on display. Too weak to rise, with huge heads and stringy, shrivelled limbs, they cowered on sheets of plastic like stranded octopi expiring in the dust.

Daisy opened her purse and distributed coins.

Her outing was assisted by Caftan, a teenage *asuqi*, or "frequenter of the market," who cleared a path through the swarm of urchins clamoring to carry her basket.

"This market takes place on Tuesdays, Thursdays and Saturdays." Caftan spoke with the authority of a guide. "It's a late market and doesn't get underway until noon, so there's no point in arriving early."

In this he proved to be correct, which confirmed Daisy's view that she must ally herself with Moroccans.

With children starving outside, the market was bursting with food. Daisy was astonished by the amount of fresh produce, attractively displayed by the diligent Berber grocers.

"This is the vegetable market, where you can buy blue desert onions. For melons you must go to Rsani, as these are inferior. But beware of desert types!" Caftan warned as they entered another shopping square. "They steal everything!"

The women clustered around her, touching and exclaiming. Their flamboyant way of dressing and lively smiling faces, prettily tattooed, contrasted strongly with the sombre backdrop of the desert and belied the life of drudgery they endured. They performed all the housework, did the cooking, fetched water from the well, minded the cattle, collected firewood and took vegetables to market – in fact every duty except ploughing seemed to fall to their lot.

Sacks of American flour were being sold right from under the nose of a tough-looking American soldier. Each sack was stamped with the message:

FROM THE PEOPLE OF THE UNITED STATES OF AMERICA
TO THE PEOPLE OF MOROCCO

Corruption and venality were common throughout the Moroccan political system; government officials routinely confiscated food aid destined for the needy, sold it to the highest bidder, and pocketed the proceeds. Everybody knew, but nobody did anything about it.

Caftan summoned Mohamed, a carter, who loaded the purchases aboard his decrepit vehicle. He insisted she buy a scrawny chicken in a wicker cage.

"Do not feed this chicken. This is the stinging season. Sleeping on the floor, you may be menaced by crawling insects – the scorpion, the centipede, the tarantula. A hungry chicken will drive away these pests. The dreaded *lefâa* will not settle near this house with a hungry chicken on the loose."

By now she had sized up her new acquaintance. Strong, smart, spirited, and attractive, in America Caftan would be at the top of his class. He exuded the immortal optimism of youth. A born entrepreneur. But with little education, no job and few prospects, he was probably condemned to be an *asuqi* for the rest of his life.

Indoors was an oven; she had to be on the roof to feel the first shadows of night. She stretched out on the mat and gazed into the depths of the sky, where stars winked on one by one.

A dog barked. Elvis moaned. Tethered in the courtyard, Rucio uttered a cry like tortured sobbing, to be answered by a donkey down the wadi.

Even little Rucio had a love life, Daisy mused, or dreamed of one. A love-sick donkey is a terrible sight.

CHAPTER 38

The Tortoise

Forbes Magazine dubbed Duncan van Renseelaer "the Tortoise of Wall Street" because he plodded on to success while the quick-starters fell by the wayside. A shrewd and patient financier, he bought up failing companies for a song, stripped their assets and invested in other more successful companies he had acquired. He created the first "conglomerate," in which he sat atop a pyramid of companies under his control. His particular perch was President of The Buffalo Fibers Company, with offices in Brooklyn, where they ostensibly manufactured rope for tugboats. In reality Buffalo was a holding company with controlling interests in other much larger corporations which formed the foundation of the pyramid, all of which the Tortoise profitably managed.

The Tortoise never gave interviews, scorned any kind of luxury, drove himself to work in a Dodge Dart (one of his companies supplied spark plugs for GM), and preferred to work in secrecy. A short, balding, non-descript figure in a permanently rumpled suit (some of his own employees thought he was the janitor) he packed his boards with yes-men and over the years made a pile of money for himself, his relations and his friends.

The Tortoise was the largest contributor to the Republican Party in the State of New York. He supported the deportation of Latinos and gerrymandering. He advocated legislation to push back social security to make room for the reduction of taxes on the super-rich.

Even before Arturo's knock on the door, he had come around to the conclusion that he had once held in his arms the most beautiful of women – mother of his two children and the most exotic, the most vivacious, the most talented and the most loving of wives –

and he had thrown it all away after a golfing trip to Spain, where he learned that the name "Toledano" did not strictly apply to one who hailed from that historic city, but was a Sepharic family name from ancient days.

Via a series of exasperating transatlantic telephone calls, Arturo finally succeeded in persuading Miss Maplethope to prod Mr. Jacobi into coughing up Daisy's forwarding address. But by the time his letter, with the news that after all these years he had been reunited with their father, reached the Hotel Lisbonne, rue de Vaugirand, Paris 6ième, the girl had bolted. The missive was returned, unopened, inside another envelope containing Daisy's unpaid bill, along with an irate note from the manager. Arturo immediately sent a money order covering the debt. A few days later he telephoned the hotel. The manager, in a more conciliatory mood, reported that Daisy had run off with a Moroccan waiter. He knew nothing more.

He thanked Arturo for settling up.

It was not long after the knock on the door that the interview which Daisy had given to *The Herald Tribune* at the Chance Bar in Tangier was reprinted in *The New York Times*. Arturo spotted it and brought it to his father. The Tortoise, in a perverse paroxysm of parental pride, curiously common in absentee dads, showed it to all his friends.

The Tortoise expressed no interest in going back in time. That his daughter was in Paris was enough; he did not inquire what she was doing there. That his son was in New York was enough. He offered to buy him an apartment on Sutton Place, but Arturo felt more comfortable at the Chelsea Hotel on West 23rd Street. The Tortoise put him up for membership at the River Club, but Arturo didn't own a necktie, let alone a blue blazer or a business suit. An account was opened at Brooks Brothers, but Arturo went on buying his clothes at the Army Navy Store. A position was created on the board of Buffalo Fibers, but Arturo never turned up for a meeting. Father and son were reunited, but Arturo made no demands, and the Tortoise felt relief.

CHAPTER 39

Transhumance

The money from the Duchess finally arrived. Liberated from that anxiety, Daisy saddled up Uncle Bernon and set out for Hnabu, the Jilaliya monastery in the desert. Surrounded by tombs, the dullness of the walls contrasted with the richness of its roof. Glistening in the sun, the green glazed tiles could be seen from miles away.

She rode into the courtyard. The hour was noon, with the sun pouring out of a white hot sky. Nothing moved – not dogs or birds or humans. A naked child flopped in the dust.

Ducking under a low archway, Daisy saw nothing until her eyes adjusted to the gloom. A body materialized, lying on a bench. All that was visible were his teeth, encased within an emaciated jaw, and the whites of his eyes. A flimsy robe covered fleshless limbs.

For a minute she thought he was dead.

Raising himself up like a reanimated corpse, he took her letter and dematerialized. Daisy rested on a bench beneath the intricately patterned ceiling. Darting geckoes peeked down from hairy palm beams.

Relieved from the furnace of the midday sun, she shut her eyes. Within the thick mud walls of the monastery she did not feel the heat. The temperature of the air and her body was the same. She was neither hot nor cold. There was no resistance, no sensation of air. She felt at one with the unchanging world of Islam.

From the far side of the courtyard the nasal wail of an Arab flute oozed like oil through the heat and silence. A hoarse male voice was speaking Arabic.

The music came to an end, and silence, like a blanket, returned. The rustling of lizards caused her to look up. The child had crept in.

Daisy gazed with pity at the chubby brown face, encrusted with flies. Beckoning her forward, she brushed the insects away and wiped her eyes with her turban. Why did her mother and father fail to do this? Didn't they know trachoma blinds for life?

The figure standing before her explained that the monks had taken their flocks to the mountains for summer grazing. Handing back the letter, he apologized that the monastery was temporarily vacant.

Remounting Uncle Bernon, Daisy felt crushed by the futility of her quest. The unrelenting African sun was sapping her strength. No one knew anything about Arturo or about the Duke. Nobody cared, and nobody was going to help. This weakness she felt, it was like death. Why brush the flies from the child's face when they would return the next minute?

Moroccans say that to swat one fly in winter is like killing a thousand in summer.

On the track back to Rfud, she stopped to water Uncle Bernon at one of those springs that miraculously occur in the desert. Insufficient to support human habitation, the water trickles with a magic sound from beneath a rock and is led for a few yards by man-made furrow to slake the thirst of a few palms that have been planted or taken root close to the source. There the water disappears, absorbed by the sands. What at first seemed to be an isolated clump of palms was in fact the first of a "string of emeralds," a chain of tiny oases watered by an underground aquifer. Hidden in deep ravines eroded from the flat desert plain, the narrow little gardens were invisible until Uncle Bernon nearly stumbled into a ravine where the fronds of fully-grown palms fluttered at his feet.

She led Uncle Bernon into a depth of palms where she dismounted, dropped onto a pile of shady sand, and fell instantly asleep.

A falling rock caused her to wake. A man was leading a donkey down the zigzagging path from the desert roof into the well of the ravine. He came on slowly, for the path was steep. The donkey, its bulky load rocking from side to side, made stiff, braking steps down the narrow incline.

In this time of *siba* Daisy avoided men on her solitary rides. Her Arabic was improving but her disguise fooled few. The natural courtesy of her Moroccan neighbors in the oasis admitted that, if she wished to pass as a man, she should be treated as such; but she worried that by dressing as a man and speaking imperfect Arabic could have the opposite effect in the desert. This was Attaland, where outsiders were suspected as infidel intruders who interfered with tribal prerogatives. To know the language might be interpreted as desiring to eavesdrop; to dress as a man meant wanting to infiltrate the world of men; and to espouse the Muslim faith could be taken as a cringing lie. In the current atmosphere of hostile suspicion the result of such deception could be rape, or murder, or both.

The man stopped by the rivulet to water his animal. Laying down a heavy stick, he did not see Daisy but spotted Uncle Bernon among the palms. Daisy fingered the Ruger.

His gaze now ranged the mini-oasis, seeking the owner, but he did not see her crouching behind the hill of sand. Apparently satisfied the coast was clear, he unwrapped the turban from his face and knelt over the rivulet.

Daisy's heart thumped. It was Slim!

"*Salaam aleikoum!*" she called, conscious that Muslims do not welcome holy words from other than Muslim lips.

"Good evening," came the reply. "Why do you shout?"

Stepping from behind the dune she sat down on a fallen palm. "In the desert, I am told, it is best to be bold!" she intoned in her deepest voice.

"Then peace to you. If there is peace left in the desert, let it be here."

Daisy's own turban was drawn across her face, leaving only a slit for eyes. That he did not recognize her – her or her voice – excited her.

"This water is good," she said.

"Then my animal and I will like it, if your horse does not drink it all."

He flopped down on his belly and drank. He had been taken in by her disguise. Hands shaking, Daisy took out the *mtui*.

He watched her roll the cigarette. "Who are you?" he asked in a voice that had become suspicious.

"A student." She answered after a minute. She lit the cigarette. "From Tangier."

He sniffed the air. "So that's where you picked up that nasty habit."

"Ever been there?"

"I have a friend. He ... she told me about it."

"He? She?" Daisy managed her gruffest laugh. "Well, my boy, which one is it?" His grumpy humor told her he still loved her. She had the upper hand now.

Unable to pretend any more, she pulled the turban from her face. "Slim! I'm Moha!"

They stood facing each other across the rivulet. The last time they had been together, they made love. Snuggling for warmth beneath her burnoose they talked of the future. This time they didn't even shake hands. The rivulet was a foot wide; it might as well have been the Suez Canal.

"So, Moha, are you still riding around Morocco?"

"Did you get my letters?"

"You said you would write."

"I did write! From Tangier, from Spain, from Paris!"

"I didn't get any letters."

"That mother-fucker. What about our vegetable garden?"

"Come. I'll show you."

Leading their animals through the palms, they came to a place where an old man with a snow-white beard was tilling with a hoe, diverting the rivulet to plots of vegetables. White cattle egrets followed the flow, deftly darting to skewer the worms forced by the water from their holes.

"Late afternoon is the hour to irrigate," Slim was saying. "Now the earth will remain cool and damp through the night."

The old man stood up and saluted.

"That's Musa. We call him Papa Noel."

They exchanged salaams.

"We're growing tomatoes, broad beans, and cucumbers – vegetables rarely seen in the desert."

"Slim, you're making our dream come true!"

"The barley we planted in February. The plowing was finished by mid-March. The whole of that month was devoted to irrigation of the plots. In April we planted potatoes, corn, and in May alfalfa. In June turnips. Now we irrigate the corn, potatoes, alfalfa and turnips, and harvest the grains. The whole cycle begins again in November. August and September is the slack season between harvesting and plowing. It's the time for weddings."

"That's now."

"When there is much water, each farmer may irrigate for five days. When there is little water, five days are not enough and each farmer may take two days extra. But there are fines for taking water out of turn and for breaking the rules. When I get out of the army I plan to open a grocery store. Right now we're renting a stall in the market. Musa takes our tomatoes in the morning."

"I go to market every day, but I've never seen tomatoes like these."

"Captain Keller buys the lot."

"We must detach our fortunes from that man."

"All I need is a little capital … "

"I'm going to help you get it."

"Come on. Papa Noel will make tea."

Within a clump of palms a breezy gazebo of latticed cane had been erected. The earth had been swept and a mat laid down. Slim's bike leaned against a tree. The water ran in little ditches all around.

Daisy shed her boots and sat cross-legged on the mat. "Can we spend the night here?"

As Papa Noel passed her a glass of smoky green tea, their eyes met. A glimmer of recognition lit, for an instant, those dull old African eyes. A flaccid lip lifted. Two or three teeth appeared, like tombstones leaning at crazy angles in an abandoned cemetery. Then the mask of Africa came down. The water in the ditches, meanwhile, was turning to rubies in the setting sun. The egrets flew away to their tree.

Slim's mother had bought this plot of land. She had sent Papa Noel, a family retainer whose wife had recently died, to plant vegetables so her son would have fresh things to eat while he was far from home.

After supper the lovers went for a walk. The silence of the desert blotted out the noisiness of man. Moonlight slid among the palms like the milky sunlight of another planet. The palms reared their plumed heads like massive dark flowers of that planet.

They stopped by a reservoir being filled by a green pump.

"What a beautiful pump!"

"It's a Lister. It's English."

The silver water poured into the tank. It took five hours to fill. Either Slim or Papa Noel had to get up with the clock to shut down the Lister. In the morning there would be a reservoir full for irrigation. Slim played his flashlight over the water foaming into the basin. Clean water, but it must be boiled before drinking. One never knew if a dog or donkey had fallen into the canal. They watched turtles mating in a separate tank. Bump bump. Holding hands, they counted the turtles. Eleven in all. The odd one got left out.

Poor little turtle! No one to love!

Upon waking from a bed of love, having passed the night with her sweet, affectionate husband-to-be, feeling refreshed and naked inside, relieved of tension and, for reasons she could not define, free, Daisy was ready to return to her quest with a considerate heart and open mind. What had been locked up yesterday was released today. Like a puff of smoke, her frustration was whisked away, and once more she felt prepared to face the open horizon.

They decided to get married right away. Why wait? They picked the Fourth of July for two reasons: Slim had the day off from the army, and it gave Daisy an excuse not to go to Keller's party.

The *qadi* (judge) drew up a marriage document. She had no idea what she was signing.

CHAPTER 40

Hammam

Daisy consulted her neighbor Waffa about her obligations and was told that at the very least her body must be clean.

In the dry heat of the desert Daisy did not sweat, she evaporated. The Moroccans did not appear to sweat. The ones who stank were the Americans because they ate so much meat. She had been advised against bathing in the desert, the reason being that soap and water robbed the skin of essential oils which, when combined with the dust that entered everywhere, protected it against the sun.

Nevertheless she looked forward to being really clean. The morning of the wedding she and Waffa walked hand in hand to the *hammam*.

Diminutive Waffa had all her teeth, and when she smiled, all of Africa seemed to smile with her. Her hair had been braided into tiny plaits with red tassels woven. Solid silver earrings were supported by chains hooked into the wool. You could have slid a pencil through the holes heavy jewelry had tugged in her lobes. Silver necklaces were draped across her chest; silver bracelets decorated ankles and wrists – wedding presents from multiple husbands who had skedaddled years ago. How silver jewelry graces African skin! From head to toe she dressed in black; when she went out she draped a square of gauzy black veil over her head. She walked with a reassuring clank and gave off mingling odors of sandalwood and smoke.

The *hammam* was a windowless, domed structure near the market square. Daytime reserved for women, nights for men. Inside, water was running everywhere, with waxy bodies writhing in the gloom. In the warm room, one tremendously fat old woman was being washed down by a team of girls. Mothers patiently scrubbed their children, while one woman lay on her side by the wall, cheek on hand, snoring gently.

The hot room rang with laughter. Completely naked teenage girls – pointy breasts sticking straight out – were swinging from bars and wrestling on the floor. Daisy was coming round to the opinion that in Morocco the best color to be was black: it provided anonymity and protection from the sun. White skin attracted attention and showed the dirt.

"They're young – they're not thinking about tomorrow," Waffa commented. "They'll be married off to complete strangers, probably older men. They'll be condemned to twenty pregnancies, abortions, miscarriages, childbirth, child death, and child rearing. They'll be expected to perform back-breaking chores while their husbands sit in cafés, or till the land, if they have any."

To Daisy it was clear that in Morocco the division of labor was grossly unequal: the women worked considerably longer hours than their men. This seemed to be a basic cultural fact, especially in rural Morocco. Nevertheless, the sight of these carefree girls lifted her heart. This was why she was beginning to love Africa – Waffa's radiant smile and the girls' light-hearted spirits in face of adversity. Amid shouts for water and general hilarity, empty buckets rolled about, and streams of suds slid toward the drains. In this women-only world everything was shared, and made life jollier.

Bathed in the light of a single candle, the marble floor of the very hot room reflected an oily gleam. Undressing, Waffa displayed a pair of pendulous breasts that waggled when she walked.

"Your husband is going to love you tonight." She gave Daisy a little peck on the neck.

Waffa summoned two women – professional washers whose bodies after years in the baths had developed the supple shine of eels.

Smooth feet trod on Daisy's back, forcing her to release her air. They laid her naked body across their knees, stretched her limbs, flipped her over and cracked her spine.

Following the exercises, they doused her with warm water and rubbed her skin with disks of palm wood. The massage, along with the heat and exercise, combined to open her pores. The eel-women grinned at the appearance of the hidden dirt, which they flushed away with buckets of water.

Shampoo followed soap. After submitting to having her bush shaved, Daisy was led to the center of the room and made to squat. Bucket after bucket was sloshed over her. Buckets of hotter and hotter water were filled from the smoking spigots and slid cross the floor. Hot water became warm, turned cool, then ice cold. She was gasping for breath.

Waffa led the way to a private room where they stretched out on mats. Towels were wrapped around, sections of orange offered. The languid after-effect of the bath, the soft towel, the fresh taste of orange and, above all, the sense of being exquisitely clean, seemed luxurious.

The day after a wedding is solitary. The privacy of the happy couple is respected; they are allowed to sleep late. Daisy opened her eyes and noticed a large insect clinging to the wall above the bed. As she lay there, half asleep, she pondered what move to make. Should she poke it with a broom? The bug began to feel its way along the ceiling. If it fell now, it would land on Slim and wake him. She let it crawl a little further before grabbing the bug bomb and rolling a newspaper. Thus armed, she gassed the beast. When it hit the floor she pounded it with the paper.

Slim woke up.

"What is it?"

"A cockroach."

He went back to sleep.

A little while later they were woken by the sound of drumming.

"The Jilaliya are here!" Papa Noel called from the courtyard.

Daisy climbed the ladder to see a parade passing near the village. Led by a man in a green robe, a procession of horsemen filed among the dunes. The thunder of drums was accompanied by the warbling cries of women who had swarmed to the rooftops.

Slim joined her on the roof.

"That's Sidi Mohamed, commander of the Jilaliya." Daisy pointed at the man riding in front. "He's been to Madrid for talks."

Slim frowned. "Do you know that dervish?"

"We've played parcheesi twice – once in Tangier and once in Marrakesh."

After the horsemen came the Marabout's massed followers, whirling to the chattering rhythm of the Jilaliya beat. Some dancers threw clay pots into the air. The pots crashed on their heads. They spun around, spattering the others with holy blood.

She was startled by a blubbering sound. Slim was shaking his head from side to side. There were flecks of saliva on his cheeks.

"What are you doing? What's wrong?"

Her husband's face had turned ashen. His whole body was trembling, his feet kicking out of control. He was having some kind of fit. She hugged and held him until his body was still.

"Dervish! It makes me sick to watch! Look at those blood-stained fanatics. They're crazy!"

Waffa and the neighbors, who had crowded the rooftops to watch the procession, were laughing at the newly-weds, whom they thought were embracing on the roof.

Looking somehow smaller, Slim pedalled off to the barracks. The sight of her husband foaming at the mouth made her realize she knew next to nothing about the man she had married. Did he love her? She remembered Madame Zizou's words on the subject. Did it matter? She lay down and slept for another hour.

Waffa served coffee in the *riad*. Asthmatics know what relief caffeine can bring. Daisy loved her adobe house which she dubbed *Darna* (our home), especially the privacy of the *riad*. And the language of the constantly dripping fountain around which the green-thumbed Papa Noel was cultivating a circle of blood-red geraniums. Mosquito fish swam and wasps drank from the pool; the timid sparrows *(t'beeb)* whirred in for a bath.

Uncle Bernon and Rucio stamped in the shed. Elvis sprawled on the tiles. A black dog suffers in summer.

Papa Noel slept on a pile of sheepskins outside the door. He swept the *riad*, carried water from the well and brought fresh vegetables from the oasis. Waffa kept the house in order. Each morning she wiped soot from lantern chimneys. Caftan did odd jobs and heavy shopping. Daisy had staff: she was leading a life of elemental luxury, which enabled her to devote herself to writing, so long as the monthly instalments from the Duchess kept coming.

Antonio had died on Christmas Day, two months and one day before his 70th birthday; her mother on September 5th, two months and one day before her 55th birthday. While puzzling over this odd coincidence, Daisy penned a letter to the Marabout.

CHAPTER 41

Zawiya

The procession threaded its way across the desert to the *moussem* at Hnabu. Daisy trailed at a distance on Uncle Bernon.

The great courtyard of the monastery was covered with hundreds of multi-colored carpets. The effect was psychedelic, kaleidoscopic. The monastery reverberated with the sound of drums, flutes, ringing metal castanets, and the chanting from swaying rows of bejewelled, tattooed girls in stupendous native costumes. Daisy felt she was witnessing something absolutely fantastic.

Bees swarmed on the *shabakia* and mint tea.

Entrusting her letter to a child, the rest of the day she passed on a dune, observing the dazzling spectacle from afar. As night fell, bonfires were lit, and the leaping shadows of the dancers were cast on the walls of the *zawiya*. The child returned with a bowl of *bysar* and a chunk of bread. It had been a long day; Daisy ate, she dozed, she slept.

The child was tugging on her sleeve. The music had stopped. Night was closing in. The temperature had dropped several degrees. The desert dogs were barking. Hand in hand they made their way among the exhausted dancers bedding down for the night.

The monastery was unlit, but the confident child led Daisy along a narrow passage that ended in a half-open doorway which emitted a thin veil of light. She peered into a room as big as a barn. In a halo cast by a single candle sat the Marabout. He was alone. Daisy shed her boots and approached. The child vanished.

Daisy settled herself on the carpet while the Marabout held her letter to the candle. The monks could be heard whispering as they tiptoed past the holy chamber. Outside, the wind moaned. A dune was trying to force its way through the keyhole of a massive portal; already it had pushed a finger of orange sand half way across the floor.

The candle flame danced in the draft.

The Marabout's tightly bound turban, his enveloping robe, the soft undergarment, and pair of pointed slippers, arranged side by side, were all of an immaculate whiteness. The lines radiating from his eyes, the creases in his cheeks, the soft gray beard, and above all his sense of resignation soothed Daisy. She felt her anxiety dissolve in the presence of this gentleman-warrior her mother had compared to Robert E. Lee.

He put aside the letter. "The Sahara cannot be home for any outsider but one who passionately wishes it to be so."

"I feel strong here, master. I breathe so well in this dry land."

"We Saharans have a saying about the desert. 'God gave trees to the lands of the north. He gave grass to the lands of the south. For the Sahara He had nothing left, so He gave it His soul.'"

He picked up the letter again. "Are you still writing?"

"Yes, master."

"And what is your book about?"

"The Sahara desert, master, and the people who live in it."

"Do you understand that Sufism is not a philosophical system but a way to purification?"

"I think so, master."

"Our groups are very loose and mobile. Students travel widely seeking teachers, some earning their way, others by begging. Some teachers are also migrants."

"As a child, master, I used to watch the road, a white road that passed by our house in America. It was a dusty lane, weaving toward the unknown. I was already in love with changing horizons and unexplored places."

The Marabout nodded. "Initiation begins with an oath of allegiance."

"I am ready to take that oath."

"Many people seek initiation to establish a relationship with a source of power to use for their own purposes. This, I must warn you, is improper. When a novice joins our order it must be with the intention of renouncing the world. He is subjected to a spiritual discipline for three years. The first year is devoted to the service of the people, the second to the service of God, the third to watching over his own heart."

"And then do I wear the *darbala*?" Daisy asked.

"Not everyone succeeds. The majority of mankind are born deaf to mystical sensitivity. I should tell you the way of the Sufi is not compatible with family life."

"I have no family."

"I understand you have recently married."

"I do not plan to have children."

"You may change your mind about that. Children are a blessing from God."

"My children will be Sufis, master. I will carry them on my back."

"Be that as it may, our way of life attracts people of an adventurous temperament. You may be one of these. The call to explore unknown realms is open to those who have inquiring minds and are prepared to give up comforts."

"I am ready, master."

"Come with me."

He led her from the holy chamber. The monastery was not reserved for a few monks only; its ramparts enclosed a village of covered streets. Figures swathed in black whisked by in the gloom.

The street was blocked by a heavy door. The scents emanating from within told Daisy they were entering the women's quarter.

In a dimly lit courtyard four women were seated together. At the approach of the Marabout, three of them, like so many timid animals, soundlessly departed. The remaining woman sat cross-legged on the floor, holding something in her lap.

"She has been cursed by her father, expelled from her family, and repudiated by her tribe," the Marabout explained.

This woman was young – about seventeen or eighteen, undoubtedly very beautiful, or had been. The narrow bridge of nose, prominent cheekbones and domed forehead perhaps derived from the Ethiopians who, according to geographers of antiquity, once inhabited the Saharan oases. Her lopsided jaw indicated that teeth were missing. Her plum blue skin was more black than blue from the savage beating she had received.

"She has something for you."

The woman fumbled with the string that held a sack. She undid the knot and pulled out a parcel wrapped in blue paper.

"It is for you," the Marabout said.

Daisy accepted the parcel, a book. Her fingers trembled as she folded back the paper. It was a sketch book – bound in red leather. Her heart nearly stopped when she read the words stamped on the cover:

Casa Peira. Barrio Gotico. Barcelona

She turned it over in her hands before opening to the first page. A self-portrait of her brother stared out at her.

"Where is the child?" the Marabout asked.

"Child? Is there a child?"

CHAPTER 42

Dutch Eyes

Three years earlier, almost to the day, at La Clinica Maternal la Mila-grosa, in Agua Prieta, Mexico, Daisy had held another dark-skinned, blue-eyed baby in her arms. For one hour she had been allowed to hug her little boy before he had been whisked away and made to disappear into the arms of an affluent family in Mexico, D.F. – discretely orchestrated by Mrs. Adams to avoid *la vergüenza* in small-town Douglas. Abortion had never been an option; when Daisy saw those blue lights in that little brown face, she understood that her mother had been right.

Those precious moments with her baby, until now only dimly remembered, were suddenly summoned into high relief, as the new babe (a little girl) squirmed in her arms, the soul of Europe peeping from the face of Africa.

This time she vowed not to be robbed of her treasure. Her first instinct was to fight – for both their lives.

Her second was to apologize – profoundly, abjectly – to the Marabout for her brother's shameful, immoral, brutal, selfish and totally unforgivable behavior. In the next breath she was pleading with him to allow her to adopt mother and child. Taking full responsibility for their well-being, she would invite them into her home where she and her husband would look after their every need and raise the child according to the Muslim rite. She would add a new room to her house to accommodate them. As a fresh initiate into the Jilaliya cult, she felt duty-bound to help those less fortunate, especially a woman who had been abused by her own brother!

This emotional plea used up all her energy and half the night until the Marabout gave his consent.

Each morning, while Slimane was on duty, Daisy rode to Hnabu to spend time with her infant niece (Maloudia – for that was the mother's name – still terrified and traumatized by her tortures – retreated like some captive wild animal) and to receive instruction.

The holy men assigned to be her teachers were under no misapprehension as to her sex. If she chose to dress as a man and be known as Moha ben Abdu, the name she had adopted to go with her male disguise, that was her business. In the desert, learning is held in high esteem, and they respected her literary projects. They understood her affinity with the desert.

Daisy became absorbed in her devotion to the Jilalya (and her new family) to the neglect of everything else. The Duchess de Bremont wrote several letters asking if she had turned up any clues as to the whereabouts of her missing husband. When she received no reply, she assumed that Daisy had abandoned her investigations, and the checks stopped coming.

At this point Daisy showed herself to be a true disciple of Antonio Adams. Given his mantra of self-reliance, he would have been exceedingly proud of his step-daughter's resourcefulness. Inclusion in the brotherhood gave her a kind of mystical standing in the desert. Every member of the cult was bound by oath to give her food and shelter, even to risk his life to protect her. This bestowed on her, at the very moment when her income was cut off, the possibility of a completely nomadic existence. She didn't need the Duchess's money, or so she thought. She belonged to the Jilaliya.

Support by the Jilaliya bolstered Daisy's standing among the Moroccans, but Keller was convinced she was nothing but a trouble maker. Heretofore he had tolerated her as an immoral but harmless adventuress. Her reputation of wealth protected her. Now he saw that her inquiries into the fate of the Duke de Bremont could lead to an embarrassment for American policy. The one person who seemed to belong to both sides was Miss Daisy Adams, whose activities he now came to regard as anti-American. In addition, her presence was becoming an unsettling influence among his men. He began to think of ways of how to get rid of her; in the meantime her house in the oasis was declared officially off-limits.

CHAPTER 43

The Dead Hills

One gray November day she found herself in "The Dead Hills," so-called because of the resemblance to grave mounds. These hills were frequented by nomadic hunters – lean, hawk-like men she had seen trailing through the streets of Rfud, shouldering ancient rifles with which they were said to be deadly shots, along with gazelle skins they hoped to sell to Captain Keller. Among them, she was told, numbered deserters from the army and other lurkers from justice who sought refuge in the company of the hunters.

The day was cold. Followed by a tenacious biting wind, she detoured around a crowd of vultures stripping a dead camel.

The range of hills was broader than she expected, their uniformity disorienting. When she had attained yet another disappointing summit, all she could see ahead was more of the same brown hills, with the texture of threadbare rugs. The sky gave off a dull metallic shine, like the bottom of a tin plate.

Nervously fingering the rosary beads pinned to the inside of her burnoose, she accepted the fact she was lost. The sensible course would be to turn back, but that evil little wind was rapidly filling Uncle Bernon's tracks. Like blowing brown snow, the sand was covering and smoothing everything behind her.

She dismounted, sat down on the side of a dune, rolled a cigarette and reviewed her options. If she didn't come home tonight, Slim would go to Hnabu in the morning. Sidi Mohamed would send out trackers. They would find her tomorrow, or the day after tomorrow, but not today.

The hood of her burnoose held half a loaf of bread; she never left home without a bottle of water. These would sustain her through the night. The burnoose and turban would keep her warm. Uncle Bernon had fed that morning. Elvis would have to go without. Had it been high summer, all would have faced problems posed by thirst and dehydration; but the day was cold, and the night, if the wind rose, would be bitterly cold. The prospect of having to spend a night outside did not unduly alarm her; but she knew from experience that in the desert, for all its vast, forlorn emptiness, one is seldom alone.

Gathering twigs, she led Uncle Bernon through the hills. Her aim was to find a sheltered place to light a fire. As they descended into a shallow valley, Elvis whimpered. Uncle Bernon's ears were up. Daisy felt for the Ruger, suspended on a cord beneath her arm. She mounted up and gave Uncle Bernon a free rein.

Setting off at a brisk trot, they descended toward a gully where bushes were growing. Uncle Bernon plunged in and started browsing. Parting the bushes, Daisy found a spring.

She was filling her bottle when Elvis roared. A grotesque individual was pointing a rifle at her.

One beady eye fixed her with a menacing gaze. The other was a watery hole. His head was swathed in a ragged turban; his robe had been patched from a dozen others.

"Who are you?" he demanded fiercely. The high, sing-songy voice identified him as one who lives far from his fellow man.

"I'm lost," she said. "Can you show me the way out of these hills?"

"Name?"

"Moha."

"Not a name!" He prodded her with the rifle. "Where've you come from?"

"Hnabu."

The rifle shook; he suffered from palsy. "What was your business in Hnabu?"

She lifted the corner of her burnoose, exposing the Jilaliya chaplet.

Thin lips parted, exposing a cemetery of broken teeth. "You're one of us," he said, lowering the rifle.

Two young men appeared, carrying between them a pole slung with the carcase of a gazelle.

"My sons," the man said. "Bring your horse. Keep that dog away. You camp with us tonight."

He led the way to a cup-like depression beneath a sheltering ridge. The sons dug into the sand and drew out a teapot, glasses glazed from repeated scourings, a kettle, a bucket, a smoke-blackened pot.

The gazelle was neatly skinned and jointed. No order was given, each man knew his job. Daisy was touched by the elemental industry of these half-wild men providing for themselves in the desert.

Tahar, for that was his name, made bread. While they waited, the old man led his sons in prayer. Their prayer in no way resembled the humble, orthodox mutterings of men lined up in mosques. They didn't go down on their knees. They stood atop a dune and shouted at God. The high trailing voices were suspended in the silence of the evening sky. The chanting seemed to fill the empty space for miles around.

After about three-quarters of an hour, Tahar majestically lifted a large white loaf from the dune. Not one grain of sand was stuck to it. Then, for reasons Daisy did not understand, he rather unceremoniously beat it with a stick before reburying it in cold sand.

Daisy felt comfortable in the company of the palsied old man. His antique Remington notwithstanding, he seemed harmless enough, but his twin sons eyed her with predatory interest. The desert ages men, especially men with lives like theirs. Their identical wedge-shaped faces were swathed with scruffy beards that had never seen a razor. Sharp white teeth contrasted with swarthy complexions. They worked as a team skinning the gazelle. Each held a curved dagger, which they sharpened, one blade against the other. Like paired animals they lifted their faces and sniffed the air. Daisy regretted having doused herself with Mrakshi scent in Hnabu.

When the meat was cooked, the old man ripped the loaf apart, releasing a cloud of steam. Each dipped his piece of bread into the stew. The meat was placed to one side to await the "desert lottery."

While they ate Daisy inquired, in a manner as discrete as possible, if any of them had heard of a Christian being held captive. She did not wish to arouse suspicion by asking too many questions.

The old man cracked a bone between his teeth. "He's in the Jebel Ouarkziz," he answered matter of factly.

Daisy was astonished. "How do you know that?"

"He's with the R'guibat at Tiglite," he replied, noisily sucking out the marrow. "The Blue People poked his eyes out, cut holes in his ears, and attached sardine cans on strings." He flicked a bone toward Elvis. "The children threw stones at him as he galloped around on all fours, crying like a donkey."

The three men rocked with laughter.

Their mirth sent a chill through Daisy. The mountains known as the Jebel Ouarkziz bordered the disputed Spanish territory of Saguia el Hamra, some three or four hundred miles to the southwest. Even if he survived such tortures, she couldn't imagine how the Duke (if it was him) could be retrieved from such a distance.

The supply of twigs expired. The campfire crumbled to a mound of glowing embers. The hunters were bedding down for the night. Daisy walked away to pee in private. She checked on Uncle Bernon's hobble and prepared a place to sleep, low down out of the wind, at a little distance from the men. The saddle blanket would insulate her from the cold sand. The turban is tremendously warm head gear. When the head is warm, the rest of the body stays warm, is what they say. She doffed her boots, reversed her burnoose and dug her feet into the hood. She lay on her back gazing up at the stars avalanching the sky, and slept.

She opened her eyes because something hard was pressing upwards under her chin. Rough hands were rummaging around her crotch.

The twins were straddling each side. Their elbows pinned her arms, and their knees were hooked over her legs, forcing them apart.

The universe came down to within inches. The upward pushing knife point sealed her jaw. She could not scream while they tugged at her bloomers. The first one was thrusting within her. It was all over with a gasp of foul breath. He rolled away, the knife changed hands, and another wave of undigested meat assaulted her face, when a gunshot rang out.

CHAPTER 44

The Quarrelling Pair

She came home to find her husband slumped on the floor.

"Darling, what's wrong?"

"Where have you been?"

"I lost the track coming home."

As Slim struggled to his feet, light from the kerosene lamp picked out the drops of sweat beading his forehead. He came toward her, but each step was stilted, as though his feet were not making proper contact with the floor. He coughed so explosively he had to brace himself against the wall.

"There's something I need to tell you …"

His eyes were unfocussed; he seemed to be walking in his sleep.

"What's the matter with you?" she cried.

He pushed his wife hard on the chest. "You spent the night with that dervish priest!"

She staggered backwards. The back of her legs caught the edge of the bed. She sat heavily down.

He made a grab for her hair, pulled her toward him, and slapped the side of her head. Her ear rang from the blow. She rolled away and stood up, but a fist in the stomach bent her double. She crumpled, the wind knocked out of her, but it didn't matter because she was ready to fight, and in this they were equals.

He thought she was finished, but she grabbed his arm and swung him onto the bed.

"Ain't so high and mighty now!" she screamed. "You goddamned superior Muslim son of a bitch!"

She threw herself on top of him, pounding with both fists. She hated all men now. He got his fingers back into her hair and yanked hard. She screamed. He said he didn't care, he'd do it again. If she didn't shut up he'd pull every hair out of her head. She didn't shut up, and he lifted her by the hair and started kicking her shins. He was barefoot and she was wearing boots. She lost her balance and fell on the floor. He picked her up and looked like he was sorry, but she wasn't.

What had begun as a fight turned into a brawl. They were rolling on the floor with the furniture falling when Papa Noel came in.

"That's enough," he said. "Go to bed."

Like exhausted pugilists, they retreated to opposite corners of the room. She spotted the bottle by the bed.

"You Muslim drunk! You've made me deaf in one ear!"

"Whore!"

"All right, I'll wear a bra! I'll darn your socks! I can have children," she sobbed. "As many as you want!"

"What were you going to tell me?"

"Nothing."

"What's that blood on your neck?"

"Nothing!"

"It's all down your shirt."

"*Nothing*!"

She picked up the bottle and drank. "Are you sick?"

"I am sick. I also have bad news."

"Oh, God. What is it?"

"I'm being transferred to Oujda."

"Where's that?"

"Up north."

"Why?"

"No reason given."

She got out the map. He showed her.

"Jesus Christ is a son of a bitch! They did it with a ruler! They couldn't have posted you farther from here without running their line out to sea!"

"I have two days to get ready."

"They're doing it deliberately to separate us. This is their revenge!"

"Revenge for what, Moha?" The fight had gone out of him.

"For digging up the past! For not going to Keller's party! But mainly for falling in love with you, my darling. By sending you away, they figure they'll get rid of me, too."

The rest of the evening passed in peace; she took three aspirins and slept the sleep of the drugged. In the morning he was as affectionate as ever, when the night before they were announcing the end of marriage! She found her mother's prayer book and read the marriage vows: " ... for better for worse, for richer for poorer, in sickness and in health, to love, cherish, and to obey ... "

Together they made a vow, "to be happy today." But the day was a gloomy one – cold and overcast, with the wind shifting to the NE. She tried to raise the new wooden blind, but WHAM! the strap broke and the blind came crashing down.

Her chief concern was money. They had run up bills everywhere. All the vegetables had been sold, and Slim's tiny paycheck hardly made a dent.

She went to the yoghurt shop, hoping for a loan, but Moïses Cohen was in Casablanca on business. She went to Keller's office, where she found Tahar.

"What are you doing here?"

He pointed to a pile of gazelle skins.

She was finally admitted to Keller's office at three o'clock in the afternoon.

"Aren't you drunk, captain? Usually you prop your boots on the desk when I come in."

A look of consternation crossed Keller's face. He had been decorated for bravery but always came off the worse from these encounters with Miss Daisy Adams.

"When you have to see someone you dislike, you make them wait a few hours to soften them up. Don't you. So they won't forget who's boss. Look at you. Clean and cool, like a man who's just woken up from a nap. You've had plenty of time to put on a fresh uniform while your victim fidgets in that stuffy room. Have you deliberately bricked up the windows so no air can get in?"

"I assume you requested this interview for some purpose." He feigned a weary tone of voice.

"Is that my dossier on your desk or the Tucson phone book?"

He put the file away.

Daisy took a deep breath. "I have a favor to ask. But as soon as I see you I forget the nice things I was going to say."

"You're wasting my time … "

"What do you think you were doing with mine for the last four and a half hours?"

They were silent for a minute.

"You know, we ought to be friends." She lowered her voice. "We're American, and this is Africa. You're here on a humanitarian mission. You probably listen to Bach or something when you're missing your mother. Here I am, the only white woman for hundreds of miles, and we should be able to talk."

"I wanted to be your friend … "

She produced a letter. "This came this morning as they all do, ripped open and resealed by the authorities: *parvenu en mauvais état*. Where they get into that *mauvais état* is an enigma, but since it doesn't matter what country they've been mailed in, or which part of this country, I can only think of one place, which is here in Rfud."

"I know nothing about this."

"No, I didn't think you would … Just as my letters to Slimane disappeared in an equally mysterious way."

"Is this what you've come to complain about – your mail?"

"I came here with good intentions … " Daisy suddenly felt very weary.

"Had a late night, Miss Adams?" Keller had noticed the bruises on her face.

"I am no longer Miss Adams! I am Madame Temsemani, and I have a bone to pick with you."

The captain frowned.

"First I have a piece of news I heard from your friend."

"Well, what is it?"

"Elements of the Ait Atta, about two hundred strong, crossed the Goulmina track at Tarda in Land Rovers headed in the direction of Ksar ... "

The captain jumped up and shouted an order. A soldier appeared.

"Get that hunter back in here!" He turned to Daisy. "One good turn deserves another. Now, what is it?"

"I have a bone to pick with you ... this very big bone. May I have a glass of water?"

Keller went to the water cooler.

"A four and a half hour wait makes a person thirsty!"

She drank in sips. "You said one good turn deserves another ... "

"So I did."

"Don't send my husband to Oujda!"

Keller cocked his head. "Husband?"

"I'm married! I just told you I'm married. Because I sleep with a Moroccan you think I'm a whore!"

"You said that, not me."

"I'm going to buy Slim out of the army."

"With all that cash you carry around, that should be easy for you."

"Please use your influence so we can have time to arrange our affairs."

The interview lasted a few more minutes. It ended with a polite but glacial refusal to intervene.

She rode to Hnabu. The sanctuary swarmed with members of the brotherhood gathering for the annual pilgrimage to Rsani. After exchanging salaams with the monks she entered the great hall where the master was receiving delegations. He listened gravely while she explained her dilemma.

"Come back tonight," he said. "Bring your husband."

She cantered back to Rfud. Her marriage had gone downhill. She could hardly bring herself to believe that things had gotten so bad, so quickly. She'd lost control of the situation. Now he had to go away. Maybe forever. She was afraid they may have lost it.

Slim was in bed with fever. She fed him aspirin. Papa Noel made *bysar*. Daisy watched Slim eat. Softly, she understood where her happiness lay. It was to be found in the flickering irresistible smile of her handsome husband.

Jealousy, she thought – it was like he had been bitten by a poisonous snake!

While he slept she drew up a list of what they owed. When she totalled it up, she smacked the side of her head. How could she have let this happen?

They set out on Uncle Bernon. Slim, bundled in a burnoose, rode in front. A freezing wind blew out of the north. He was shivering. Daisy hugged him the whole way.

Black tents were pitched in the courtyard of the monastery. Fires blazed, and the drums never stilled their beat. The pilgrims were coming and going in the great hall. They had to wait.

The Marabout looked fatigued from his day-long audiences. "*De quoi s'agit-il?*" he asked.

She began. "Our situation is desperate, master … "

He raised his hand. He wanted Slim to talk, but Slim lay in a heap on the floor. Daisy coaxed him into a sitting position. The expression of dull incomprehension dissolved as his eyes wandered over the walls of the great hall, taking in the painted ceiling, the carved plaster frieze, the Fez tiles.

"So it's you we've come to in our hour of need, is it?" he said bitterly. "I thought you monks lived on bread and beans, and here we are in a palace! So it's true what everyone says – you sold the desert to the Americans and lined your pockets with gold!"

"For God's sake, Slimane! Do you know who you're talking to?"

The Marabout held up his hand. "Let him speak."

"He seduces my wife but speaks with the authority of a priest!" Slim brayed with insane laughter.

Daisy looked at him in stupefaction. "I apologize, master!"

"Does she dance in the nude for you, boss?"

"Don't say such things!"

"Does she make you smoke two pipes of *shira* before dragging you to bed?"

"Stop it! Have you no respect?"

"What about my respect?" He turned on his wife. "Every private in the army knows you sleep with this saint!"

If the Commander of the Jilaliya was stung by these insults, he retained his composure.

"As a result of this sanctified affair, which neither of you has denied, I am served up with the ultimate indignity – to come and kiss your feet and beg for money! Ah ha ha ha!"

He subsided in a fit of sobs.

"I apologize a thousand times, master!"

"Let him be. He is sick. Tell me what you need."

She explained their predicament. The Marabout went out. There was silence in the hall. The drums had stopped. Wind moaned. The candle flame fluttered as eddying sand whirled over the floor. The encroaching dune had advanced another foot or so. The weight of it looked as though it would push down the door.

The Marabout returned with a handful of bills. "Take this," he said. "You may repay me when your book is published."

Daisy saw it wasn't enough.

"Come with me tomorrow to Rsani," he said. "The merchants will be there. Among them will be members of the brotherhood. They will lend you what you need."

Daisy nodded. "Thank you, master."

Together they lifted Slim to his feet.

"Look, darling." She held the cash for him to see.

Snatching the bills from her, Slim tried to cram them into his pants. There was a tussle, and the money scattered on the floor. He was making horrifying noises, like a donkey. Suddenly he went limp and fell down.

Daisy gathered the bills, dragged him up again, and helped him from the room. Grave and impassive, the Marabout watched them go.

Silence awaited them. The moon was sinking toward the cemetery where the Marabout's children were buried. The world seemed plagued with sadness. They mounted up. They had behaved like children, and the master's children were dead.

CHAPTER 45

Rsani

During the night the wind shifted to the SE. Moaning around the corners of the house, it woke Daisy before dawn. While Papa Noel readied Uncle Bernon in the *riad*, she dipped the *churros* into a glass of sweet coffee.

Pulling over her shoulders the snow-white burnoose (*silhem*) she had had made in Marrakesh, and wrapping the indigo turban (*fibrane*), she headed off into the gale.

The sky was colored orange with flying sand. It penetrated every-where – the eyes, the nose. She could taste the grit between her teeth.

With the wind at her back she cantered across the plain. Whole sections of the earth were lifted up and blown away. Everything was moving; the air was filled with a hissing, soughing marine sound. The desert was sighing because it had once been a meadow, so the saying goes.

At Hnabu she joined the pilgrims setting out for Rsani. This was supposed to be a day of celebration, but the wind put a stop to that. With drums muffled and flags furled, long lines of people and animals trailed across the plain. Whole columns disappeared behind moving walls of sand; then suddenly the air cleared to reveal proces-sions of trudging figures where none had been before. There were hundreds of pilgrims leaning into the wind, each alone in his battle against the elements. Daisy rode beside the Marabout. Wrapped around her face, her turban covered nose and mouth, leaving only a slit for the eyes. No one spoke.

Normally a sleepy, sun-baked village dominated by the snowy dome of the tomb of Sidi Abdelkader Jilani, patron saint of the Jilaliya, Rsani comes to life each Wednesday when merchants arrive from as far away as Fez and Marrakesh to mingle with the nomads for a day of barter and exchange. Once a year this market coincides with the feast day of the saint, and tribesmen trek for miles with their animals and tents, which they set up on a volcanic hill known as "the black dune" to the east of the village.

The village boomed with the sound of gunfire and drums. The Marabout's followers were there and so were their rivals – other brotherhoods who had come to judge the numbers and strength of the Jilaliya. United Nations officials, who administered a food distribution center in the area, judiciously took the day off. The shaikhs had come to hear a report of Sidi Mohamed's negotiations in Madrid; they were also curious to get a glimpse of his companion, the American *roumia*, whom he had admitted to his cult.

He ordered Daisy not to leave his side. Together they cleaved the teeming throng and entered the sanctuary.

Pilgrims were huddled within the walls of the tomb. The fine sand sprayed above their heads and drifted down to weave orange seams in the folds of their indigo robes. There were musicians among them; the buzzing voice of flute and nervous patter of drum rose and fell with the volume of wind.

There was a shout, followed by a chorus of screams. The music stopped. The pilgrims were pointing over the wall.

"God save us!" one shouted. "Agadir! Agadir!"*

The pink and orange cloud, which must have been a mile high and covered the plain from horizon to horizon, was advancing on the village like a colossal churning wave. Everything in its path – clumps of palms, the dune with its clutter of tents – was swallowed and apparently obliterated forever. There was no place to hide or time to think; in less than a minute it was upon them.

The wind abruptly dropped, and the sanctuary was swallowed by a mist of swirling dust. Voices became muffled and vision vague. The

---

* Where a calamitous earthquake hit, several years earlier.

dust, fine as powder, was falling like snow, and the silence which followed was not unlike the hush that accompanies a snowstorm. The world was suffused by a mysterious saffron-colored light. It was peaceful, and those who had been afraid cautiously raised their heads and looked about. Everybody sat quietly and waited, because there was nothing else to do. The light, meanwhile, was fading fast. With dust thickening, the saffron glow darkened to amber. When the sunlight was shut out altogether, people groped about calling names. It was blacker than the blackest night, so it was safer not to move at all.

The Marabout touched Daisy's shoulder. "Stay close to me," he whispered. "There are enemies among us."

She felt for the Ruger beneath her arm.

They pulled their turbans across their faces and for the better part of an hour did not speak. As when one vigilantly waits the dawn, yet is taken unawares by the first light, Daisy opened her eyes to an amber glow that had returned to illuminate the mist. The pilgrims began to stir as though waking from a dream. The swirling dust was once more permeated with saffron light.

Then things happened very quickly. The wind began to blow again, and the world grew brighter and more distinct. The breeze freshened and became colder; the temperature had dropped several degrees. Daisy poked her head above the wall as the dust storm rolled away. The air was clear. She could see for miles.

Daisy was sitting cross-legged in a doorway, beside a heavy block of wood used for chopping kindling. She had taken out her notebook and was making notes when a man with an orange beard entered the sanctuary. He was holding something – a stick. A shadow fell across the paper. The hood of her burnoose had fallen forward, preventing her from looking up. She was conscious of someone standing over her.

A woman screamed. Daisy simultaneously felt a blow on her head. She toppled over backwards groping for the Ruger, but could not move her arm. She was aware that a tumult had erupted. She rolled on her side. This was the movement that saved her life. Another heavy blow landed near her head.

With the help of others Sidi Mohamed carried her into the tomb and lay her on a bench. While she lay there stunned, not knowing what had happened, the Marabout unwrapped her turban. An ugly gash on the side of her head was bleeding profusely. The burnoose was cut away to reveal another wound on her shoulder. The hand appeared to be nearly severed at the wrist.

A mob of Jilaliya, outraged that the tomb of their saint had been desecrated, pressed around the sanctuary. The Marabout ordered the gate shut.

Daisy's wounds were wrapped to staunch the flow of blood, and she was given some tea to drink.

It was an ax the man was carrying. He stood before Daisy in the doorway of the tomb, where she was absorbed in her writing. When she looked up he struck, aiming the ax at her head. Incredibly, he missed. Instead of cleaving her skull, the blade was deflected by a wire clothesline strung above her head. It glanced off the side of her head, which was protected by the woolly hood of her burnoose and several layers of turban, sliced across her shoulder and sank into her wrist.

A pilgrim grappled with the assassin, but he threw him away like a doll. Raising the ax again and shouting, "This time I'll chop her head off!" he brought it down just as Daisy rolled away. The ax imbedded itself in the wooden block, rendering it a useless instrument. He was subdued by several men.

After she had recovered a little, she asked to see her aggressor.

He was dragged in and thrown on the floor. He was a small man with broad shoulders. He was slobbering. His eyes were rolled up so only the whites were visible.

"Who is he?" Daisy whispered.

The man did not answer.

"Who are you?" the Marabout demanded. "Speak!"

His tongue lolled out. He was making growling noises like an animal

"I know him!" piped up the woman who was bandaging Daisy. "He's a wood chopper from the oasis. His name is Allal. He has a wife and six children. His wife says he has visions. He's talking to himself when we pass on the road, but I've never seen him behave like this!"

The man scooped up a handful of sand and started to eat it.

"At home he wears a nice clean robe," the woman added. "He has a job cutting wood for the Americans."

"So you work for the Americans, do you?" the Marabout said. "Have they sent you to defile the sanctuary of Moulay Abdelkader?"

The man snarled.

"Murderer! Kill him!" A voice shouted and was echoed by an angry roar from outside.

"If you can't talk like a human being I'll throw you to the mob! You can growl while they twist your arms off!"

The man sat up and wiped his nose.

"So you're not as crazy as you pretend." The Marabout paced in a circle about him. "You have a name and, apparently, a family. Do you know what you've done?"

"Carve him up!" the voice called.

"You nearly killed this woman! Thanks to God, she's not dead. But you've hurt her badly! What do you have to say?"

The man had the eyes of a stricken animal.

"Allal," came Daisy's faint speech from the bench. "I don't think I've seen you before. Do you know me?"

"No, miss, I do not," he answered in a strangely civil voice.

"What have you got against me?"

"Nothing, miss."

"Do you hate me?"

"No, miss, I do not."

"Then why did you try to kill me?"

"I was following orders."

"Whose orders?"

"I was told to kill the infidel woman."

"Who told you that?" Sidi Mohamed roared.

"A voice."

"What voice, dog?" The anger of the Marabout was a fearful thing.

"God."

"So God gives orders to murder these days, does He? Blasphemy, coward! You're hide will be ripped off for saying such things!"

"If you've never seen me before," Daisy said, "how did you know who I was?"

"The voice said the *roumia* would be wearing a white *silhelm* and blue *fibrane*. She was coming to Rsani to visit the Sanctuary of Sidi Abdelkader Djilani."

"Those are very precise instructions." Sidi Mohamed said. "Who paid you to do this? Who are the others involved?"

The man shook his head.

"Do you repent, now that you've come to your senses and seen the terrible thing you've done?"

"I'm sorry I hurt you, miss," he said apologetically. "But if these men let me go, I will try to kill you again. As long as I am alive I will go on killing you, even with my bare hands. Sooner or later, I will kill you, or someone else will kill you. And if he does not kill you, the earth will kill you. And if the earth does not kill you, the sky will kill you. And if not the sky, water ... because it has been ordered by God for you to die ... "

These words, spoken with simple-minded conviction, overwhelmed Daisy. Exhausted and in pain, she lay back on the bench.

A Moroccan doctor examined her wounds by candlelight. The cuts on her head and shoulder would require stitches, but the wrist was more serious. The tendons had been cut. The bone was chipped but not broken. She was weakened from loss of blood.

She was taken to the military hospital in Rfud. Already a rumor had started that it was God's finger that had deflected the blow.

CHAPTER 46

Meet the VR's

Inevitably, Arturo began to meet his Van Renseelaer cousins. Most had graduated from Ivy League colleges; home-educated, he had never been to school. An attempt was made to find common ground. Two of his affluent girl cousins rode to the hounds: one in Far Hills, NJ, the other in the Worthington Valley, MD; Arturo had roped calves in AZ and worked as a trick rider for a Polish circus in Sevilla.

They had grown up on a diet of Hemingway and Scott Fitzgerald; he had read *Under the Volcano* and *On the Road*, not much else. They smoked Marlboro Lights and filtered Luckies; he went for roll-ups and weed. They drank white wine and gin and tonics; his tipples were tequila and Mexican brown beer.

One cousin had spent his junior year of college in France; Arturo had lived rough for a year in Andalusia. Another cousin had served as an officer in the Navy; Arturo did not mention he was a deserter from the U.S. Army.

For his birthday the Tortoise presented him with the keys to a dove-gray Impala convertible with red leather seats. Arturo drove it once around the block, pushed the keys through the mail slot of his father's apartment at 14 Sutton Place South and walked back to the Chelsea.

In the Café Moro next to the hotel he met Samson, a rich hippy from Acapulco who ran an art gallery in the East Village.

Arturo had been busy in his studio apartment at the Chelsea. He showed Samson the drawings he had made during his trek across Africa: trans-Sahara from Tindouf to Timbuktu, and along the Niger and Senegal rivers.

From these drawings he had developed a series of canvases depicting his subjects in a harsh African light that obliterated depth and made them seem strangely two-dimensional:

A portrait of the turbanned, gap-toothed, grinning Mejdoubi, filling his pipe;

In a family group Maloudia sits before the tent between her mother with the circus hair and her son, busy with his nut. Enveloped in yards of indigo, she gazes brazenly at the viewer, her Ethiopian features frozen in an imperious mask. Behind the tent dunes rise like golden domes;

Two naked maidens of exquisite posture standing in a flimsy dugout canoe. They have flung out the weighted net and are hauling in the teeming, flashing fish. Their smiles radiate across yards of water;

In another river scene dugout canoes nose like spokes around an above-water mound. On the mound a fire is burning. Over the fire an animal of some kind is being turned on a spit. Around the mound stand the naked Africans, knee-deep in water. Tall, slim muscular warriors, some with spear in hand, stand beside young maidens, tiny g-strings hiding the pubic area but nothing else;

In a nude portrait the lovely Paloma, in a melancholy pose, contemplates a love bird in the palm of her hand.

Samson took the lot and the show, entitled "From Timbuktu to Tapachula," sold out.

CHAPTER 47

The Sand Catcher

The hospital room was blue, splashed with pigments which had not been fully mixed. Wavy white lines rippled the cool blue walls. Was this the artisan's signature flourish, or was he too lazy to stir the paint. Moroccan blue discourages flies, Slim said. So does the fragrant basil plant. Even the floor was blue.

Slim was on his way to a distant corner of the country, leaving no forwarding address, and she had no idea how to get in touch with him. And now the Girard Perregaux, about the last decent item in her possession that she had inherited from her mother, was missing. The hospital nurses pick your pockets while bandaging your wounds. This was the last straw. She hated this fucking country.

The thing poised on the window-sill appeared as a blur. At first she thought it a leaf, a colorful autumn leaf that had blown in through the open window and landed on the sill.

She rubbed away the tears and looked again. Long spindly legs gripped an area as broad as her hand. The black ovoid thorax pulsated like an obscene heart. A single black eye bulged from the middle of its pointed orange head. Tarantulas like wood. They cling to window sills and leap on their prey. They can deliver a sharp bite which is painful to humans but not poisonous.

Scorpions crawl into openings or under things. Caftan had warned her to give her slippers a good shake before putting them on in the morning. The *lefâa* vibrates itself into the soil. At the vital moment it unleashes its coils in a spray of sand. It was a miracle Arturo had survived.

With a rolled up copy of *The Herald Tribune* in her good hand, she was easing herself from bed to deal with this critter, when the door opened.

The good doctor was standing by the bed.

"Let me help you, mademoiselle."

"Madame." She pointed at the window.

He stepped across the room and with a finger flicked the beast outside.

"Gerrymander," he said.

"In America that's a political fiddle."

"*Galeodas*. Huge, hideous, but harmless. How's my patient?"

"The cramps in my arm won't let me sleep."

"I've had to sew the ligaments back together. They contract as they heal. They may tickle a little."

"Tickle they do not. They hurt like hell."

Doctor Parodis was a bald, spare Frenchman in gray slacks, a loose white shirt, not exactly clean, and sandals. He ate little and drank only water, but smoked one thick yellow (*papier maïs*) French cigarette after another. He was a vegetarian and knew a great deal about grains, upon which he largely subsisted.

Dr. Parodis was interested in "Sufi technology" – solar energy, windmills – but agronomy was his hobby. During the seven years he had spent as a doctor in North Africa, he had made a study of Saharan agriculture. Daisy was eager to learn about this study, so she could pass the details along to Slim.

The doctor had concluded that a sedentary family of eight could subsist wholly and comfortably on one hectare of land, provided the land received an adequate supply of water.

That was Daisy's dream. A little farm and a little grocery store.

With the doctor's help she gingerly slid from the bed. He guided her little steps onto the balcony.

Part of the old French fort had been converted into a hospital, and the balcony overlooked the parade ground. To one side stood the barracks, now occupied by the Americans. A square building that had once been the kitchen was now a prison. On the high red rampart two soldiers shouldered arms with bayonets fixed. They paced with measured tread and gazed listlessly at the limitless desert.

The pebbly orange plain, cut through with diagonal streaks of black, zigzagged to eternity. A suggestion of dunes trembled on the horizon. The air was still veiled with dust swept up by the storm. Bits of earth danced high in the yellow sky. A swirl of brown mist hovered about the sun, like iron filings sucked in by a magnet. It was three o'clock in the afternoon. The sun – small, pale and metallic – an Elmyr sun – was warm, but the air felt cool.

They leaned on the railing and lit cigarettes.

"You've had a lucky escape."

"Saved by a clothesline. How romantic." Daisy blew out some smoke. "But do you know what it was about that brush with death that really scared me? The realization that I haven't published anything. I haven't told the world about this life that is like no other life. I feel an urgency now. Writing is my insurance policy. It's what I'll leave behind. Writing is my only hedge against death, which Allal made me realize could be right around the corner."

Their conversation was interrupted by a shouted order. The prison door creaked open, and two soldiers escorted a prisoner from the cells. There was a rattle of chains as the shackles were removed from his feet.

"What are they doing?"

"I believe the man in the middle is the one who tried to kill you."

"Allal?"

The sight of the diminutive African, hands chained together, shuffling between two blond giants, brought tears to Daisy's eyes. She gripped the doctor's arm.

"Are you frightened of him?"

"No! Look how small he is! I've turned the crime over and over in my head, and each time my thoughts keep returning to that insignificant little man. Do you know what impressed me about him? His sincerity. I believe he did hear voices, or thought he heard them."

"You don't think he was manipulated by others?"

"Keller you mean?"

"There is a rumor that the Marabout Sidi Mohamed ordered the assassination," Dr. Parodis said.

"Never!" Daisy reacted fiercely. "Well, what exactly did you hear?"

"He paid one of his followers to kill you."

"Why?"

"To counteract certain rumors … "

"That we're lovers, is that it? I've heard all this before."

"And this Allal, being properly obedient, proclaimed himself to be a member of a rival sect so they would be blamed."

"That's just bullshit invented by Keller because I didn't go to his party. No, no. Allal wasn't being manipulated. I believed his story then and I still do. He's a fanatic. Sincerity is the purest form of fanaticism."

The little group was making its way across the parade ground.

"What are they doing?"

"They're going to turn him over to the Jilaliya for violating their sanctuary."

"Who ordered this?"

"In cases like this the Saharans administer their own justice."

With the soldiers pushing, the great gate swung open. Outside, a knot of tribesmen squatted in a semi-circle, their camels couched on the sand.

The manacles were removed. The prisoner was handed over. The soldiers returned to the fort. The gate was swung shut and secured.

Daisy strained to see where the group had gone. She heard singing. At last the little procession came into view beyond the wall.

Tethered between two riders, Allal walked to his destiny.

"*Allah akbar*! God is great!" The single frail voice seemed to fill the desert all around.

"Where are they taking him?"

"They're going to put him in the sand catcher."

"What's that?"

"A wattle fence about a meter high and two meters wide, built across the prevailing wind. You plant tamarisk stakes and weave them with the tough groping roots of the spider plant. On the leeward side a post is banged into the ground. The Jilaliya will push Allal down and tie him in a sitting position to the post. Within hours or days, depending on the wind, a dune will begin to build behind the fence. It will gradually bury him as he shouts his last prayers at God."

A cold wind began to moan around the corners of the hospital. In it Daisy decoded that comfortless message meant for herself. The dense air sweeping down from the icy peaks of the High Atlas meets little resistance on the high plateaux of the stony, pre-Saharan region of the Moroccan south. She was shivering beneath the pitiless yellow sky shot through with patches of blue. Dr. Parodis escorted her back to the room. He helped her into bed and tucked the burnoose around her.

Lying on her side, her knees drawn up for warmth, Daisy cried for Allal. The Girard Perregaux appeared as a blur. There it was – inside her orange slipper that sat on the low blue bench, next to the basil plant – just where she had put it.

CHAPTER 48

Bouârfa

Bouârfa had to be one of the drabbest, dreariest, most depressing one-horse towns she had ever had the misfortune to find herself in. And there wasn't even a horse, just one sodden donkey, head down in the rain. It was raining, it was sleeting, it was freezing cold – the kind of damp that goes straight for the bones. But, tucked away among the tin-roofed shanties and melting mud walls was a hotel, not a *fondak* but an actual hotel, the Hotel Terminus, a relic from French colonial days, the only one for hundreds of Saharan miles. Monsieur Jacques showed her a room that, miracle of miracles, had hot water in its pipes. The window overlooked the railroad tracks. How incongruously correct they seemed, how shiny in a dull world as they snaked out of the desert streaked with mist like a northern wintry sea.

Monsieur Jacques, ex-legionnaire with long service in Indochina and Algeria, poured a double scotch as soon as she walked into the bar. He understood her need.

In Africa the contrasts are terrific. In the end you ask yourself: which was the more memorable, the hardship or the relief? The answer is neither. Or both. One defines the other. Together they make the experience unforgettable.

He showed her an article from *Liberation,* describing the incident at Rsani. *"La Bonne Nomade"* she was now known as. She was famous now.

Her head ached, the arm was a mess, sore as hell and still bleeding where the stitches had been yanked out. Her feet were so cold and clammy she could hardly believe those dying things belonged to her. She was just settling into her bath, a little sitzbath, an unparalleled pleasure even though the hot water failed after a couple of inches, when she heard noises outside. Excited shouts and the slamming of car doors. Familiar-sounding female voices. She went to the window and looked out; a mud-spattered Pontiac station wagon was pulled up in front of the hotel.

Downstairs she found Amalia and Carmen established at a table by the fire, already well-advanced on a bottle of Old Cornstalk, which they were slugging down neat.

Amalia appeared regal as ever in the voluminous black burnoose, gray-green eyes embedded like pale emeralds in chocolaty skin, what the Portuguese call *moro-coloniale*, the color of ancient families who have for centuries been embedded in the tropical colonies of Angola, Mozambique, Goa.

Carmen, by contrast, had upgraded to beige: buckskin jacket with tassels and beads, two-toned jodhpurs, black riding boots, and a chauffeur's hat.

Daisy understood instantly: Carmen steered the massive Pontiac while *la princesse* reclined in back. In this royal mode they sailed through the police barricades established during "the troubles" on every main road in Morocco. Half-frozen officers stepped aside to salute the Queen of Sheba and were warmed by her passage.

Like a lemur Carmen sprang from her chair and wrapped Daisy in a muscular embrace.

Like the giant forest toad Amalia seemed to swell on her bench as she waited for Daisy to lean across her lunar breasts for a kiss.

They were on their way to Beni-Abbès in Algeria, to spend the cold North African winter months at the Hotel des Palmiers, snuggled among the golden, sun-drenched dunes of the Grand Erg Occidental.

The platter, delivered to the table by Monsieur Jacques himself, was piled with the multiple blackened heads of some small animal, which the ladies proceeded to dismantle with knowing, surgical skill. Each charred skull had been split in two. The twin halves lay like clamshells side by side, from which they were scooping the gray-white brains with silver teaspoons. With squeaks of delighted ravishment they peeled away the angry black lips and nibbled tiny morsels of roasted cheek. Sharp white teeth gleamed like rows of pearls against the burned bone and flesh. The miniature tongues were filleted with razor-sharp knives, the slivers sprinkled with a mixture of salt and cumin.

Daisy watched with morbid curiosity. Would they eat the eyeballs? They did, deftly skewering them from the sockets and popping them into their mouths.

"It's Monsieur Jacques' specialty," Carmen gasped. "Every year we come from Tangier to enjoy."

"What is it?"

"Baby gazelle."

The Good Nomad, translated from the original article in *Liberation*, was spotted by Arturo in *The New York Times*. It mentioned the Duchess de Bremont, whom he was able to contact in Paris.

Over the phone Cajan filled him in on her meeting with Daisy in Elmyr's studio. She described *The Girl with the Shaved Head*, which Elmyr considered to be his masterpiece. It was now on show under his own name in the Iris Clert Gallery.

Finally she got around to revealing her bitter disappointment with Daisy. Instead of making use of her exceptional abilities to scour the desert for her missing husband, the dizzy girl had married a Moroccan soldier! The generous sums advanced to her she had squandered on a house in the oasis and had taken up farming!

Worse, she had fallen under the spell of a renegade Sufi saint, an enemy of America. She had joined his fanatical cult, and had been involved in some tribal scrape which had nearly cost her life.

The last Cajan heard, Daisy had left hospital in pursuit of her errant husband.

CHAPTER 49

Train of Shame

The coal train from Colomb-Béchar was due in at midnight. A company of soldiers arrived by truck. It had begun to snow. Daisy shared a bottle of Old Cornstalk (parting gift from *les deux madames*), with Ed the academic and Danny the Missouri farm boy, the duo who the year before had bought her drinks Chez Zizou. Heavy wet flakes the size of potato chips slapped against their faces. There was no shelter from the stinging force of the wind.

The ancient engine rattled out of the storm towing boxcars packed with Moroccan troops, who had providently stuffed them with straw. The pair of obsolete French (S.N.C.F.) passenger cars at the rear had been reserved for the Americans. Daisy boarded with her friends.

As the train began to move, the blizzard struck in earnest. All dimension was lost, all depth nullified by the seething whiteness. The railroad car must have been fifty years old, with gaps between the floorboards and some windows broken. As the train picked up speed, a freezing gale sprinkled with snowflakes swept through the car. The exhausted soldiers plugged some holes with burlap, wrapped themselves in ponchos and tried to get some sleep.

In the middle of the car stood a cast iron stove with an HORS DE SERVICE sign on it. A chimney pipe went up through the roof.

"Does it work?"

"I don't see anything wrong with it."

Using his M16 as a club, Danny demolished an antique wooden bench. He got a fire going and fed the pieces to the flames. For a while no one spoke; they were preoccupied with the important challenge of warming up. By degrees the chill went out of the air. The windows steamed up as the top of the car filled with smoke floating from the leaking chimney pipe.

"I think that's enough wood, Danny," Daisy said. "That thing can't get any hotter."

"Hey, what's happening?"

The stove had suddenly gone cockeyed. It was beginning to sink. First one foot went through the wooden floorboards, then the other. Our companions could do nothing because the stove was too hot to touch. It was burning itself into the floor.

"I think I know what the problem is," Ed observed mildly. "The asbestos pad it's supposed to sit on is missing."

All four legs dropped through. The stove disconnected itself from the chimney and sat on its bottom, belching sparks and smoke. As it wallowed deeper into the floor, the flames spread. The jiggling of the train was easing the stove down through the burning planks. Then suddenly it dropped down and banged away along the tracks. The old wooden floor began to blaze like tinder in the gale blowing up through the hole. As the car filled with smoke and freezing air, the weary soldiers began to wake up. Danny made a half-hearted attempt to put out the blaze by pissing on it, but the fire was out of control. There was no panic, just a little grumbling as the soldiers collected their gear, edged past the fire, and moved to the car ahead.

Within a few minutes the car was completely alight, with flames pouring out the windows. The train stopped. The Moroccan engineer came back and uncoupled the burning car. The train started up again. The old S.N.C.F. passenger car was left blazing like a torch in the middle of the snow-blown night.

As Daisy attempted to pass into the car ahead, an officer pulled her arm.

"No natives in here!" He yanked her back. "Wait a minute! Who are you?" he barked, suddenly realizing he held a woman in his arms.

CHAPTER 50

Down and Out in Malaga and Tangier

Daisy tried to jump train as it pulled into Oujda but was grabbed by the guard. At the station MP's were waiting. Ed and Danny were handcuffed and driven away. She was taken before an American officer. The interrogation went something like this:

"Name?"

"Moha ben Abdu."

"Is that the name you were born with?"

"It's the name I use."

"I don't want any aliases. What was your name at birth?"

"Elizabeth Wilhelmina van Rensselaer."

"The name in your passport is Daisy Adams. This is the name we'll use. You are the daughter of Antonio Adamski."

"Step daughter. That's his nom de guerre."

"Speak English. You have the same name."

"He gave it to me. I didn't ask for it."

"He is a member of the Mexican communist party."

"That was pre-me."

"You are an excellent rider."

"Is that a compliment?"

"Age?"

"Twenty-one."

"Place of birth?"

"New York City."

"Profession?"

"*Homme de lettres.*"

"Speak English!"

"Writer."

"What do you write about?"

"The desert, and the people who live in it."

"Well, Miss Daisy Adams, you won't be writing about the desert any more, unless it's from memory, because you're being deported from Morocco."

"Why?"

"For destroying military property. We have about thirty witnesses who swear you and your friends set fire to the train." He picked up a sheet of paper. "This comes from the American Embassy in Rabat. It refers specifically to you and recommends your immediate expulsion if you commit any act considered contrary to American interests in Morocco."

"This isn't your country. You can't throw me out!"

"We're not. The Moroccans are."

"But I'm Moroccan! This is my country!"

"You're American."

"I'm married to a Moroccan, therefore I am Moroccan!"

"Marrying an Eskimo doesn't make you one."

"I am Muslim and am governed by *sharia*!"

"Speak English!"

Daisy jumped up and went to the window. "That's my husband out there! He knows I'm here! I must speak to him!"

"I'm sorry. You're under arrest."

"You're not a bit sorry!" She wiped away the tears. "You want to separate me from the man I love and ruin my life."

For three days she was confined to a cage-like cell. It was solitary confinement in the open air. She did not know who said what to whom, but on the fourth morning she and a police woman were in a taxi on their way to the Spanish *presidio* of Melilla.

Aisha, the tough-looking Berber policewoman with blue tattoos on her chin, shared her cigarettes and called for shots of Fundador, twice. She understood Daisy's need.

They hugged on the quayside. She handed Daisy her passport and for the first time smiled, showing shiny gold teeth. Inside the passport was a slip of paper with Slimane's address.

In Malaga she attempted to buy a ferry ticket to Tangier, but was told by the ticket seller that a cholera epidemic had broken out. Cholera vaccinations were required for anyone planning to visit. It was not permitted to sell passage to Morocco to anyone who did not have proof of vaccination. She could go to the hospital on the hill, have the required injection, come back in ten days, and he would sell her the ticket. While he was telling her all this, the *portero* had picked up her basket and was running for the boat. She chased after him and found herself in a line of passengers waiting to have their passports stamped. The *portero* by-passed the line and dashed through an open gate heading for the ferry which was about to depart. Afraid of losing her basket, she raced after him. An outcry erupted from the customs inspectors. On the gangway stood a tall man elegantly attired in a camel hair coat and astrakhan hat. With a black mustache and Nasser smile, he exuded authority and calm. Daisy instinctively attached herself to him. He waved off the customs officials who were crowding the gangway. Like a pack of curs they backed off before the larger, stronger animal. Everyone stood respectfully aside as they boarded the ferry. He tipped the *portero*. On the first class deck he bought her a club sandwich and a beer before joining his friends. He, too, understood her need.

Disembarking in Tangier she stayed close by his side. There was no police or customs for this man of grand standing. Without exchanging a word she allowed herself to become lost in the crowd. She later recalled him as one of Jâafar's dinner guests.

In winter there is no place colder than the Med. Sitting up late in the truckers' cafés, she worked on her book. When she wrote, she drank. Writing and drinking, drinking and writing – she couldn't separate the two. When she was writing well, she didn't care (or remember) how much she drank. While her mind was floating her body was going down the drain.

Daisy was at a fork in the road. When you encounter the spiritual realm, nothing else will do. She hadn't yet, but she'd gotten a whiff.

How she longed for a sea of yellow sand!

One morning in early spring, sickened by the wretched circumstances to which her life had descended, and wanting to remind herself how the other half lived, Daisy ducked under the wire and went for a walk along the narrow beach below the Casbah wall. Scaling a seaside cliff, she found herself in the Marshan, one of Tangier's residential districts.

She paused before a large square "merchant's" house set back from the street behind a sturdy iron fence. Something about this house attracted her. The blue wisteria flowers festooning the gables reminded her of Villa Arida Zona; or was it the antique Spanish tiles framing the doorway? Her mother had a collection of tiles like those.

The sun was hot and the blinds were drawn. A street cleaner came by, pushing his cart. She asked who lived in the big house.

"Rich Jew," was the snarled reply.

This is the moment to be bold, she told herself. Nothing I do here can make things worse off than they are already.

She went to the gate and pulled the chain.

There was an eruption of dogs. She stepped back while they threw themselves against the heavy bars of the fence.

Someone was watching from an upstairs window.

Whoever it is probably thinks I'm another down and out bum looking for a handout or a job or worse ... she said to herself, which wasn't far from the truth.

A wooden blind was cranked open. A figure in a faded blue caftan leaned out.

"Can I help you?" he called in Arabic.

She could not make herself heard above the racket the dogs were making.

He seemed to understand this. A minute later the front door opened, and the blue caftan appeared on the step. The dogs ran to him; he calmed them down one by one.

About ten feet from the fence he stopped. He looked about fifty, maybe not so old, bald, with soft, dark, deep set eyes. He looked sad: Daisy thought he looked like an undertaker. He was slim and elegant in a simple caftan and yellow slippers that could be bought for next to nothing in the native market.

"Can I help you?" he repeated.

"I am Daisy Adams, daughter of Estrella Toledano."

As he took in this bit of information his expression did not change, but he looked at her more closely. Daisy wished he wouldn't. Her clothes were dirty. She hadn't bathed. It was hot. The dogs lay down on the drive.

The vestige of a smile lifted the otherwise deadpan features. "You must be … Moha."

"Do you know me? And you are … ?"

"Jacob Toledano." He freed the huge padlock that held the gates together. "Your mother and I were first cousins."

Jacob Toledano, son of Yamin – the premier tea baron of Morocco – grew up in Tangier, was educated at Yale and lived in Paris collecting art and automobiles. He had married an American but was divorced, the cause of much sadness in the family. He left Paris and recently returned to Tangier to look after Rackel, his ageing mother.

He led Daisy inside and made her sit while he cranked up the shutters. Sunlight flowed into a room packed with antique furniture. Paintings hung frame to frame across the walls.

"It's hot for March, isn't it?" He pulled a bell chain. "Do you like champagne, Moha?"

"Well, I … " The question almost reduced her to tears.

A servant padded in.

"A bottle of Krug and two glasses, Mustafa, please!"

Catching a glimpse of herself in a mirror, Daisy cringed with shame.

Her hands were dirty. Her feet were filthy! A stained and dented fez topped her shaven head. She felt out of place in Jacob's elegant salon.

"May I call you cousin, Moha?"

"Yes, of course. Anything." She gazed about the room. "It's pure fate I happened to come down your street … what if I'd turned left at the corner instead of walking straight ahead?"

"Have you just arrived from the desert?"

"No, I've been here a while … "

"Are you staying at El Minzah?"

"No, no … " Daisy clenched her eyes. The tears squirted.

Jacob stepped closer. "Are you all right, cousin?"

She shot a blurry glance at his sad and worried face. "I mean … " The tears were running down her cheeks. "*Fondak* Waller." She had made them come. Now they were real. She couldn't stop them.

Jacob poured the champagne. "Drink this."

Daisy smiled through the tears. "I shouldn't be here."

"Oh?"

"I've been kicked out of Morocco."

"Why?"

"Oh, for all sorts of reasons … my husband was there, right outside the gate, but they wouldn't let me see him … that's cruel – isn't it? – not to allow a man and his wife to share a moment together before forcibly separating them? After the publicity surrounding the incident at Rsani … they decided to get rid of me … They thought I was dangerous … me, the *victim*."

As she rolled and smoked a cigarette, Daisy spoke slowly, as if searching for words, in her flat, nasal Arizona drawl. When she laughed, which was seldom, she hid her teeth, which were not good. A typical gesture was to lift, with her left hand (the good hand) the cigarette to her lips while the other (injured one) rested upon her knee. Her bearing was dignified, even grave. She was no longer the exuberant and optimistic young woman who had arrived in Morocco two years ago. Desert life had taken its toll, but it was a life like no other life and she would have no other.

Jacob smiled his worried smile. "Well, we'll see what can be done to rectify this sad state of affairs."

Alcohol on an empty stomach was beginning to have an effect. "This champagne is a step up from Whiskey Abdullah and Matarata – the moonshine the stevedores mix up in the port … you know, my mother and I became Muslims before she died … we're Muslims."

"I don't think there's anyone in Tangier, Paris, or New York for that matter who doesn't know you're a Muslim."

"Is that so?"

"It's not just through *Liberation* and *The Herald Tribune* I've kept track of you, Moha. Old Cohen in Rfud used to send me messages … "

"Moïses? I owe him money."

"Not to worry. He is a cousin of ours."

"Cousin?" Daisy seemed completely non-plussed. "That old goat?"

"You have many cousins in Morocco, Moha, some rich, some poor, some young and some very, very old. I'm particularly delighted to see you since I missed my trip to New York this spring. My mother is ill."

He poured out more champagne.

"Nanny usually looks after her, but Nanny went to Mecca this year, so I've had to play nurse." He got to his feet. "Now, if you'll excuse me, it's the hour to take her out. She loves to go for a drive in the open car. In the meantime, there's a room for you. Please make yourself at home."

Mustafa led the way up a staircase spiralling toward an oval skylight that let a pale luminosity into the house. Another shutter was cranked open, and light flooded in. The bed, so high a little stool had been provided, was stiff with linen sheets. The bathroom was full of antique chrome gadgetry whose function she failed to fathom. For the first time since Bouârfa she had a bath – an unimaginable luxury. Standing before a full-length mirror, she was horrified by the transformation that had come over her body. Her ribs stuck out like an accordion. Her boobs had gone into hiding. She slipped into a robe Mustafa had laid out and, filled with an unaccustomed sense of well-being, climbed onto the bed. She was about to shut her eyes when she heard voices.

She went to the window.

Mustafa came out of the house carrying a woman in his arms. Jake opened the door of the Cadillac. The sight of this gentle trio filled Daisy with a strong sense of predestination. She could hear them speaking Ladino, the archaic Judeo-Spanish language of Andalucia.

Dr. McGregor x-rayed her shoulder, put the arm in a sling, and showed her how to protect it. Jake paid Dr. Decrop, the French dentist, to fit a bridge to fill the gap left by the missing molars.

What with the Arab telegraph, news travels fast in Tangier. One morning she came downstairs to find Mina and Sobrina waiting in the kitchen.

Mina brought letters, months old. Maître Jacoubi reported that Villa Arida Zona had been sealed and boarded up, pending a legal settlement. Thieves had broken in and stolen the best furniture. The property had finally been sold to Lord Denby, but at a fraction of its value, due to the collapse of the real estate market. Most of that was eaten up by legal fees.

Daisy would never receive her legacy.

It turned out that Jake had been a classmate of Gluglu de Bremont at Yale, where he was known as "The French Oak" for his exploits on the football field.

Small world!

Jake put a call through to Cajan in Paris. Daisy filled her in on what she had learned from the hunters – that the Duke had been seen in a place called Tiglite, in SW Morocco, adding that the Marabout Sidi Mohamed knew he was in Tiglite. That her husband had been tortured she did not reveal.

Daisy's most passionate need was to return to her little family in the desert. But she didn't have dime one – not a bean!

Once again Cajan provided a way forward. In the wake of a series of skirmishes in southern Morocco, the press was sending correspondents to report. She found Daisy a job at one of her husband's newspapers, *The Tangier Gazette,* as war correspondent.

CHAPTER 51

¡Harka!

A *harka* is not an army. It is a huge, shambling assemblage of men, women, children and animals. It resembles an amoeba, blob-like, shapeless but self-sufficient, feeding off the land. It moves in a series of lumpy, irregular spasms. Its marching order is haphazard: proud young men with modern weapons on Arab stallions are followed on foot by their less fortunate comrades carrying an assortment of antique rifles, their stocks emblazoned with inscriptions in Arabic exhorting their owners to throw back the infidel.

Women lead donkeys burdened with household equipment. Camels carry the tents, mules the tent poles and other heavy items, including stones. Expert children race about with slings, keeping goats obedient. Ravenous chickens dart beneath the feet of man and beast. Everywhere there is dust, a cacophony of dogs barking, the loud, protesting groans from the pack animals, and above all the shrill warbling notes of the *zaqâreet*, the female war-cry which incites their men to battle.

The sole military tactic of the *harka* is to overwhelm, envelop, ingest.

At the U.S. Military Academy, where the cadets analyze every military formation in recorded history, from hoplites to the Afrikakorps, the *harka* has never made it onto the curriculum. West Point would have done well to have exchanged notes with St. Cyr, its brother academy outside Versailles, some of whose graduates had suffered grievously at the many hands of the *harka*. Even at St. Cyr the word has disappeared into the history books as a military anomaly, which is not surprising as the *harka's* last recorded appearance on the field of battle was in 1903.

Tarhit was the last of a series of military outposts established along the Zousfana "River," or wadi, in Sud Oranais, Algeria, close to the ill-defined border with Morocco. (Except for the rare occurrences of flash floods, Saharan "rivers" tend to flow underground, which prevents them from becoming totally extinct.) In those isolated forts, where small garrisons kept long, lonely watch over the empty landscape, many young legionnaires succumbed to the desert curse known as *le cafard*.

(N.B: the word *cafard* (cockroach), Foreign Legion argot for boredom, ennui, which can add up to a kind of hopeless case of the desert blues, comes from spending long periods of time without women – a condition which can slip into despondency and a corresponding inability to take orders, even when shots are fired.)

That summer of 1903 was particularly oppressive. The power of the Saharan sun seemed capable of baking the mud walls of the post to powder. In August, three powerful Moroccan tribes from the Tafilalet – Oulad Djeria, the Doaui-Menia, and the Ait Atta – crowded into the village of Béchar for a powwow. They were prepared to suspend their eternal blood-feuds to oppose French imperial designs being devised by General Hubert Lyautey, the future founder of modern Morocco. The native informers, upon whom French officers depended for intelligence, sensing the storm that was about to break, melted away. Consequently, Captain de Latour was clueless at the very moment when 8,000 Moroccan warriors and their followers chose to up sticks and move against him.

On the morning of August 15, one of his scouts galloped into the fort. A *harka*, a big one, had left Béchar two days ago, its destination Tarhit.

The next day at dawn the *harka* was looped over the dunes like a gigantic serpent, its tail in the wadi, its fangs about to close on the fort.

Fighting in the Sahara, especially during high summer, is thirsty work. In a protracted siege, water becomes more precious than bullets. De Latour cursed the architect of Tarhit: the walled enclosure was more *fondak* than fortress, with the sole source of water down in the oasis. The only solution was to defend the fort from the outside.

The tactics employed by the Moroccans were brave but not brilliant. The young, hot-blooded warriors raced their horses to within inches of the French rifles, stood up in the stirrups, and, with the reins in the left hand and the butts of their rifles tucked under the right arm, fired and withdrew. (Even today, visitors to Morocco can witness re-enactments of this colorful cavalry tactic, called *fantasías*, at government-sponsored tourist events.) The combination of French discipline and magazine-fed Lebels gave the legionnaires an enormous advantage. It was like shooting fish in a barrel. Hundreds of Moroccans fell. Others tried to retreat, but were blocked from behind by the tightly packed scrum of men, women, animals and children. At last, under withering fire, the *harka* seemed to hesitate, quiver, and withdraw. The wounded reptile slowly recoiled down the hill.

Morale in the French camp was not high. The attack had been repulsed, but 8,000 Moroccans were still camped in the wadi. Every tree in the oasis had been cut down to feed their cook fires. The smell of roasting lamb tortured the legionnaires penned behind mud walls. The drumming and the chanting went on through the night.

The Ait Atta and the tribes from the Tafilalet may have been discouraged, but they agreed on one thing: they had not been defeated. It could not be called a true *baroud* (hand to hand combat). The legionnaires just stood there, loaded and reloaded, and shot everyone down. The French were the richest tribe in the desert. Their convoys were an inexhaustible supply of booty.

"Allah, but how many bullets they have!"

At dawn the Moroccans mysteriously decamped. De Latour, too exhausted to pursue, watched the *harka* slither away among the dunes.

CHAPTER 52

Tent Life

Part I

For the third time in two years, Daisy crossed the High Atlas range. She had made the trip on the back of Uncle Bernon, and by Cessna. This time she travelled by taxi, paid for by *The Tangier Gazette*. She now owned a bank account and a check book. Overjoyed, she arrived in style, only to find her house in ruins! A freak rainstorm had left a large puddle on the flat roof, which went undetected. In her absence the notched palm log ladder had rotted through, and Papa Noel had been unable to climb up and inspect. Finally, the weight of water collapsed the supporting palm beam and lath structure beneath.

The house would have been vandalized, had not the loyal Papa Noel stayed *fidèle à sa poste* with his knotted walking stick, sleeping on a pile of sheepskins in the stable. The old boy had the skills to make the necessary repairs but lacked the funds for materials. These Daisy readily provided, and hired Caftan to do the heavy lifting. With the ladder broken she instructed them to build an outdoor staircase to the roof, plus an extra room to accommodate Maloudia and her daughter.

She called on "Cousin" Cohen in his yoghurt shop, paid her debts and led her animals home. But her little family was not yet complete.

Slimane was a poor correspondent. When he did write, his chief preoccupation was to persuade his wife to change her costume, which he believed to be responsible for their troubles with the Americans. He proposed to do some shopping in Casablanca and urged her to procure a wig to conceal her shaven head.

Daisy replied:

"You cannot buy European clothes for me. You have no idea what is well-made, stylish or just cheap, and you don't have a clue what they cost! The shopgirls will laugh at you. They will humiliate you while charging three times what the clothes are worth. <u>I formally forbid you to incur a penny's worth of debt.</u> And I do not want to hear another word about dressing me as a woman. You know me, and you know that I am ready to obey you in everything, but not to give in when you suggest something completely <u>out of the question</u>."

Moha

As the ongoing repairs rendered her house (*Darna*) uninhabitable, she purchased a summer lease on a bedouin tent (*haima*) in the nomad encampment in the desert outside Rfud. To accompany her as cook, housekeeper, chaperone, nanny, bodyguard and general factotum, she engaged Waffa .

Waffa was petite, five foot at most, with friendly boobs and a resolute confidence among men. Her skin was coal black, blacker than black, a kind of blue-black, the color of some exotic anthracite. Her Hausa grandmother, stolen from the family home in the Sudan, had been dragged in irons across the burning sands to work in the oases of the Moroccan South. Beyond her dear granny Waffa knew nothing of her history, not even the family name; but she was well versed in the arts of voodoo, hand-drumming, and poison. How many children she had borne, she wasn't quite sure, but she stayed in touch with two grown daughters. As with many Moroccans of her generation, her date of birth had gone unrecorded, but in her case was related to a memorable national event: the birth of the Sultan. In other words Waffa, like S.A.R., was about fifty years old.

She could neither read nor write but prayed five times daily. She and Daisy prayed together. She taught Daisy how to pray.

Off no man did she take sass – not soldier, not policeman – and could deploy a battery of epithets that would make a sailor blush.

She'd had it with men, and had little use for Slimane, but his wife she adored. Somewhere on her person, concealed beneath enveloping robes, resided a delicate little shiv, a razor-sharp utensil that knew its way between a man's ribs.

CHAPTER 53

Tarjijsht

The oasis of Tarjijsht comes close to earthly paradise. Situated on the *Piste de Mauritanie*, one of the trans-Saharan caravan routes leading from Morocco to Timbuktu, it lies at the center, like a yolk in a fried egg, of a huge basin of shiny black rock. In season, palm trees are laden with an abundance of the highly-regarded "boufeggou" dates. Barley, oats, alfalfa and assorted vegetables flourish in tiny shaded plots. Water runs in the ditches. Black birds with orange beaks flit through the air which is both warm and cool.

By some miracle (God is Great!) the oasis of Tarjijsht had been spared the plague. The numberless locusts, in a cloud so dense that it blotted the sun, had flown straight overhead, continued north-wards, and pounced on the fertile valleys of Tafraoute, stripping the almond trees, all in pink blossom, before surging up the Souss Valley.

There was rejoicing in Tarjijsht. Allah had held his hand over the beloved oasis, shielding it from the locusts as they flew past. The sullen, seething xenophobic tribes in the surrounding hills who had kept to themselves with Americans about, woke to the news that a miracle had occurred. They descended on the oasis to share in the good fortune.

Market comes twice a week to Tarjijsht – *Souk el Khemis* (Thursday) and *Souk el Had* (Sunday) – when the villagers mingle with the tribesmen who with their women and children arrive on foot, on the backs of camels and donkeys, or by truck and taxi from the hills for a day of barter and exchange. The market square is packed, and the *fondak* teems with large animals in a violent rage to expend their surreal sexual appetites.

As Tarjijsht sits astride the *Piste de Mauritanie*, the old Foreign

Legion post was occupied by a small American military contingent whose job it was to monitor the route for elements of the Polisario, once Spain's nemesis and now Morocco's, filtering up from Rio de Oro.

As a general rule the young Americans got on tolerably well with their Moroccan hosts, often frequenting the market for local produce. None of them spoke more than a few words of Arabic and so, to avoid any possible misunderstanding, they were under orders not to haggle with merchants, but to pay the full asking price, or walk away.

On this particular Sunday morning a soldier had come down to the market square to buy fresh eggs for his breakfast, and an event of some kind occurred. The full truth will never be known, but apparently an altercation broke out between the American and a Berber woman over the price of eggs. Now some of those clear-skinned, blue-eyed Berber women of the Anti-Atlas Mountains are classic beauties. They go about unveiled, strong and confident in the prime of their young lives. Primarily vegetarian, they don't smoke and have never tasted alcohol. They work hard and lead a hearty outdoor life, which you can see in the high color of their bronzed cheeks. They mature early, they marry early, and their men-folk don't like strangers looking at them.

The father of the beauty in question happened to be nearby. The red-bearded patriarch – a man of some standing in his village – was in the process of haggling with a well-heeled neighbor over the bride-price – that is, the price at which he might be persuaded to sell his highly eligible daughter. Overhearing the contretemps behind him and fearing that his bargaining position might already be compromised by his affluent neighbor's instant appraisal of "damaged goods," he stepped forward and with both hands gave the soldier a hard push on the chest.

The flimsy paper sack, which contained the still-warm eggs he had just purchased, split open, and its contents fell to earth.

Whatever the circumstances, American soldiers are not used to being "pushed around." Instead of taking the heavy-handed hint and "pushing off," he stood his ground, pointed to the broken eggs at his feet and demanded to be compensated.

The father, certainly misunderstanding, perhaps believing that the soldier, in his incomprehensible infidel tongue, was making fresh advances in full view of his daughter's prospective husband, or his "nest egg," fumbled beneath his voluminous robes, produced an antique revolver, and shot the imagined pretender dead.

The horrified spectators drew back from the scene of the crime. The father, a tall man, taking advantage of the space suddenly created around him, delivered a soap-box diatribe against not only the young soldier, but against the infidel Americans in general, illegally occupying the southern and "holy half" of Morocco, and, in particular, against those who occupied the old French fort a few yards away, who, at the sound of a gunshot had rushed to the ramparts in their underwear, clutching and loading their weapons.

Something strange began to happen. As the insulted murderer ranted on, perhaps in the not so vain hope that the more the words he piled on the deeper he would bury the still warm corpse at his feet, an invisible sign, like a shiver or a spasm, or a pin-prick, passed through the crowd in the market square. The entire population – men, women, children, even the chickens, turned as one and began to move against the fort.

That mob in Tarjijsht later became known at St. Cyr as the first "*ad hoc*," "*spontané*," or "*combustible*" *harka*, terms not previously coined in any military manual, French or American, because they hadn't been invented.

There they were, all twenty-three of them, against two or three thousand screaming fanatics advancing in a human wave across the square. Not just men firing Kalashnikovs, but women and children and animals were coming to murder them. The women were making that deafening banshee noise, urging their men to battle. Donkeys were braying, and children were screaming. It was a living nightmare in which all of humanity had come together to chuck them out of the universe. There was no way the defenders could have held off such a horde.

The helicopters arrived too late. With women and children milling about, stripping the corpses, the crews had no choice but to hold their fire.

Senior Berber women, all their lives brutalized by men, took savage revenge on the fallen. The soldiers, young enough to be their own sons, were mutilated. Arms and legs were severed, tongues pulled out and eyes gouged. Some were beheaded. One was found sawn in two. Gutted stomachs were filled with stones and straw. Their hands were tied up with their own intestines. Genitals were hacked off and stuffed into crying mouths.

Nothing appeared in the press because the U.S. military command made a frenzied effort to keep it hushed up.

Reprisals followed quickly. Rocket fire from helicopter gunships was directed at mud walls with predictable effect.

A fresh strategy was needed without delay.

CHAPTER 54

Haimasinc

The order, which originated in Washington, and transmitted to the Embassy in Rabat and channelled via the Palais Royal, had senior tent-makers at HAIMASINC scratching their heads. Hamid K. Kamili et Fils, Ets., enjoyed a long and distinguished record of producing tents for grand occasions – diplomatic tents, wedding tents, tribal tents – tents traditional and tents modern. They had made tents for S.A.R. and for his father to celebrate diplomatic and military triumphs. At the Casablanca Conference in 1943 Kamili canvas had shielded the tender Anglo-Saxon complexions of Winston Churchill and F.D.R. from the fierce North African sun. Over the intervening years HAIMASINC had received and filled innumerable lucrative orders from Kuwait, Kazakhstan, Iraq, Pakistan, Saudia, Jordan and the King Ranch. Kamili tents were famous all over the world.

We are not talking about Omar the tent-maker here. Tents are big business in oil-soaked Arab lands. They speak of a noble and nomadic past, perhaps the most romantic image of how man once lived – not cooped up in castles, isolated in igloos or cowering in caves – but in flowing robes, free and forever on the move across an endless, blazing, spiritual landscape, in restless pursuit of union with the Almighty and a bit of R & R in the next oasis. Sweet are the oases in the Sahara.

In all their colorful, quixotic dealings with some of the most undeservedly wealthy people in the world, Kamili et Fils had never handled an order quite like this. And it had to be filled quick-time, delivered and erected in two months flat. An order like this, with so many demanding, decorative specifics – the outer fabric to be woven of the finest goat hair for warmth and weatherproofing, lined with Chinese silks of a dozen different hues, stretched with hempen ropes from India, supported by poles of Aleppo pine, secured by stakes hand-carved from Lebanese cedar, with all metal fittings 100% damascene – must be the whimsy of some fabulously rich and eccentric shaikh who had lived under canvas all his life.

Because of its imprimatur from the Palais Royal, the tent had to be produced to these exact demands. With no questions and asked and no corners cut, it was to be delivered on a certain date, to a particular secret spot in the desert. For the moment we shall refer to this spot as Spot X.

And it had to arrive in the traditional manner, that is, by camel train, with the caravan visiting each of the string of oases which make up the Tafilalet with its royal antecedents, to announce to locals that an all-powerful shaikh was approaching their desert. (Transport to be included in the price of manufacture.)

In a preliminary assessment by senior tentmakers at Kamili et Fils, the tent, with its labyrinthine passageways and secret rooms, would be ample enough to accommodate the Shaikh and his harem, the Shaikh and his entourage, the Shaikh and his extended family, the Shaikh and his tribe!

Design top-secret, but already the rumor had leaked out that the fabric required would keep sun and rain off a football field.

But who was this American Shaikh?

CHAPTER 55

Puer Eternalis

Unlike most officers who follow orders and expect everyone else to do the same, David Ben Jalloud was a soldier of a different stripe, with a broader vision, both pragmatic and idealistic. Promoted when he was thirty-nine, to his sister in America he wrote: "Each time one of my officers calls me 'general,' I turn around to see if he's serious!" He peppered his family with such expressions as, "Africa! Africa! Magic! Magic! Here is the Sun-king, and here is the Sun-god. What a healthy, independent, fully virile life I am leading now!"

While expressing many such surges of aesthetic and ascetic delight with his new life in the desert, he developed a penchant for the burnoose, eating with his fingers, and other Arab cultural habits.

A West Point graduate, he had been sent to Africa on a six-month "study trip." He chose Morocco because his romantic imagination was stirred by the landscape south of the Atlas. Also, Tangier at the time was very much in fashion for eccentric adventure, ex-patriot art and literature, decadence and exoticism. At Sun Beach, the gay *balneario*, he ran into our own Elmyr, studying through a magnifying glass the remains of a scorpion being consumed by ants. Having completed his examination, he incinerated the mangled corpse with said glass.

This young man of Lebanese background who, like General Douglas McArthur, had been a sickly child, was dazzled by this new environment, also by the discovery of enjoyment of the male body. He described a formative visit to a Moroccan household: two "nearly naked young men" led him along a dark passage with heavy soft drapes brushing his skin. They undressed him and took him by the hand to a marble steam bath for a massage by an ageless Moor "with the slippery, unjointed body of an eel." Afterwards he was enfolded in towels and invited to stretch out on a divan with other young men.

Already "avid for mysticism," he learned classical Arabic, studied the Koran, and plunged himself into Muslim culture. All this ensured that he and our heroine would establish an early rapport, plus the fact they both suffered from *le cafard*, "the loveless desert despair," for which there is but one remedy.

A photograph on the cover of *Time* showed the general striking a pose against a backdrop of palm trees and sand. His uniform is partially draped by a cape thrown over one shoulder. In place of a military hat he wears a fez. A pearl-handled revolver dangles from a cartridge belt fashioned from leopard skin – a souvenir of his Sudanese campaign. He holds a curved sword of oriental design. There is little to suggest the iron-willed commander who sank the Sudd pirates with air-boats imported from the Everglades, and crushed the Hoggar rebellion.

The purpose of the American mission in Morocco had already been blurred by the so-called "Vietnam syndrome" – the fear of getting too deeply involved in a military expedition from which it might be difficult to emerge with credit. More study had been spent by State Department officials planning the withdrawal of American troops from Morocco than on what they were supposed to do while they were there.

Ben Jalloud's plan to bring peace to southern Morocco was not, as had proved successful in Niger, endless small "bulldog attacks" against resistants who could "dematerialise" before a modern army could respond, but to systematically win over the cooperation of wavering tribes. The resolutely hostile must be bent to submission by denying them the oases, upon which they were dependent for survival. This was the so-called "Ben Jalloud method," which came to be known as the "Tafilalet Resolution," with psychological contacts and multi-leveled conquest, always with a strong flavor of asceticism or "localism," or the "hearts, souls, minds, and bodies no-frills" directive. Ben Jalloud envisioned creating "a center of seduction and not a pole of repulsion," and described his overall goal as "pacific penetration," akin to the sexual act.

"Muslims spend their whole lives waiting. I, too, know how to wait. I will not bring America to Morocco. No air-conditioning allowed. I will employ Muslim means to ease the fears of our Muslim friends. While in Morocco, we will convert. We Americans will become Muslims among Muslims."

The agitators were able to infiltrate the oases of the Tafilalet because the Algero-Moroccan boundary dispute had never been resolved. The land in between, the *Hammada de Guir*, a vast pebbly plain, had never been plowed or inhabited. From time to time it served as pasturage for nomads who came from both countries for the grazing and water that were necessary to them. The empty landscape provided the bandits with a limitless refuge into which they were adept at vanishing without a trace. One officer described the conflict as "searching for mice on a tennis court."

Ben Jalloud's trump card, the prize which he must deny the enemy at any cost, were the oases of the Tafilalet. This was where the water was, and it was the population center. It was the only part of the desert worth having. For this reason he parked his tent outside Rfud and had bulldozers push up a series of massive "berms" or sand walls, around the Tafilalet, effectively dividing the desert into what was useful and "theirs."

CHAPTER 56

Tent Life

Part II

At the nomad encampment each day began with the ritualistic slaughter of a camel. A decrepit, protesting beast was led in from the desert and made to couch on the sand. A rope was looped around his knee to ensure he would never rise again. The head of the animal, whose loud groans indicated he knew his end was near, was forced backwards over the hump, exposing the base of the neck. The black-turbaned Bedouin drew from his indigo robe a curved knife which he plunged into the jugular, giving the blade a few twists to widen the hole. The camel emitted a swooning groan as the blood gushed out. The head was released, and he was allowed to rest it on the sand for the last few seconds of his life.

Next came the grisly business of cutting him up. The head was amputated and the hooves lopped off. The belly was split and the guts scooped out. The prized liver was put to one side; the intestines were emptied and carried away in baskets. The hide was stripped off in one piece. Women gathered with buckets to haggle over the price of meat. The flies arrived. Soon nothing remained but reddish clots on the sand, lapped by pariahs.

Tent city resembled a fleet of ancient sailing ships, moored in confusion. The desert stretched away in every direction, there were miles of empty space all around, but the tents crowded together as though real estate were at a premium. By day they were occupied mainly by women and children, with the men away tending camels. A maze of ropes webbed the spaces between the tents, making passage difficult and sometimes dangerous. Like sailors at sea, women were continuously rushing out to adjust bucking tent flaps as the wind changed. They pounded in stakes and weighed down shifting tent edges with rocks. Violent arguments broke out over the ownership of rocks (in a sand desert, rocks are rare), spillage of water, and the pranks of wandering children. With the men away, a libertine, harem-like atmosphere prevailed. The temperature was hot, few clothes were worn, with breasts and private parts carelessly exposed. In the encampment the puritanical dress code demanded by the fundamentalists fell on deaf ears.

The bedouin women who camped outside the oasis were stronger than the village girls. They flaunted a raw elegance that Daisy termed "how to wear rags." Their physical charms could be seen through the holes in their indigo robes as they paraded without timidity before men of other tribes. It was a challenge and selection of the fittest.

By night the hubbub subsided as the children dropped off to sleep. The flies mercifully departed. Men were about, giving orders. Grown-ups became involved with the all-important business of food and sex. Silhouettes moved on the tent walls, and laughter could be heard from within. A dog barked, another answered. The moon shined down on the flotilla of tents that heaved with murmurs of the rut.

Listening to those shrill moaning cries and stifled sobs, Daisy felt "*cactosa*" – the joke word for "horny" she and Arturo had invented while smoking weed in AZ. Yes, she was "*cactosa*" as hell, because she missed her man.

"*Estoy cactosa.*"

"*Sí.*"

"*Muy cactosa.*"

"*Tambien.*"

"*Demasiado cactosa.*"

"*Vamos.*"

CHAPTER 57

Tent Life

Part III

Daisy's *haima* was not the largest in the encampment, nor was it by any means the smallest. The dense, heavy fabric, tightly woven in an austere black and white pattern from oily goat hair, insured it would be warm and rainproof. It was supported by polished eucalyptus poles, tethered to iron stakes with ends weighed down by rocks.

Daisy's summer home could have housed a family, but she had it to herself. Hanging blankets partitioned the area into three sections: two areas at the back, one for sleeping, the other for cooking. The frontal area was her "office" – where she wrote and received guests. Flush with money from her new job, she had splashed out on Berber carpets, camel hide hassocks from Mauritania, and cushions embroidered in Fez. Light was provided by kerosene lamps suspended from the supporting posts.

Three small pieces of furniture completed her office décor: *taifor* – a low round table for serving tea – and an inlaid walnut writing slope of English design, which she had spotted at the Bazaar Tindouf in Tangier. Its several drawers contained her writing materials, a flashlight, a magnetic compass and the Swiss army knife. In the bottom drawer, next to her knee, rested the Ruger, loaded.

The third item was a porcelain box connected by a rubber tube to a blue bottle. This was the mini gas fridge which contained scorpion serum, the viper serum and the all-important ice tray.

A monk-like figure in a blue robe, shaven head topped by the embroidered skull-cap, Daisy sat cross-legged on the carpet before the slope.

The tent flap parted.

"A gentleman to see you!" Waffa's face was wide with excitement.

"Who?" Daisy responded irritably. This was the evening hour when she got her writing done.

"Ben Jalloud," came an authoritative voice.

A man stepped into the tent. The sight of Daisy, pen in hand, made him pause.

"I'm interrupting your writing."

"No, you're not ... " Flustered by this unexpected visit, she attempted to rise, but her guest had already sat down.

"I got used to tent life in Mali," he said, settling himself on the carpet.

He was dressed in a loose, open-neck, sand-colored shirt. Baggy legionnaire trousers (*sirwal*) billowed from the knee. Red-topped riding boots denoted respect for local custom. A soft gray burnoose (*silhem*) seemed to float over his shoulders. He carried a battered Moroccan satchel (*shqara*) which he set on the carpet beside him. Daisy glanced at it and frowned: the *shqara* looked oddly familiar.

"I bring greetings from Elmyr. He sent me the article from *The Herald Tribune*," he said, "but of course the adventures of *La Bonne Nomade* are the subject of gossip all over Morocco."

Daisy, thrilled by the unexpected presence in her tent of this powerful, older man, instinctively reached for her tobacco.

"How is dear Elmyr? If it wasn't for him, I wouldn't be here today."

"For once the news is good."

"I owe everything to Elmyr. He plucked me from the Parisian cold, and fed and warmed me in his apartment. He introduced me to my patron, the Duchess de Bremont."

"He claims to have stumbled on an invention that will make him rich."

"Will you have something to drink, *mon général?*"

"Tea would be very nice."

"I meant whiskey."

"Even better."

"Waffa! Two glasses and the bottle!"

Waffa scampered away like a rabbit.

"It seems he was in the south of France, riding along on a bus. It was one of those dead straight roads in Provence, originally laid down by the Romans, with plane trees planted, with strict French correctness, exactly twenty meters apart. It was late afternoon. The sun was low. Elmyr had had a good lunch. He was settling into a white wine nap, with his head resting on the back of the seat, sideways, facing the window, when he experienced a kaleidoscopic swirl of colors within his closed eyes. Similar, he said, to the visions St. Paul must have experienced on the road to Damascus."

"That scallawag never thinks small, but I've never heard him promoting himself for sainthood."

"In Aix-en-Provence he picked up a math student from Princeton and described the phenomenon. The young genius immediately twigged. What had seemed to Elmyr to be an act of God turned out to be a well-known scientific phenomenon. Alpha waves, corresponding to a certain number of pulses per second, can produce visions from the optic nerve. The prodigy went back to Princeton and built a contraption, a perforated cylinder mounted on a victrola turntable. A light bulb suspended within the spinning vertical tube reproduced in the viewing eye the same swirls of light that Elmyr experienced on that road in Provence."

The general watched Daisy flick the *mechero*.

"What is it?"

"A Spanish goatherd's tinder-lighter. It doesn't blow out in the wind."

"Elmyr is applying for a patent. Your duchess is backing the project. The Iris Clert Gallery is putting on a show. Elmyr calls his gadget 'The Dreamachine,' – the only work of art you look at with your eyes closed!"

Jewelry clanking, Waffa sliced like a knife through the curtains. Dipping to her knees before the general, she set a tray on the *taifor*. On the tray sat two cut glass tumblers and a bottle of Old Cornstalk.

A glimmer of ivory told Daisy she was enjoying this little ritual. With an extra wiggle for the general to hear the clank, she slipped away behind the curtain.

Daisy cracked the ice tray and poured the whiskey.

"*De l'eau, mon général?*"

"Just the way it is."

Daisy blew out some smoke. "Is that a new airport on the hill, general, or your tent?"

"A major new tribe is coming to the desert. I am the leader of this tribe. In the desert the strength of a man is judged by the size of his tent. It is a symbolic element of a broader plan to bring peace to the Sahara."

"And how are you going to do that?"

"By convincing my enemies that I am the most powerful shaikh in their desert. Capitulation you see … " He smiled. "Must be a gentle process. The Smithsonian has already requested the tent as an emblem of American military authority."

Daisy was studying the general's close-cropped hair and flat brown cheeks. His full sensuous lips were of a brownish-purple color.

"No-one must lose face. It is easier to submit when the victor is all-powerful."

With a face like that, she thought, he could be Moroccan, or Spanish, or Italian, or from anywhere in the Middle East. Another golden-eyed god, come down to earth to rule over brown men.

"When I arrived here," he said, "I requested your dossier."

"Did it take a camel to carry it, like your tent? I saw it once, on Captain Keller's desk. I thought it was the Tangier phone book."

The general ignored the banter. "You speak *darija*."

Daisy sipped the whiskey.

"You've been admitted to the brotherhood of the Jilaliya."

"I'm a novice, a *khouan*. A low monk."

"You are a friend of the Rogue."

"You mustn't call him that," she answered sharply.

"Mustn't I?"

"No, you mustn't."

"Why?"

"Because it is a bastardization of the word Rogui, which means Pretender to the throne of Morocco, which he is not. His proper name is Sidi Mohamed ould Brahim."

"I need to get in touch with him."

"I may be able to help you with that."

"How do you know him?"

"We met at a dinner party in Tangier. Does that sound frivolous to you?"

"No."

"Did you expect something less social from a desert chieftain?"

"He is a well-travelled, highly-educated desert chieftain."

"Yes, as educated as you, and a whole lot better than me." Daisy said defensively. "His niece is a student at the American School. He opposes the Americans in the desert, while paying for her education in Tangier. What does that tell you?"

The general smiled.

"My late mother was exceedingly fond of the Marabout. She compared him to Robert E. Lee. Coming from her, that was the highest praise possible."

"Why Lee?" The general looked surprised.

"For her Lee was the epitome of a Southern gentleman. The protector of women, children and tradition. He fought to keep the Yankees from burning his house down."

"That he did."

"Like the Marabout is doing now."

The general smiled. It was a queer, enigmatic smile. Daisy wasn't quite sure whether she liked that smile.

Upon entering the tent, framed by the billowing burnoose and baggy trousers, Ben Jalloud had initially looked enormous to Daisy – like Superman; but now, in a sitting position with trousers deflated to his thighs, the burnoose collapsed around his shoulders, he seemed more like Clark Kent. Like the other men she had loved

– Cowboy Slim, Arturo, Slimane – he had a slender, average build. She didn't want heavy men lying on top of her.

"First of all, apologies must be made."

"By all means, but to whom?"

"To the Marabout. For the rumor that he organized my murder. By the way, what's happened to Keller?"

"I sent him to Mrheimine to work on the sand wall. Aside from your mother's romantic notion, what is your opinion of the Marabout?"

"He is a spiritual leader and a gentleman. His children are dead. He lives for his people."

"That may be so, but we find his tracks everywhere. All our troubles begin with him. With him we will have to finish."

"How do you expect the Marabout to preach peace in an atmosphere of insecurity? His followers are the poorest people on earth. They're starving! They have nothing! American food aid is not enough. Most of it is confiscated by corrupt government officials. His people are on the outside. They want to come in. They need to trade in order to survive. Make the Tafilalet irresistible to them and they'll come, not to fight, but peacefully, on your terms."

"How do you propose we do this?"

"Open markets, let the tribes see the economic advantage of your presence. Your advance across the desert ought to be measured not by military success, but by the spread of wealth. Let the Jews play a role."

"Why the Jews?"

"They're not strictly allied with either Muslims or Christians. They can do business with both. They speak the languages. Let them open markets for you, instead of wasting your time on that sand wall."

"The Egyptians of the twelfth dynasty built a wall from Heliopolis to Pelusium to discourage Bedouin incursions. The Assyrians put up a barrier across the Euphrates to repel the Medes, and the Persians erected a wall against the Huns. The Great Wall of China was the final defense against the Mongols. Each of those great works was designed to put an end to the recurring raids from the arid upon the sown."

"I say let the Jews be your agents."

"Are you Jewish?"

"Was. Now Muslim."

"My sand wall is keeping the bandits out of the Tafilalet."

"I've heard it's so bugged with listening devices a dung beetle can't roll a camel turd across it without them hearing about it in the White House. I say let the Jews of the region get on with this job, the ones who speak the local dialects."

A child toddled into the room. Daisy pulled her into her lap and kissed her.

"This is Nabilah, my niece. Bedtime, darling."

The general pushed the satchel toward her.

"That looks like my old *shqara*."

"That it is."

She pulled it open.

"What's all this?"

"Forty-nine hundred dollars."

CHAPTER 58

"The Method"

In a speech before the shaikhs of the assembled tribes (the Ida Ocblal, who camped on both sides of the Drâa; the Ait ou Mribet, who also roamed the Drâa; the Oulad Delim, whose range extended to Mauritania where they bought slaves to sell north; and the Lemtouna, or men of the *litam* – veil – another important Berber tribe), Ben Jalloud made it clear that, if attacked, he would reply with overwhelming force, but he remained open to any overture which might lead to peace. Daisy sat at his side and translated.

The general envisioned an oil stain that would spread slowly, inexorably, alternatively playing on all the local elements, and utilizing the divisions and rivalries between the tribes. The ultimate solution must be underpinned by political and economic policies which would ensure that an indelible pro-American "memory" would be left behind. This was the essence of the Ben Jalloud 'method.'

As the general expanded his perimeters, the Rogue began to feel the pressure. Two tribes begged for mercy. 1350 tents of the Arib, who lived in tents between the Tafilalet and the Drâa, had a *ksar* at Zair and spoke Arabic and claimed to be Arabs, moved to Rsani; and 1742 tents of the nomadic Tajakant, using tents with a ksar at Tindouf, resettled near Foum el Hassan. On May 4th a deputation of the Braber, a slave-owning section of the Ait Atta, asked to see the general. The Marabout had written a letter. The general summoned Daisy to his tent; together they formulated a reply.

"When the Rogue falls, or is brought to heel, the problems of southern Morocco will fall with him."

"You must distribute seed to the working populations in the oases. What have you done to compensate the families of Moroccan troops? Have you contacted the Beni Israel in the valleys behind Rich? Those Israelites of the Atlas live under the protection of the Ait Atta. They have been the Ait Atta's bankers for centuries. We're talking about old money here."

"Not one of my officers understands Morocco like you."

"Not one of your officers loves Morocco like I do."

"The day after tomorrow I'm off on a reconnaissance tour to test the strength of the Rogue."

"How many times do I have to ask you not to call him that?"

"I want you to come along."

The favorite, now almost twenty-two years old, raced around Rfud in a frenzy of excitement, buying clothes and doling out cash. Throughout the tour she attached herself to the general like a devoted squire from the Middle Ages, which stirred up resentment among his staff, who branded her "la Rasputeen" for bewitching their commander. She was the first into the tent each morning to demand the news of the night. She prepared his coffee and arranged the burnoose over his shoulders.

Soon she was in the tent. They discovered a shared passion for pingpong, and played two out of three games each night after supper. The general then retired to his office to write his report, Daisy to a cubicle where she had access to a typewriter. The tent provided her with the peace and privacy she needed to turn out articles for *The Tangier Gazette*.

Women on the Edge

Here in Saharan Morocco women stay on the edge. They are hesitant, they hover in the background while the men do the talking. With their babies on their backs, holding little ones by the hand, the women watch and listen.

In Africa public space belongs to men, but I have learned that if I want to hear the full story, space must be made for the women. Recently, in the commune of Ain Jrane I met a group of men who had come out to talk about the digging of a new well to bring life back to a tiny oasis picked clean by the locusts. There was absolutely nothing left; the palm fronds had been chewed down to their stems; it looked like a battlefield. The entire community depended on food aid from America.

"Someone is missing," I said.

"No, we are all here," replied the men who had gathered about me.

"So Jrane is the only commune in Morocco where there are just men?"

This prompted much laughter. Slowly the women, who had been invisible until now, began to edge forward.

There was a lone protesting voice – the eternal long-suffering voice of women who know that their men are fools and children, but indispensable. .

A discussion with women always starts with laughter. A western woman, asking questions, makes for an interesting encounter. A universal camaraderie exists among all women.

We found a way to understand one another through shared experiences – always having too much to do, the relentless sexual demands of men. And everywhere motherhood is the same.

The women told me how they were planning to expand the new water source: they were going to dig fresh channels to grow potatoes, onions, lettuce and carrots to add variety to their diet.

Laughter was replaced by seriousness as the women described the harshness of their lives devastated by the locust invasion. What could I do to give their children a better hope for the future?

It was a simple question, one with many answers, none easy. Mothers worry about feeding their children, and anxiety grows amid fluctuating weather patterns, erratic rainfall, conflict, and especially the locust plague which visited southern Morocco.

In the endless debate about the effectiveness of humanitarian aid, people say, "Why bother?" "It's too costly." "Charity should begin at home." "The governments in those countries are corrupt." "The aid never reaches the people who need it most." Then there is the alarming suggestion to let nature take its course – a kind of heartless mechanism to manage population growth.

One small ray of hope is that in Morocco the alarm bell rang early. There is hope for these women living on the edge. The child strapped to the mother's back could be my child, or yours. All women share the same hope. Without America's help these women and their children would face a darker destiny.

"The Cathedral," the main Jilaliya *zawiya*, was located on a chott or salt pan – one of the vast saline plains that occupy more than a fifth of the Sahara, residues of prehistoric seas. This chott *djerid* (locust leg) was located SW of the Tafilalet, in a desert region with no fixed frontier accepted by either Moroccan or Algerian authorities. The Rogue used it as his headquarters in winter because no one could get at him there. With the first rains, the chott quickly transformed into a deadly quicksand of mud and mire, rendering the monastery impregnable to overland attack.

The winter before, a U.N. helicopter, delivering a high-ranking official to negotiate with the Marabout, attempted to land on the chott. Wild celebrations echoed from the ramparts of the *zawiya* as the flailing monster, like some gigantic trapped insect, was slowly gulped down in big hungry slurps of mud, saltwater and sand.

In summer, however, the chott becomes as hard and flat as a tennis court. The fast camels of the Attaoui gallop over it.

While the General kept to his tent, Daisy got some writing done in hers, awaiting the summons she was certain must come.

Finally it did.

"The Rogue is in the Cathedral and the chott is dry."

"That can only mean he wants to talk."

"A message arrived. He wants you to go to him. He has something for you. Or, should I say, someone … "

"Oh my God. The Duke!"

CHAPTER 59

Time Marches On

When he passed away, Duncan van Renseelaer, to the considerable dismay of his relatives, left the bulk of his estate to Arturo and Daisy. Arturo moved from the Chelsea Hotel into a brownstone at 231 West 11th Street. Dear old Miss Bushy, once more rescued from skid row, served as his live-in housekeeper.

Now a wealthy young man about town, and with a promising art career, Arturo had hardly changed his ways. He was still, as Daisy called him, "a walkin' dude." Cowboy-lean, road-hardened, he tried to shed his demons on the road, like his namesake, Arthur Rimbaud.

An inch or two under six foot, high-colored like his sister, with the rugged good looks of a middle-weight prize fighter, he thought nothing of hiking from Manhattan to the Jersey Shore, sleeping on the beach at Mantoloking and hanging out with the seagulls. His sketchbook and a change of socks he toted in a beat-up German rucksack with wooden slats. His long legs calmly covered the ground in enormous strides, like a horse. He marched all the way to the Delaware Water Gap and explored on foot the Catskill Mountains and the fabled lands of his ancestors – the Hudson River Valley. But where he felt most at home was at the New Jersey end of the Holland Tunnel. Speaking Spanish in low-life Dominican bars in Hoboken and Perth Amboy liberated him, somewhat. In the Church of Santa Ana in Jersey City he found a kind of earthly solace.

But was he desecrating the altar because of his illicit love? Was it even love or just a feeling of pity in return for such affectionate little-sisterly devotion? He tried in vain to excuse himself. You know how to take care of yourself, Antonio had taught. You can suffer but not be lost. But did he know how to care for others? In church he still was a spectator, one of the multitude around the cross over whom the gaze of Christ must have passed. Daisy had borne a child by him in one agony; in another had watched while it was taken away. It seemed to Arturo that he had run away from everything.

But in the church of Santa Ana he had for the first time in his life the odd sensation that the burden of his guilt had shifted elsewhere. Somewhere behind it all was the love of God, bestowed on him by his mother. This love now stirred him. The love one always feels for what one has lost – a child, a woman, even a pet. He carried a wound, one that would not heal. In church his artistic ambitions came back to him as something faintly comic. But for a truly peaceful life he needed human company. Aloneness posed a threat of worse things to come.

Twenty-seven and single, with one of the oldest names in Manhattan (he never used it), he was considered quite a catch. Women were after him, but he wouldn't commit. He was a loner. Something was holding him back.

Cajan was back on the phone from Paris, with the news that Daisy had surfaced in Tangier. She had been accused of some kind of crime for which she had been thrown into jail. She had been kicked out of Morocco, but somehow had managed to sneak back in. Arturo fired off a letter with the news that she needn't worry about money any longer because she was the co-beneficiary of their father's will to the address Cajan had sent him.

Poste Restante,
Rfud,
Tafilalet,
Maroc.

By the time the letter threaded its way through the creaking Moroccan postal system and crossed the Atlas Mountains by dusty desert bus, Daisy had again flown the coop, this time seeking her destiny on the track to Khettamia.

CHAPTER 60

The White Road

June 16 10.15 AM
At 2.30 AM they crept past the sentries. Guides and camels were waiting in the wadi. After walking fast and riding hard for the rest of the night and half the morning they stopped for tea.

A man approached. They threw themselves down. The rifles were out. Everything was tense in this land of *baroud*. But it turned out to be a friend.

8.36 PM
At dusk they stopped again and pitched camp beneath a mountain of yellow sand. Erg Chebbi. Forty-five kilometers she figured they'd made. Loot prayed. A single human voice raised in song can fill an entire desert.

She sat at a little distance from the others and listened to the talk. The voices of the Saharans are uniform. They are gentle but can be raised and carry a long way.

These must be old-fashioned voices of people who have not gathered in sufficient numbers or who lack sufficient reason to form permanent communities.

Brahim made bread. They ate the inner organs of the animal, talked about desert crossings, and drank glass after glass of tea. Before turning in she peeked at the contents of the box which Ben Jalloud had entrusted to her: the sealed letter for the Marabout and medicine for the his mother. (She suffered from diabetes.) Plus viper serum, scorpion serum, syringes.

June 17

They stopped in a wadi for lunch: the remains of last night's bread, cheese, the world's best apricots. Her back was sore. Her legs were sore. Her shoulders were sore from sleeping on the ground. Her new sandals were rubbing the tops of her toes. Her feet were killing her.

Loot: full of energy and cheer. Now he made tea again. Gray, close shaven head, turban covered. Forty-two, he looked fifty-five. A gentleman in harsh surroundings. They were following the same route he and the Duke took. The mythological route; now she was on it.

8.30 PM

In the evening they camped in another dry riverbed – Oued Amri, in a nest of Barshan dunes. Brahim was atop one, rifle across knee, keeping watch. Tomorrow they would see big sand – Erg er Raoui.

She figured they made 59 kilometers. Loot said 60. Brahim said 65.

Brahim said they made 5 kilometers per hour. Loot said 4. She figured 4.

Now they numbered 7 men, 4 camels, 4 asses. People knew they had meat. Loot held the young men with his tales. He examined the stitch marks on her arm where Dr. Parodis had sewed her up.

"Ohhh!" He touched his finger to the scar. "Ohhhhh." He mimicked the sound of pain. "Ahhhhhh." Then he smiled.

Hassi Sidi Rouidane was a primitive oasis where they stopped to wash. Folded *haimas* and other desert equipment lay in neat bundles all around, on the tops of boulders and in the branches of the *arganiers*. The Ait Atta left this baggage behind while they were off raiding. It was never disturbed because the saint in his tomb guarded it.

Everyone bathed but her. The camel men chided her for being too prudish to take off her clothes. Did they think she was a man, or were they hoping she was a woman? She saw them conspiring like schoolboys and feared they would throw her in.

"Then work!" Loot tossed her the Kalashnikov and pointed to a pile of rocks. She knew how to handle a shotgun (quail), a rifle (peccary), and a revolver (sidewinder), but had never before held a man-killing instrument.

Down! Flat! Two Hueys flashed overhead.

June 19

Her djellaba, burnoose, the Swiss knife, the Ruger, – especially her writing – were of great interest to all.

Loot was the old desert hand, but Brahim knew the way almost as well. Loot said the trip to Taodeni took thirty-seven days not pressing the pace.

Desert people talk and talk. All they do is talk, in long monologues, to be answered by another long monologue.

Their way of eating, which she found sensible, was to eat something as soon as a stop was made, even a crust of yesterday's bread. This cut the appetite and one could wait patiently while the hot meal is prepared. Nothing was done in a hurry. When they pray, they pray briefly, rifles beside them.

While dinner cooked, she lay inside the tent with her notebook before a candle stuck in the sand. (Her companions regarded her candles as a luxury.) Outside, a fire blazed, men talked, a pot bubbled, and stars shone down on a perfectly still Saharan night.

She consumed, on the average day, twelve small glasses of the strong smoky sweet green tea. Most liquid was consumed in this manner. This was where the energy came from.

When Daisy walked away from the fire to pee in private, she took in the stars. Some nights the desert seemed dangerous and inhospitable, others tender and vulnerable, because it was so unprotected. Polished stones glittered like coins in the moonlight. The desert was littered with invaluable and inconvertible treasure; no wonder it engendered dreams of priceless spirituality.

June 21
Locusts:

These birdlike insects flittering on feeble glassy wings – we saw an infinite flight of them drifting on the evening wind, a diaphanous tongue caressing the sky. On the ground they look like grasshoppers. At first white, they turn black within three days and grayish within the space of a month. They have two pairs of wings and six legs, three on each side, the back pair longer than those in front. When fully grown they reach the length of a couple of thumbs.

June 22
Her feet ached, her toes had blood blisters. Even the camels were bushed. One collapsed on the sand. Loot kicked it. "Dog!" There is no place for the weak in the desert.

She wondered how much more of this she could take. Most of the afternoon they wandered among dunes which were beautiful to look at, but oven hot. She started off barefoot but scorched the soles of her feet, which accounted for the soreness. Even in sandals it was too hot to walk. She mounted her camel but had to get down every hour. Sometimes every ½ hour. Shit and more shit. Watery.

9.15 PM
The sun was going down. It was warm and windless. She ate two boiled eggs, crunched some aspirin and felt better, as depression departed with fever, fatigue, boredom and exposure.

Only one thing exists out here: time. The soft explosions of sunrise and sunset are the main events in this land without echoes.

June 25 11.18 AM

This morning, just after setting out, we came across a member of the Marabout's camel corps. Or he came across us, cantering across the plain on his snow white mehari. He was one of the most ter-rifying men I'd ever laid eyes on. Sitting high on his beast, with an AK47 across his lap, dressed ordinarily, that is, in an indigo blue robe with white turban and a white sash wrapped around his waist and criss-crossing his chest and back. His skin was blue-black, the features fine Arab. Incredibly haughty, he did not greet me but stared down at me (I had not yet mounted my camel) as he exchanged lengthy salutations with the others. While he examined my laissez-passer, I examined him. He looked cruel and beautiful and tough as nails. My master has some meanies on his side. No wonder Ben Jalloud has his hands full taming men like these.

2 PM

They rode on for a few hours until they met another group of Saha-rans with about forty camels. Women were present.

They lunched in the dunes. It was hot, they had no cover, and the exposed meat drew a swarm of flies. While she waited for Boahinin and Loot to fetch water from the *hassi*, Ali, age ten, entertained her with songs from Mauritania and showed her his Spanish knife.

In a wasteland like this a Spanish knife has the entertainment value of the Marx Bros.

June 26

Jebel Gouman: country of hope – because it is empty.

When the wind begins to rise in the middle of the night, and unknown things begin to move about, and the world beneath the moon seems a ghastly place, I am more than grateful for my com-panions the camel-men, for their reassuring company and unerring knowledge of the desert, and especially for the presence of their sleeping forms just a few feet away.

Her feet: she couldn't remember what they looked like before, but now they looked different – bigger, with toes splayed, heels cracked. They looked more like hooves than feet. She would have to buy a new pair of shoes (if she ever wore shoes again).

June 27/28?

Horrible day – the sun set in the middle of the sky. The sand is blowing. We made 15 km. only. I'm slowing everyone down.

CHAPTER 61

Khettamia

The sun rose above a ghastly world where no sign of life was visible. The vast salt pan stretched to infinity, welding itself to the white hot sky. For hours they had been traversing a perfect flatness, toward a horizon obliterated by an infernal blaze of dancing heat.

In the middle of the pan, of a whiteness passing to blue as the throbbing sun sank through the sky, the rose-colored towers of Khettamia materialized above the dark vegetation of its gardens.

The first and most powerful impression was made by the large number of slaves. Uniformly dressed in snow-white turbans and ivory gowns, gliding silently on bare feet, these towering, elegant, but timid men communicated in a twittering African tongue. Daisy felt she had arrived at the last outpost of civilization. Next stop Timbuktu, whence the ancestors of these blacks had originally come, driven along, chained together, not so long ago.

While the slave prepared coffee, her eyes grew accustomed to the gloom. After the blazing light reflecting off the salt pan, her chamber seemed almost dark. It had its own water supply, fed from above by a hanging goatskin, dripping onto a copper basin.

When the slave departed, she examined the chamber from the point of view of security. The door could not be locked. Outside was a terrace with a fifty foot drop. The massive walls of the *zawiya* bristled with such terraces, for cooking and sleeping beneath the stars. She slipped the Ruger beneath a cushion and slept for twelve hours.

The Marabout was not in residence but Lalla, his mother, was. Daisy sent the medicine.

Confined to her quarters, she spent her mornings writing, her afternoons on the terrace gazing at a great golden dune banked up against a cliff behind the Ksar.

At the top of the cliff, near the summit of the dune, a lone pistachio tree had taken root. Daisy felt a strange kinship with this tree whose solitary existence, she imagined, was not unlike her own. After observing the tree for several days, she became certain that the dark lump beneath was not a rock but a man, sitting in its shade. Daisy watched him from afar. Each morning he was in the same place. In the evening he dematerialized.

Lalla expressed her gratitude by sending Mamadu. The bowl of pomegranates decorated with cornflowers told Daisy she was personally supervising the preparation of her food. She realized that she was being looked after, and a kind of nursery peace descended.

Recovered from fever, she worked on the manuscript; but when she tried to leave her apartment she found the way blocked by the slave.

"Why don't they let me out, Mamadu? I love my solitude, but this room is beginning to resemble a cell!"

Mamadu shrugged. "Orders are orders."

"Who gave them?"

"The Marabout."

"But he's not here."

"Here or not here, his word remains."

The dune became her symbol of eternity, her mountain of light. The hill of golden sand, blown by the wind, changed its shape and color from hour to hour, but forever remained the same.

"Who is that out there, Mamadu?" she asked. "The one who sits beneath the tree?"

"A hermit."

"He makes me think of the early Christian hermits, sitting all their lives before caves in Sinai."

"That's what people say he is – a Christian."

"Why do they say that?"

"He does not pray. He speaks a language no one understands."

"I want to talk to him."

"You can talk, but he won't talk back."

"Why?"

"He has no tongue."

"That's impossible!"

"He has a forked tongue, like the *lefâa*."

"What?"

"His tongue was cut in two. He can only talk gibberish."

My God! Daisy said to herself. Could that be the Duke?

The Marabout returned. Daisy sent a note protesting her confinement. The reply was a basket full of clothes. She had to change from her riding costume, which came from *bled-al-askar*, or "governed" Morocco which would arouse suspicion if she ventured abroad.

She selected a cool blue robe. With Mamadu as her guide, she shuffled into the light.

They scaled the cliff and made their way toward the tree. Rocks glittered in the sun. The dune shimmered in the noonday heat. Only the tree seemed stable. A man, or something, was under it – a lump in the shade.

"Your Grace!" Daisy called.

No answer. She crept closer. "The Duke de Bremont! Is that you?"

The tree began to move, or was it the man? He leapt from the shadows where he had been sitting almost invisible and ran straight toward her. He was a huge man, a giant.

Mamadu fled.

His eyes were blank. Slobber dripped from his lips and beard. Through the rents in his tattered robe Daisy could see skin that was milky white, but with face and arms charred like overcooked meat. He moved with heavy legs, barefoot. He carried part of the tree in his hand – a stick.

Bellowing and gesticulating, he lurched forward in a stiff, halting run.

"Gluglu?"

The giant bared his teeth, roared and jabbered to himself. Daisy jumped aside as he ran right by.

"He doesn't see anything but his own visions!" Mamadu popped up from behind a boulder. "The Blue People poked his eyes out. He sits there day after day babbling incantations with that forked tongue of his."

"How does he live?"

"Kind people bring him bread, dates from the oasis. He likes a cigarette. A Jew brings him wine."

"That's not gibberish he's talking – it's French!"

Fever returned, time stopped, and Daisy spent long hours on the terrace, facing the flaming horizon. Lalla sent her sympathies, her infusions and her servants, but could not visit. In order to preserve his identity, Moha had to be treated as a man.

Was it July now, or August? She lost track of days. The Marabout himself came to her cell, in his arms lifted and carried her to his apartment, where she lay among carpets and cushions. She experienced some doleful respites, lucid and voluptuous. Night after night she lay half-awake on the terrace – white nights of infinite transparency. The moonlight, reflecting off the frozen lake of the desert, picked its way across the mat, over the tips of her fingers, up her sleeve, to her face.

September was the month of *sherqi*, when the dust-filled air penetrated every crevice. The temperature rarely dropped below 100°, day or night, and Daisy lived through seventeen days of fever. Even Mamadu fell sick, and once more she was attended by the moody slave. She began to think she might die in that place. For minutes that seemed like years she imagined the relief she would feel when, at her order, the slave would take away the copper basin, and the drops of water from the goatskin would fall on the beaten earth with a flat, dull sound. But she did not have the strength to command, and the drops kept falling, ringing forever on the polished copper.

CHAPTER 62

Fata Morgana

The vast, lifeless and apparently immutable *hammada* was strewn with trilobites, each perfectly embalmed in basalt, with fanning wadis ending in moraines of boulders the size of ashcans, once pushed along by phantom rivers. Dancing like vaporized marionettes, spiralling dust-devils whispered of an age when all was water.

A mighty surf once thundered against cretaceous beaches now blown over by Saharan sands; dunes roll over ancient sea-beds where plesiosaurs sported, gulping down ganoid fish the size of canoes. Leather-winged reptilians – twenty-eight feet from wing-tip to tip – patrolled these coasts; even today's descendants, wandering seagulls blown a thousand miles off course by Atlantic gales, have found an ancestral home.

Mirages mocked them every step of the way. The effect produced a kind of monomania: would they ever find their way out of this hell of mirrors? The gravel plain, featureless but for the monogamy of shimmering images, ended with the sky.

For months nobody knew if she was dead or alive. Then one day she reappeared, spectral as the glittering mirages that lapped at her heels, supported by the boy who accompanied her. The Duke de Bremont trailed along on the end of a rope.

The pack camel having collapsed – she put the poor beast out of its misery with the Ruger – they fell into the dunes outside the fort at Tawaz to await the light. Their ordeal was nearly over, or so they thought.

"In a few hours," she said to Mamadu, "someone will be offering you a cup of water."

"*Insh'Allah.*"

"Or a glass of champagne," the Duke gasped.

"What is champagne, your highness?"

"Liquid kif. Only more refreshing. You'll love it."

"We're in Morocco now, Mamadu," Daisy said.

"This fighting Morocco I do not like."

"Tomorrow you will be a free man."

"What is free, Moha?"

"You will belong to nobody. You can do what you like."

"Si Moha, who caught you when you fell from the camel at Hassi Bizbooz?" Mamadu pleaded. "Who found the well at Rouidane and made His Highness drink? Who baked your bread in the sand dunes of Morocco? Your bones would be there now, crunched by the jackals, if it weren't for me. You are my master – you cannot leave me like this."

"Your master I am not."

"Si Mohammed gave me to you, in front of the assembled shaikhs at Khettamia. To be abandoned now would be a grave humiliation."

"In gratitude for the many favors you have done, I am giving you your freedom."

"Is this the reward I get for saving your life?"

"My son, what greater gift is there than freedom?" whispered the blind Duke.

Mamadu sincerely thought Gluglu was mocking him.

"Your highness," he whined, "all my life I have been pro-tected, housed, clothed and treated as a respected member of Sidi Mohamed's household. Now Si Moha throws me out!"

"You don't want to be free?"

"What is this freedom? I want food and new clothes. White bread and a roof over my head, a master to arrange my marriage. It is shameful to be sixteen and not married."

"Come with me, my boy," he rasped. "You may take care of me in my enfeebled state."

"I swear on my mother's unmarked grave, I would rather die of thirst in the Grand Sahara than be free."

"Do not fret. I will take you in."

"But where is this England, sire? I do not wish to leave the holy lands of Islam. What is this *madrassa* you speak of, where elderly white Christian men will beat me with sticks if I do not learn to read and write?"

"They will make a gentleman of you."

"What is a 'gentleman,' your highness?"

"A gentleman … is a man who lives in a great tent and has many women."

"Oh, yes!"

"Perhaps an Eton education is a bit fanciful, my boy, although I do believe a strapping lad like you could win your colors in a rugby shirt. Moha has rescued me from the Saharan sun, which I cannot now do without. In one of the oases of the Tafilalet I shall build a Casbah. You shall be my servant."

"Do you not object, Si Moha?"

"I give you to him."

"Will you cook my food?" asked the Duke.

"Yes, sire."

"And bring me women?"

"Oh, yes."

"Many women."

"Of course."

"You shall be the judge of their beauty."

"It is a slave's job, sire."

"And I shall find a slave woman to bear your children."

"Just one?"

"One at a time."

"That sounds so peaceful, sire. A garden with many women – it is the dream of every slave."

Mamadu kept watch while Daisy and the Duke dozed in the sand.

"Darling Duke, after chasing the phantom of a man I did not know, I too begin to feel a strange kinship."

"Ditto." He squeezed her hand. "If I were not so feeble, Moha, I would ask you to be my wife."

"Gluglu, you already have a wife!"

"In Tiglite I was forcibly converted to Islam. Koranic law allows a man to possess four wives."

"Then I would accept."

"But you too are married."

"Among the Tuareg people, the men go veiled and a woman can take more than one man."

"True."

"So, darling Duke, I would ask you to be my number two."

"And I too would accept."

At first light Daisy put her head above the dune, and ducked back down as bullets from the fort thumped into the sand. So there they were – exhausted, weakened by thirst and pinned down by her own countrymen. Having trekked hundreds of miles, they were unable to walk the last two hundred yards or so for the drink that would save their lives.

The day began to stoke up. Thirst became a torment. Each time Daisy poked her head up, bullets spattered the sand. There seemed to be no way out of this absurd but potentially lethal predicament.

By midday the sand was baked to furnace-heat. It was burning through the soles of her sandals. Soft and shapely as they appeared, the sickle dunes were heat-traps. With encircling arms they collect the heat.

The horizon oscillated. Dune crests quivered like custard. A sheet of blue water appeared.

"Look!" Mamadu shouted. "Do you see the trees? The water – how pure it is, how cool!"

Poor boy, Daisy thought, he's lost it.

"After so much false water, your highness, to taste some of the real. Just one drop!"

Gluglu was mute. He was fading fast.

As they crept along, the silvery water gradually retreated, expiring at their feet.

Daisy saw the Duke was too weak to go on. If she did not find help soon, he might not make it. She made a plan.

"Listen," she whispered into his ear as he lay on the side of a dune. "Mamadu and I are going to creep around and try to communicate with the fort on the Rsani side, where they might not be so trigger-happy. Don't move from here. Keep your head down."

He found her hand and squeezed. "My fate is in your hands."

"I love you, darling Gluglu."

He squeezed again. "Ditto."

"Goodbye for now. Stay low. We'll be back in an hour. *Insh'Allah*."

Crawling on their hands and knees, she and Mamadu made their way among the dunes.

Just when they needed it, they were running out of sand. The dunes had slumped with the wind. The spreading sea of sandy waves, swell after swell, had reduced to ripples. They bellied along, keeping low profiles to avoid being targeted. A vulture circled overhead. Ahead lay the hard desert floor with no cover at all.

The shadow of the vulture, looping lazily over the dunes, made her stop. Mamadu looked absolutely bushed.

Why am I strong? she wondered, when I feel so weak?

She unwound the turban, revealing the livid, crescent-shaped scar on the side of her head.

The voluminous jellaba, essential for sleeping beneath the stars, she lifted away. Beneath the jellaba she wore a lightweight *fokia* of glistening indigo, delicately embroidered with golden thread, a gift from the Marabout; under the *fokia* a loose-fitting, long-sleeve shapeless cotton shirt, a paler blue.

Mamadu was roused from his stupor by the thud of the Ruger hitting the sand next to his head.

"Take care of that."

Mamadu had never quite believed Daisy was a man; nor was he convinced she was a woman in disguise. His eyes grew big.

The buttonless shirt came away over her head. Daisy had not worn a bra since her mother died.

Mamadu gasped. "Miss, you mustn't."

"Mustn't I?"

She was fiddling with the knotted cord that held up her bloomers. Mamadu held his breath. The bloomers dropped to earth. She stepped out of them. Mamadu's eyes grew big as he stared at the pubic triangle.

"No, miss, you mustn't. It's shameful. *Hshuma.*"

To describe Daisy as muscle-bound would not be accurate, but every muscle in her body was visible. She had been ill, she had subsisted on a poor diet, she was nearing the end of a punishing trek. Her arms and shoulders were not so much muscular as sculpted from carrying buckets from the well. The muscles behind her shoulders were bunched from the same effort, her thighs solid from long hours aboard Uncle Bernon.

Mamadu did not like the muscles. His eyes instinctively gravitated to the comfort zones – her breasts, her hips, her calloused *montes veneris* with the tattoo of a leaping mustang. Muslim women traditionally clean shave theirs. As a small boy, visits with his auntie to the *hammam* during the women's hour led him to deduct that a bush properly belonged to men only. But here it was, in full view, minus the usual equipment. For one desperate moment he thought she might strap it on, as and when required. These mad speculations, in a brain already addled by the desert sun, only served to confuse the poor boy even further as to the true nature of Daisy's sex.

"Miss, you mustn't."

"How else are we going to dig ourselves out of this hole?"

Naked but for her sandals, she strode to the top of the dune and stood, legs apart, in full view. Unfurling the white turban and waving it strenuously above her head, she started walking forward, chanting as she walked.

Not a shot was fired.

The vulture gave up and floated away.

CHAPTER 63

Visiting Hours

Gluglu never made it out of the dunes. As befitting his title of the first Duke of France, Robert de Bremont was buried with full military honors in the Foreign Legion cemetery at Ksar. Daisy was too ill to attend.

Slimane had grown a mustache. What with his sallow complexion and bedroom eyes, he liked to think he looked a little like Ringo Starr.

He was impressed by the changes that had come over Rfud. Café Zizi was full of Spanish and Greek workers, and several new shops had opened on main street. The flimsy cane-and-palm frond stalls in market square had been replaced by wood and stone. According to Radio Maroc, engineers in California had come up with a plan to bring water from the Atlas to the Tafilalet via a series of underground channels. A Swiss firm was studying a project to bore a tunnel through the mountains, and extend the railroad all the way from Tangier to Timbuktu!

The arrival of a wounded soldier was causing a commotion at the hospital. Slimane caught sight of Dr. Parodis.

"Tell that wife of yours," the doctor called, "to take a toothbrush into the desert instead of a revolver!"

Slimane found her sitting up in bed.

"Slim, darling, you've come." She stretched out her arms.

She had lost so much weight her jaw stuck out like a monkey's.

They embraced, but not with the warmth of former days. Slimane did not find his wife attractive.

Her manner was grave, her movements deliberate. Her fingers, brown and coarsened, with nails not exactly clean, splayed against the hospital sheets. A dented fez partially covered the rusty stubble. Her arms were sinewy, her chest emaciated. It was as though she had gone somewhere far away, but only part of her had come back. As if in compensation for the loss of flesh, her soft brown eyes seemed larger and more luminous.

On the bedside table sat a cracked pocket mirror, the *sebsi*, the *mtui* and the *mechero*. The battered *shqara* bulged with writing materials.

A black boy, squatting on his heels near the foot of the bed, crept forward and submissively kissed Slimane on the shoulder.

"Bring us some tea, please, Mamadu."

"Who's that?" Slimane asked after the boy had gone.

"A gift from the Marabout."

"A slave-owner now, are you?"

"Don't be like that, darling. I thought I'd never get out of there alive. The day I finally felt strong enough to leave, Sidi Mohamed led his retinue to the monastery gate to see me off. I thanked him for his hospitality and for sending Mamadu. 'I give him to you,' the Marabout said. He saw I was too weak to travel alone. It would have been impolite to refuse, so I whispered that when I reached Rsani, I would send him back. 'No, he's yours to keep,' he insisted. 'He wants to see the world. Who better to show it to him than you? Farewell, Moha.' And so forth. And let me tell you, Slim, it was hard going. When we crossed the Wad Ziz, I said, 'You are a free man now, Mamadu. We are in Morocco.' He was indignant! I couldn't get rid of him. But when not threatened by freedom he is the personification of honesty and calm."

Daisy turned her face away. "Don't look at me like that." She picked up the pocket mirror.

"What's happened to you?"

"Some bug I picked up in the salt marshes that knocked me out, so nothing serious. Between bouts of fever I worked on my book. I'm calling it *hobo*, from the notes I've taken."

"What about our grocery store?"

"We need to make money first. As soon as I get out of here I'm going to send the manuscript to a publisher. General Ben Jalloud gave me the name of one in London. What with the publicity Morocco has been getting, he thinks it might be a best seller."

"Writing takes too long."

Slimane experienced a strong aversion to his wife whom he thought he once loved. She was too thin. She looked sick. Her neck was scrawny like a chicken's. Already she dreamed of another desert crossing – she was beginning to talk like she was crazy.

She lay a hand on his arm.

"You've got to get me out of here, darling! Tomorrow they're going to do something awful to me. They're going to pull out my teeth!"

CHAPTER 64

Home Sweet Home

Against the wishes of Dr. Parodis she checked out of the hospital the next day. He tried to persuade her stay a while longer, to rest up and get her strength back, but once more she insisted. She leaned on Slimane's arm as they made their way through the sandy streets of Rfud. Her mouth was sore, she did not wish to talk, but she bent to hug the children who ran to kiss her sleeve.

To the north, the sky flickered with silent lightning.

"It is raining in the Atlas," Daisy murmured. "God is great. He is bringing life to the desert."

Daisy's house was cluttered with souvenirs from her wanderings in the desert. An oryx skin was nailed to one wall. Gazelle horns, ostrich eggs and vulture feathers, evil-looking daggers and ornamental swords lay scattered about. An antique Arab rifle, inlaid with silver and ivory, leaned in the corner. A coiled cartridge belt, cowrie shell amulets, an assortment of camel udder boxes, and *thuya* wood sculptures. A jumble of tack, Spanish and Arab, hung outside. A chain of worn-out dog collars looped from a wooden peg. A raw ax handle to discourage uninvited guests. The Ruger dangled by its trigger guard on a nail. The row of battered riding boots spoke for themselves.

Silent lightning played across the sky.

"It's still raining," she said. An anxious look crossed her face. "It must be an absolute cloudburst."

"Why should it worry you?" Slimane asked.

"I've never seen such a big storm over the Atlas."

Slimane woke early and found Mamadu preparing coffee. Daisy had taught him to do it her mother's way – Brazilian style – with a sock.

He went out for *churros*, a crispy doughnut his wife craved. It was a clear Saharan morning, with the sun already warm, the air still cool. Not a cloud in the sky, not a whisper of air. The world stood ominously still, as though holding its breath. Slimane stopped, he listened.

Returning to the house, he heard laughter within. His wife was in a happy mood. He handed over the *churros* on a palmetto string.

"Desert mornings – I can't get enough of them." She took a deep breath. "These are the sweet days of autumn: blue skies, hot sun on cool sand – perfection."

"What's happened to the birds?"

"What?"

"Where are they?"

"What are you talking about?"

"Have the children killed them all with their slingshots?"

"What?"

"The birds are silent."

With the morning so fine, it was decided to breakfast on the roof. It was about nine o'clock. Mamadu was pouring coffee when an unfamiliar noise – a kind of muffled roar – made everyone look up. Mamadu pointed to a cloud of dust rolling down the dry riverbed of the Ziz.

"What is it?" Slimane wondered. "A sand storm?"

Daisy frowned. "The sand wind never comes from the north."

Mamadu sniffed the air. "There's no wind."

"It is a train?"

"There is no train."

The noise grew louder. It did sound like the roar of an approaching train. Something very strange was happening.

"My God!" Daisy was leaning over the wall. "It's not wind, it's ... *water!*"

People down in the street began to run and shout, "River! River!"

Slimane did not understand. "What river?"

"Oh my God! It's the river! The fucking river is coming!"

A wall of foaming brown water appeared at the top of the street. It was crashing among the houses, pushing them down, and carrying everything before it – a rolling tide of trees, bushes, masses of rubbish, and the bodies of animals and people, some already drowned, with others waving and struggling to stay afloat.

Daisy and Slimane stared speechless as the flood raced down the street and invaded the quarter where they lived. Mud houses were melting and collapsing. People on a nearby roof waved and screamed, then they, too, were gone. In the blink of an eye.

By some miracle Daisy's house stood alone in a sea of swirling mud. The massive gate kept the water out. On all sides the pandemonium quickly subsided as the neighbors were swallowed.

"Get out of here!" Daisy picked up the *shqara* and pushed Slim down the stairs. "This place won't last another minute! Lose that djellaba!"

She neglected to take off her own.

"Open the gate!" she shouted to Slimane. "Mamadu, grab something to hang on to!"

But there wasn't enough time and there weren't any planks. The water was spurting around the edges of the gate. It looked as though it would burst open any second.

"Open the gate, Slim! We must get out! Push! I can feel it! The house is moving!"

He couldn't open because of the violence of the flood.

All of a sudden the current took the gate, ripping it off its hinges. Slimane grabbed hold and was carried away as a tide of water flooded neck deep into the *riad*.

He was washed down the wadi where the destruction was going on. People waved but he could not help. Their woolen robes filled with water and dragged them down. Nobody knew how to swim. For what seemed like hours he clung to the gate while he was carried on a current of liquid mud.

Hours later he came to his senses, washed up on soft watery mud littered with wreckage from the flood. The experience was so far beyond his ken he thought it had been a nightmare. Corpses of goats and donkeys were entangled with branches and debris. There were human bodies – trapped under trees, floating in water, half buried in mud with feet sticking out.

The great flood that had swallowed so many houses and lives had in turn been swallowed by the desert and was no more. In a daze, Slimane staggered through what was left of the village. A squad of soldiers was picking over the ruins, looking for survivors. The wailings of the bereaved filled the sky. The destruction had so altered the landscape he hardly knew where he was. After some difficulty he came to the place where Villa Darna once stood.

A man stepped from among the ruins. The hood of his burnoose fell forward, partially concealing his face.

"What is your business here?"

"This was my wife's house. I was with her when the flood hit."

"What happened to her?"

"We were having breakfast. We tried to get out."

"How did you escape and she did not?"

Slimane realized it was General Ben Jalloud he was speaking to. He described how the flood had swept him away.

All that day they led the lives of people shipwrecked, pulling survivors from the mud and consoling the families of the drowned. There were stories of miraculous preservation from the current, but none of escape from those caught in its tremendous rush. Old and young alike were overwhelmed in one fearful death, and grown men and unweaned children lay side by side in makeshift wards erected for the reception of the dead.

With night, hope faded that Daisy would be found alive. Slimane and the General met again near the ruins of her house.

"Whatever happens today, I will always treasure the memory of my friendship with your wife." His face rippled. He wiped his eyes. "She had many loves, but the one she gave herself to without reservation was the desert!"

These words from the commander of the Americans made Slimane proud.

The next day the general directed a squad of soldiers to look for Daisy's body. They scoured the wreckage and unearthed corpses across the desert. The Saharan heat returned with a ferocity. During the night the bloated remains of man and beast were savaged by jackals. Pariahs congregated in packs. They sniffed out corpses and dug them up. A storm of vultures descended on the rest.

Slimane declined to participate any further in the search. He sat in the bar of the Zizi and awaited news of the inevitable.

The general was growing impatient. On the third day he ordered his men to search the ruins of Daisy's home. There were rumors of a large black dog in the area, howling and frightening people. The soldiers shot him.

As they approached what was left of the house, the stench emanating from the rubble told what they would find. The soldiers dug down and there, crushed beneath the carcass of Uncle Bernon she was attempting to free, lay Daisy's crumpled corpse, surrounded by a mass of muddy papers.

Mamadu's body was never found.

The general directed his men to make a thorough search and collect whatever writings they could find. Notably missing was the *ms.* of her novel, which she had shown him in the hospital.

He gave orders for the funeral to take place.

Waffa and Maloudia washed the body according to the Muslim rite. Four men carried the litter to the cemetery. The body was placed in a shallow grave, already filling with blowing sand. A Jilaliya holy man stayed by the graveside, chanting the prayer of farewell.

A handsome stone of gray basalt, hewn from the desert floor, with trilobites and other Palaeozoic creatures swimming in it, inscribed in English on one side and Arabic on the other, was put into place. The Duchess de Bremont paid for it.

DAISY ADAMS

dit Moha ben Abdu

Writer, explorer of the desert
Dead at 22
Perished in the Great Catastrophe of Rfud

She loved Morocco

Facing the dunes, the tomb looks toward Mecca like the others.

Post Mortem

The news reached Arturo in the form of an article in *Libération*, sent from Paris by the Duchess de Bremont:

"La Bonne Nomade a quitté La Table."

The *Hammada*, a.k.a. *La Table*, located between SE Morocco and Algeria – claimed by both countries, occupied by neither, inhabited by no one – is a vast stony plateau with nothing to break the horizon. The hard flat soil is without water or vegetation. Here begins the great desert from which crop primary rocks incrusted with marine fossils. The region however was not always so desolate: as the numerous rock drawings attest, this was once the lower valley of the River Drâa. The ancient authors who knew it as the *Flumen Darat* (Pliny), the *Dyris* (Vitrovius) or the *Daradai* (Ptolemy) all relate, especially Polybius, that it was once infested with crocodiles.

It does not rain on the *Hammada*. In summer temperatures soar and hover while the east wind (*sherqi*) blows. Pilots report towering clouds of orange dust, as though the whole region was on fire. In winter the mercury plunges below freezing, causing rocks to split with a sound like gunfire. Temperatures can change as much as 100° in a single day. Bedouins avoid the area. They don't take their animals because there is nothing to eat, nothing to drink, there is nothing. Even scorpions get thirsty.

La Bonne Nomade was raised in the Arizona desert, USA. One thing about her was certain: she knew how to handle a horse. Her mother was American, English, Spanish, maybe Moroccan. She seems to have had two fathers – one Mexican, the other Dutch. One was a Communist, the other a Capitalist. She called herself Adams, Toledano, van Renseelaer and Temsemani. This desert damsel had more aliases than Billy the Kid. She was Christian, Jew, and Muslim – in which order is not clear. She dressed as a man; some thought it was the other way around. The question was finally settled when like Alice through the looking glass she stepped from the mirage and walked naked across the dunes chanting the Yale College football fight song. The guns fell silent. The American army held its fire and dreamed of love.

Not so for the Duke de Bremont, ex-alcoholic, drug fiend and serial philanderer, rescued by the Good Nomad from the butcheries of the rapacious R'guibat. She accomplished this near-impossible feat by crossing the formidable *hammada* in high summer, when the brutal *sherqi* pulverizes the earth. The Blue People had made a plaything of our Duke, spearing his eyes and bifurcating his tongue. Within meters of safety the old boy clambered blindly to the top of a dune and got riddled by American bullets.

A few days later the Good Nomad perished in the great catastrophe at Rfud. It is said that more people drown in the Sahara than die of thirst.

Women are the peace-makers; traditionally they do it in bed. It sometimes happens (in modern romantic novels, mainly American), that rival lovers become reconciled once the woman they shared departs the scene. This seems to have been the case in the Moroccan desert, where what the Americans call their "Tar Baby War" has been sputtering for a couple of years. The antagonists, the colorful American General David Ben Jalloud, and the reclusive holy man, the Sufi Marabout Sidi Mohamed Ould Brahim, were seen shaking hands.

Our nomad evidently preferred senior gents; she even fell for the Duke.

In deepest Morocco, along the edges of the *hammada*, the people whisper a sacred word, *Baraka*. It means grace, and implies a kind of charisma which attracts people, and can rub off on others. The Good Nomad, it seems, had *Baraka* in spades.

Arturo booked himself on a Royal Air Maroc flight to Casablanca. Withdrawing $10,000 in cash from the bank, he pressed a wad of $50 notes into Miss Bushy's protesting palm (he had given her an American Express card, but she was forever forgetting her PIN) knowing she would blow it on the ponies as a way of assuaging her grief.

The day before he was scheduled to depart, a parcel arrived from the Duchess de Bremont. From the FedEx packaging emerged an object wrapped in brown paper and tied with string. Arturo undid the multiple knots. The contents were further bound in layers of hospital gauze. With trembling hands he lifted it away. It was like unwrapping a mummy. Each successive layer yielded the antique, dusty odor of arid Africa.

The mass of tightly packed pages nearly exploded in his hands.

hobo
A Tale of Wandering

by
Moha Temsemani,
Villa Darna,
Trik Sidi Masmoudi,
Rfud,
Tafilalet,
Maroc.

Cajan had included a note: Daisy's husband, Slimane Temsemani, B.P. 608, Berkane ppl., Maroc, had been released from the army. He was asking for a $5,000 reward for having salvaged the manuscript from the flood. His plan was to open a bicycle shop.

Arturo wrote out the check, sent it off, and sat up the whole night reading.

At 35,000 feet over the Atlantic, the truth hit home. The responsibility for his family tragedy lay squarely on his shoulders. Had he not impulsively enlisted for Morocco, nor been foolishly negligent about staying in touch with his mother, the anguish of uncertainty might not have pierced her aneurism. She might be alive today and, under her and Daisy's care, Antonio's life could also have been prolonged. The dogs would have survived; the little family would still be together under the same roof at Villa Arida Zona in Balaguer.

No, it was worse, far worse than that. He was five years older than Daisy. Naturally, little sister looked up to big brother. She expected to follow, to be guided, and above all to be protected. And what had he done with this adoring devotion? Violated every moral principle and made her pregnant! And, like his father before him, brought shame upon his mother – in both instances, compelling her to uproot her children from the family home and move to some foreign sanctuary. Like father like son! But for Arturo, the family need never to have left Douglas at all. His selfish actions had set in motion a concatenation of events that led to the annihilation of his family, with the sole other surviving member swallowed by the yellow smog of Mexico, D.F., never to call him father.

The damned must be in a special category. Here he was, destined for some unhealthy foreign shore, where he would be fiendishly absolved from the balm of daily toil, so the worst might stay alive. This is what comes of knowing the worst – one is left with the worst – and it is almost like peace because there is nothing else. He was damned for all eternity – unless a miracle happened.

He wept over the pain he had inflicted. The Moroccan air hostess inquired. (He was flying first class.) Looking up into that caring brown face, he could have sworn he saw Maloudia.

At Marrakesh airport he rented a Toyota Land Cruiser with a massive roof rack. (In more peaceful days it had ferried film crews and their equipment around the desert.) He exchanged dollars for dirhams at the Hotel Mamounia and called on Mr. Hans Rutishauser, the Swiss manager, who discretely alluded to his sister's one-night *debacle*. Arturo settled the unpaid bill.

Over the High Atlas he motored, beneath peaks already sugared with the first snows of autumn. The U.S. base at Boulmaln had been dismantled, all wire removed. Captain Keller's crow's nest had reverted to its former function: an adobe tower for storing fruit and nuts, with rose buds fragrant on top.

He visited the Gorges du Todra by car and the oasis of Tinerhir on foot. He picnicked alone on a stony ridge far from the road, far from everything but the mineral silence that envelops this pre-Saharan region.

Ridge beyond stony ridge, where the stone broke off in flat geometrical shapes, ideal for building material. The Moroccans came in trucks to rip the black rocks from the crumbling ridge. The dry stone walls were fitted together with the tight combinations of a jigsaw puzzle.

On that flaking ridge above the oasis Arturo finally came to grips with the instinct which had brought him back to Morocco: to try to fit the pieces of the jigsaw together, to complete the mosaic. He could no longer endure the suffering, because he caused it all the time.

At Ksar the hard road dipped south and followed the Wad Ziz, arrowing through palm forests that carpeted the canyons. The hand of man had done much to add to the majesty of the scene by perching great mud castles, rich in decorated towers, on every pinnacle of rock.

He called on General Ben Jalloud in his tent. Daisy's notebooks and papers, some soiled by mud, some utterly spoiled by water, had been arranged on the pingpong table, ready for collection.

Also on the pingpong table: the Girard-Perregaux, the *darbala*, the *mechero*, the *shqara*, a handsome pair of turquoise cufflinks in a camel udder box. The Ruger.

For a few minutes Arturo and the general stood by her tomb.

"Your sister was what attracted me more than anything else," he said. "She was a rebel. Her integrity derived from that enviable single-mindedness of the writer, who knows where the truth is and has the means of getting at it."

They walked through the palmeraie to the ruins of Villa Darna which the general was having rebuilt. Papa Noel casually informed Arturo that Maloudia and her daughter were still out in Daisy's *haima*, being looked after by the faithful Waffa.

Arturo staggered backwards, as though he had been struck by a physical blow. Dropping everything and taking Caftan along as interpreter, he sped to tent city. Maloudia scooped up her child and vanished among curtains to escape this terrifying apparition, the source of all her misery. But Waffa stood her ground. Arturo pressed a roll of bills into her palm and instructed her to have mother and daughter ready in three days. One glimpse of that blue-eyed child had triggered in him a near savage rush of compassion. He was taking them to America.

Waffa caught up with him by the Land Cruiser. Her granddaughter Kinza had passed her baccalaureate. She could read and write French and Arabic. She was healthy and strong. Her ambition was to be a teacher, but men were after her. Already there was an offer of marriage. She didn't stand a chance.

Please.

She did not have to ask twice. Arturo added more bills to the roll. "Buy her new clothes."

Waffa sank to her knees and kissed the cuffs of his trousers.

Arturo drove back to Rfud overcome by a blinding happiness. His was one of those strange discoveries a man can make: life, however you lead it, contains moments of extreme exhilaration. He had given away to despair. From being alone, in darkness, with the rain falling and the hail rattling in, with the horizontal curtain ends snapping at him like a pair of phantom snakes, without love or pity, a human soul had emerged.

In the hour before dawn came a tap on the door. Mr. Lebaddy, manager of the Hotel Zizi, apologized for disturbing. He handed Arturo a letter written in courtly, antique Spanish on a kind of vellum.

It was antelope skin.

Four tribesmen, armed with sword and sabre, decked out in Saharan finery, were waiting beneath the palms. A syce held the horses. With the rising sun on their backs they cantered across the desert to the *zawiya* at Hnabu.

Sidi Mohamed received Arturo in the Great Hall. Beside him sat a demure young woman. Embarka spoke English, Spanish and French as well as her native Arabic. The Marabout mused that his niece had become "a true Tangerine." As a graduate of the American School she had been accepted at the Columbia School of Nursing in New York. She had a passport and could pay her own way. The Marabout desired that she accompany Arturo to America. Arturo solemnly declared that it would be an honor to perform such a service. For him, so undeserving, to be given responsibility for another young person, he could hardly contain his elation.

He paid a final visit to the grave:

I am sitting by your side, sister, I am near you on the sand. The clouds have parted. The new moon and her companion Venus glide in a sky that has not yet lost all its light. In Arizona, this was our favorite hour, with the sun poised on the western wall of the world, bathing the desert in her luminous glow. Voices hush and motors fade before the forces that rule us all. Without the sun we are nothing. Without loving the earth and each other, we are nothing.

Now the sky is shot through with shafts of red light, but not the fiery streams of tracer bullets. I like to think of God's fingers reaching down to draw a healing caress over this divine land.

Already the wind has built a little dune around the edges of the stone. And a fine stone it is, sister – rounded on top, inscribed in English on one side, Arabic on the side that faces east.

Some will not believe your story. Others might say you never existed. But I know that you do – for me you still do – and that your story is a true one.

You needed all the skills Antonio taught to survive that trek over the Atlas, and I can see that prison cell in Oujda you described in detail. Even as they prepared to have you deported and separated from your husband, your accusers swept your body with the male gaze of desire. But you, with your amazing resourcefulness – and a bit of good luck – overturned all that and were reunited with the country and the man you loved, before this cruel and ironic fate.

They branded you a whore and a spy, but the Moroccans disdained this name-calling and will keep you for themselves.

God has withdrawn His hand now. The desert is dark and at peace. The silence is nearing absolute. I have not yet learned the whole story, sister. Not even you could know it. I have your notebooks, those which were not destroyed or lost. I have your novel. Our family perished, but your priceless account, or most of it, has survived.

Even with its huge roof rack the Land Cruiser could not hold it all. Caftan had to run to market for blue rope to secure the baskets, the bundles, the sacks, the carpets.

After multiple farewells boarding commenced. Embarka, with her English, sat up front, with Maloudia and Kinza in back and Nabilah, Arturo's daughter, between.

Arturo looked at the child. His was the love he now felt for every soul in the world. All the fear and the wish to save were concentrated in one child. He was aware of an immense load of responsibility.

I love you. I am your father and I love you. One day I hope you will try to understand this.

Very soon he would have to establish some sort of vital contact with the child, and with the mother, but not just yet.

Generous tips had been distributed to Waffa, Papa Noel, and Caftan.

Arturo took the wheel. The engine roared. Amidst warbling shrieks the Nazarene drove away with his entourage – three eighteen year-old unmarried, unchaperoned Muslim women and the child. It was a scandal!

Mr. Hans Rutishauser thought he had seen his celebrity guests do it all – Mick Jagger, turtle-like on his elbows and knees, howling at the moon; John Lennon, comatose, flat on his back, pushing up daisies; Tennessee Williams bawling for bourbon; Irene Pappas and Anthony Quinn cavorting naked in the pool during the shooting of the life of the Prophet; and that Kuwaiti shaikh with his caravan of Mercedes limos – rolling air-conditioned cages of peregrine falcons to plunder the bustards of the Moroccan south – but these three turbanned, tattooed, hennaed, dusky desert women, wrapped in yards of indigo, with one kohled eye shining, spilling from the Land Cruiser with a clank of silver – many clanks – bringing his well-heeled guests galloping, gawking, snapping – took the cake, for authenticity at least; definitely for business.

It was arranged for the harem to be lodged in the Churchill Suite, with the master in a separate room on the floor below.

Next morning early, in a state of repressed euphoria, he went to market and came back with a battery of massive counterfeit "Elizabeth Taylor" Louis Vuitton suitcases. A tearful palaver ensued as the girls were persuaded to jettison most of their worldly goods – the carpets, the bedrolls, the cushions, the blackened kettles and blue teapots, the octagonal tea glasses (designed to be packed in straw for desert crossings), sugar loaves in distinctive blue paper wrapping, tins of Temple of Heaven "Gunpowder" green tea, a cast-iron mortar and pestle (this alone weighed in at three kilos), charcoal, firewood, and the razor-sharp knives they would not be needing in the Big Apple.

Embarka was allowed to keep her tennis racket.

At Boukhalf, Tangier's airport, Arturo rented a people carrier and a van for the luggage. The massive wooden portal to Jâafar's palace swung wide; his household had gathered to greet the Saharans with Jilaliya chanting, clacking metal castanets, and drums. Jâafar used his influence at town hall to obtain passports for Maloudia, Nabilah, and Kinza. Mina and Sobrina were tracked down to receive their tips. Arturo couldn't give it away fast enough. Mad to meet the girls, Amalia and Carmen came to tea. Jacob invited the whole team to Villa Toledano.

Arturo scattered breadcrumbs over his mother's grave at Sidi Bouarakia.

Monsieur Charles Joly, manager of the Ritz Hotel in Paris, definitely had seen it all. Cajan used her considerable pull with the American Ambassador (the andirons in his fireplace once belonged to her ancestor, General Zachary Taylor, 12th President of the U.S.) to obtain the necessary visas. She arranged for the girls to tour the city (Eiffel Tower, Arc de Triomphe, the Great Mosque, with a ride on a *bateau mouche*) with an Arabic-speaking guide, while Arturo visited Elmyr in his studio. Arturo's rugged good looks and ecstatic mood made Elmyr think of the inebriated young man staring from Velasquez's *Bacchus*. He collected the "Saharan Suns" triptych Daisy had paid for, and commissioned portraits of the girls; but with Embarka due to begin her nursing course at Columbia, there was no time for sittings. Cajan paid a society photographer to capture them in their Saharan finery, for Elmyr to copy. As *The Girl with the Shaved Head* had been sold to a dealer in Dallas, Arturo left with Elmyr a photo of Daisy, taken at Guadalquivir Ranch – cowboy-hatted – sitting on a horse – a rodeo winner at sixteen – already pretty serious.

Then all upped sticks and went to America.

THE END

JOHN HOPKINS, a Princeton graduate, lived for many years in Tangier and was a central figure in the bohemian literary crowd of the 1960s and 1970s.